"Mind if I join you?

Shrugging, she turn

water. Had he seen the

over her lips? "Suit yourself."

The dirt crunched as Nick settled himself beside her. The closeness of him was almost palpable. Once he was situated, Dallas turned to look at him. While his gaze had strayed out over the river, the muscle twitching in his jaw told her he wasn't ignorant of her presence. "What do you want, Nick?"

"To talk to you." His gaze stayed forward. "About lesson number six."

"Oh." She frowned. There was something about Nick tonight. Something tightly leashed and dangerous, humming just below the surface, but she couldn't quite put her finger on it.

"You ready?" He rubbed the nape of his neck with his hand as though he was massaging away a soreness. Then he looked at her and Dallas's breath caught. His eyes captured the moonlight and sent it back to her in penetrating, deep blue shards.

Her heart did a crazy flip-flop and her palms were oddly moist as she waited breathlessly for him to continue. "What is lesson number six? Tell me . . . please?"

The muscles in his jaw bunched and his blue eyes darkened, burning into her. "Kissing, darlin'. Lesson number six is kissing."

REBECCA SINCLAIR
SWEET TEXAS KISS

ZEBRA BOOKS
KENSINGTON PUBLISHING CORP.

To
Courtney and Adam . . .
who make each day special.

ZEBRA BOOKS are published by

Kensington Publishing Corp.
475 Park Avenue South
New York, NY 10016

First Printing: March, 1994

Printed in the United States of America

Chapter One

"You'll change his mind, Dallas. You always do."

Lisa Cameron's words rang sharply in her sister's ears. Oh, how Dallas wished the girl was right. But she doubted it.

Lisa hadn't been the one closeted in their father's study for the better part of the morning. Lisa hadn't been the angry recipient of Ian Cameron's determined glares. Dallas had, and she wasn't at all certain she could change their father's mind. Not this time. This time, Dallas had a feeling Ian Cameron was going to be stubborn.

Sighing, Dallas smoothed the tawny bangs back from her brow. "You didn't see the look on his face. If you had, you'd know this time is different. This time"—she sucked in an agitated breath and shrugged—"this time I think he really means it."

Lisa chuckled. Although the girl was barely thirteen years old, Dallas thought her sister's laughter packed years of seduction behind it. It was, she mused, a laugh that would make a man sit up and take notice; high, musical, soft—the exact opposite of Dallas's own whiskey-raw timbre.

"Don't look at me like that," Dallas said as she perched on the edge of the bed. She sent Lisa, who sat primly in a chair wedged into the opposite corner of the sparsely decorated bedroom, a sharp glance. "Seriously, you weren't there. You don't know what he said, the way he acted."

Lisa shrugged and laced her fingers atop her lap. It was an unconsciously feminine gesture; one Dallas knew she would need to practice diligently to achieve the same fluid poise.

Such was the way things had always been between them. Lisa was the elegant one, the sweet one, the good-natured one. Dallas never had time for such feminine nonsense. Instead, she'd channeled her growing up years into molding herself into the son Ian Cameron had never had, but always yearned for. She hadn't succeeded, as her father's ultimatum of a few short hours ago proved; the man wouldn't have dared to make such outrageous demands of a son!

"Well?" Lisa prodded. "Are you going to tell me what happened, or am I going to have to wheedle it out of Maria? You realize, of course, by the time the story works its way through the kitchen it will sound a lot juicier than it actually was."

"Doesn't it always?" Dallas agreed, an emotionless grin tugging at her lips. The Bar None wasn't any different from other moderately-sized Texas spread. Gossip spread hotter and faster than brushfire; by the time the story reached town—and it would, it always

6

did—only the names of the players would be the same. The tale itself wouldn't even *sound* familiar.

Lisa leaned forward. A few honey blond curls spilled over her brow as she propped her elbows on her thighs and cushioned her delicately molded chin on the heels of her palms. "Well? Don't keep me in suspense, Dallas. What did Papa say to you? More important, what did *you* say to *him?*"

Dallas squirmed on the bed, pulling her legs beneath her in a cross-legged sit. "I already told you." She tucked her chin against her collarbone, so the soft underside resembled their father's jowls. Her already husky voice dropped two determined pitches. "Three things I want out of life, girly. Only three." A slender finger counted off each of Ian Cameron's unbearable orders. "Grandsons. Yours. Now."

"He didn't," Lisa gasped. Dallas's pursed lips told her sister that Ian Cameron most certainly *had*—that, and more. "And what did you say?"

"I laughed." Dallas's smile was cold and forced. At her sister's horrified expression, she added, "Well, what was I *supposed* to do?! I mean, I heard what he was saying, but to be honest, I didn't believe a word of it. I thought . . . well, I thought it was a joke. A very cruel one."

"Papa never jokes." Lisa shook her head, which sent her springy blond curls bouncing around her slender shoulders.

Closing her eyes, Dallas sighed heavily. "I know. I guess I was hoping he'd made an exception this once. Actually, I was *praying to God* he had." Her eyes opened. The chocolate brown irises were dazed with the much too fresh memory. "The look on his face told me that he was dead-set serious."

"And you said . . . ?" Lisa prodded.

Dallas, surrendering to a sudden burst of energy, thrust herself off the bed. The spurs hooked over her boot heels—which had torn a few unnoticed slices in the bedspread—jangled as she paced the room. "What could I say? He didn't *ask* me to find a husband, he *demanded* it." Her gaze sharpened on her sister. Wide-eyed and staring, Lisa greedily devoured every juicy tidbit of the story. "I"—Dallas shrugged, crossed her arms over her chest, spun on her heel, and continued her anxious pacing—"I told him no."

"You didn't."

This time the amused sparkle in her eyes and the smile that curled over Dallas's lips were genuine. "I most certainly did. At least a dozen times, if I remember correctly. But you know Papa. I really don't think he heard me." Again, her chin and voice dropped in a mocking imitation of their father. " 'Three things, girly,' he kept saying to me. 'Grandsons. Yours. Now.' I swear, Lisa, if he'd said that one more time, I would have either screamed or strangled him."

"Did you two argue very much?" Lisa asked. Her voice was hushed with awe. Obviously, she couldn't imagine anyone having the nerve to argue with their father. Ian Cameron could be very intimidating when angered. Lisa did her best *never* to anger him. As it was, the man seemed to frighten his youngest daughter senseless when he was happy!

"We argued," Dallas confirmed with a brisk nod. "Very, *very* much. Not that it mattered, of course.

Does arguing ever accomplish anything with Papa?" She spun on her heel, her pace quickening. "Do you know what his last words to me were?" Lisa shook her head. This time when she quoted Ian Cameron, Dallas did not imitate him. His words were much too serious for that. "He told me that I have until the end of the fall drive to 'rope myself a husband.' He thinks that's more than enough time, if I start today. Oh, and since he said he was feeling generous, he gave me until spring roundup to have the man 'hobbled to the altar.' "

"Hobbled?"

"His words, not mine," Dallas clarified caustically. "As though I were roping a maverick!"

"Well," Lisa said calmly, diplomatically, in a way only Lisa Cameron could, "in a way, you are. Papa's always saying that men and horses are more alike than either will ever admit. Both buck until you throw the saddle on, but it's all for show. Give them a gentle hand, they'll calm soon enough."

"Please, do *not* repeat that man's words to me today. I'm in no mood to hear any more of them."

The room was thick with tension, the only sounds that of the inner seams of Dallas's denim pants rubbing together as she paced, the agitated click of her boot heels, and the *chink* of her spurs atop the roughly hewn planked floor.

"I wish you were older," Dallas said. "Then maybe he'd be doing this to you instead of me."

Lisa sent her sister a shy grin, and released a breathy, wistful little sigh. "So do I. I wouldn't mind nearly as much as you do. *I've* always wanted to marry."

Dallas snorted her contempt of matrimony. "That's only one of the hundreds of things that make us so different." Then, to lighten the mood that had grown much too dim, she sent her sister a crooked smile. "Are you *sure* Ian Cameron is your father? You may look like him, but I have my doubts."

Lisa grinned and sat back in the chair. "We've had this conversation before."

"I know. And I still have trouble believing you're my sister. You're too . . . too . . . delicate." She shuddered.

"Mama was delicate and small. Just like me."

Dallas forced her voice to sound light and airy—the exact opposite of the way she felt. "Mama was also married to that ogre we call Papa for twenty-five years, which proves that, while she may have been small and delicate and pretty to look at, Laura Cameron was *not* very bright. Really," she huffed, shaking her head, "I don't know how she stood the man that long without killing him."

The sound of her sister's laughter floated through the air, tickling Dallas's ears, reminding her that, unlike Lisa, Dallas had nothing to laugh about.

"So what happens next?" Lisa asked when her good humor subsided. "Will you find a husband, like Papa said you have to? Or will you defy him?" The girl's voice went soft and nervous. "What do you think he'll do if you *do* decide to defy him? Did he say? What did he threaten you with?"

"Nothing," Dallas said, her jaw hardening. Approaching the open window, she leaned her shoulder against the corner of the frame and flicked back the sky-blue, thin cotton curtain. A slight draft of dry heat blew her bangs into her eyes. Flipping them back with a toss of her head, her gaze fixed on the dirty, sweaty cowpunchers who were working horses in the crudely built coral in the front yard. "Absolutely nothing."

"Nothing?" Lisa echoed, surprised. "You mean he didn't threaten to disinherit you? Didn't threaten to boot you off the ranch, disown you, or worse, both?" Dallas shook her head, her attention still outside. Behind her, Lisa groaned. "Oh my."

" 'Oh my' is right," Dallas grumbled.

A clock on top of the bureau ticked off one tension-heavy minute. Another.

"And what did you do?" Lisa's tone rose a shocked pitch. "Goodness, Dallas, you didn't agree to do it, did you?!"

"I already told you, I said no." Dallas swallowed hard. Shaking her head, she pushed back the wispy bangs that had, again, rebelliously fallen over her brow and into her eyes. "Lisa, after three very long, very *boring* hours of badgering, I got to the point where I could no longer fight with him. In the end, I told him I'd think about it."

"My goodness, Dallas, do you realize how little time that gives you to find a husband?" Lisa murmured, and her sister nodded.

"Of course I do," Dallas snapped, then realizing her bad mood wasn't Lisa's fault, sent her sister a tight, apologetic smile.

Pushing from the chair, Lisa crossed the room and stood by her sister's side. The distressed glint in Dallas's eyes made her want to reach out and wrap her

11

arms around her sister, but she didn't dare. The rigid set to Dallas's shoulders, the hard bunch of her jaw, said sympathy was the *last* thing Dallas wanted right now. A ready solution to this whole mess, that's what her sister needed.

"Did you have anyone in mind?" Lisa asked softly.

Dallas shook her head.

Lisa sighed. "Are you open to suggestions?"

"Depends. Who'd you have in mind?"

"David Parker."

Dallas shivered. "Lisa, please be serious. I need help, not jokes."

"I *am* serious. David isn't so bad," Lisa said, and the tempered patience in her tone made Dallas wonder which of them was really the oldest. "Well, he isn't," the girl continued defensively. "I'll admit that he isn't the handsomest man I've ever seen, but he isn't *bad* to look at. And he's very nice."

"To you, maybe." Dallas's expression indicated that niceness was not a trait to be bragged about. To her, it really wasn't. Since Lisa didn't work the ranch—not the way Dallas did—it stood to reason that Lisa hadn't spent as much time with the punchers and wranglers as her sister had.

Dallas, on the other hand, had seen the inside of the men's bunkhouse when she was six. She'd learned to rope proficiently when she was ten. She'd gone on her first roundup when she was barely thirteen.

Lisa had done none of that. And it showed. The men clammed up whenever Lisa was around. They tripped over their feet—and their tongues—when forced to be around the youngest Cameron.

They never acted that way with Dallas. Thank God! Of course, they had no reason to. They were used to her, had treated her as one of them—with only a few exceptions—for as long as she could remember. To the punchers who worked The Bar None, Dallas Cameron wasn't merely the boss's daughter, and hadn't been for a very long time.

In turn, Dallas was used to the men. How could she explain to a young, innocent girl like Lisa that a quiet, sensitive man like David Parker was . . . well, dammit, he was *dull* compared to the weathered saltiness she was accustomed to.

"What about the TLP?" Lisa asked, referring to the Parkers' spread, which bordered the Camerons'.

Dallas could tell by the glint in her sister's baby-blue eyes that Lisa was playing her trump card. And way too soon, in her estimation. Then again, the girl *did* manage to snag her attention, so maybe it wasn't too soon after all?

"What about it?" Dallas asked warily.

"Winston Parker is sickly, has been forever. Even Doc Praed says it's a miracle the man is still alive. What do you think will happen to the TLP when he dies? Who do you think will inherit the ranch?"

"David, of course," Dallas answered automatically.

Lisa grinned. "Exactly."

Dallas shook her head, confused. "What are you getting at?"

"Dallas, there are times you can be so *thick.*" Lisa rolled her eyes and sent her sister an impatient, I-don't-believe-you-haven't-figured-this-out-yet glare. "Winston Parker is going to die eventually. When he

13

does, his son will inherit the ranch that borders ours. A good-sized ranch, I might add. Now, if you were to marry David, and join the two families together . . . Think about it!"

Dallas had *never* thought about it, never even considered it in passing. She thought about it now, and thought about it hard.

If the families were joined through a marriage between herself and David, if they took their two moderate-sized ranches and merged them together . . . ?

Dallas's eyes grew wide.

So did Lisa's grin. "It's unbelievable, isn't it?"

"Well, it's something to think about."

"Better think quick, because the drive starts in a week. You are still planning to go on it, aren't you?"

"I haven't missed a drive since I was thirteen." Dallas's chin tipped up a proud notch.

"Then you'd better hurry. You don't have much time to decide."

Again, Dallas nodded. A scowl furrowed her brow as the seed of the idea Lisa had planted began to flourish. David Parker. Could she stand being married to such a soft, sensitive man for the rest of her life? Could she stand to—?

No, *that* was something Dallas refused to contemplate. She turned her thoughts in another direction, and her scowl deepened.

"It won't work," Dallas said, surprised to feel a stab of disappointment. While the thought of marrying and living under the same roof as David Parker held no appeal to her, the thought of merging their two

14

spreads together held more appeal by the minute. Pity it would never happen. "Not with David Parker."

"Why not?" Lisa demanded, her hands uncharacteristically planted on her slender hips. "I think it would be an ideal arrangement."

"Oddly enough, so do I. There's only one problem, and it's a big one."

"Name it."

"David Parker. He'd never agree." When her sister sent her a blank look, Dallas elaborated, "He doesn't like me, Lisa. Or did you forget the shouting match we had the last time our families got together?"

Lisa winced. "I remember. I also remember what caused it. You two wouldn't have argued if you hadn't told David that he was roping that calf all wrong."

"He *was!*"

"Maybe so, but you shouldn't have *told* him, Dallas. And if you absolutely *had* to tell him, you shouldn't have done it in front of his men. Of course he yelled at you." Lisa sighed impatiently, tapping the toe of her shoe on the floor. "You made a fool out of him in front of his men. He was embarrassed."

"That's no excuse for him to scream at me the way he did."

"You screamed at him first," Lisa reminded her sister patiently. "Besides, he had every reason to be angry. He's a man, isn't he?" she asked, as though that explained everything. And in a way, it did.

"I suppose you're right," Dallas grumbled, her gaze shifting back out the window. "But that doesn't change the fact that David would prefer to be skinned alive and roasted on a spit over an open campfire than ever *consider* marriage to me."

"So change his mind."

"Uh-huh," Dallas huffed. "I stand about as much chance of doing that as I do in bringing Momma back from the grave. Even if I could talk to him about this, he won't listen to me. He never has. I don't think he likes me."

"Don't be a ninny. He likes you fine . . . in all the ways that matter. I've seen the way he looks at you when you aren't looking. Seems to me, he just doesn't know what to do with you, is all. You aren't," Lisa hesitated, shrugged, then continued tactfully, "like most of the women around Prospect."

That comment won Lisa a glare, but Dallas didn't argue. How could she? The girl may be thirteen, but her sister's judgment had always been years more mature.

Besides, there was no arguing with the truth. Which made Dallas all the more certain David Parker would never consider her for a wife. So why was the prospect of marrying him sounding more and more lucrative by the minute? She wasn't sure, and tried hard not to look too closely at her reasons, but she had a feeling there was something about the challenge of it all . . .

No, Dallas reminded herself, it won't work. David's taste ran toward very feminine women. Like Lisa. He'd want a wife who was content to clean and cook and sew, not one who rode like a demon, and who could rope a calf in her sleep a far cry better than he could when he was awake.

That decided, Dallas explained her logic to her sister, counting off on her fingers the reasons David would never marry her. She ended with, "And even if I *did* stand a chance with him, you know as well as me that I don't have a clue as to what a woman does with a man."

Lisa blushed to the roots of her honey-blond hair. "You mean you don't know about—?"

"Of course, I know about *that,*" Dallas snapped, cutting her short. She cleared her throat and rushed on, "What I *don't* know about is . . . well, you know."

"No, I don't think I do. Explain it to me, please."

Dallas's mind scrambled for the right words. "Lisa, I haven't a clue what men and women talk about if they aren't discussing horses and cows. Not only that, but I don't know how a man likes a woman to dress, how he likes her to act, what he likes her to think about and do. I don't . . . dammit, I just don't know how to act right with them." She gestured briskly outside. "Except the punchers. Those men, I get along with fine. But other men . . . well, they make me nervous."

Lisa rolled her lips inward, her dainty brow furrowing as her gaze strayed out the window. "I'm sorry, I can't help you there," she said. "I'm only thirteen, remember? My experience with men isn't just limited, it's nonexistent."

Dallas decided not to point out that Lisa, at thirteen, seemed to know more about men than Dallas did at twenty-five.

"You need someone to teach you," Lisa said slowly, thoughtfully. "You know, show you the ropes—er, so to speak."

Dallas laughed. It was a throaty, seductive sound, but to her own ears sounded rough and gravelly and not nearly as appealing as her sister's soft, light laughter. "Who did you have in mind? Or don't I want to know?"

"No one," Lisa admitted, though the attention she gave to the goings-on down in the corral sharpened. "Then again . . ."

Dallas noticed the change in her sister. Squinting, her gaze followed Lisa's, rooting instantly on the men inside the corral as they tried to toss a saddle onto the back of a frisky maverick who, obviously, had other ideas.

"Hickory Pete?" Dallas asked, her voice thick with amusement as her gaze shifted to the cowpuncher who was trying to catch the maverick's reins. The tall, rangy old man bounded after the horse, but the maverick was too quick and Pete landed face first in the dirt for his efforts. "You want me to ask that old coot how to rope a husband? Lisa, I doubt he even remembers being roped himself, he's so old and it was so long ago."

"No, not him," Lisa murmured, distracted. Her attention had caught on one of the other cowpunchers. Whomever he was, the girl was studying the man intently.

"All right," Lisa said, still distracted, "let's think this through before we do anything rash. What are your choices? You can't go to Maria, because she'll blab to everyone that you don't know how to catch yourself a husband. That would be humiliating for you. You can't ride into Prospect and ask any of the

18

women there, because then *they'll* blab to everyone, and it would be even more humiliating. If you asked Papa, he'd laugh you off the ranch. But . . ."

"But?" Dallas prompted, curious despite herself.

Lisa's head came up, her blue eyes sparkling with enthusiasm as their gazes met. "What you need is an expert."

"An expert . . . what?"

"Not a 'what,' silly, a *'who.'*" Leaning forward, Lisa whispered conspiratorially, "What you need is an expert on women. A man who knows what a man likes," she reasoned, "is a man who knows what he likes himself. And what one man likes . . ."

"They all like," Dallas finished for her, nodding. It was starting to make sense now. Unfortunately. "I see what you're driving at. Again, do you have someone particular in mind?"

Lisa's grin said that she did.

Dallas's gaze drifted back out to the corral. The horse had finally been saddled, and a rider was now climbing on the bucking maverick's back. The maverick, in turn, was putting up one hell of a good fight, much to the delight of the rest of the punchers. "I don't see a single man out there who isn't an expert on women, Lisa. Except Pete."

"Neither do I," her sister agreed, a sly smile curving her lips. "However, I do see *one* man who's more of an expert than the others. That is, if all the gossip about him has any weight to it, which I don't doubt for a second. Think about it, Dallas. Who down there has made no secret that he's 'sworn off ladies?' And wouldn't a man who knew what to stay away from also know what a lady is?"

Lisa nodded to the men below, who laughed good-naturedly when the rider was thrown from the saddle. The man landed face down in the dirt. A cloud of dust billowed up around him. Grunting an off-color reply to the other men, he pushed to his feet and set out after the now happily prancing maverick.

"Which one?" Dallas asked, never taking her eyes off the men.

"Don't you know?" was her sister's snappy reply. "Isn't it obvious?"

No, it wasn't obvious. She must be overlooking something, because even as she scrutinized each familiar face and body, none looked any more knowledgeable about "ladies" than the next. Every one of them had more women than they could count waiting in one rowdy cowtown or another. And not a single one looked to be—

Dallas's brown eyes narrowed as one man, who'd been leaning against the end of the split rail corral, broke away from the rest. His broad-brimmed hat shadowed his face, but there was no disguising his cocky swagger as he made his way over to the drinking well near the barn.

Dallas recognized him immediately, recognized, too, the ragged fringe of sun-faded blond hair peeking from beneath his hat. She didn't need to see it to know the mustache curling over his upper lip was the same rich shade of sun-streaked blond as the hairs pelting his thick, tanned forearms and the firm wedge of his chest.

As she watched, he took the dipper from the pail and lifted it to his lips. When he finished drinking, he removed his hat, scooped up another dipper, and poured this one over his head. The water plastered the hair to his scalp, sparkling in the sunlight as it ignited the rich gold undertones in each strand that, like the man, was wind-tossed and unruly.

Dampness seeped beneath his dusty, collarless shirt, coating the light blue cotton to a back that long days—make that long *years*—of hard work had broadened to a firm wedge of muscle. Ranch work had also done wonderful things to his thighs, making them heavy and thickly muscled from clinging to a saddle for more hours out of a day than he walked. Even from this distance, Dallas could see the bands of sinew beneath the coarse denim trousers, could see the leanness of hips beneath the gun belt he was rarely without, and that was customarily strapped arrogantly low on his hips.

After shaking his head like a dog shaking off its bath, and sending shards of crystalline droplets scattering everywhere, he settled the hat back on his head. He tugged the brim down low, and swaggered back to the corral.

Dallas watched him hook the stacked heel of his left boot over the lowest timber, and cushioned his crossed forearms over the top one, his spine bowing slightly forward as he assessed the goings-on inside the corral. The gesture set his hips—of which, at this angle, Dallas had an exceedingly good view—at an arrogant slant. The stance, she noted, feeling somewhat dazed, was flagrantly, unabashedly male.

He must have sensed her stare, for his head came up, and his attention whipped over his shoulder. Dallas had looked into the man's eyes every day for the past fifteen years; she didn't need to see them to know how very blue they were.

His gaze scanned the house, settling on her window. For a split second, she fought the urge to step back into the shadows so he wouldn't know she'd been staring at him.

Of course, she did no such thing, knowing he'd only tease her unmercifully about it later. Instead, he dragged the hat off his head and waved it in her general direction, his smile wide and friendly. Dallas smiled and waved back as though she hadn't a care in the world.

She didn't look at Lisa—who, she now realized, had been watching her intently—until, apparently satisfied with what he'd seen, the man again shifted his attention back to the corral.

The sisters' gazes met; confident blue collided with shocked-into-speechless brown.

When the two spoke, they spoke at once, their voices tripping over each other. Though they said the same thing, at the same time, the words had completely different inflections.

"Nick Langston!"

Chapter Two

"Nick Langston," Dallas whispered six hours later, after she'd retired to her bedroom for the night.

Supper had been a very uncomfortable, very tense meal. At the time, Dallas had wondered if it would never end. The meal *had* ended, finally—after dozens of hot, angry glares were swapped between Ian Cameron and herself. Father and eldest daughter hadn't spoken a word to each beyond the initial "You *will!*"—by him, followed by an equally firm "I will *not!*"—by her.

Their furious glances had then commenced.

There had been other types of glances cast about tonight. Quite a few of them. It was those glances Dallas remembered now, for they'd been exchanged with someone else.

They'd been exchanged with Nick Langston.

As foreman of the Bar None, Nick took his meals with the family. It was common practice. No one thought anything of seeing his ruggedly handsome face across the table. It wasn't abnormal for Nick to fill the gaps in the conversation by talking to Ian or Dallas about the problems, or successes, of the day.

Tonight had been different.

Tonight, there hadn't been anything normal about sharing a meal with Nick Langston—especially when, more times than not, Dallas had found her gaze straying to him, and any words she might have said clogged in her throat right along with the oddly tasteless meal.

Damn it, why had she been so tongue-tied around Nick? That wasn't like her. God knows Dallas had talked to him often enough in the past. Daily, sometimes hourly. She'd always smiled and laughed at his dry, witty jokes. Occasionally, she would ask his advice about something . . . even more rarely, she'd take it.

Never before had Dallas noticed Nick the way she'd noticed him tonight. Never had she been aware of the way he often said something outrageous, then his blue, *blue* eyes would seek Lisa. He'd grin that familiar, lopsided grin when the girl blushed furiously. Nor did Dallas remember him flirting so shamelessly with Maria, a woman twice his age, and size. Yet, judging by the way the large Mexican woman blushed and flirted as good as she got, this was obviously a regular occurrence.

Why hadn't Dallas noticed any of these things before?

The mattress crunched as she tossed restlessly beneath the sheet. There was another troublesome little something she hadn't noticed about Nick Langston until tonight: Nick *never* teased her father, and his teasing was rarely directed at Dallas. Until that instant, that *second,* she also hadn't realized how much Nick's lack of teasing bothered her. She wasn't sure why.

The air was hot and dry. Dallas kicked off the thin cotton sheet. She told herself it was the heat that accounted for the hot, sweeping sensation that spread like liquid fire through her body. But that was a lie she couldn't convince herself to believe.

Slipping her legs over the side of the bed, she stood and shrugged into her robe. Tying the cotton sash around her waist, she tugged her heavy blond hair from beneath the collar while creeping to the door. A quick listen at the crack separating door from jamb told her no one was rambling through the halls.

Not surprising, that. The ranch hands awoke before dawn, ready to work. The rest of the house got up with them. Nights on the Bar None never seemed to last long enough. Anyone with half a brain would be asleep by now, although the hour wasn't late.

Grateful for the solitude, Dallas opened the door and slipped from the room. Her bare feet padded over the unadorned planked flooring; Ian Cameron didn't believe in expensive frivolities like rugs, meant only to impress people he "didn't give a hoot about." Quietly, Dallas crept down the hall, down the stairs, and out the front door.

It was a lovely night; the sky was huge and starry. The moon was a full, shimmering disk that bathed the endlessly flat land in a breathtaking haze of glistening quicksilver.

Sighing, Dallas pillowed her wrists atop the roughly hewn timber of the corral, her hands dangling limply over the side. In the distance, she heard the bay of a coyote, the whicker of bedded-down horses, the lowing of cows in a trail drive passing nearby. Well, nearby Texas-style. If she squinted, she could see on the horizon—much, much farther away than it appeared to be—the faint orange semiring of light, close to land, given off by the drive's campfire. Though she knew she couldn't, Dallas imagined smelling the charred aroma of smoke curling up into the air, scented with a hint of the steak and beans the cook had pan-fried for supper.

"What do you think, Squirt?" someone, close to her right, asked, his voice deep and low, thick with its customary lazy drawl. The familiar timbre brought an automatic, friendly grin to Dallas's lips. "Thirty miles? Maybe thirty-five?"

Mentally, she assessed the distance between the Bar None and the campfire that was a mere flicker on the horizon. Her nose wrinkled thoughtfully. "Thirty-five, but not an inch more. We couldn't see them if they were any farther away than that."

"True enough," Nick Langston said. He was standing close enough for Dallas to feel his warm breath wash over her cheek and neck as he spoke. A peculiar sensation curled through her. It was . . . warm, oddly stirring. "You know, as I was walking over here, I could have sworn I heard the critters lowing. 'Course, since they're so far away, don't guess that's possible, huh?"

"No, it isn't," she agreed, then added, "but I thought the same thing. Even if it's imaginary, the

26

sound gives the night a pleasant, peaceful ring to it. Don't you think?"

The wistfulness in her tone must have taken Nick off guard, because Dallas noticed he didn't say anything right away. Dallas heard cloth rustle, and imagined his shrug when he finally answered, "Yeah, I expect."

They stood in companionable silence for a few minutes, while Nick fished the makings of a cigarette out of the leather pouch tucked in his vest pocket. Though Dallas had yet to look *at* him, his hands, hooked over the timber, were within view.

She studied them as though she'd never seen them before. Nick's fingers were thick-knuckled, long, and tanned a rich copper-brown. Dirt was embedded beneath his bluntly-cut fingernails. With quick, deft motions that unaccountably fascinated her, Dallas watched him roll a cigarette, watched him bring it to his mouth and lick the paper to make it stick. When he was done, his left hand disappeared to tuck away the pouch. The right one tapped down the cigarette against the timber, packing the tobacco firmly inside the freshly sealed paper.

He had nice hands. Strong and capable, reliable, the kind of hands Dallas was accustomed to seeing on a man. His fingertips were work-roughened, as were his large, solid palms. The richly tanned skin on the back, and the flesh separating the joints of each knuckle, were sprinkled with sun-bleached hair that shimmered a snowy white in the moonlight.

All too soon, his right hand also disappeared. It wasn't until Dallas heard him fetch a match from the leather strip—the one trimmed with silver conchas—

on the inside of his hat brim, that she glanced up. Well, she *almost* glanced up. She might have looked Nick in the eye, had her gaze not snagged on the way he dragged the tip of the match up the coarse, outer seam of his snug-fitting denims.

The match flared to life. Dallas tracked its progress as it ascended to the cigarette, which now dangled out of one corner of Nick Langston's mouth. The light from the match cast his ruggedly carved face in a soft, flattering orange glow.

Dallas blinked hard. She was staring, and she knew it, but she couldn't bring herself to stop. With effort, she forbade her jaw to sag open the way it wanted to do. However, that didn't stop her eyes from widening in surprise and, yes, appreciation.

Had Nick always been this handsome, she wondered. Oh, she'd known he was. Subconsciously. But had he always been this . . . this . . . all-fired *good looking?!*

Of course he's good looking, you ninny, Dallas thought to herself. You've always known that. Always. Why else would the women in every cowtown from here to Abilene be so happy to see Nick every time one of the Bar None's drives hauled in?

The women were always happy to see Nick. Exceptionally happy, now that she thought about it. Dallas tried not to think about it.

Yes, the women were always happy enough to see the other men, too, but not as happy as they were to spot Nick Langston. For years Dallas had watched barmaids sidle up to him, their eyes glistening with a hunger she didn't comprehend, their ripe bodies press-

28

ing against his shoulder as they poured him a drink, against his outer thigh as they sauntered away. Very few left his table without whispering something in his ear.

Dallas never knew what they said, except that whatever it was, it was the focus of at least one ribald joke. She wondered now what those women had said to Nick. She wondered now about a lot of things she'd never had the time or inclination to wonder about before.

Why did women go out of their way for even a platonic touch from Nick Langston? Even when he made it clear by words and action that that's all they were going to get? What was it about Nick's touch . . . ?

Fast on the heels of that thought came every sordid bunkhouse tale Dallas had ever heard told about him. There were quite a few, and though none had ever been confirmed, neither had they been denied. Nick wasn't the sort to boast or to lie.

She swallowed hard, only to find that her throat had gone as dry as the dirt underfoot. A whimper—*hers? she hoped not!*—whispered through the still night air.

Nick must have heard it, too, for his head came up. Their gazes meshed. In the indigo-blue irises of his eyes, Dallas saw a distorted reflection of herself—she looked flushed and confused—and the flickering glow of the match a split second before he shook the flame out.

The haze of moonlight didn't penetrate the shadows cast by the brim of Nick's hat. Dallas was thankful for that. Now, if she could convince her heart there was no reason for it to be slamming against her ribs, she'd be all set!

"You were quiet at supper tonight," Nick said.

"Was I?" Was it Dallas's imagination, or did her voice sound strangely husky and breathless? If it did, apparently she was the only one to notice.

"Uh-hmmm. Mind telling me why? While you're at it, you can also tell me why you and your daddy kept glaring at each other like a pair of rabid coyotes." The way he pronounced the last word, there was no "e" in it. "Lord, I don't remember ever seeing Ian so mad. What'd you do, pull out of going on the drive?"

"I—um—" Dallas tried to concentrate on what Nick was saying. It simply wasn't possible. How could she be expected to think coherently when, in a repeat of that afternoon, she watched him hook his left boot heel on the bottom timber of the corral, and cross his arms—*had he always been* that *sinewy and firm?*—over the top one. The difference between then and now was that this time Nick was close enough for Dallas to feel the heat of him seep through her too-thin cotton wrapper and nightgown, close enough to smell his intriguing, leather-and-spice-and-tobacco scent.

Her uncommonly acute senses screamed that this was *much* different from watching him from afar.

"You all right?" Nick asked softly, but Dallas could barely hear him over the throbbing of her heart in her ears. "Dallas!"

"What?!" she snapped with equal force. In the shadows beneath Nick's hat, she saw a corner of his thick sun-gold mustache tip up in that familiar, lazy grin. What wasn't familiar was the way her stomach somersaulted at the sight . . . a split second before it plunged all the way to her toes.

"I asked if you're all right," he repeated around the cigarette clamped firmly between a line of even white teeth. He was squinting at her through the cloud of smoke curling up from the glowing red end, regarding her oddly. That was fine by Dallas; she felt a bit odd right now. "Your cheeks are all red and . . ." he scowled, "you're breathing a might funny, Squirt."

"Am I? I hadn't noticed," she said. And noticed. She *was* breathing funny, dragging air into her lungs in quick, rapid-fire succession. A light, dizzy feeling circled in her head, and she leaned weakly against the timbered corral.

Had Nick always called her "Squirt?" Yes. Had it ever aggravated her before? No. Not until tonight.

"You and Ian must've had one doozey of a fight," Nick remarked on an exhale of thick gray smoke. "Can't remember ever seeing you so skittish before. You're acting like a virgin mare, you know." He slanted her a glance from beneath thick, honey-tipped lashes; a glance that made Dallas's heart rate inexplicably quicken, and her knees go as inexplicably weak. "Wanna talk about it?"

"No. Yes! I mean . . ." Dallas snapped her mouth shut. She didn't know what she meant. Worse, she didn't know how to tell *Nick* that she didn't know what she meant. Forcefully, she reminded herself that she was talking to Nick Langston here; a man she'd known most of her life, a man who wasn't just another cowpuncher, but her long-time *friend.*

There was only one flaw in that otherwise reasonable vein of logic. The thoughts Dallas had been entertaining about Nick for the past few hours weren't the kind one friend had for another.

She tried not to think about that. She had enough on her mind without complicating matters more than they already were.

Tearing her gaze from Nick, she again focused on the distant glow of the campfire. This time, she didn't really see it. "I have a problem, Nick," she said finally, softly. "A *big* problem." Something in her tone must have caught his attention, for she felt his gaze warm her profile. Dallas refused to look at him. Feeling him beside her was another matter entirely. Indeed, she felt more of Nick Langston right now than she'd ever felt of him in her life. The observation was alarming.

"Something I can help you with?" he asked after an almost imperceptible pause.

She heard him shift against the corral. Her gaze dipped to the hand he'd dangled over the top timber. The tip of his cigarette, wedged between calloused index finger and middle, smoldered red-hot in the moonlight.

"I don't know." She sighed, and wondered if her sister was right. Dallas wasn't so sure. There was only one thing that, no matter how much she thought on the matter, never wavered. Nick Langston's reputation with women was something to be reckoned with. If any man on the Bar None knew what a man liked and wanted from a woman, it would be him.

Those facts couldn't even be disputed mentally. Dallas knew. She'd tried. For the past six hours. But facts were facts.

"You're not going on the drive," Nick said, when she remained silent. "That's it, isn't it?"

"I'm going."

Nick angled his head, glancing at her. In the shadows beneath his hat, only the rich blueness of his eyes shone through; his gaze was so hot it burned. "Then what?"

Should she tell him? Why not? By this time tomorrow, Maria's wagging tongue would make sure the entire ranch, the entire *county,* knew what was going on. "Papa said he wants grandchildren," Dallas said finally, miserably.

Looking at the flames on the horizon, she imagined Nick's thick blond brows rising high in his sun-copper forehead. "So?"

On top of the roughly hewn rail, her fingers interlaced, twisting tightly. That familiar prick of anger stabbed through her, and her tone sharpened. "You don't understand, Nick, he wants *my* grandchildren. Grand*sons* to be exact."

Nick pulled in a deep drag of the cigarette. "He's always wanted that, Squirt. Can't remember a time when he didn't."

"Yes, well, he's being a little more vocal about it these days. He told me this morning that he wants to see me married by spring roundup. No," she amended, "he didn't tell me, he *ordered* me."

A long, slow whistle hissed through Nick's teeth as he turned his head and fixed his gaze on the glowing tip of his cigarette. "You said no, right?"

Dallas smiled weakly, and shrugged. "Not exactly."

She felt his surprise; it matched her own. "You told him *yes?*"

Her forced grin faded. "Not exactly."

" 'Not exactly,' " he growled. "What the hell's *that* supposed to mean? Either you said yes or you didn't, Dallas. Which is it?"

"No," she said firmly. "I told him no."

"But . . . ?" he prodded, correctly sensing the indecision in her tone.

"Buuut," she echoed, "I've been thinking, and . . ."

Briefly, Dallas related Lisa's idea about David Parker—the more she'd thought about it, the better the plan seemed—although she was careful never to divulge the idea as being Lisa's. For some reason, Dallas wanted Nick to think the idea was her own. Nor did she tell Nick in exactly what capacity his help was going to be needed. Yet. She wanted to save that—the worst—until after she'd assessed his initial reaction.

His initial reaction wasn't what she'd expected.

With a flick of his middle finger and thumb, Nick sent the stubby remains of the cigarette careening into the middle of the empty corral. Somehow, he made the gesture one of tightly leashed anger.

The feel of his fingers wrapping around her upper arms pushed a surprised gasp from her. She and Nick often worked together, but they rarely touched. Now she knew why. The heat and strength of his fingers sent tingling currents of shock rippling down to Dallas's wrists, up through her shoulders. Her heart started hammering again.

Nick angled his head until the tips of their noses

touched. This close, Dallas could see the angry red beneath the tan in his sharply chiseled cheeks, could see the thin, tight line of his mouth beneath the curl of his mustache. And she could feel the ragged wash of his breath on her face.

"The truth, Cameron," he demanded. "I want the truth and I want it *now.*"

His grip tightened. Dallas squirmed, but he refused to let her go. What had brought this on? "I *told* you the truth, Langston," she insisted breathlessly.

"Like hell you did!" A muscle just beneath his left cheekbone jerked. Like a magnet, Dallas's gaze was drawn there. Her eyes narrowed when she realized she'd never noticed that instinctive flexing before; yet she had a feeling Nick did it often, usually when upset. "Ian dotes on you, Dallas. Always has, always will. He'd *never . . .*"

She watched Nick's blue eyes darken. Whatever thoughts were running through his mind, they obviously didn't please him. If possible, his agitation increased.

"Who?" The single word was brisk and razor sharp. It sliced straight down Dallas's spine. The intense glare of indigo-blue eyes boring into her demanded an answer.

Pity, Dallas didn't know what the devil Nick was talking about! "Who . . . what?" she asked, confused.

"Who?!" he repeated furiously. "Give me his name, dammit, and I swear I'll rip the bastard apart with my bare hands!

The fingers wrapped tightly around her arms, cutting off her circulation, told Dallas that he was serious.

So did the murderous glint in his eyes. "Nick, I don't know what you're talking about. Whose name?"

"The guy who . . . who . . ." Though his words faltered, the gaze that raked Dallas from the top of her head to the bare tips of her toes did not. It told her all she needed to know.

Her cheeks blazed from the onslaught of his gaze. Good God, for the second time in one night, she was blushing. That was a record! Oh, who was she trying to fool? Her *entire body* was as hot as her cheeks. The feelings had little to do with Nick's unspoken, unfounded accusations; they had everything to do with the feel of his hands biting into her flesh, and the way his gaze roamed freely over a robe that suddenly felt so transparent it may as well have been made of gauze.

"There's no one to name," she assured him, the words leaving her in a husky rush. When his gaze flashed her a challenge, she met it with an even one of her own.

"I don't believe you."

Dallas forced a chuckle. "Why would I lie? Better yet, why would I lie to *you?* I've always been honest with you, Nick. Always. We're . . ." for some reason, her tongue stumbled over the word, "friends, aren't we?"

His grip loosened, but he didn't let her go. The look he sent her said that, though his anger was tempered, it wasn't doused. "I'll take you over my knee and wallop your bare butt if I find out you're lying to me, *friend.*"

The grittily uttered threat was spoken like a protective father to his wayward daughter. Only it wasn't

36

received as such. Not by a long shot! The words sent a bolt of hot sensation through Dallas. She was glad Nick's fingers were still coiled around her arms; if not for the quiet strength of his grip, her knees might have buckled, the way they kept threatening to do.

She sucked in a shaky breath, her attention riveted on a single, flat copper button in the middle of his shirt. It was, she thought, a safe place to look. Safe, that is, if one could discount the firm wedge of muscle sketched beneath the cloth.

Without warning, Nick let her go.

Dallas stumbled, her shaky knees supporting her only long enough for her to lean weakly against the timbered rail of the corral. The dry night air cut into her burning lungs as she dragged in deep breath after equally ragged deep breath. She discovered that no amount of air helped clear the fog that had settled over her senses, nor did it help douse the odd, fiery sizzle of awareness pumping hot and fast through her blood.

Nick must have thought her bizarre reaction stemmed from the ultimatum her father had issued, for he guided the conversation in that direction. "I don't think Ian means it. Whatever he said to you, he'll change his mind. That, or you'll change it for him. Just like you always do."

"Not this time," she grumbled miserably.

Nick was silent for a minute. "Well then, Squirt, what's the worst that can happen? You find yourself a husband, settle down, raise a pack of brats. Lots of gals have done it and lived. *You* should have done it years ago."

"I didn't want to do it years ago," she argued stubbornly. "I don't *want* to do it now."

Nick shrugged and adjusted the hat lower on his brow. "Doesn't look like Ian's giving you much of a choice."

Now, a little voice inside her screamed. *Ask him now, before you lose your nerve!*

"Nick, I need your help," she said, and her voice sounded high and shaky, even to her own ears. Before he could say anything, she hurried on. "If Papa doesn't back down on this . . . that is to say, if he really *does* intend to see me married . . . I mean, if for some reason I can't make him change his mind, I . . . um, I'll need your help."

She glanced up in time to see Nick's eyes narrow to cautious blue slits. "How so?"

How should she phrase this? Exactly how *did* a woman go about asking a man to teach her the things she needed to know to make another man notice her? Damned if Dallas knew! After a brief debate, she decided to go with the unvarnished truth. This was Nick Langston, after all; she'd never had to sugarcoat her words with him. "I've already told you who I have in mind for a husband, right?"

Nick shrugged and again adjusted his hat, until the brim was fairly riding the bridge of his long, straight nose, which gave him a deceptively lazy demeanor. It was a casualness in attitude that the tension radiating from his body denied. "David Parker," he replied, his tone as devoid of emotion as his face. "So?"

"Sooooo . . . I need you to help me."

A tense pause slipped passed, during which neither

Nick nor Dallas moved a muscle. Neither of them breathed.

Nick broke the silence by asking, "Help you do what?"

She could tell by the tone of his voice that he didn't really want to know. "Help me . . . well, you know."

"No," he said, his voice edgy but still relatively flat, "I'm hoping I don't. Why don't you tell me?"

Distance, Dallas thought. She needed to put some distance between herself and Nick. She was noticing the heat of his body washing over her again, noticing the sharp, spicy scent of him on the air and the way the enticing aroma overrode all others until it wrapped around her like a thick, impenetrable blanket. With a bit of distance, she hoped that maybe—just *maybe*—she'd be able to think coherently.

The robe swirled around her legs as she pivoted on her heel and started pacing the dirt beside him. The hot night air, she noted, felt oddly cool as it sneaked beneath the robe, seeping past the barrier of thin white nightgown to caress the flesh of her legs like icy fingers.

Shivering, Dallas wrapped her arms around her waist and quickened her pace. "I've been working on this ranch my entire life," she said finally. "Everything I have, everything I *am*, is the Bar None. I've never had much time for men. You know that."

"Uh-huh. So?"

Had his tone hardened, she wondered, or was her imagination taking over? "So," she continued, "because of that, the only men I've ever had much to do with are the punchers on this ranch. Since Papa made it clear a ranch hand was *not* what he had in mind for a son-in-law, I'm left with trying to catch a real man for a husband. You know, a man who owns property, or one who will someday." She sighed helplessly. "I need someone respectable."

"Like David Parker."

It wasn't her imagination; Nick's tone *was* harder, and degrees colder. "Yes," she said, "like David Parker."

"What do you want me to do, Squirt? Talk to him for you? Maybe put in a good word or two?"

"No, that's not it. What I need for you to do is . . ." Dallas cleared her throat nervously. "Nick, I want you to show me what a man likes, what a man wants from a woman, so I'll know how to win David."

"You what?!"

Dallas froze, her bare feet rooted to the dry, gritty dirt. Her spine stiffened, and she fought the urge to look over her shoulder and gauge Nick's reaction beyond the roaring anger in his voice. "You heard me."

"No, I don't think I did. In fact, I think I damn well better have heard you *wrong,* Cameron."

His boot heels crunched in the dirt. Even without the sound of his approaching steps, Dallas would have known when Nick stopped close behind her. She could smell him—a sharp, spicy male tang in the air. Worse, with every fiercely alive fiber of her being she could *feel* him. And he felt . . . well, damn good, that's how he felt!

They stood for what felt like a very long, very ago-nizing lifetime. Finally, mustering up the last of her courage, Dallas hugged her arms tightly around her

40

waist and said, "You heard me right, Nick. I want you to—"

"Seduce you," he growled. Again, his fingers cut into her upper arms. His grip was punishing as he spun her around to face him. His eyes sparkled with furious blue fire as he bellowed into her upturned face, *"Are you out of your cotton pickin' mind, gal?!* Your daddy would kill me just for *thinking* about doing something so all-fired stupid!"

Dallas's cheeks drained of color. "No! God, Nick, that's not what I mean! I don't want you to . . . to . . . ." She couldn't say it. She simply *could not* force the word past the lump of breath that had clogged somewhere between her burning lungs and her painfully dry throat. "Oh no," she murmured. "All I want is for you to show me how to *act* like a lady. That's it. *Nothing* more."

"I don't know many ladies," he growled. Only the fingers he flexed tightly around her arms told Dallas just how close Nick was to *really* losing his temper with her. "And those I do know, I stay the hell away from."

"But you *are* a man," she argued. "Surely you know what *you* like in a woman. You know how a woman is supposed to act, how she should talk and move to make a man interested in her, and let him know she's interested in him. Think about it, Nick. Please. *You* know what draws a man to one woman instead of another. *I don't."* Her eyes widened, the chocolate brown depths pleading with him to understand, to help. "All I'm asking is for you to teach me those things."

"Sweetheart, about the only thing I'm likely to teach you is how to sit comfortably after I take a strap to your bare—" Nick's mouth snapped shut, as though his mind was no longer able to form the image or the words he'd just moments ago been able to speak with ease. The fingers digging into her soft upper arms shook, but only a little.

"Please, Nick?" she begged to his silence. *"Please!"*

"No!"

Dallas's jaw hardened. "All right, that's fine," she snapped. Her chin tilted proudly, her gaze sparkling with defiance as it locked with his. "If you won't help me, I'll find someone who will."

Judging by his expression, the force with which she spoke the words left no doubt in Nick's mind that she'd do exactly that. Damned if she wouldn't!

Stunned, his fingers loosened. Dallas seized the advantage and tore herself from his grip. Dirt and sage nipped at the sensitive soles of her bare feet when, after sending him a final, searing glare, she spun on her heel and stalked toward the house.

She made it to the halfway point between the corral and the porch steps. That was as far as Nick allowed her to retreat.

"Ian will kill any man stupid enough to lay a hand on you. You know that," a deep, gravely, aggravatingly controlled voice taunted from behind her.

Dallas hesitated. "I don't care. This is all Papa's fault to begin with. I'm not doing this because I think it will be *fun,* Nick, I'm doing it because I'm being forced to."

"I don't think Ian's gonna see things that way."

Very slowly, Dallas turned to face him. The sky was dark, but the moonlight was strong. It washed over Nick Langston's rugged frame, carving and defining the raw strength of him.

"Papa isn't going to see things in any way at all," she said, while trying to ignore the way her heart raced beneath her breasts when Nick took a step toward her. "I don't plan on him ever finding out about this. *And,*" she added harshly, "I don't plan on letting any man except my husband touch me. Like I said, I need to learn how to be a lady that men take notice of, not a . . . a whore."

"Then let this be your first lesson, Cameron. Men take as much notice of whores as they do of ladies. Most of the time, more," he said, his voice seductively husky as he closed in another step. He stopped when the scarred leather tips of his boots grazed the shell-pink curls of her toes.

Dallas tilted her head to look up into his gaze, and found there was something else she'd never noticed about Nick before; how tall and imposing he was up close. He dwarfed her. The top of her head barely cleared the broad shelf of his shoulders. The wedge of his chest spanned what seemed like yards. By comparison, she felt small, insignificant. For the first time in her life, Dallas Louise Cameron actually felt . . . feminine.

"Lesson?" she asked, when Nick's words finally seeped into her churning mind. One tawny brow arched him a challenge—even as she mentally challenged her body to stop the odd shivers that were gnawing at her from the inside out. The night was hot, so why was she shivering? "Does that mean you'll help me? You'll teach me what I need to know?"

Nick's eyes darkened, narrowing to stormy blue slits. "Are you still threatening to find another man for the job?"

"It wasn't a threat," she answered defensively, then thought it funny that she should do that. She wasn't feeling defensive. What she felt was all weak and tingly and warm. "If I have to, I *will* ask someone else but . . ." She shrugged, her gaze again dropping to his flat copper buttons, which shimmered in the moonlight. She studied them intently, refusing to contemplate the chest muscles rippling beneath. "I'd rather it was you, Nick," she admitted softly.

The feel of his roughened index finger scraping the line of her jaw was unexpected. Dallas startled, but allowed him to hook his knuckle under her chin and drag her gaze back to his.

"Why me?" he asked raggedly. It was unclear whether he was asking her the question, or himself.

"Because I know you. Because I've always felt comfortable around you. Because we're f-friends. And because you promised me once that if I ever had a problem, you'd help me as best you could."

"I must have been damn drunk when I said that." Though his tone was light, his gaze was not. His blue eyes were searching her face, looking for . . . something.

"You were. But that doesn't mean I won't hold you to your word, Langston. Will you help me?"

The muscle in his cheek ticked rhythmically. After one throbbing heartbeat had slipped past, he nodded.

44

"Yeah," he said, sighing reluctantly, "fool that I am, I'll help you. Which brings us to lesson number two, Cameron."

His gaze sharpened on her, even as his hand turned inward. His calloused palm cradled her chin, his fingers vising her jaw, holding her steady when she would have looked away.

Slowly, his head dipped.

Dallas's gaze fixed on the golden curl of his mustache. Through it, she could see the sensuous turn of his lips. The racket her heart was making was disgraceful, as was the blush that flamed in her cheeks. Try though she might, she couldn't tear her gaze away.

Was Nick going to kiss her? Dear God, what would she do if he did?

His lips hovered a mere inch from hers, so close she could feel the heat of them brand her mouth, as though the searing contact had been made, not threatened.

She swallowed hard, her tongue instinctively stroking the upper palate of her mouth. What would Nick Langston taste like? Sharp and tangy, she guessed a masculine combination of strong coffee laced with the sting of tobacco.

"Lesson number two," Nick repeated, "is that a lady never backs a man into a corner the way you backed me into one tonight. Not ever. You got that, Cameron?"

"Yes," Dallas answered, the single word slipping past her lips on an embarrassingly airy sigh.

"Good." Nick's penetrating gaze held hers ensnared, his eyes a glaring reinforcement of lesson number two. The tip of his calloused thumb feathered the line of her jaw before he took his hand away. His arm dropped to his side, but he didn't step back. His lips were still poised one hot, tantalizing inch from hers. "Now, unless you smarten up between now and tomorrow, we'll have lesson number three tomorrow night."

"Tomorrow night," she repeated, her voice dazed. "Where?"

"Nine o'clock, on the riverbank where the cows gather every April." He stepped away from her then. Pinching the brim of his hat with his index finger and thumb, he sauntered past her, until Dallas had only the fading crunch of his heels in the dirt.

She wasn't sure, but she could have sworn she heard him mutter something under his breath before he'd rounded the corner of the house, disappearing in the direction of the bunkhouse. "Don't be late, Squirt," she thought he'd said, his voice oddly husky and raw. "I'll be waiting."

Soon, there was nothing but the sounds of the night, and the beating of her heart.

Shivering, Dallas clutched the gaping folds of the robe tightly around her, forcing her trembling knees to carry her back into the house.

Even once she was again tucked safely away in her bed, it was a long time before sleep claimed her. When it did, her dreams were filled with strangely erotic images of Nick Langston.

In her dreams, Nick was a far cry from being a "friend."

* * *

There wasn't much a body could say to Nick Langston that he didn't have a ready answer for. The man thought on his feet better than most. His sharp, dry wit had earned him a reputation on the Bar None, as well as throughout Prospect. A reputation that almost exceeded his reputation for being damn good in bed.

There was only one line he could be handed that would tie his tongue—as well as his gut!—up in knots. *If you don't help me, I'll find someone who will* was it, and the words had been slapped in his face by a gal he felt a brand loyalty to protect.

Brand loyalty.

Those two words gave Dallas Cameron's ultimatum a bitter sting.

At the time she'd said it, Nick hadn't been pleased to find his supply of scathing comebacks fresh out, his supply of words in general as dry as his throat.

He didn't know how she'd done it, but damned if Squirt hadn't coerced him into helping her. Now, three restlessly long hours later, Nick regretted giving in so easily. If things progressed the way Dallas intended for them to, he had a feeling he'd be regretting the error with his life shortly.

Why?

One reason was because Ian Cameron was going to kill him.

"Dammit," Nick growled as, still fully clothed, he thrust himself off the lumpy cot.

His bed in the bunkhouse was situated between Pea-eye Thompson's snores and Hickory Pete's midnight

47

ramblings. Most nights, Nick didn't notice the all-too-familiar sounds. He was used to them. Christ, they were almost comforting. But tonight, the racket aggravated the hell out of him.

Nick stood, pausing next to his cot, his gaze volleying between the thin, lumpy mattress and the door. Slivers of moonlight slanted in through the planks of the latter. Though he knew he needed a cigarette and a breath of fresh air—ironic mix, that—to clear his head.

Hickory Pete's tired old voice crooning in his sleep to the cows he was driving spurred Nick to leave. A few of the other punchers stirred as he stalked down the shadowy center aisle and slammed out the door. The dry midnight heat hit him like a slap. So did the sight of the corral—a looming shadow in the not very far distance.

It didn't take much imagination to conjure up the image that had greeted Nick the last time he'd set foot over the bunkhouse threshold.

Dallas Cameron, looking tiny and strangely pretty in her flowing white nightgown and robe, her hair cascading down her back like a wave of tawny silk, each strand highlighted by moonlight. When she'd leaned her wrists against the top timber, the silvery light had shimmered in through the gaping placket of her robe, silhouetting firm legs, lean hips, the pert, temptingly firm thrust of her . . .

Nick groaned. With effort, he forced the image away, and dug into his vest pocket for the leather pouch that would at least bring a meager amount of comfort. Lord knows, the fresh air and moonlight weren't doing a damn thing to make him feel better.

His gaze was still fixed on the corral. Unable to tear his attention away, he rolled a cigarette from memory. It wasn't until he'd jammed it into the corner of his mouth that he remembered his matches were in his hat, and his hat was in the bunkhouse.

Ripping the cigarette from his mouth, he started to pitch it into the dirt, then thought better of it. On a foreman's wages, tobacco was expensive. He shoved the freshly rolled cigarette into his vest pocket, plowed his hands through his hair, then agitatedly thrust them into the front pockets of his denims.

He started to walk, no direction in mind.

Nick made it all the way to the riverbank before realizing that, hell, it didn't matter where he went. Massachusetts wouldn't be far enough to get away from the promise he'd left with Dallas Cameron only three short hours before. Like a ghost, that promise followed him. Haunted him.

"You're a fool, Langston," he growled as, bending, he picked up a fist-sized rock and hurled it into the water. The splash was loud; the ripples the rock created shimmered like quicksilver in the moonlight, and seemed to go on for miles. So did the repercussions of his vow to show Dallas Cameron how to be a lady.

In Nick's estimation that wasn't a promise he was likely to keep. Not from lack of effort on his part, but lack of ability on hers. That girl couldn't act like a lady if someone put a loaded Colt to her pretty blond head and demanded it. It wasn't in her nature.

That was part of Dallas's charm.

And *all* of Nick's current problem.

He wondered how was he supposed to go about teaching the chit to act ladylike when she insisted on telling other punchers, in no uncertain terms, that they didn't know squat about roping? And, worse, ladylike or not, how the hell did Dallas expect to get David Parker—that lily-livered son of a bitch—to marry her, especially when *Parker* was the one she'd humiliated repeatedly over the years, ever since the two were in short pants?

It wasn't going to happen. Nope, as far as Nick was concerned turning Dallas into a lady was a truly Herculean feat; one he was about as likely to accomplish as Dallas was in getting the Parker kid to marry up with her.

The hell of it was, none of that mattered.

When it came right down to it, even if Dallas wasn't successful with Parker, her failure didn't exonerate Nick from his promise. Helen Langston had raised no slouch. When her son gave his word, he kept it, by God!

Nick snatched up another rock, testing the weight of it in his fist before chucking it into the river to join the first. The amount of energy he expended was minimal, not satisfying. At this hour of the night, it would have to do.

"I could kill her," Nick muttered under his breath halfheartedly. The thought of wrapping his fingers around her little throat . . .

Little?

The word reverberated through Nick's mind, much like the ripples that still swirled in the moonlit water in the wake of the last rock. Dallas Cameron was short, true—his chin cleared the top of her head with room to spare—but there wasn't much "little" about her. Oh, sure, she was a tiny, small-boned thing . . . but that wasn't the part of her that Nick's mind had settled on. His memory flashed him a traitorous picture of her wrapped in a long white robe, with the moonlight filtering in through the thin, cottony material, outlining the more than generous curve of her . . .

He'd rarely thought of Dallas as anything but a hell of a good rider and roper but, with her smart-aleck mouth and cowpuncher's ways, a pain in the butt more times than not.

Tonight, he was reminded that she was a beautiful, desirable woman.

Nick decided he must be in a self-torturing mood, because his cruel mind also decided to flash him another picture. This one was of Dallas, her chin tipped up, her lips softly parted as she waited breathlessly to see if he would kiss her.

The hell of it was, he almost had. He'd wanted to. God, how he'd wanted to crush his mouth over hers! The urge had been as unreasonable as it was strong. He'd wanted to kiss her so badly he could taste it, could actually feel the throbbing need to do it pumping hot and sure in his blood. The only thing that stopped him was the minuscule sliver of reason that had, at the last second, shot through his head like a bolt of lightning.

If Ian found out Nick had kissed his daughter, Ian would kill him.

That wasn't speculation. It was cold, hard fact.

51

The boss made brand rules crystal clear to every man who hired onto the Bar None. Ian Cameron promised competitive wages and hours no more or less than those on any other spread. In the same breath, he told you just-as-calm-as-you-please that if he ever found out you'd touched either of his daughters in a less than brotherly fashion, you were a dead man.

Ian was taken at his word. Every puncher on the ranch knew that, in this matter, the boss was dead-set serious.

It hadn't been a problem, until Dallas had grown up.

Exactly when that had happened, Nick couldn't say. Sometime in the last two years would be his guess. He frowned. No, that couldn't be right. Dallas was twenty-five. It had to have happened before that. It was only in the last two years that Nick had started to notice the changes. It seemed like one minute the gal was wearing frilly little pinafores, the next she was filling out a calico bodice like nobody's business. Not that she wore a dress often, but when she *did* . . .

The problem, Langston. Keep your mind on the problem!

Something had to be done about the promise he'd given Dallas. But what? And how could he risk "doing something" about it without also risking her finding some other man to teach her the things she wanted to know? She *would* find another teacher if he said no, Nick didn't doubt it. The girl was as stubborn as a bucking maverick, and twice as illogical sometimes.

If someone had to teach her, Nick knew it would have to be himself. Dammit, he didn't definitely trust any of the other men to teach her in words, not in action.

He wasn't entirely sure he trusted himself.

Tonight, for the first time, he'd noticed how very soft Dallas's skin felt when it slid beneath his fingertips. Tonight, he'd noticed how deliciously tempting and full and pink her lips were, and how great his desire was to drink of their sweetness.

Nick Langston was no fool. He knew lust when he felt it. Hell, it was kicking up a storm in his gut right now! Luckily, he also had the sense to know when such a feeling was misplaced.

That doesn't mean I won't hold you to your word, Langston.

"Ah, damn, back to that again," Nick growled, and kicked his booted toe deep in the dirt. Yeah, he'd given her his word and, yeah, he'd be damned if he wouldn't keep it, but . . .

His blue eyes narrowed. His shoulders tensed as an idea sparked in his mind. The first ray of hope he'd felt all night quickened in his blood.

He'd given Dallas his word, and there was no going back on it now. Yet there was nothing in their bargain that said *Dallas* had to go through with any of it. She could back out any time, no questions asked.

Nick grinned. If he thought on it hard enough, wouldn't he be able to figure out a way to insure she would go to no other man for the information she'd asked Nick to furnish? There had to be a way. He may not have thought of it yet, but if he set his mind to it, surely he'd come up with some plan to show Dallas how a scheme this all-fired stupid could never work.

His grin broadened as he hooked his thumbs in his belt loops, rocked back on his heels, and looked out over the moonlit water.

The water was still. Nick's thoughts were not. His thoughts churned. The more he thought, the wider he grinned.

Yup, there *had* to be a way . . .

Chapter Three

"I'm tired," Dallas announced, and at the same time pushed herself from the thinly padded chair with more energy than her words suggested.

Lisa glanced up from their father's shirt, which she was mending, the needle pausing in midstitch. Ian Cameron, his face hidden behind a newspaper thats publication date was over three months old, grunted and turned the page.

"Yes," Dallas elaborated awkwardly, covering her mouth with her hand as though stifling a yawn. "Very tired. I think I'll go to bed now. Good night."

"So soon?" Lisa remarked, turning her attention back to her mending. "Mornings come early around here, Dallas, but not *that* early."

Dallas hesitated. Her mind scrambled to find a logical excuse that would explain why she was going to bed an hour early when she'd never done so before. The one she settled on sounded lame, even to herself. "It was a long day and I'm, um, not feeling well."

Now *that* comment brought Ian Cameron's attention out from behind the newspaper. His hard brown eyes raked his eldest daughter from head to toe, and his bushy white brows pinched in his customary scowl. "Look fine to me, girly," he muttered. The paper crinkled as he snapped it back into place.

After spending another agonizingly long supper seated across the table from Nick Langston, Dallas felt anything *but* fine. During the meal, her stomach had fluttered nervously every time Nick had glanced her way. She wasn't positive but—heaven forbid!—she thought she may have blushed once. Oh, no, she felt far from "fine!"

"Now that you mention it, you do look a bit flushed," Lisa remarked. Though her honey-blond head remained bent over her sewing, she sent Dallas a sly glance from the corner of her eye. "And you're shaking. Come here, let me see if you have a fever."

Dallas glanced at the clock and swallowed a groan. It was now ten past the hour. She was supposed to meet Nick in less than forty minutes. She'd barely have enough time to change and get to the river. Of course, it stood to reason that it would take her much longer to get out of the house if she raised a fuss.

With a sigh, Dallas dutifully crossed to her sister's chair and knelt beside it.

Lisa laid a cool, enviably smooth palm against her sister's brow. "Dallas, you—"

Dallas sent her sister a meaningful look and shook her head vigorously.

Lisa frowned. Her voice raising to an uncertain timbre, she continued, "Feel warm?"

Dallas croaked out a "yes."

Lisa's frown deepened. "Not too warm, mind you, but a bit. Where"—Lisa cleared her throat—"where don't you feel well?"

"Everywhere," Dallas improvised, her gaze sharpening on her sister, who regarded her oddly, before straying meaningfully between the newspaper shielding their father, and the door. When her gaze again met Lisa's, she hoped her meaning was clear.

"Bed rest," Lisa blurted, then winced and softened her tone to one of confused concern. "That's what you need. Bed rest. And lots of it."

Dallas grinned.

Lisa shook her head. It was clear from her expression that she didn't like being part of what was obviously a lie. Dallas wasn't surprised; Lisa told a lie with less ease than her sister. "I'm sure you'll feel much better after, um, a good night's sleep. Won't you?"

"I hope so," Dallas replied, then feigned what she hoped was a weary sigh. It wasn't easy to push herself to her feet in a way that looked tired and weak, especially when her too-awake body craved activity.

"Well, then," Lisa said, and the look she sent Dallas before bending her head back to mending indicated she expected a *full* explanation for this in the morning, "what are you waiting for? Go upstairs and crawl into bed. I know it's hot tonight, but ask Maria to give you an extra blanket anyway. That will ward off a chill." Her blue gaze lifted, locking on Dallas. "Stay in bed. I'll make sure no one disturbs you."

"If you insist," Dallas said, her gaze shifting to their father as he briskly turned another page, and grumbled something about politics beneath his breath. She felt a pinch of guilt, but not a large one. Papa was the one to blame for all this, she reminded herself as she turned and headed for the door, her boot heels clicking sharply on the bare, planked floor. If not for his ultimatum of yesterday afternoon . . .

Dallas left the parlor the way someone who didn't feel well would; head down, shoulders slumped, feet dragging. It wasn't until she'd latched the door firmly behind her that she broke into a run.

She cleared the stairs two at a time, reaching her bedroom before she'd managed to drag three deep breaths into her lungs. It was as she was searching through the saddlebag she'd tossed atop her bed before supper that she realized she really shouldn't enjoy lying to her father quite so much.

While she could fib with ease when necessary, outright lying to her father was something Dallas had never done before. Until tonight, she'd never *had* to! Still . . . dammit, this whole mess *was* Papa's fault! Ian Cameron had no one but himself to blame for the drastic measures his daughter was now forced to take in order to win herself a husband.

It did occur to her that, maybe if she acted a wee bit more sedate—*pretend if she had to!*—winning a husband wouldn't be such a time-consuming, laborious chore. Then even David Parker might have been able to abide her just fine.

David Parker.

When Lisa had first suggested him, Dallas had been torn between the urges to laugh hysterically and to throttle the girl on the spot. The idea had been ludicrous. Now that she'd had a day to think on the matter, though . . .

All right, so Dallas still didn't find the thought of spending time with David appealing. But the notion of joining the Bar None with the TLP had an appeal all its own. A very *strong* appeal. Besides, since she was being forced to marry and beget grandsons anyway, did it really matter *whom* she took as a husband? So long as her intended wasn't one of the hired hands—Papa had been most adamant about that—the man's identity was inconsequential.

Truth be told, David Parker was the perfect candidate. In fact, if Dallas didn't know better, she might have realized that it was precisely David's intense dislike of her that made the thought of winning him all the more enticing. Dallas Cameron had never backed down from a challenge in her life; she wasn't about to start now.

As she saw it, Nick Langston was her key to winning David Parker.

Nick.

A slight shiver curled down her spine as her fingers closed around the object she'd been searching for inside the saddlebag. From the cool, leathery depths, she pulled out her grandfather's antique gold pocket watch. The cover *clicked* as she snapped it open, checked the time—it was now eight twenty-three—then snapped it shut and tucked the watch into the pocket of her vest. If Nick was so much as a second late for their meeting, Dallas wanted to know it.

Straightening up, she ran her palms down the thighs of the worn blue denims that encased her from waist to ankle; the cuffs of the pants were tucked into the tops of her riding boots. She was still dusty from working in the corral that afternoon, but there was no time to clean up and change now.

Retucking the blue plaid shirt into the waistband of her pants, Dallas straightened the brown leather vest hanging from her shoulders, reknotted the red and blue bandanna around her neck, and then, boot heels clicking atop the scarred plank floor, headed for the door.

The hat and spurs that completed the outfit were left hanging on a wooden peg by her bureau.

"Lesson number three," a grittily familiar voice said from somewhere in the darkness, the same instant Dallas stepped up to the riverbank. "Women dress like women, *not* ranch hands."

Dallas, her breaths coming hard and fast from running the last hundred or so yards, spun on her heel. Squinting, she searched the moonswept darkness. Except for a silhouetted stand of cottonwoods edging the riverbank, she couldn't see much. One thing she definitely couldn't see was where Nick Langston was standing.

Dallas didn't need to see Nick to know he was there. Somehow she could *feel* his presence, *feel* his gaze on her. For some reason that was twice as unnerving as actually looking into those penetrating blue eyes of his.

She imagined Nick's scrutinizing gaze rove over the tawny wisps escaping her braid, the bangs that puffed lightly against her brow, the wayward strands that curled softly against her temple and cheeks.

She dreamed his attention dip, as his gaze swept over her mouth, lingering there for a heartbeat too long. Her cheeks felt unaccountably warm when she visualized his gaze latch on to the pulse drumming erratically in the base of her throat.

She felt his gaze dip lower.

"Where are you, Langston?" she called out finally. "And what the devil is wrong with my clothes? I work a ranch, remember? These duds is practical."

"No, ma'am. Those duds is ugly," he chuckled. "Take my word for it, Squirt. The clothes I see you wearing every day wouldn't attract a cow."

Dallas continued to scan the trees, but though his voice gave her a general direction to look in, Nick remained well hidden. "I've never wanted to be attractive before," she argued defensively.

"Obviously." His dry chuckle felt like sandpaper scraping down her spine. "But you do now. Those clothes'll have to go."

"What?"

"You heard me. Strip!"

Dallas's throat went dry. She would have stumbled back a step, had she not been aware the river was directly behind her. The water wasn't deep, the current lazy, and she was a good swimmer; drowning wasn't a concern. Humiliating herself was, and she was thinking of more than merely taking a tumble into an icy river.

Nick peeked out from behind the tree trunk he'd been leaning against. His gaze latched onto Dallas.

She was standing statue-still a few steps in front of the riverbank, her athletically slender figure outlined enticingly by the pale moonlight. The splash of color in her cheeks would have been bright in a pitch-black room. So would the wide, shocked roundness of her normally narrow gaze.

Cautiousness and uncertainty were not expressions Nick was used to seeing on this girl, but they suited his purpose just fine. He grinned, and pictured her running for home at any minute. "Well? What the hell you waiting for, Cameron?"

"You, Langston," Dallas snapped. "I want to see your face when I slap that silly grin off it."

The lopsided grin in question didn't waver. Instead of stepping into the moonlight, Nick bent and retrieved the pile of clothes he'd neatly folded and stacked on the ground next to his booted feet. The cotton felt cool and smooth in his hand, soft and feminine. And so it should, he thought moodily, since the damn dress had set him back a month's wages—never mind the time it had taken to fetch the frilly thing!

Nick didn't begrudge the expense, or the wasted hours in the saddle riding into Prospect and back. If this dress was what it took to bring Dallas Cameron to her senses, and scurrying back home where she belonged, so be it. He would have paid twice that amount and considered it well worth the sacrifice!

"You naked yet?" he asked calmly.

"No."

"Let's get a move on. It's getting late, and I've gotta be up early tomorrow. So do you."

Her response came to him as a feral growl that might have been a word, although Nick didn't think so. At least, it was no word that any lady he knew would repeat. Then again, like he'd told Dallas last night, he knew very few ladies—and those he did, he stayed the hell away from. She should have listened.

The last lady he'd been associated with was a schoolmarm from Kansas. That was three years ago. He'd hooked up with Kathleen at the end of a too-long, too-tiring trail drive. She'd been walking past the Prospect saloon as he was walking out of it . . . he found out later. At the time, he'd swallowed down enough rotgut to think she worked there. Maybe if he hadn't been so drunk, he would have seen her for the lady she was.

Nick sighed, remembering Kathleen's long, lustrous brown hair and bright blue eyes that sparkled and smiled every time she looked at him. Every time, that is, until the fall drive came up and he told her he didn't suspect he'd need her company when he returned.

By then Nick had sobered up and realized Kathleen was a lady to the core. But by then it was too late.

She wanted marriage and babies and a prairie cottage with a picket fence and wildflowers. He wanted nothing to do with any of that; after a week, he was hankering to be alone with the wilds again.

When Kathleen had broken down in tears, it had torn Nick up inside.

Even now, three years later, he could hear her gut-wrenching sobs in his ears, still feel the twist of emotion that had wedged in his throat when he saw the tears streaming down her cheeks. He'd broken her heart. Kathleen had told him.

Nick had never forgiven himself. Never, he'd sworn, never again would he hurt a woman that way. It wasn't a vow he intended to break. Yes, he stayed away from ladies.

The sound of Dallas's feet crunching over dirt and sage clumps dragged at Nick's attention. She'd commenced pacing. His grin broadened as he pictured her eyes; they should be a murderous shade of brown right now. She was probably clenching and unclenching her fists at her sides, he laughed to himself.

If Nick Langston had been standing in front of her at that moment, Dallas would have gladly carried through on her previous threat and sent one of her fists hurdling into his arrogant jaw.

"That's really clever, Langston," she called out, her tone only slightly high, only slightly strained. "But, unfortunately for you, not clever enough. You know me better than that. I don't scare off so easily."

"Maybe I don't know you as well as I'd thought. And who said anything about scaring you off, sweetheart?" His tone was so insolent—so damn *casual!*—it made Dallas's spine stiffen, made the tawny hair curling at her nape prickle. "I promised I'd teach you how to act ladylike, and that's exactly what I'm aiming to do. Unless, of course, you've changed your mind and no longer want my help . . . ?"

"I want it," she snapped irritably. In fact, when it came right down to it, she didn't just want Nick's help, she *needed* it. Why else would she be here now? Her agitated gaze narrowed, fixing on the sketchy silhouette of cottonwoods. What was Nick up to, demanding she strip? "I'm *not* taking off my clothes." She paused as, frowning, she tapped her index finger against her pursed lips. "And even if I *did* agree to stri—er, get undressed—which I won't, but if I *did*—I couldn't. I don't have anything else to wear."

"Nothing?" His tongue wrapped around the word, steeping it with a sexual connotation that Dallas had never heard in Nick's voice before.

A wave of heat sizzled through her blood; though she refused to acknowledge the sensation—or its dizzying aftereffects—Dallas couldn't deny the peculiar way she went both hot and cold at the same time. She was torn between wanting to shiver, and fan herself with her hand.

Spinning on her heel, she resumed her pacing. "So much for lesson number three," she said finally. "Let's move on to lesson number four."

"Not on your life. We haven't finished this lesson yet. And we're gonna." It was, Nick realized only as he said the words, a lesson he would lay down his life to see to its bittersweet conclusion. Exactly why that was, he couldn't say . . . or wouldn't acknowledge.

"I just told you, Langston, I don't have anything to—"

He peeked from around the tree only long enough to chuck the pile of clothes at Dallas's feet. "What was that you were saying, Squirt?"

The crunch of her boot heels on dirt came to an abrupt halt. After what felt like a very long time, she broke the silence. "Where did you get these?"

Nick's grin returned in force when he recalled the

lithe, busty blonde who'd been wearing the dress when he'd bought it, quite literally, off the woman's back. "You don't wanna know. Just put the damn thing on and get it over with, okay?"

"Are you crazy? First you won't let me see you then you tell me to strip—no doubt so you can get a kick out of watching? Just how stupid do you think I am?"

Nick plowed all ten fingers through his sun-streaked hair and leaned back against the tree. He kept his opinion of Dallas's intelligence to himself. "If you don't trust me, then do you mind telling me what the hell you think you're doing meeting me out here? In the dark? *Alone?*"

Dallas's hands dropped limply to her sides, her lips clamping around an answer that refused to form. She looked at the clothes she was now clenching tightly in her fists. The rose and yellow calico glistened an attractive shade of silver in the play of moonlight and shadows. The cotton underriggings were a splash of vibrant white.

Where *had* Nick gotten the garments, she wondered, and in the same instant her traitorous mind wondered if they would fit. And if they did, would the fabric feel as soft and cool against her skin as it felt against her fingertips? Would the bodice cling and flatter, and would the skirt make seductive, whispery sounds when she walked, the way Lisa's always did?

"Okay, Squirt, pay attention. The way I see it, you've got three choices. Either you smarten up and go home, or you strip and put that dress on."

She waited, but that was all he said. Slowly, Dallas's head came up, her gaze focusing on the thick shadow

66

of trees. "You said three choices. That was only two."

The silence suddenly seemed thicker, crackling with staticlike tension. The croak of a bullfrog downstream, and the distant bay of a coyote, sounded unnaturally loud. His husky timbre wrapped around her like a warm, familiar blanket.

"Choice number three is *I* take that getup you're wearing off you and put on the dress myself."

This was *not* a humorous situation. Far from it, in fact. Dallas struggled to remember that when she felt a grin tug at her lips, and heard the words that automatically tumbled off her tongue before she could bite them back. "Can if you want, but I don't think it'll fit you, Nick."

"Dammit, Cameron, I'm serious. What's it gonna be?" he growled, his voice low and menacing. "You ready to go home yet?"

"Not hardly." Her shoulders squared. If she'd suspected before that Nick was trying to scare her into running away, now she was positive. Pity she refused to be scared. "I'll take choice number three," she called out, her tone forcefully light. "The dress will probably look better on you anyway."

A twig snapped. That was Dallas's first indication that Nick was no longer content to hide behind the cottonwoods—if hiding had ever been what he was doing, and she doubted it. Leaves crunched beneath large, booted feet. The bark of one of the trees shifted, or so the flickering moonlight, filtering down through the thick ceiling of leaves, made it appear.

Squinting, Dallas picked out a tall, rugged figure as

it pushed away from one of the cottonwood trunks and took an angry step toward her.

Her grin wilted. A shiver of apprehension raced down her spine. Teasing Nick Langston when she couldn't see him was one thing; teasing him while looking into those angry, piercing blue eyes of his was something else entirely.

"You made a bad choice," he said, his voice low and ragged. His eyes were narrowed, but not so much that Dallas missed the glint of determination sparkling in the dark indigo depths. "A real bad choice."

He took a step closer.

Dallas took a quick, instinctive counterstep back. Her heels sank into the soft sand, alerting her to the fact that she'd reached the edge of the riverbank. Her area of retreat was painfully small. "Don't come any closer, Nick. For crying out loud, it was only a joke."

"I'm not in a joking mood." He stopped a foot away from her, and his expression was hard, impassive. In the bath of moonlight and twisting shadows, his features looked like they'd been carved from granite. "You made your choice, Squirt. Come here."

Dallas shook her head. Even if she'd wanted to move—which she didn't—she couldn't. Her boots felt abruptly leadened, the muscles in her legs oddly weak and watery. Her knees shook, threatening to buckle. Had there been anything handy to support her weight, she would have made a grab for it. There was nothing. Except Nick Langston but she didn't think touching him right now would be a smart idea.

"Go away, Nick," she said, her voice high, and almost as shaky as the rest of her. "Go back behind the trees, and promise not to look. I'll put on the dress myself."

The mustache blanketing his upper lip quirked up at one corner. The grin didn't reach his eyes, which remained cold and emotionless as he lifted a hand, extending it to her palm upward. "I said 'come here.'"

Her gaze dipped. His fingers were long, thick-knuckled. A dusting of sun-gold curls pelted his wrist, disappeared beneath the cuff of his sleeve; a sleeve that couldn't hide the bunch of muscle in his forearms. Swallowing hard, she traced each steely band of sinew by memory, stopping only when she reached the stretch of his shoulders, and the fringe of unruly, sun-streaked blond hair that scraped the dusty, faded blue cotton. His hand was big, strong, capable of breaking her in two without expending much effort, Dallas thought, and at the same time felt her heart plummet to her toes. Her gaze lifted, locking with determined blue. Absently, she fisted the collar of her shirt beneath her chin. The other arm hugged her waist. "No. Langston, I made a joke. A *joke.*" Her brown eyes sparkled with defiance. "What the hell is *your* problem? You've always had a wonderful sense of humor, Nick. Remember the time you—?"

"Maybe I didn't think this particular joke was funny," he said tersely, cutting her short. His blue eyes darkened, and the muscle in his cheek ticked. He took that last step forward. The step Dallas had been dreading. "Come here."

Without thinking, she took another step back. The ledge of the riverbank wasn't steep, only about a yard in height, but it was enough to toss Dallas off balance

when her foot sank into air where ground should be
. . . and wasn't. Her left knee carried through on its
previous threat: it buckled.

She gasped when she felt herself falling backward.
Her view shifted abruptly from Nick Langston to star-
studded sky. Her arms flailed. She tried to right herself, but the momentum of the fall was too great; she
couldn't compensate for it.

Throwing out a hand to offset her fall, Dallas was
surprised to feel something rough and warm scrape
her palm. Nick's hand. Instinctively, her fingers curled
inward, clutching at him, hoping to save herself a tumble in the ice-cold river. For a split second, she thought
he had her, but before he could get a good grip and
yank her to safety, her small hand slipped from his.

Dallas landed in the water with a loud splash, and
a cuss that would have made a Union soldier blush.
Her swears came to a halt only when her head plunged
under the icy depths.

She came up spitting. With cold, jerky motions, she
swiped back the saturated hair now plastered to her
face. Her ears were ringing, but not so much that she
missed hearing a rumble of male laughter.

"Y-you think this is f-funny, Langston?" she demanded through ice-numbed lips. Her entire body had
set to shivering, and Dallas wondered briefly if she'd
ever feel warm again.

Nick tried, but failed to suppress his laughter.
"Looks like my sense of humor's come back, Squirt,"
he said and hunkered down beside the riverbank.

The look she sent him was so hot Nick was surprised
the water didn't set to boiling. God knows the blood

pumping through his veins did! Her furious glare made him think better of extending a hand to offer help. He'd a feeling that, if he did, she'd either pull him in with her or ignore him entirely. It was a toss-up that would have been more damaging to his ego.

Lifting her chin, and straightening her spine as regally as a shivering woman could, Dallas stood in the thigh-deep water and stalked from the river. A ribbon of water trailed out behind her, turning the dirt to mud.

She didn't need to glance back to know Nick was dogging her heels. Dallas could hear the ground crunch under his feet, feel the liquid heat of him seep through the drenched cloth plastered to her back.

"No need to get so mad, Squirt. It's not like I pushed you in."

Her cheeks were hot with equal parts humiliation and fury. It was, she noted wryly, the only warm spot on her body—besides the places where the heat of Nick's nearness penetrated her wet clothes.

Her gaze shifted to the dress and underriggings Nick had hurled at her earlier, which were still laying on the ground only a few feet away. Dallas may not know where they'd come from but they were warm and soft and enviably dry. She took a step toward them. Only when she felt a sudden coolness wash over her back did she realize Nick hadn't moved to follow her.

"I'm going to get changed," she said as firmly as her chattering teeth would allow. She unknotted the bandanna from her throat and let it drop soggily to the ground. Her vest was quick to follow. "I suggest you hurry and find those trees you were hiding behind."

When he said nothing, Dallas scowled and spun on her heel to face him. The look on Nick's face set her fingers trembling and poised in the act of releasing the top button of her blouse.

Nick swallowed hard. His throat suddenly felt all dry and thick, while the bandanna knotted around his neck felt unaccountably tight. So did his pants, now that he thought about it. The coarse denim, normally more than roomy enough, felt two sizes too small.

His gaze swept over Dallas. Her hair was water-darkened, sticking to her cheeks and brow. The brisk-ness of the river had flushed her cheeks a becoming shade of pink. Her eyelashes shimmered in the moon-light; the water clotted the sweep of curls together, making them look longer, thicker than normal. More water beaded on the tanned porcelain of her skin, clinging, each drop a crystalline caress, shimmering in the moonlight.

Wet, Nick thought, and sucked in a deep, uneven breath. Everywhere he looked, she was wet. His gaze snagged on a drop of water that beaded against her temple. Fascinated, he watched the drop trail down her cheek, ribbon a temptingly moist path down her neck, pause for a split second on the pulse throbbing in her throat, then slowly wind down and disappear beneath the drenched collar of her shirt.

Though he could no longer see the tantalizing drop, his gaze continued to track its progress. A groan rum-bled in the back of his throat. The water-slickened shirt looked like it had been painted on her body, concealing nothing. Through it, he could see not only the tantalizing shape and size of her breasts, but as he watched, her nipples hardened, beading beneath the cloth.

If he'd needed·proof that Ian Cameron's eldest daughter had grown up, that proof now punched Nick in the jaw. There was no comparison between the flat-chested little spitfire who, at ten, had demanded he teach her to rope, and this woman who, a spinster at twenty-five, had enough firm, ripe curves to drive a sane man crazy.

His hands clenched into fists at his sides, so tight his knuckles hurt. He forced his elbows to lock, forced his arms to remain rigid by his sides for fear he would do something *really* stupid. Something that would get him shot come sunup.

That something was to reach out and see if Dallas's breasts would feel as satisfyingly heavy—and soft and warm and firm—in his hands as they looked like they would. Could they be molded to fit his palms? Nick fought an overpowering urge to find out. From the look, her breasts would nestle in his hands perfectly, with enough overflow to satisfy his gut-wrenching need to lick and taste.

Taste.

The muscle in Nick's cheek ticked erratically. Did her skin taste as creamy and sweet as it looked? How would it feel to have that straining nipple pebbling against the center of his open palm? Against his darting tongue? If he touched her, would the feel of her wet skin sliding beneath his hands, beneath his mouth, have the earth-shattering effect on him that just imagining it did?

Dallas had been looked at by dozens of men in

dozens of ways. Yet the way Nick Langston was looking at her now . . . well, she'd never been looked at like *this* in her life! His gaze was hot, searing, as though it had the power to peel away the saturated shirt and see and touch what lay beneath.

She dragged in a ragged breath, noticing that her breasts felt tingly and warm with his gaze. Her skin smoldered, as though his fingers were caressing and searching her, not his eyes. A rush of sensation swept through her, alarming in its intensity, but not as alarming as she thought it should be. Far from it! And, oh how that scared the hell out of Dallas!

"Nick? I need to get out of these wet things," she said timidly.

The shyness in her tone jarred Nick to his senses. He blinked hard, yanking his gaze to hers. Her brown eyes were wide, shimmering in the moonlight as she searched his face, looking for . . . well, Nick didn't know what the hell she was looking for. Nor was his churning mind able to push his erotic fantasies aside long enough for him to pool his thoughts together and figure it out.

He swallowed again. It was a hard, dry thing that clogged somewhere between his parched throat and his gut, which was kicking up a storm. His voice, when it came, was so rough it was barely recognizable as his own. "Get dressed, dammit! Now!" Gritting his teeth, he stalked around her before he could change his mind. Nick felt her gaze follow him as he stomped back toward the relative safety of the cottonwoods, but there was no help for it. He knew if he didn't put some sanity-saving distance between them—now!—

well, God only knows what would happen. And if she didn't get out of those wet, clinging clothes and into something nice and baggy and safe . . . dammit, he wouldn't be held responsible.

His breaths were tearing through his lungs by the time he reached the shaded safety of the trees. The air seemed to feel cooler here, but that might have been because he was no longer looking at Dallas Cameron's breasts. Nick's blood had stopped boiling in his veins, content now to simmer from the memory of the sweetly tempting sight.

He leaned a shoulder heavily against a solid tree trunk. The bark felt gritty, biting through his shirt, scratching the flesh beneath. He barely noticed as, with trembling fingers, he tugged the familiar pouch out of his vest pocket and rolled himself a much needed cigarette. His fingers were shaking, making the chore take twice as long as it should have. By the time he was done, there wasn't a swear in his extensive vocabulary he hadn't used at least once.

Dallas stripped out of the wet clothes quickly. It took her a while to dress, her frozen fingers having trouble with how the underriggings worked. It was after she'd changed, as she was twisting the remaining water out of her hair, letting it splash to the dirt at her feet, that she heard a crunch of leaves and dirt behind her.

The sight of two large leather boots filled her vision as Nick stopped at her side. The spicy, tobacco-laced smell of him filled her senses at the same time the heat of his body warmed her still-chilled side.

She glanced up.

He glanced down.

Impassive indigo blue met cautious chocolate brown. And held. For an uncomfortably long time.

"Did I embarrass you?" It seemed inconceivable to her; men like Nick didn't *get* embarrassed.

"No," he said, his voice as sharp as a razor. Was it her imagination, or was his stance unnaturally rigid, as if he was being extra careful to make sure no part of his body came in contact with hers? "You ready to go home yet, Cameron?"

"Nick?" She placed a hand on his arm when he turned to walk away. Another mistake. The feel of his muscles hardening beneath her fingertips was electric.

Nick felt it, too. A thrilling current of excitement surged through him, so powerful it pushed the breath from his lungs and made his heart hammer like an adolescent's. He stopped abruptly, and glanced down at her. One golden brow arched the question his suddenly numb tongue refused to form.

"You, um . . ." Dallas licked her lips nervously, and noticed the way the arm beneath her fingers turned to bands of inflexible steel. "You didn't say whether or not you liked me in the dress."

"I'm not the guy you're trying to impress, remember? It doesn't matter what I like, Squirt," he said, forcing the youthful endearment off his tongue, hoping it would remind him of the defiant little girl Dallas used to be. It didn't.

"Your opinion matters to me," she said softly. "It always has. Do I"—she sucked in an uneven breath and, her trembling palms smoothing out a wrinkle in

76

the soft rose and yellow calico covering her thighs, mustered up the last of her courage—"look pretty?"

The uncertainty in her tone—Christ, he couldn't remember Dallas Cameron *ever* sounding so frightened and unsure!—tugged at Nick's heart. Still holding her gaze, he did something he knew damn well he would regret. But she looked so vulnerable, and he felt the last of his willpower snap like a brittle twig. How could he resist?

Nick cupped her cheeks in his hands. Her skin felt smooth beneath his work-roughened palms, silky and warm and right. Too damn much so! His voice husky and raw, he said, "You look beautiful, Dallas."

A hesitant smile, as though she really didn't believe him but wanted very badly to, played over her lips. "Nick, I—"

Whatever else Dallas might have said was lost to the thunder of an approaching horse.

Before Dallas knew what was happening, Nick's arm shot out. His elbow slammed roughly into the side of her waist as he shoved her behind him. Crouching slightly, he cleared the Colt .45 from its holster, and primed the hammer. The barrel was leveled expertly at the trees.

A split second later the lone rider broke into the clearing.

"Jesus, Langston, you almost gave me a heart attack! Put that thing away before you hurt somebody." Ian Cameron's voice cut through the night like a knife. A cloud of dirt billowed beneath his horse's hooves as he reined the stallion in. His narrow brown gaze then pierced his daughter, who was blushing guiltily and settled on Nick Langston.

"Ian," Nick greeted flatly, tipping his hat respectfully, as though he'd just crossed paths with the older man while they were both out riding the range, not by a moonlit river while Nick was touching the man's daughter. "How'd you know where to find me?"

"Pete saw you moseying this way." Ian's glare pierced his daughter. "Didn't say anything about you tagging along with him, girly. Someone mind telling me what the devil's going on here!" he demanded. If fury had an expression, Ian Cameron was wearing it. His glare sliced into his daughter. "I thought you took to your bed sick. And as for you, Langston . . ."

"Papa, I can explain," Dallas said, her tone smooth and controlled as she stepped out from behind Nick. The anger in her father's gaze threatened to melt her on the spot, but she refused to cower. She met her father's glare with a level one of her own and shrugged, as though the reason she was out here with Nick was simplistically reasonable. "It must be my fever, because I couldn't sleep, so I decided to take a walk. Of course, I had no idea Nick was going to be—"

"Save it." The hand Ian sliced through the air, as well as the bite of his tone, cut her explanation painfully short. "I'll expect a full explanation from you both, don't think I won't, but it'll have to wait until morning. Right now, we've got a crisis. Fire's been spotted over at the TLP." That said, he spun the stallion around and charged back the way he'd come.

Dallas's gaze met Nick's. Years of unspoken experience passed between them. Neither were novices to ranching. No one had to tell them how devastating a fire could be when the summer was as hot and dry as this one had been. Even a tiny brushfire could be deadly if it wasn't tamed quickly.

That the TLP was in danger went without saying. However, if a wind picked up, the Bar None would be in jeopardy as well.

Chapter Four

The pain was lifting. Not a lot, but a bit. Instead of the heavy, constricting agony of a few moments ago, the ache had begun to ease and throb dully. He could breathe better. The nausea and dizziness had subsided. Only the sweating remained, but that could have been caused by the dry heat of the fire, now under control, that had burned the TLP's barn to the ground.

Clumps of smoldering timber were the only thing left of the structure. The roof had collapsed before the mad rush of Bar None punchers could get there to help. The fire had been under control even sooner than that. Soot ashened the trampled ground. Smoke blanketed the area, scenting the hot night air with a charred, bitter sting.

Ian Cameron, sitting on the ground, levered his weight up on the stiff-elbowed right arm he'd extended behind him. His sore left arm hurt as he massaged the dulling pain in his chest, his gaze sweeping over the destruction all around him.

It could have been worse. The summer had been dry

and hot, the range grass seasoned on the stalk, ready for any excuse to go up in flames. Damn good thing Parker's men had caught the fire early. TLP hands had brought the fire in the barn under control with unprecedented speed. The smaller flames, caused by shooting sparks, had been doused before they'd had a chance to spread.

Damn good thing. If the grass went, the herd's winter food went. *Nobody* needed an explanation as to what the effects of a range fire right now would mean to all of them. The magnitude of a disaster such as that was painfully obvious.

Ian wiped his stinging, watery eyes with the tail of his bandanna. Smoke clung to the coarse cloth, filling his nostrils as he wiped away the sweat dotting his brow and upper lip. His hand, he was less than thrilled to notice, was trembling. Aftereffects of the fire? Or aftereffects of the pain that still shot through his chest and down his left arm at sluggishly erratic intervals.

Ian's gaze shifted, fixing on his eldest daughter. His brown eyes narrowed. The dress Dallas had been wearing when he'd found her with Langston by the river was now dusted with black soot. The skirt, once full and crisp, drooped limply from her nipped-in waist to the tops of her small, masculinely booted feet. Dark smudges marred her face, he noticed, as he watched her chin tip up and her gaze cautiously meet that of the man standing beside her.

Another stab of pain knifed through Ian's chest as his attention swept over David Parker. He was lanky and tall, his dark head towering a good foot over Dallas's. Reluctantly, Ian had to admit the contrast between Dallas's slender, tawny lightness, and Parker's lanky, midnight darkness, complimented each other perfectly. Standing side by side, they made a striking couple, one that made a body do a double take if he noticed the two just in passing.

That was as far as generous comparisons went.

Dallas and Parker weren't only dissimilar in coloring and frame, but were night and day when it came to personality and attitude. Where Dallas lived and breathed the Bar None, Parker whittled away his time on the TLP, grudgingly doing what was expected of him, never completely happy. He made no secret of wishing his father's health improved enough so he could travel back East and finish his inane schooling.

Schooling, Ian thought with a huff. As though book-smarts would help him run a cattle ranch! Not hardly.

Ian's gaze again narrowed on his daughter. Though he could see Dallas's lips moving, he was too far away to hear what she was saying. Not that he had to, of course. The angry flush stealing over Parker's cheeks told Ian that his daughter was giving Parker a tongue-lashing . . . again.

Ian grinned and shifted his attention. The smile faded when he saw the familiar shape of Nick Langston. The man was standing amid the punchers from the Bar None who wandered here and there, gathering the firefighting supplies they'd brought with them, throwing them in the buckboards as they wearily prepared to head for home.

The first thing Ian noticed was that Langston wasn't helping the others. The second, that the blue eyes Ian knew so well were narrowed to slits, and trained on

Dallas. Langston was staring at the girl intently, the expression on his chiseled face similar to that of a kid who'd trapped a fly under a glass jar and was watching from the outside to see what it would do.

Ian's gaze lit with interest as his attention volleyed between Langston and Parker. Comparisons were inevitable, but again Ian thought there *was* no comparison to make. Physically, the two men were worlds apart; where Langston was all raw muscle and coiled strength, there was a physical softness to Parker that couldn't be denied. One was tall and lanky, the other broad and ranch-worked firm. One had an open, welcoming expression, the other's face was a hard, weather-tanned shield.

Ian sighed. It wasn't that he disliked Parker. Nor did he like the man. David Parker was merely . . . there, always trying to live up to what was expected of him, always going about it totally wrong, always failing. You could tell David had no enjoyment in anything he did, that he worked the TLP spread merely because he had no choice.

That wasn't the way with Nick Langston, though. Langston enjoyed the open range almost as much as he enjoyed a good woman. The hours long and hard, the work lonely, often times backbreaking, but Langston lived for it. You could tell it by the way he sat on his horse, by the way his eyes roamed almost lovingly over the flat, endless stretch of land around him. His touch with the animals was good, instinctive; his judgment in a crisis quick and distinctive; his decisions born of a life of hard-won experience.

Langston lived his simple dreams every day under

an unbelievably huge sky on the wide Texas range. Parker wasted his time daydreaming of things he could never have.

There was no comparison.

A thought struck Ian then, and it sliced through his mind at the same time another pain twisted in his chest. If given a choice, there was no question which one Ian would pick for a son-in-law. Langston, hands down. Cowpuncher or not, he was the best man for the job—and the only person alive who stood a snowball's chance of taming the wild streak in Dallas.

This knowledge struck Ian hard. If he'd been standing, the realization would have brought him to his knees.

He'd never wanted Dallas to wed-up with one of the hired hands. That had never been a consideration; she deserved far better. Ian wanted Dallas's husband to be a man with a little money behind his name, someone respectable. Of course, since the gal was twenty-five and never even been engaged, *any* husband who was still warm and breathing would be an unexpected coup.

Yet . . . a *cowpuncher?* Christ, Ian had fought so many damn years to make sure things never came to *that*.

The question was, was a marriage between Dallas and someone like Parker any better? Ian shivered at the thought. No, it wasn't. In fact, hate though he did to think of his daughter married to a mere ranch hand, the thought of her saddled with a boring book-smart like Parker was untenable.

What to do, what to do? Ian's mind churned. His

thoughts, blessedly, made him forget for a little while about the pain that was fading slowly in his chest. While his idea didn't please him—Dallas married to Nick Langston?—Ian also knew that he didn't have much time left in this world to rope her a better husband. Besides, except for the fact he was a puncher, what was wrong with Nick? Langston was a hardworking, loyal man. Always had been, always would be. At the spinsterish age of twenty-five, Dallas wasn't likely to do much better. Not with *her* waspish tongue and fiery disposition!

It could work. No, make that it *would.*

That fast, the decision was made.

Ian, with his customary ability to effortlessly switch courses midstream, turned his mind to figuring out how best to go about seeing his wishes carried through.

With Lisa, it would have been easy; tell her, she'd do it. Things had never been that simple with Dallas. If Ian demanded she marry Langston, he'd have one hell of a rip-roaring fight on his hands. The gal's stubbornness was unequaled.

On the other hand, if Dallas somehow thought *she'd* come up with the idea or, even better, if Ian kept doing what he'd always done, kept adamantly insisting a hired hand was off limits . . .

Ian grinned, remembering how Dallas and Nick had flushed guiltily to be discovered alone by the river. What was it they said about the forbidden fruit? Didn't it always taste sweeter?

There was only one thing that worried Ian. He was doing Langston a disservice, and he knew it. Paying back years of loyalty by making the man think he was going against his boss's wishes was contemptable. The obvious thing to do would be to tell Nick that he wanted the boy to marry his daughter. There was one drawback there: Dallas had a way of getting information out of people. She'd find out, and she'd refuse him just to be her ornery self. No, if she knew what was happening, she wouldn't go through with any of it.

And she *had* to go through with it. Ian *had* to know she'd be taken care of when he was no longer around to do the job himself. Also, he *had* to know he'd left the Bar None in capable hands. Besides his daughters, it was his only legacy.

His plan may have been hastily concocted, deceptive, and mean, but as much as he hated it, circumstances were such that he simply didn't have a choice. If he'd been firmer with Dallas when she was a child, if he'd started the marriage ball rolling years ago, maybe he'd have had the time to do things right by Dallas and Nick.

As it was, the pain in Ian's chest told him firmly that time was one luxury he did not have.

Nick heard the threads of conversation long before he approached Dallas and Parker. As usual, Dallas was furious. As usual, Parker had his customary scowl locked firmly in place. Nick thought the man's cheeks, normally pink from the sun, looked redder than usual. And Parker's left eye had begun to twitch at the outer corner, a sure sign of growing fury.

Nick groaned.

"Low, David. Trust me, I would know better than you would," Dallas snapped. Curling her fingers inward, she planted her fists atop slender hips. The still damp tawny braid slapped her back and waist when she gave a toss of her head and glared up at Parker, her eyes flashing with liquid brown fire.

"You would know?" David sputtered. His gaze hardened to shards of emerald ice. *"You* would know? Oh, please! Dallas, I'd hardly think *you* to be an expert on—"

"Think again. I've lived on the Bar None all my life, *and,"* gaze narrowing, she thrust the blatant meaning of her next words home, "I've *worked* my ranch. I think that qualifies me as an expert, don't you?"

Parker's chin hiked up an indignant notch. "No, I don't. In fact, in my opinion about the only thing you're qualified for is being an obstinate, spoiled, rotten brat. Ian should have taken a strap to you years ago, Dallas. God knows why he didn't."

While David may not have noticed Nick's rugged form materializing at his side, Dallas did. In the split second it took her to sum Nick up in a glance, he distracted her from her indignation—not only by his unexpected presence, but by her own breathless reaction to it.

"What?" she asked David, blinking hard and frowning as she pulled the tall, lanky man into focus once more. But her gaze didn't want to stay there, and she had to fight the urge to let it return to Nick.

"I said I'll do whatever the hell I please," David growled, glaring down his nose at her. "High or low, it's my decision."

"Of course it is," Dallas murmured, distracted as she wondered what had caused the odd fluttering sensation in the pit of her stomach. And why was her heart racing as though she'd just run a mile? Why were her cheeks all hot and warm with the knowledge of Nick Langston's gaze? Nervously, she cleared her throat and added, "Do what you want. Makes no difference to me if you get yourself killed."

"I won't," David insisted. "Ask Langston here. He'll tell you I'm a decent shot."

Dallas finally had an excuse to look at Nick. Her gaze pounced on it, sweeping to him quickly, devouring the hard yet smooth lines of his impassively set face. Her tawny brows rose with the question she belatedly remembered was her excuse for looking at him. "Well?" she asked. As her gaze met Nick's, she felt her pulse throb to life. "Are you going to lie for him?"

"He's a decent shot," Nick confirmed, his blue eyes fixed on Dallas. The way he unconsciously stressed "decent" indicated Parker could be a better shot if he tried.

"But there's room for improvement, right?" Dallas insisted.

Nick shot her a warning glance, but knew by the determined set to her jaw that she either wasn't paying attention, or chose to overlook what his eyes were trying to tell her. He opened his mouth to reply, but David's words stopped him short.

"I'm no worse than you are, I'll wager," David said to Dallas, his baby-smooth jaw tilted proudly. There was a glint of challenge in both his gaze and his tight smile.

Dallas grinned like one who smelled the lure of easy money in the air. Her brown eyes sparkled in the moonlight as she crossed her arms over her chest. Her gaze dropped meaningfully to the gun strapped to David's hip. Not his thigh, his hip. The carved mahogany butt of a pistol that looked as though it hadn't been fired more than twice. The new leather holster was stiff, the holster itself set too high for a quick draw and clean shot, she thought.

"I don't suppose you'd care to back those words up with a friendly bet?" Dallas asked. Her grin broadened when her gaze strayed over David's narrow shoulder. Their conversation had drawn more than just Nick's attention. A few of the Bar None punchers had begun gathering around them, murmuring curiously, and some TLP hands were quickly joining in. It would be difficult for David to refuse the challenge without losing face—which was exactly what Dallas had counted on.

"Dallas . . ." Nick's gravelly voice warned, but she paid him no mind.

David's gaze slid over the growing semicircle of men that was quickly forming around them. Bets were already being placed as to who they thought would win the contest. David was less than pleased to hear that precious few would match bets placed against him.

His attention sharpened angrily on Dallas's grinning face. "Depends," he growled, cheeks flushing, eye twitching. "What did you have in mind?"

Dallas pursed her lips and tapped the side of her index finger against them thoughtfully. It was clear from the look in her eyes that she'd already decided what she wanted *when* she won. Losing was never a consideration—after all, Nick Langston had been the one who'd taught her how to shoot. "How about . . . a picnic? If I win, I want you to take me on a picnic. Sound fair enough?"

"A *picnic?*" Two male voices growled in unison. Dallas couldn't decide who looked more surprised, Nick or David?

"Yes, a picnic," she insisted, and shot Nick a glance that said she had the entire situation under control. The glance he shot back told her he doubted that very much. "I don't think that's unreasonable. I'm sure the Bar None wouldn't miss me for one afternoon. And the TLP, well they get along just fine without you every day. Probably won't even know you're gone."

Scowling, David jammed his fists deep in the pockets of his dingy brown trousers. His expression was tight and cautious as he ignored the jibe. "That's all you want? A picnic?"

Dallas shrugged demurely as she imagined her sister would do. "I *would* like to give you a shooting lesson after we eat. I guess you'd say that was part of the deal, too."

"*If* I lose," David insisted.

Dallas sent him a look that said there was never a doubt of that. Still, remembering she was going to have to be nicer to David if she hoped to marry him, she humored him by answering, "Yes, of course."

"And if I *win?*"

The skeptical glint filtered back into her eyes. In a voice that said she was still humoring him, she asked, "If you do?"

"What do I get?" David pressed.

"That depends, David," she said, batting her thick, sweeping gold lashes the way she'd seen Maria do last night while flirting with Nick. For some reason, the gesture didn't have the same effect on David that it had had on Nick. "What do you want?"

David's answer was immediate and sure. "Six months away from you. That means for twenty-four blessed weeks I don't have to see or hear from you. I don't want to even know you *exist* until after Christmas."

Dallas's gaze widened in alarm, then narrowed with self-assurance. It went without saying that if David won, she would have a devil of a time trying to court him—so to speak—if she wasn't allowed near him. Then again, what were the chances of David winning? "Slim" and "none" sprang immediately to mind. Of course, there was still a *chance*. On the other hand, she could hardly back down now—not when so many of the men she worked with every day were witnessing this exchange. She had a reputation in the Bar None's bunkhouse to protect!

"All right," she conceded amicably. "If you win, I promise to stay away from you for the next six months. But if *I* win, I get my picnic and you get your shooting lesson. Agreed?"

David looked at the small hand she extended to him as though it was a snake. Eventually, reluctantly, he took it, pumped it as briefly as possible, then dropped it quickly and spun on his heel. Mumbling something about finding some bottles, he disappeared into the crowd of men who were now betting heavily.

Dallas scowled down at the now limp, soiled dress. Deciding she couldn't shoot like this, she searched out the bunkhouse. A few minutes later she returned wearing an outfit that was a good deal more comfortable than the calico dress. The borrowed trousers were two sizes too big, but they were clean. So was the soft red flannel shirt that hung loosely from her shoulders, the tail of which was crammed haphazardly into the baggy waistband of the pants that she'd cinched with a strip of hemp.

She stopped on the fringes of the men, looking around to see if David had returned yet. If so, she didn't spot him.

"Smart, Squirt," a husky voice said close enough to Dallas's ear to cause her to jump. "Real smart. I can see the guy's just counting the days until he can get down on his knees and propose wedded bliss to you."

Dallas sent Nick a scathing glare. "I know exactly what I'm doing, Langston. Why else do you think I asked for that stupid picnic?" she hissed softly, so none of the other men could hear. Her mind, however, wasn't on what she was saying; it was too busy remembering the soft, cool dampness of David's hand in hers—weak fingers; smooth, gentle grip—and the lack of excitement the touch evoked. Clearing her throat, she continued, "You know damn well that I'd much rather have that mustang he likes so much. I could've said I wanted that, but I didn't."

"And I'll bet it just killed you, didn't it, Squirt?" he asked, his voice steeped in sarcasm.

"As a matter of fact, it did. You know how hard I've

been trying to convince David to sell me that horse. I—"

"Botched up," Nick cut her off sharply, "that's what you did. Admit it. That kid's never gonna marry you after you prove you're a better shot than him. And in front of his own men! Christ, I'm starting to hope he *does* win. I don't particularly care for him, but he's sure as hell earned a break from you."

Dallas sucked in a long, deep breath. It was either that, or risk saying something she would live to regret. It didn't work, the urge to slap Nick soundly was incredibly strong, barely tempered.

"Thanks, Langston," she snapped. "It's reassuring to know you're backing me in all of this." With a toss of her head, Dallas spun on her heel and stalked away.

Nick let her get exactly two angry footsteps from him before his hand shot out. His fingers coiled around her upper arm—God, she was small!—and dragged her back. Hard. "You're forgetting one very important point, Squirt," he growled so close to her ear that Dallas felt the hot wash of his breath sizzle over her.

She shivered.

Nick grinned.

Her gaze lifted, defiantly meeting his. Her brown eyes sparkled murderously. His blue ones glinted hard, his gaze unmercifully determined.

"What have I forgotten, Nick?"

"You blackmailed me into helping you rope Parker, remember?" The way she averted her gaze, then quickly dragged it back to him, said she did.

"I remember. So what?"

94

His grip tightened, then immediately loosened when she winced and tried to pull away. He pulled her closer, until her arm, from shoulder to elbow, pressed against his chest. "So nothing. You want the poor guy roped, then you do exactly what I tell you to do. And if you don't"—his eyes narrowed with deep blue conviction—"you find someone else to help you. Before you take me up on that, Squirt, remember that the second you break our deal, I'll go straight to your daddy and tell him what you're up to. Is that clear?"

"Now who's blackmailing whom?"

Though her words were sarcastic, Nick could tell by the scowl furrowing her brow that she believed him. Good. Because he hadn't been lying. If he had to insure she wouldn't go to another man by snitching on her, so be it. It wouldn't boost his pride any to do it—such a slimy tactic was repulsive—but the possible consequences of what another man would do with Dallas's offer was worse.

Nick grinned coldly. "This time *I'm* blackmailing *you,* darlin'. Make no mistake about it."

The tense silence that followed was filled with the mumbles of the punchers who, bets placed, were now speculating on how much Dallas would win the makeshift shooting match by. Dallas's shoulders squared proudly when she realized she was the obvious choice to win—and that everyone seemed to know it.

"All right, Nick," she said finally, tightly. She kept her gaze averted, although she was very aware of his eyes boring hotly into her. "What do you want me to do? *Besides* intentionally loose. That, I will not do."

"Obviously, you can't," he drawled. "No one would believe it. However, that doesn't mean you have to show the kid up, either. Win by *one* bottle, Dallas. If he hits five, you hit six. If he shoots ten, you shoot eleven. Whatever." The crook of his index finger—warm and rough—hooked beneath her chin, tilting it up, forcing her to return his level stare. "Just—and this is the important part, so pay attention—just *almost* miss the last one. I don't care how you do it, but make it look like a lucky shot."

Dallas's eyes sparked with indignation, her outraged glare sweeping back to Nick. Her voice was surprisingly calm. "You taught me how to shoot. We both know I can do better than winning by a single bottle."

"Fine," Nick growled. "So we'll both know it. Just don't *do* it. Let Parker think you won by a very small margin." Letting go of her chin, he plowed the fingers of that hand through his tousled, smoky-smelling hair. "Christ, Dallas, leave the kid a scrap of pride."

"And if I don't?"

Nick's eyes bored into her. "Then start looking for another husband. You heard what Parker wants if he wins. A rest from you. Hardly sounds like a man who's thinking of getting hitched up with you, does it? You've humiliated him one too many times."

Dallas frowned thoughtfully. Damned if Nick wasn't right. David was angrier tonight than normal. Humiliating him in a shooting contest was not the way to convince a man she was good wife material. It would be no incentive to marriage.

Sucking in a deep breath, Dallas nodded. She felt

96

Nick's body relax by slow degrees, the way his breaths went from ragged to even. She noticed other things as well—like the beat of his heart hammering beneath her arm, the charred scent clinging to both their clothes, the way her arm tingled from where it pressed against his sinewy chest, and . . .

". . . use mine."

Dallas blinked hard. Though she was struggling to hear what Nick had said, she was more aware of the way his breath sizzled over her face when he'd said it.

"Wh-what?" she asked, noticing suddenly that his fingers were no longer curled around her arm, no longer holding her to his chest. She was now leaning against him of her own accord. She enjoyed the feel of his muscular firmness against her much more than she should have. "I . . . did you say something about a gun?"

"Not listening, Squirt?" he asked, and sent her that infernal lopsided grin. Her heart skipped, then plunged, and Dallas was aware that her easy acceptance of that reaction meant she was getting used to the effects his smile had on her. The smile, at least, was friendly and familiar, even if the man who bore it no longer seemed to be.

Her gaze drifted up past the mustached lips, settling on his eyes. The blue depths said he knew exactly what she'd been thinking. Dallas felt an immediate need to lie. Pushing away from him, and supporting herself on her own two watery legs, she said shakily, "I was just thinking about . . ." The blue eyes challenged her to say it. She couldn't. Lying to Nick had never been easy for her. That was one thing between them that hadn't changed. Perhaps, the only thing. She shook her head. "Never mind, it doesn't matter. What did you say?"

Nick angled his head, one eye squinting, and sent her a curious glance. Then, shrugging, he said, "I told you to use my gun." His gaze strayed purposely down to her hips. "You didn't bring one."

A strangled "Oh" was about all she could manage, because with Nick's gaze came the memory of him, many years ago, hoisting her onto the back of a horse. She'd been ten years old, though she still remembered like it was yesterday, the safe feel of his rugged hands cupping the hips his gaze had just now seared. The gesture then had been made with brotherly affection; an intimacy that was really no intimacy at all. It hadn't bothered her. Then. Why would it? It was merely Nick teaching her how to ride bareback.

The flash of memory disturbed Dallas now. Quite a bit. Enough to make a shiver coil down her spine. Her attention snagged on Nick's hands, watching intently as those thick, calloused fingers lowered to the gun belt strapped to his hips.

Now was probably not the right time to wonder if that man in California had made coarse-clinging denims with Nick Langston's lean-hipped frame in mind. But she did wonder. And she thought that, yes, Levi Strauss must have done exactly that, because Dallas couldn't remember ever seeing a man who wore denims quite like Nick did. The tough material was weather-faded and worn—which made it all the more appealing to look at. The coarse blue cloth stretched around his hips, clung to his thighs, cupped his taut buttocks. Appealing creases—light melting into

98

dark—shot out from the junction between his legs, emphasizing the way the pants molded and defined the enticing bulge of his—

"Dallas!"

Jarred and breathless, her guilty gaze snapped up. She met Nick's all-knowing eyes, and knew she was blushing because she felt the stain of hot color in her cheeks. "What?" she said, straining to keep her voice soft.

"Here." He held out the gun belt. When she looked at it dumbly Nick sighed and, taking her hands, placed the heavy, tooled leather in her grip. He had to curl her limp fingers around it, otherwise, it would have slipped from her still slack grasp. "Put it on, Dallas."

Nick cussed softly as he watched her trying, and failing, to tuck the leather strap through the wrought silver buckle. It was her third attempt, yet even that easy chore seemed beyond her. "Oh, for Christ's sake," he growled, swatting her hands away.

But Dallas wanted to do it herself—it was a matter of pride now—and her hands returned. She fumbled around, trying to work around Nick's insistent fingers. Her fingertips seared over hot, calloused flesh more times than she could count. She remembered each and every touch, each slide of flesh, each shiver.

Her interference, and his, made the chore impossible.

"Hold still, dammit!" Nick grabbed her hands, wrapping his powerful fingers around them. He felt her trembling. And his own. There was a hot flush in her cheeks and her brown eyes looked wide and confused. In that instant, Nick remembered where Dallas had been looking when all of her odd behavior had begun.

Dropping her hands, Nick snapped, "Do it yourself," then stalked away.

It took her awhile, but without Nick Langston nearby, Dallas managed to wrap the gun belt around her hips. The strap she'd tied around her upper thigh was not too tight, the holster and gun felt heavy. It was a familiar weight; it didn't bother her. What *did* bother her—a lot—was the raw heat of Nick's body that still warmed the leather from where it had rested intimately against his body, in the same places it now rested against hers. The lingering male heat, in turn, seeped through the coarse material of Dallas's borrowed pants, warming her skin. It was a hot, branding feeling. Disturbing in that it was not nearly disturbing enough.

"You ready to lose, Dallas?" David Parker asked. His tone was good-natured, with not a hint of his previous anger.

Though he was standing directly in front of her, and looked as though he had been for at least a full minute, Dallas jumped. Her fingers fluttered to her throat in an unconsciously feminine gesture that for some reason made him frown.

His green eyes narrowed, straying downward. The frown puckered into a scowl when he apparently noticed—really noticed—her change of clothes. "What happened to your dress?"

The question surprised her, since she hadn't realized David had been aware of the dress before. Of course, why would he? They'd been busy toting buckets and hefting weighted gunnysacks. Still, after the fire had been controlled, there'd been plenty of time for him to acknowledge her change of appearance. He hadn't said a word.

"I—er—changed. Skirts and guns don't mix." Dallas shrugged nervously and realized that, for the first time in her life, she was having a normal conversation with this man. Well, almost. It made her uneasy. "Nowhere to tie the bootstraps," she elaborated, and waved to the leather thongs in question.

Was it her imagination, or did David's gaze darken as it traveled over her hips, gliding down the length of her thighs? One thing she knew was genuine was the way the little muscle in his left eye twitched. His jaw bunched when his gaze strayed back up the same shapely path.

Dallas fought a grin. In the past, when not wearing pants, she'd always worn split skirts. While not quite the same as a dress, they were almost as bulky and full. The pants she now wore were loose, but not *that* loose. The size and shape of her legs were easy to trace beneath the cloth. It gave her a thrill to know David was indeed looking, and that his eyes glinted with appreciation—whether he admitted to it or not.

Had Nick also noticed? she wondered, and the thought made the small, heady thrill ebb. Not because there was a chance he hadn't looked, but because she was disappointed to think he might not have *wanted* to look. Perhaps he didn't find her pretty enough to ogle.

"Since when do you want to be ogled, girl?" Dallas snapped, softly enough for only her own ears to catch. "Since when do you care about being pretty?" She

101

purposely used her father's brisk tone, hoping it would snap her back to her senses.

Her chin lifted, her gaze met David's. He was looking at her oddly, as though he'd never seen her before. Ah, well, Dallas had expected that. Lesson number three: women dress like women, not ranch hands. Probably that glint she saw in David's eyes was disgust. She told herself the stab of regret she felt came from knowing she would now have to work harder to get David to recognize her as a woman. It had nothing at all to do with female vanity—whatever that was. No, of course not.

"Are you ready?" she asked tightly.

He nodded, apparently distracted by the buttons running up the front placket of her borrowed shirt.

Dallas turned and started working her way through the men, over to where David had lined up an even dozen bottles atop a split-rail fence. A dozen or so more were stacked beside it. She'd taken no more than three steps when David called out her name. Glancing back at him from over her shoulder, she lifted a tawny brow in question.

"Would you . . . I mean, if you win, that is . . . would you . . . ?"

"Would I what?" she asked, and wondered what had made his prominent cheeks darken to a shade redder than his sunburnt normal. "Would I do what?" she repeated.

"Would you clean up that dress . . . I mean, wash out the soot and smell of smoke and, um . . . ?" His voice was as stiff as his stance. "Would you wear it again? On our picnic? If you win."

"Do you want me to?" she asked, eyeing him carefully. His cheeks darkened still more when he nodded. "All right then, I will." To ease the tension that had abruptly sprung up between them, Dallas nodded to the fence, and the men who were quickly—and quite verbally—growing impatient. "Come on, Parker, let's get this over with."

Without a second glance at him, Dallas strode over to the line someone had drawn in the dirt with the tip of a charred chunk of wood. In her opinion, it was ridiculously close to the bottles lined up, barely a hundred feet away. She made no complaint, knowing David would shoot better at a lesser distance.

"This little contest here is to prove more than aim," the man who had been chosen as judge said, his drawl as thick as the tension that raced through the gathered spectators. "Dallas, David, you each'll get points for accuracy, but you'll get more points for speed on the draw. Understand?"

Dallas nodded, her attention focused solely on the bottles as she unsnapped the strap holding Nick's pistol in place. Her fingers flexed, then poised over the plain wooden butt.

"Shoot when you're ready, Dallas," the man told her.

She drew the way Nick Langston had taught her.

Dallas shot from the hip.

Winston Parker was dying.

Nobody had come right out and told him so, even his doctor, but Winston wasn't stupid. He knew. His mortality was written on every face that came through his bedroom door. It was always the same. First they'd glance at the bed, then they'd focus intently on his chest. Once assured he was still breathing, he'd hear the soft, inevitable sigh of relief, and see the glint of sympathy in their eyes.

This had gone on for months. With every person who came into his room, the annoying ritual was repeated.

Lately, though, a different expression had been added to their faces. Curious. As though they wondered if maybe, just maybe, the old goat wouldn't hold on for a while after all.

Everybody had expected him to be dead by now, including Winston himself. If he didn't have one more thing to do, maybe he would have had the common decency to oblige them all. Then again, maybe not. If it was one thing Winston Parker was not known for, it was decency. Of any sort. Why should dying be any different?

With labored movements, Winston rolled onto his side. He grimaced at the pain that cut through his chest. He should be used to it by now—since the onset of his sickness, the searing pain in his lungs had grown progressively worse—but he wasn't. Four months ago he'd been an active man. To be inactive now, to have every movement pained and labored, was more than annoying; it was downright humiliating.

It didn't help that there wasn't a damn thing he could do about it. Nothing he could do about the pain, about his health, about *anything*.

He sucked in a breath, and noticed the air in the

room was cloying and hot and . . . well, sickly smelling. His room stank of imminent death. It wasn't a pleasant odor, but a familiar one; like most things that bothered him lately, he'd learned to ignore it.

There was only one thing Winston could not—*would* not—ignore, and that was his son. Ever since David had come home, Winston had been on edge. David bothered him, plain and simple. That idiotic schooling mattered to him more than the TLP, and that was one thing Winston could never understand.

The fire in the barn was a good example. Winston had smelled the smoke—Christ, this time of year that scent was enough to send shivers down anyone's spine!—and he'd somehow managed to climb out of his sickbed and stagger over to the window. He'd watched the wooden structure he'd built with his own two hands and sweat burn to ashes. And he'd watched his son stand helplessly by, watching while *others* doused the blaze.

David hadn't helped fight the fire. David hadn't known *how* to help fight it.

Winston shook his head sadly and sighed into his pillow. Where had he gone wrong with his son? What could he have done differently to make David grow up right?

He didn't know. What's more, he was sick of asking himself that question and never finding an answer. As a father, Winston had gone wrong with David. Somehow. Somewhere. He knew that, had known it for a long time. The hows and whys no longer mattered. The here and now did.

The here and now said that in the very near future

David was going to *have* to set his idealistic goals aside and come through for the TLP. It was the only way the ranch, Winston's legacy, could live on after he'd breathed his last. It was also the only financial support his son had.

Winston tensed, feeling the burning itch that anxiety always brought on in his chest. He could have tried to suppress the inevitable, but why bother? Suppression stalled, but didn't make the problem go away. He grappled amid the bed linen, his once thick fingers, now bony and weak, searching for the stack of folded handkerchiefs he was never without.

The first wracking cough tore from him before he'd grabbed two of the course squares of linen and pressed them to his mouth. It took five long, painful minutes for the coughing to stop. By then, his lungs felt as though someone had cut them open with a very dull knife, and the two handkerchiefs were smattered with blood.

Winston collapsed back against the pillows with a groan. *Soon, David,* a tired voice echoed in his mind. *Soon.*

As though his thoughts had conjured up his son, he heard David's voice shoot out from the doorway.

"I heard the coughing. Are you all right?"

Winston grunted, and wondered how a man like himself could have spawned such a thoughtful, soft-spoken thing for a son. It just didn't seem right. "They gone yet?" he grumbled, waving the stained handkerchief he clutched in his fist at the window.

"Hours ago. I came up earlier to tell you what happened, but you were asleep. I didn't want to wake you."

Winston grunted again. This time he had to bite down on his parched lower lip to keep from speaking his mind. Instead, he guided the conversation to the topic that had been eating at him for weeks. And, he suspected, eating at his lily-livered son. "Did you ask her?"

David shook his head and closed the door behind him. The hour was late, the room lit only by the moonlight slicing in through the windows. He settled on the chair beside his father's bed. "No, I haven't asked her."

"Why the hell not?" Winston kept his voice low. His lungs hurt with every scorching breath; yelling would only start up the dreaded coughing again. He wasn't up to another bout.

David shrugged. "The time wasn't right."

"You've been home for three months now. The time's never been right."

"Soon, Dad. I promise."

Winston's glare told his son exactly what he thought of the promise David had been spouting—then, as far as Winston was concerned, ignoring—for months. "It damn well *better* be soon. There isn't much time left. The drive starts in a week. Mark my words, that girl's as stubborn as her father. She'll be on that drive. You can't woo her when she isn't here."

David's glare pierced the darkness. For just a second, the look of leashed fury on his son's face brought a stab of admiration to Winston. It was a small stab, though, and it went away quickly. But it had been there.

"I'll do it before she leaves," David said, his voice edgy as he shifted in the chair.

Winston grunted, only then noticing the charred scent still clinging to his son's clothes. An instinctive shiver born of years of dreading that smell shimmied through him. Still, even that hated aroma was better than the sickness and decay he'd been smelling night and day for far too long. His gaze narrowed, locking with David's. "When?" he demanded. Though his voice was wispy, out of respect to his aching lungs, his tone was hard and demanding.

David glanced away, his gaze fixed on the nightstand and the bottles of medicine scattered atop it. "I . . . did you see any of what happened?" He glanced up long enough to see his father's dark head nod. "Then you know about the shooting match?"

"Yes," Winston grumbled with disgust. "I know you made an ass out of yourself. *Again.* Is there anything else about it that I should know?"

David shrugged, and quickly explained the stakes he and Dallas had been wagering on. He didn't miss the speculative glint in his father's eyes at the mention of the now unavoidable picnic.

Winston's lips pursed. He scowled thoughtfully, even as his fingers tightened around the soiled handkerchiefs. "When is this picnic of hers?"

"She didn't say. In a few days, I presume."

"Goddammit, boy!" Winston bellowed. "You can't *presume* anything with Dallas Cameron. Haven't you

108

learned that yet? When it comes to women like her . . . you have . . . have to—"

The angry words were choked off by another vicious bout of coughing. This time, the spasms cut through more than Winston's lungs, they cut through his entire body.

The coughing eventually eased, but only after three more handkerchiefs had been soiled.

"Do it, David," Winston wheezed, his breathing not yet fully recovered. "Just . . . just *do it!* Propose to her, make her accept, then marry her before she realizes what she's doing and changes her mind. Don't do it for me. Do it for the ranch. It's our only hope." As much as it pained him to say it, to even admit it to himself, Winston added, *"You* are the TLP's only hope."

The carpet muffled the scrape of chair legs as David pushed to his feet. He stood beside his father's bed, looking down at the sickly body that had, just months ago, been hearty and robust. The night shadows played over Winston Parker's face, emphasizing the gaunt hollows and angles, the thick smudge of shadows under his eyes. The pale face staring back at David hardly looked familiar anymore.

David sighed and turned toward the door, the click of his boot heels absorbed by the carpet. "I'll *tell* Dallas when the picnic is going to be, and I'll *make sure* she keeps the date. I'll . . ." his fingers poised over the doorknob, "I'll propose to her then. We'll be married the week after that."

"And if she says no?" Winston rasped. "What will you do then?"

David turned slowly. His gaze, when it met his fa-

109

ther's, glinted in the moonlight. Winston saw a flash of determination in both his son's eyes and his expression. He'd never seen that in David before. The spark of admiration fired again in his chest; this time it stayed a few seconds before flickering out.

"I'm a Parker," David said solemnly, his words clipped and low and precise. "I'll do whatever has to be done."

Like his expression, that confident tone was also unfamiliar to Winston. Unfamiliar, but welcome. It gave Winston hope that David might yet succeed.

David's rare determination worked like a salve on Winston. He didn't feel better physically, but the churning of his mind had eased a little.

David turned back toward the door. As he left, he said over his shoulder, "I'll send someone up to change the sheets."

The door clicked into place behind him. A surge of anger had been riding David from the second he'd walked into his father's room. Only once the door had been shut between them did he allow his raw fury to show. Had anyone seen it, they would have thought the transformation astounding. Meek, mild David Parker's face twisted in rage. His green eyes were never so murderously bright.

But his expression *was* furious, and his eyes were lit with the thoughts whirling through his brain. He could feel the blood drum in his temples, feel his muscles harden with the need to hit something hard.

His father was asking a lot of him. Too damn much!

But Winston Parker didn't care that he was demanding his son marry a little hoyden like Dallas

Cameron. Why should he? Winston didn't have to live with the bitch. Winston didn't care about the price he was asking his son to pay for a ranch David didn't even like. But David knew. Just like David knew the only way he was going to be able to afford to continue his schooling was if the TLP survived. He had no other source of income—had never thought he'd need one. The TLP had always seemed rock solid. Because he'd spent the last four years in Boston, David hadn't seen the years chipping away at the spread he'd thought would be there for him whenever he needed it.

To say the Parkers had had a bad year would be a massive understatement. Winston's illness had summoned David home. What David had found astounded him.

Cattle gout had destroyed almost half the herd before it could be treated. The TLP's credit was overextended; no bank would lend them more. Half the hands had been let go; there was no money to pay their wages, already four months overdue. With the herd badly depleted, and a severe lack of help to run the ranch, David knew the situation was hopeless. They *could* drive what was left of the herd to market, but even if they'd sold every head at top dollar, the money wouldn't be enough to save the ranch.

As Winston had said when his son had first come home from Boston, and as David now grudgingly believed, the only way the TLP was going to survive was if it merged with another spread.

The obvious choice was the Bar None.

Who would have expected so many years ago that Ian Cameron's little ranch would turn such a fine profit? Not Winston or David Parker! But, despite the odds, Ian had done just that. And it was a damn good thing he had, too, because now the TLP was going to profit from Ian's good business sense.

In the last seven years, Ian had bought out two neighboring ranches, adding more lucrative land to his original investment. There was no doubt Ian would snap at the chance to, if not own outright, at least *merge* the TLP with the Bar None. Of course he would. As long as the merger was made by a marriage, and the land officially stayed in Parker hands, the arrangement would benefit everyone concerned.

Everyone, that is, except David. Because in order for the merger to take place, he was going to have to marry Dallas Cameron. A woman he'd never liked, and whom he hated now.

His jaw flexed when he clamped his teeth together. One fist ground into his softly muscled thigh. Could anything be more reprehensible than marrying Dallas? Nothing David could think of. But what David thought and wanted no longer mattered. Saving the TLP did. There was only one way to save the ranch, and save it quickly. Before the creditors were no longer knocking politely at their door, but kicking it down.

He'd bite his tongue, smile, continue to act like the simpering fool. It was what people expected of him, after all. David had learned early that if he simply gave people what they expected, and nothing more, they could be so easily manipulated into doing what he wanted them to do.

Somehow, he would manipulate this situation so that Dallas Cameron would be his wife. Yes, he'd marry the detestable girl if it killed him! But he swore the marriage wouldn't last a second longer than it took for the ink on the merger papers to dry and the marriage to be consummated.

Afterward, if she was smart, Dallas would give him the land he wanted and a quick divorce. If not . . . Well, there were ways to be found.

While David Parker wasn't an overly violent person at heart, he knew that, considering the alternative . . . yes, he could stomach committing a crime if it meant not being saddled with Dallas for the rest of his life.

A sly grin curled over David's lips as he pushed from the door and stalked down the hallway toward his own room. "I'm a Parker," he muttered under his breath savagely. "I'll do whatever it takes. Damned if I won't!"

Chapter Five

Ian Cameron's heels clicked sharply atop the planked floor as he paced back and forth behind the oak desk in his study. His gaze shifted to Dallas, who sat in the padded, wing-backed chair across from him. His brown eyes shimmered approval. "Thirty-three out of thirty-six," he said, his chest swelling with pride. "Impressive. Don't you agree, Langston?"

Nick had tucked his rugged body into the mate of Dallas's chair. If there was a spot on him that wasn't dusty from spending the better part of the morning in the corral roping and branding calves, she couldn't find it.

The brim of his hat rode low on his brow, shadowing the upper portion of Nick's face. His slouched, lazy posture gave the impression of a man who'd fallen asleep. A noncommittal grunt, coupled with the tightening of his lips beneath the weather-bleached mustache, said he was awake. Wide awake. And not as impressed as Ian with her skillful display the night before.

115

Sensing Nick's quietly leashed fury, Dallas squirmed. She wavered between the urge to bask in her father's rare words of praise, or be anxious Nick was upset with her . . . again. In the end, she decided on the latter. After all, Ian *did,* when the mood struck, shower her with stingy words of praise. But never could she remember Nick being this all-fired angry at her.

"Yup," Ian continued, "gotta hand it to you, girly. You really put Parker in his place this time."

Dallas smiled weakly, and lowered her gaze to the hands she'd clenched tightly in her lap. "That, um, wasn't the plan," she murmured.

Nick grumbled under his breath. Though Dallas didn't catch the words, she knew the tone. Her jaw hardened, and the fingers in her lap twisted.

Ian stopped pacing only long enough to send her a curious glance. "What plan? Never mind, doesn't matter. Just so long as you whip that boy into shape before you hog-tie him to the altar. Won't have no sissy for a son-in-law. No sir-ee."

"David's not a sissy," she said, pushing to her feet. Though defending Parker left a bitter taste in her mouth, if she was going to marry the boy, she'd better get used to it.

Both Nick's and her father's gaze tracked her as she commenced pacing in front of the desk, while Ian resumed pacing behind it.

"He's just . . ." She sighed. "Well, he has other interests besides cows and horses, is all." Her gaze narrowed, brushing over Nick; she felt his interest perk. "There's nothing wrong with a man wanting to better himself."

"Better himself?" Ian sputtered, coming to a dead stop behind his chair. Crossing his arms atop the scuffed oak backrest, he leaned forward and glared at his daughter. *"Better* himself? You call burying his nose in a book when he could be out riding the range *'bettering himself?'* " He shook his snow-white head. "Lordy, I thought you were smarter than that."

Dallas met her father's glare with a level one of her own. Now that he was yelling at her and no longer lavishing praise, her feet were on familiar ground. "I'm very smart. I take after Mother that way." Dallas grinned. "For example, I'm smart enough to know there's more to life than ranches, cattle, roping, and branding. David knows that, too. That's why he wants to go back East and finish his schooling. He wants to be a . . ." She frowned. What did her soon-to-be-fiancé want to be? If he'd ever told her, she couldn't remember. "He wants to make something of himself."

"He already has," Ian growled. "He's made himself a real pain in the a—"

"Papa!"

Ian's fist pounded the desk hard enough to make the pen holder and ink bottle bounce and clatter together. "It's the truth, girly, and you damn well know it. Just ask Nick here. He'll tell you what a sissy-boy Parker is. Ain't that right, Nick? Nick!"

"Hmmm? Oh, yeah. Parker'll come around eventually, I expect," Nick said, his drawl so lazy that Dallas had an urge to slap him hard just to rouse some emotion in him. "Like you said, boss, Dallas will see to it."

"She will see to no such thing!" Fists on hips, Dallas glared at them, disgusted. Why should she care whether David went back East to school after they were married? It wasn't as though she intended to go with him. There'd be enough work joining the TLP and Bar None together to keep her busy. "If David wants to finish his schooling that's his business, not mine."

"Wrong." Ian resumed his own angry pacing behind the chair. It was Dallas's turn to stop and glare. "Once you're his wife, everything that sissy-boy does damn well *is* your business." His eyes narrowed to piercing brown slits as his gaze fixed on his daughter. "And mine. Make *no* mistake about that."

The hem of her fawn-colored split skirt sputtered corral dust and flared just above her ankles as Dallas spun sharply on her heel. Spurs *chinked* atop the floor planks as she stalked to the door. "The only mistake I'm guilty of making is having stayed in this room for so long listening to you!"

Her fingers wrapped around the doorknob. It was Nick's lazy drawl that stopped her from turning it.

"Just outta curiosity, boss . . . what makes you think Dallas could rope Parker even if she wanted to?"

She glanced over her shoulder just in time to see a thoughtful scowl pinch her father's snowy brow.

"What makes *you* think she couldn't?" Ian countered.

The red leather creaked as, in slow, lazy movements, Nick pushed himself up in the chair. With the crook of his knuckle, he angled his hat back and met his employer's gaze. "After last night, I'd think the last person Parker wants to marry is Dallas." Nick's attention shifted, locked with Dallas's. His next words hit their mark quite nicely. "A man doesn't like a women who outshoots, outropes, outrides, out . . . hell, out*everythings* him! Don't you know that?"

Against her will, Dallas flinched.

"Never bothered me," Ian grunted.

One sun-bleached brow slanted up. "Laura ever outshoot you, boss?" Nick asked casually.

Ian chuckled harshly. "Nah. She was just a tiny thing. Like Lisa. The recoil would've taken her shoulder off."

"She ever outrope you? Beat you in a race?" Nick's gaze sharpened on Dallas, though his words were still aimed at his boss. "Did she ever scream at you in front of your men?"

"Laura?" Ian's bushy brows rose in surprise. "Hell no! She'd never dare." He paused, then grunted, "I see your point, Langston, but I don't think you see mine. Laura was a woman—a good one, mind you, but a woman all the same. While sissy-boy may act like one sometimes, the fact is, Parker's a man. Not much of one, but there you have it. Now, if *I* were him and *I* had a gal like Dallas chasing after me, why I'd—"

"You ain't Parker," Nick cut in dryly. "He's not cut out of the same cloth as you and me. You can't even begin to guess what a kid like that's looking for in a wife."

Nick's gaze volleyed between Dallas and her father. It was obvious those too-blue eyes of his were trying to tell her that whatever David Parker was looking for in a wife, she wasn't it, and never would be.

Dallas's spine stiffened, her chin notched up proudly. Her glare would have melted butter; Nick Langston was, unfortunately, made of much sturdier stock. Opening her mouth to voice a hot retaliation, she was cut short by a clipped rap on the opposite side of the door.

Thankful for any excuse to expend her sudden burst of energy, Dallas yanked the door open. Hickory Pete stood framed in the doorway.

Dallas didn't realize she was glaring at the man until she saw the old coot take a quick step back into the hallway.

"I—I came to see the boss," Pete stammered, even as he yanked the hat off his wispy head, setting a cloud of dirt and dust scattering the air in all directions.

The clomp of her father's footsteps approached Dallas from behind. She stepped aside to let Ian pass. Ranch business always came first.

"We'll talk in the hallway, Pete," Ian said as he draped an arm around the older man's scrawny shoulders and guided Pete farther away from the study door. "From the looks, they're about to start yammering at each other, and I won't be able to hear a word you say over the ruckus."

Yammering, Dallas thought as she slammed the door closed with the heel of her palm. Oh, yes, she was about to yammer, all right!

The hem of her split skirt whipping around her ankles, Dallas spun angrily around and faced Nick. If he felt even an ounce of her indignation, it didn't show. Damn him!

"Was that lesson number four, Langston?" she

snapped. "That a woman shouldn't pursue a man who doesn't want her?"

"No, darlin'," Nick drawled, his shrug lazy, "that's lesson number five. Lesson number four was 'a woman doesn't show up the man she wants to marry in front of his ranch hands and hers.' You flunked that one."

Dallas gritted her teeth and counted to ten. Twice. It didn't help a bit. "I was trying to *help* David! What good would losing by one bottle—when I know damn well I can do better—do him? He needs to know that in order to survive around here, he needs to learn how to shoot right."

Nick angled his head, his gaze slowly scanning her from head to anxiously tapping toe. An emotionless grin curled up only one corner of his mouth. "And you're gonna teach him, is that it?"

Her chin lifted higher still. "Someone has to. It might as well be me."

"And what, exactly, is it you plan to teach him? That you can humiliate him whenever you feel the urge?"

"I'm teaching him how to shoot. How to protect himself if he ever has to."

A muscle in Nick's jaw flexed, but his tone remained cold, detached. "The kid's twenty-six years old, darlin'. If he had a hankering to know how to shoot, he'd have found someone to teach him long ago. Someone who wouldn't humiliate him into learning the lesson."

"For the last time, I did *not* humil—" The words choked in Dallas's throat when the door opened and her father stepped back into the study.

Ian's gaze volleyed assessively between Dallas and Nick before he resumed his seat behind the desk.

"Everything all right?" Nick asked cautiously.

"Fine," Ian said. "South fence needs some repairing, but it's nothing serious."

Nick nodded. "I'll get it fixed this afternoon."

"Damn straight you will." A hint of a smile ticked at one corner of Ian's mouth. "That's what I pay you for, Langston. Now"—his gaze shifted to his daughter—"what did I miss here?"

Dallas forced her voice to sound calm and controlled—everything she didn't feel. "Not much. I was just about to tell Nick that everything worked out fine last night. David agreed to a picnic if I won. I did. Even he wouldn't go back on his word. Now I'll get the chance to work on him with no one else around." She glanced at Nick. "You know, Nick, I really think I'm starting to get to David because he . . ."

"What?" Ian prodded, while Nick stiffened unexpectedly in his chair. "He what?"

"He, um, asked me to wear the dress again. On our picnic." Dallas couldn't contain her condescending grin. Her brown eyes flashed with triumph when she met Nick's suddenly narrowed gaze.

Nick, on the other hand, was forcing himself to stay seated. He was fighting an almost overpowering urge to push to his feet and start pacing right along with them. The only thing stopping him—besides the thought of how foolish the three of them would look, of course—was knowing that if he did get up right now he would stalk across the room and shake Dallas Cameron until her teeth rattled.

He'd been angry last night when she'd outshot Parker six to one after he'd told her not to. Oh, hell, he'd been *furious*. It was nothing compared to the way he felt right now, though.

For some reason, the thought of Parker finally noticing the hidden, feminine side of Dallas irked the hell out of Nick! *Damn it! That's my dress. Bought and paid for with my wages. Let Parker buy his own if he wants to see Dallas wearing one!*

Anger threaded through Nick, coiling like a white-hot knot in his gut. His reaction was as irrational as it was intense, he knew, but right now Nick had a very strong urge to hit something. Hard. The image of Parker's baby-smooth face sprang to mind. To counter the impulse, he swallowed hard and curled his fingers inward. His ragged nails scratched the padded armrests as he clenched and unclenched his fists.

To Dallas's keen eye, only the angry color beneath Nick's tan was obvious. His expression remained alert and controlled, although she might not have thought so had she glanced down to see his knuckles whiten with the force of his empty grip.

"So, he wants to see you in a dress again, eh, girly?" Ian said, his gaze bouncing back and forth between Dallas and Nick. They were glaring at each other, and he had a gut feeling they'd forgotten he was in the room again. Normally, he would have been offended. Right now, he fought the urge to laugh. "That's a good sign. I can almost hear those grandsons of mine running through the halls."

Ian's words won him an angry glare from his daughter. Nick's shoulders tightened to bands of granite beneath the dusty cotton shirt and clinging leather vest.

No one spoke. Tense moments were ticked off by the mantel clock resting amid the clutter atop Ian's desk.

When Dallas could stand it no longer, she spun on her heel and wrenched open the door with more force than she'd intended. The door swung open, crashing against the wall behind it. The racket masked the jingle of spurs and the click of boot heels as she stalked down the hall, then slammed out of the house.

Ian's whistle was low and appreciative. "That's some girl I've got there. Wouldn't you agree, Langston?"

"Yeah," Nick growled, and pushed to his feet. Outside, he could hear Dallas screaming orders to the other punchers. "She's something all right. I just ain't sure what."

"Special," Ian said, which stopped Nick's clomping footsteps at the midway point between chair and door. "Wouldn't you say Dallas is special?"

Nick's head came around. Between the shadows cast by the brim of his hat, he knew his eyes couldn't be seen. Good. Nick didn't want anyone—*especially* Ian—to see the confusion that flashed in his gaze.

"Well?" Ian pressed, leaning his elbows atop the backrest of his chair, "wouldn't you say my Dallas is special?"

"Depends, boss," Nick drawled sarcastically, his attention locking on a man he'd known most of his adult life. There was no reading Ian's expression. That disturbed Nick. "You paying me to agree with you?"

Ian straightened. A flash of indignation—God, he looked like Dallas sometimes—lit, in his brown eyes, only to be immediately doused. "I'm paying you for the truth. Same as always."

Nick turned his attention back to the door. He hoped that, viewed from behind, his shrug looked careless; it felt unusually stiff and awkward. He had an uneasy feeling Ian was playing with him, that the older man's words only scraped the surface of their meaning—whatever the hell *that* was.

"Yeah," Nick said finally, his voice hard, "Dallas is special. But don't ever expect Parker to see that. The kid's city blind."

"For now," Ian conceded tightly. "But eventually he'll see her for what she's worth. Like you said before, Dallas'll bring him around."

"Wouldn't count on that, either."

"Why not?"

Again, Nick shrugged. "She ain't his type of woman. We both know it. No matter how many dresses she wears, ain't no way she'll ever get him to marry her. No way in hell."

"We'll see," Ian said, but his mind had wandered in another direction—to the pain that was again making itself known in his chest. Tightening. Throbbing. Building.

"Yeah, well, just try not to be too disappointed if things don't work out the way you planned," Nick muttered.

Ian opened his mouth to reply, but it was too late. With the stealth of a cat, Nick Langston was gone from the room. His spurs jangled atop the planks in

125

the hall, and the front door slammed with no less force than it had a few short minutes ago.

Sighing, Ian swiveled the chair around and slowly lowered himself onto it. His gaze strayed out the window, over the vast, endless range behind the smudged pane of glass. His right hand massaged the tearing ache in his chest.

By the time nine o'clock rolled around, Dallas was so tired she had only enough energy to drag her clothes off, shrug into a nightgown, and climb between the covers of her bed.

Roping and branding were hard work on days when her emotions weren't all tangled up. Today, the chore had been exhausting. It didn't help that she was, as always, partnered with Nick. The two had been roping together for more years than she could count. She'd never thought a thing of it . . .

Until today.

In preceding years she and Nick had cut the hard tedium of the work by bantering. Their easy conversations had always made the time slip by quicker, make the hard work seem less difficult.

But not today. Nick would have to be speaking to her for them to share their easy camaraderie of years gone by. He wasn't. He hadn't said a word from the moment he'd stepped into the corral until they'd both led their tired horses away.

Dallas hadn't tried to draw him into a conversation. There was no talking to him when he was in one of those moods. Besides, she'd caught his angry glare on her enough times to know he wanted no part of her today.

Maybe tomorrow? she thought as she tossed onto her side. Her muscles ached, but it was a welcome pain, one that reminded her of the full day's work she'd put in. Physical exertion was like a narcotic, it had always soothed her to sleep at night.

Yet, for some reason, tonight the drug wasn't working. Though she was tired and achy, she wasn't close to falling asleep. Her mind churned. She thought of Nick, of the way he'd avoided her, the way he'd treated her like she had the plague. She remembered the few times she'd caught him looking at her when he thought she wasn't looking. His blue eyes had sparkled in the bath of lemony sunlight. She remembered the emotion she thought she'd glimpsed in his gaze— an emotion she'd never seen in Nick Langston's eyes before—and one that disturbed her all the same.

Releasing a frustrated sigh, Dallas flipped onto her back. The mattress crunched beneath her as she strained her vision, finally pulling the clock on her bedside table into focus.

Quarter past eleven.

The house was dead quiet. Anyone with half a grain of sense had been asleep for hours. Tomorrow's work would be much the same as today's—long hours of backbreaking labor—they'd need all the rest they could get.

Damned if she felt tired, though! If only she could shut down her mind so her exhausted body could get some sleep. She didn't. Couldn't. Though her muscles were sore, at the same time they itched with an abundance of restless energy.

Gritting her teeth, Dallas finally kicked the sheet off and scrambled out of bed. She'd pulled on her robe as she padded downstairs and out the front door.

Her gaze lit on the moonlit corral. A warm shiver curled down her spine. Clutching her robe tightly together, she quickly moved past the corral. Her bare feet shuffled in the dirt as she started to trace the path leading to the riverbank.

She froze. The last thing she needed was to be reminded of Nick Langston . . . and the dress . . . and his jeering. Bad enough she hadn't been able to push any of it from her mind, she didn't need to go searching for more reminders.

Changing course, she headed for the barn. Again, she stopped short. The barn. That was where Nick had started teaching her how to ride so many years ago. Right there, in the shadowy apron of the barn, was the place Nick had pillowed his large hands on her hips for the very first time.

No, not the barn. Anywhere but the barn.

Her gaze shifted to the bunkhouse. Her cheeks flamed. She certainly couldn't go there! Nick was there, sleeping in his bunk. The thought of his features softened in sleep tugged at Dallas. So did the question of how much clothes he slept in. Did he wear his denim trousers to bed, like some other punchers, or just his cottony white underdrawers, like a lot of them did in warm weather?

Dallas groaned and had to force the image of Nick wearing nothing but a scrap of white cotton from her mind. Not all of it vanished. The odd, tingling heat in her blood lingered long after she'd shifted direction again, and started to go . . .

Where? Where on this entire ranch could she possibly go that wouldn't remind her of Nick in one fashion or another?

The answer was simple and immediate.

There was nowhere.

Dallas sucked in a breath of warm, dry night air and released it in a long, slow sigh. She should have stayed in bed. At least Nick Langston had never been *there.* The erotic dreams she'd had these last two night's flashed through her mind. Good Lord, even her bed wasn't sacred from Nick anymore. While he may not have visited it in the flesh, he'd visited it in mind. That was just as bad. No, worse. Her nighttime fantasies knew no inhibitions.

Dallas swore under her breath as, with a burst of defiance, she stomped down the path leading toward the river. "I *refuse* to let him do this to me. This is my ranch. I'll go wherever I please. Damned if I won't!"

Where she pleased to go was the river. The gurgle of water and rustle of cottonwood leaves had always soothed her nerves when they were chaffed. She *would not* let Nick's actions the other night ruin this spot for her.

Dirt and dry leaves crunched under Dallas's bare feet as she rounded the stand of trees and stepped into the clearing.

Immediately, she felt better. The moonlight gave the spiky carpet of grass that tickled her bare feet and ankles a pale, quicksilver cast. The sluggishly churning water reflected the star-sprinkled sky, the rustling tops of the trees, and Dallas's own reflection as she stepped to the bank and gazed down.

On impulse, she plunked herself down on the steep-but-not-high incline of dirt and, lifting the skirt of her nightgown, dunked her feet in the water. The coolness lapped at her calves, and made goose bumps sprout on her legs and arms. She barely noticed, so intent was she on gazing at the water. Her mind wandered, latching onto words that had been spoken years ago.

No, Squirt, keep your head up. And move your arms. You look like a dog who don't know how to paddle.

I can't, Nick. The tide's up and the current keeps pulling me under.

The current ain't that strong.

It feels like it is.

Well, it ain't. Lay down on your stomach, over my arms. Yeah, like that. Now, stretch your arms out over your head and pretend you're rowing with your hands. I said stretch. Keep your elbows straight, Squirt. No, straight. Straight, dammit!

Like this?

Yeah, like that. You're doing fine. Now—argh! What the hell'd you do that for?

I felt like splashing you, Nick.

And what if I said I felt like splashing you back, brat?

I'd say you're welcome to try.

Nick hadn't just splashed her. No, no, instead he'd caught her in those big, powerful arms of his and, maneuvering them nearer to the shallow bank, dunked her head under the water briefly but repeatedly. He hadn't stopped until she'd cried out in good-natured defeat. Eventually, they'd clung to each other laughing and splashing. Eventually, after a few more lessons, she'd learned how to swim.

That was thirteen years ago, but the memory was still sharp in Dallas's mind. Ian Cameron was scared to death of the water; it was the only weakness of her father's that she knew of. Not only had he refused to teach his daughters how to swim, he'd also been adamant that no one else teach them.

Lisa had no desire to learn how to swim. Dallas, on the other hand, had a *great* desire for it. Probably, like most things, because it was forbidden. She'd hounded Nick until, finally, he'd grudgingly and for the first time ignored one of Ian Cameron's orders. Secretly, he'd taught Dallas what she wanted to know.

"Remember when I taught you to swim Squirt?" The voice, deep and familiar, shot out from behind her.

Dallas startled, and her legs jerked reflexively. Her feet slapped at the water, sending up a splash that wet her legs up to the knees and dampened the hem of her robe and nightgown. Her head snapped around so fast she felt a crick of pain in her neck.

"Nick," she gasped, her heart racing when she saw him standing only a few feet behind her. She had the uncomfortable feeling he'd been there for a while, watching her. Why hadn't the tangy male scent of him—so obvious now—and the heat of his body, seeping through the poor barrier of soft cloth, not alerted her to his presence when she was so painfully aware of them now? "What are you doing up?"

"Same as you, I expect. Couldn't sleep." Nick

131

shrugged and jutted his chin to the strip of moonlit dirt stretching emptily out by her side. "Mind if I join you?"

Dallas swallowed back her immediate reply. Truly, she shouldn't be sitting out here at this hour talking amiably to a man who hadn't spoken to her most of the day. And she still remembered Nick's hot, piercing glares. Unfortunately, she'd never been able to stay mad at Nick for long. He could charm the fur off a cat if he set his mind to it; he could certainly charm Dallas out of a snit. At least *that* hadn't changed.

Shrugging, she turned her attention back to the water. Had he seen the grin that threatened to curve over her lips? "Suit yourself. *If* you think you can stand my company."

"I'll manage."

A few uneasy seconds slipped by.

The dirt crunched as Nick settled himself beside her. The closeness of him was almost palpable. Once he was situated, she turned to look at him. While his gaze had strayed out over the river, he wasn't ignorant of her presence. The muscle twitching his jaw told her that. "What do you want, Nick?"

"To talk to you." His gaze stayed trained forward. Again, the muscle flexed beneath its covering of taut, sun-copper flesh. "About lesson number six."

"Oh." Her spirits sank. To mask a surge of irritation, Dallas swirled her feet restlessly in the water. She'd grown used to the icy temperature, it no longer felt cold . . . unlike the gaze Nick sent her; now *that* chilled her to the bone. "What about it?"

"You ready?"

She frowned. There was something about Nick to-night. Something tightly leashed and dangerous, humming just below the surface, but she couldn't quite put her finger on it. "Ready for what?"

He rubbed the nape of his neck with his hand, as though he was massaging away a soreness. "Lesson number six." He looked at her, and Dallas's breath caught. He was hatless tonight, and without the shadowy brim for concealment his eyes caught the moonlight and sent it back to her in penetrating, deep blue shards.

Her heart did a crazy flip-flop, the beat staggering as it slammed a rhythm against her ribs. Her palms were oddly moist as she waited breathlessly for him to continue. The curiosity was eating at her. "What is lesson number six? Tell me . . . please."

His attention dipped, slowly, slowly descending to her lips. The muscles in his jaw bunched, and his blue eyes darkened, burning into her. "Kissing, darlin'. Lesson number six is kissing."

Chapter Six

Dallas's cheeks felt hot with color, her heart was hammering, and she was suddenly having a good deal of trouble drawing breath.

Was this Nick's idea of a joke? *Him* kiss *her?* Why, the thought was ludicrous. Laughable, even. Then why wasn't she laughing?

Maybe she'd heard him wrong? There was only one way to know for sure. She had to bolster her abruptly flagging courage and risk looking at him. Those indigo eyes had never lied to her.

There was only one problem. What if she did meet his gaze, only to see that she had indeed heard him correctly . . . ?

"The branding will be over in a couple of days." The words came out in a rush; her tone was unusually low and throaty. Dallas cringed, and thought she didn't sound too much better than a bullfrog croaking upriver. "The—er—trail drive'll be starting soon. Papa said he wants to go on this one, said it was past time, that he hasn't been on a drive in years and it'd do

135

him some good. I'm not so sure, though. I told him—"

"You hear what I said, Dallas?" Nick interrupted huskily.

Dallas hadn't been aware she'd fisted clumps of dirt in her hands until she felt the granules filter grittily through her fingers. Her grip slackened. His gaze, she was disturbed to feel, still caressed her face. "I told him I didn't think it was such a great idea. Maybe next year. He hasn't been looking too good lately. Have you noticed that, Nick? He's—"

"I said lesson number six is kissing, darlin'. Man/ woman kissing."

Dallas paused only long enough to suck in a gulp. "—pale lately. Real pale. And grumpier than usual. I mean, well, Papa's always grumpy, 'course, but *lately* . . . ! And I've seen him rubbing his chest every now and again when he thinks I'm not looking. You don't think he's sick do you? Oh, God, I hope not. He can be ornery as a bear sometimes, but he *is* still my father. Just because I don't particularly *like* him right now— grandsons, and all that foolishness!—doesn't mean I don't—"

Nick's hand came out of nowhere. His grip was firm as he cradled her chin in the warm webbing between powerful thumb and calloused index finger. His knuckles formed an unbreakable vise on either side of her jaw as he turned her head toward him.

Dallas's eyes remained stubbornly downcast, until she forced herself to focus . . . and noticed that what she was looking at was an appealing bulge of denim, enticingly located in the front of Nick Langston's pants. When he nudged her chin up, she made her gaze lift with it, thinking that looking at Nick's ruggedly handsome face *had* to be safer than what she'd just dragged her attention away from!

She'd been wrong before. There was nothing safe about the way her gaze settled on Nick's mouth, the way her eyes devoured each sensuously carved detail of his lips, nearly concealed beneath the thick blond mustache.

Odd. While she'd seen Nick Langston's mouth before, never had she looked at it just after he'd threatened to kiss her. Then again, Nick had never threatened to kiss her before, never even hinted at it, which explained the delicious little shivers that were racing down Dallas's spine. Her entire body quivered, reminding her that she had to get ahold of herself. She was noticing the tips of his mustache curled inward, scraping against his lips. Enough pink flesh was visible beneath the ragged fringe to make the sight intriguing.

Forcing her attention up, her gaze locked with Nick's.

Dallas scanned his rugged, familiar features, searching for a hint of the Nick Langston she knew. Where was the man who'd so patiently taught her to swim and ride and rope and shoot? Nowhere that she could see. Instead of Nick-Langston-The-Friend, she was staring—dumbfounded, openmouthed—at Nick-Langston-*The-Man*. The difference between the two was not subtle; it jarred her all the way to her toes.

His eyes pierced her to the soul. The irises—shards of indigo steel, shimmering hot in the moonlight—were half obscured by eyelids that were thick and hooded. In the swirled depths of his eyes, Dallas could see her reflection staring back at her. She looked confused, amazed . . . and more than a little nervous.

Her fingers were shaking; she folded her hands in her lap, hiding them inside the folds of her robe and nightgown so Nick wouldn't see. She tried to turn her head away, but his grip on her chin wouldn't allow it. She settled for averting her gaze to something she knew was safe—one flickering pinprick of star in the huge stretch of black velvet behind him.

"—love him." Dallas lamely finished the sentence she had started what felt like a lifetime ago.

Nick's stare was a constant, driving force. It never wavered. Dallas knew, because she felt the rush of heat in her cheeks that seemed to go hand in hand with the hot caress of his eyes.

Her tongue felt thick, even as she forced it to form words she had to push past her lips. "Is this your idea of a joke, Langston? Your way of getting back at me for the way I joked with you last night? Because if it *is*—"

"No joke." The fingers gripping her jaw flexed. "I'd never joke about kissing you, darlin'. I just figured it was only fair to warn you first."

Dallas blinked slowly, absorbing this. When her lashes flickered up, she again sought out the star, latching onto the sight like a drowning woman latched onto a sliver of driftwood.

"Why?" The unnaturally high timbre of her voice made her wince. So did Nick's next words—but only because the formation of them made his breath puff hotly across her face.

"David Parker. Your picnic. Or did you already

138

forget about that? If you play your cards right, Squirt"—from the corner of her eye, she saw him wince, and felt his grip tighten on her chin—"David's bound to try and kiss you. If he does, you'd best know what you're doing, right?"

"Don't be silly. A kiss is a kiss is a kiss, Nick." She felt Nick stiffen. A scowl pinched Dallas's brow as her gaze unconsciously strayed back to him—and she found a matching scowl furrowing his. "I mean, there's not that much difference between kisses."

The corners of Nick's mouth quirked down, the grip on her jaw loosened but didn't fall away. Instead, his fingers skimmed over the delicate line of her jaw. His thumb traced the column of her throat in hot, slow strokes. Lightly, he held the calloused pad of his thumb against her wildly leaping pulse. At the same time, his other fingers hooked around the back of her neck.

Without thinking about what he was doing—what he'd been *going* to do—he'd angled his head to the side. His lashes had already begun their descent. He was aware of her every whisper-soft breath warming his face, and every ragged breath that left his lungs in answer to it. His mouth hovered mere inches from hers.

Nick had already mentally braced himself for the contact. He was confident he could carry through with the threatened kiss and remain emotionally detached. He was ready for it. What he wasn't ready for at all was the feel of Dallas's hair against his hand. The strands were silky soft; they tickled his work-roughened knuckles. Nor had he prepared himself for her sweet, earthy scent, or the way it washed over him, swelled inside him, threatening to drown him.

He closed his eyes. It made his next words easier. "You ever been kissed"—he swallowed hard, twice, and forced the youthful endearment off his oddly dry tongue—"Squirt?"

"Of course."

Closing his eyes, Nick realized with a groan, had been a real bad idea. His other senses were kicking in, making him notice things he otherwise wouldn't. Like how soft and smooth Dallas's skin felt beneath his palm, and how sweet and warm her breath felt puffing over his lips. His voice went husky. "Okay, Cameron, let me rephrase that. You ever been kissed by a man who ain't your daddy?"

"Oh, well . . . I, um . . ."

"The truth," he growled impatiently. His eyes snapped open, the determined glint in them telling her he would settle for nothing less than honesty.

"You know I haven't," she answered weakly, all the while wishing to God that her voice sounded stronger. It didn't, of course. Some things were simply beyond capability; like stringing two logical thoughts together when Nick Langston was touching her, threatening to kiss her. "Papa would never let a man close enough to try. If any had dared, they'd have been dead come sunup." She hesitated only long enough to try to regulate her oddly erratic breathing, and failed. "I'm surprised you're willing to take the chance, Langston."

"I've always been a gambling man, Cameron. You know that."

Dallas started to nod, but Nick's grip on her jaw

140

didn't provide enough slack for it. "I know. Just like I know that if you do kiss me, you'll be gambling with your job. Maybe even your life. If Papa ever finds out, he'll either kill you or show you the property stakes. Is it really worth the risk?"

His grin was wicked and quick. "I'll have to get back to you on that. *After* I've kissed you . . . Squirt."

It took Dallas a moment to speak. Nick Langston was merely offering to teach her how a woman kissed a man. She would learn this the way she'd learned so many other things. Nick would teach her. Nothing more than a "lesson" was being offered. Nothing more than a "lesson" would be expected or accepted. Surely if she tried hard enough she could remain cool and detached.

"All right," Dallas said finally. "Explain what I should do. Tell me how a man likes to be kissed, then we'll give it a shot."

His grin never faltered, though one golden brow did arch high. The muscle in his cheek flexed once, drawing her attention to the way the soft glow of moonlight deepened the hollow beneath. "Tell you?" he asked, and she nodded. He shook his head. "Un-uh. This time we do things my way."

Dallas felt decidedly warm and uncomfortable. It didn't help that Nick's attention had dropped from her eyes to her lips. She could have sworn she heard him groan.

"We just do it," he said simply as his other hand slipped around her waist. "I'll give you instructions as we go. How's that sound?"

141

It sounded dangerous, Dallas thought, and opened her mouth to tell him so.

That was when he tugged her forward.

The unexpected movement pitched her off balance. Dallas did what came natural. She righted herself by splaying her hands over his hard, warm chest and squirming to the side, coming up on her knees facing him. She hadn't expected Nick to move with her, doing the same thing.

The hand he'd wrapped around her neck had come away when they'd moved. His large palm was now pillowed atop her shoulder, his fingers digging into her flesh. His grip, while not painful, was firm.

The arm around her waist tightened, dragging her forward.

From hip to knee, the front of their thighs met. The collision of hard against soft was jarring. The effect it had on Dallas was akin to being hit by lightning. A bolt of awareness shot down her spine. The sensation soaked through her blood like a charged current, making it simmer and tingle in her veins. Her heart clapped like thunder in her ears, obliterating every sound but that of her own breathing. And Nick's. A part of her noticed how easily the two ragged whispers melded into one.

"Tip your chin up," Nick ordered.

Dallas hadn't been aware her chin was down. It was, her gaze fixed unseeingly on the flat metal buttons of his shirt. She traced the row up to his neck—thick, solid, tanned—and past his hard, sun-kissed jaw. She skimmed the muscle now jerking in his moonlight-sculpted cheek, seeking out his eyes. They were as dark as midnight.

"Higher," he rasped.

Her shoulders went back, her spine instinctively arching. Her breasts grazed his chest. The lightning came back in force; Dallas felt as though it had rended her in two. This time the center of the hot, tingling currents was located in her nipples; they tingled, burned, ached . . .

Excruciatingly aware of every spot where their bodies pressed intimately together, she tried to pull away. Nick's arm tightened. His gaze held hers captive as his head lowered by tormentingly slow degrees.

Kissing this woman gently had not been a consideration. From the second he'd felt her thighs against his, Nick had wanted to slam his mouth over hers, kiss her hard, devour her with his lips and tongue. He wanted to drink the sweetness from her mouth, drain her dry, and hopefully in so doing satisfy this newly awakened yet insatiable thirst he had for her.

What prevented him was a single, piercing thought. Parker would never kiss Dallas that way. The man was too soft for hard, mouth-eating kisses. Nick told himself that was the reason he brushed his lips back and forth over hers when he would rather have crushed her to him, under him.

He pulled her forward until, from knee to soft, swollen breasts, her body was plastered to his. His tongue bathed her lower lip in moist, flicking strokes, then he sucked it into his mouth. He nibbled the tender, quivering flesh even as his fingers tunneled into the silky hair at the base of her braid.

143

He cupped her scalp, hugged her tiny waist tightly to him, deepening the kiss, covering her mouth fully. She shuddered in his arms, and he swallowed her gasp of surprise . . . even as she swallowed his low moan of raw pleasure.

She tasted good, sweet, like freshly gathered honey. Nick savored the flavor; it was more intoxicating than the best whiskey greenbacks could buy. He took a good, long sip of her, then flicked his tongue impatiently over the crease separating her top lip from her bottom.

She whimpered, and he felt the rush of it in a soft, warm burst against his cheek. Her breath was hot, searing. Nick shivered and pulled back. Slightly. Their lips were separated by a tantalizing fraction of an inch, yet still close enough for his mustache to tickle her lips when he spoke. "You needed lesson number six worse than I thought, Cameron," he said huskily. "That'll never do."

Her lashes flickered up, her gaze as dazed as the rest of her. She should be offended by Nick's comment. She wasn't. She was too busy wishing he would kiss her again to be able to think of anything other than the taste of him—sharp and strong—and the way his flavor lingered on her tongue.

"What do you want me to do?" she asked softly, throatily. The sliver of her mind still capable of rational thought said she'd phrased the question all wrong. She should be asking Nick what David Parker would want her to do. And she would have . . . had she cared. Dallas wanted to know what Nick wanted, expected from a kiss. The need for that knowledge was all-

144

consuming. In her frustration to learn, she squirmed against him. "Teach me, Nick. I want to know how to please yo—er, a man."

His eyelids lowered, hooding his gaze, but not before Dallas caught the flash of desire that shimmered there like liquid blue fire. The sight, though quickly gone, thrilled her senseless.

The hand at her waist loosened, straying down to cup her bottom and draw her firmly against him. "Wiggling like that's bound to please a dead man, darlin'," he said, his tone low and gritty. "But it ain't too safe. Now keep still before you end up getting more than a lesson in kissing."

Dallas nodded mutely. She couldn't have answered him right then even if she'd had the voice for it; his words had made her acutely aware of the solid heat radiating from his body to hers. The core of the fire centered where their hips met. It was a wild, hot, pulsating warmth. Was Nick aware of it, too?

His fingers had tightened into fists around her hair. His grip loosened, and his hand opened. His fingers skimmed lightly downward, until his roughened palm was caressing her cheek and jaw. "Let's try again. Only this time, I want you to kiss me back. And pretend like you mean it, okay?"

"I don't have to pretend anything, Nick," was her husky reply. "I meant it last time."

"Yeah," he said just as softly, and leaned his forehead against hers, "that's what I was afraid you'd say. You ready?" he added, knowing he sure as hell wasn't. The first taste of her had left him parched for more. Much, much more. Somehow, he'd leashed his control

145

with their last kiss. Would he be able to do it again? Nick had his doubts. "Time for lesson number seven, Squir—darlin'. Women who like kissing do it with their mouths open. And they use their tongue."

The picture his words painted rocked Dallas to the core. The image was intriguing. She opened her mouth to ask exactly what these women did with their tongues.

Nick, never one for words when swift action would suffice, silenced her with his lips.

If his last kiss was day, this kiss was night; dark and erotically consuming. His mouth was hard and grinding as it worked its magic over hers, his tongue demanding, insistent when it darted out to find her lips tightly closed.

Dallas tensed. She felt each hot, moist flick batter down her sudden need to refuse entrance, and inflame what was quickly becoming an insatiable need to touch and taste in equal measure. Slowly, her lips parted, and she opened herself up to him.

Nick moaned, crushing her to him as he plunged his tongue into her mouth. Nothing in his life had ever tasted this good. The need to teach was gone, forgotten to the more potent need to devour. And *be* devoured, in turn.

Her back arched. Her breasts made a swollen, straining pillow for his chest. Nick leaned into her, bending her back further. Unconsciously, he made a bed for her out of his arm. His elbow supported her waist, his forearm her spine, his open palm cradled the hollow beneath her shoulder blades. His free hand found the fists she'd unconsciously curled atop his chest, fists that were now tightly wedged between their bodies.

His knuckles brushed the outer swell of her breasts. The sizzling contact made him hesitate a full minute before he was able to seize one small hand and drag it upward, wrapping her arm around his neck. Her other hand was quick to follow.

There was nothing to separate them now but insignificant layers of light cotton. The barrier was thin, not nearly enough padding to muffle the frantic heartbeats slamming against each other. Each was excruciatingly aware of the other's wild tempo, and the way their own raced to match it.

Nick Langston, a man who'd always prided himself on steely self-control, felt his restraint snap when her hot, moist tongue hesitantly snuck out and touched his own. Either he was a better teacher than he'd thought, or she was one damn fast learner. In one heartbeat she seemed to have grasped what little he'd taught her so far. In the second, she'd begun to improvise, spicing the ingredients of the kiss to her satisfaction.

Nick's tongue swirled. Dallas's counterswirled and boldly stroked. He thrust. She parried, then launched her own sweet attack. He surrounded the tip of her tongue with his lips and suctioned it into his mouth. He absorbed her instinctive tremors of pleasure with his body, and matched them with his own.

The thought came to Nick that this woman had learned all she needed to know about kissing. Jesus, if she got any better, she'd drive Parker to his knees! Lord knows, Nick was close to being there himself.

The thought also came to him that he wasn't going

to stop kissing her. He couldn't. Not now. He'd carried the lesson too far.

His free hand, the one he noticed only now had been stroking the curve of her upper arm in the rhythm of hot, frantic lovemaking, wrapped around her waist. Twisting his torso, he lowered them both to the ground.

His lips never left hers as he spread himself out on the grass; half at her side, half on it. Her left breast nudged the center of his chest. Even through her robe and nightgown and his shirt, he could feel her nipple pebble. His palms itched to make reality of the visions his mind unwisely entertained.

It was getting harder and harder to remember that the woman in his arms, the one he was now crushing beneath him, was Ian Cameron's daughter. All he'd planned to do was teach her how to kiss. He shouldn't even be considering touching Dallas the way he wanted to so badly right now. He'd had no *intention* of touching her like that. He had no right. He was a dirt-poor cowpuncher, for Christ's sake. Off limits to someone like Dallas Cameron. Ian had made that clear long ago, and Nick had always respected it. Never questioned or resented it . . .

Until now.

But Ian wasn't here now.

Dallas was.

It was difficult not to think about taking her right here, right now, the way his body craved to do. And it was damn near impossible to remember Ian and his threats; they were just wisps of a memory that didn't even seem real at the moment. He was only a man, after all, and as such, Nick couldn't think of sense or consequence when the woman in his arms was kissing him like this. What was restraint, anyway? He sure as hell didn't know—not Dallas arched beneath him as though she wanted, *needed* for him to touch her almost as much as he needed, *craved* to touch her. Her plaintive little whimpers, the ones he caught with his mouth, were driving Nick insane.

Against his better judgment, the hand cupping her waist inched up. Her stomach rose and fell unevenly beneath his palm, her ribs vibrated with each hard thud of her heart. Even her breasts seemed to quiver, he thought, as he turned his hand inward and stroked the soft underswell with the back of his calloused knuckles. He ached to cup her fully, to . . . Oh, who the hell was he kidding? His hand—his entire *body*—ached to rip off her robe and nightgown and feel her flesh to hot, hungry flesh.

He didn't, of course. Wouldn't. He'd settle for tasting and touching her, just this once, just for a little while.

Before Nick's mouth had claimed Dallas, branded her, ignited in her desires she hadn't known existed. The feel of his hair tickling her palm was magic. The feel of his heart slamming against her breasts was erotically powerful. His hot breath washed over her face in rhythmic waves. His hands and his tongue . . .

Dear Lord, his tongue!

She couldn't stand much more of this. His taste was sharp, his heat inflaming. If he touched her where she ached so badly for him to touch, she was going to explode. She knew that as surely as she knew she had to stop him. Or never stop him at all.

Her fingers untangled from his hair, slipped down over his neck, and formed fists that she ground against his tightly bunched shoulders. She pushed and, to her shock, he moved.

Cool air rushed over her hot flesh as Nick grunted in resignation and ended the kiss, slowly, slowly peeling the upper half of his body from her. His hand was no longer stroking the underside of her breast, but was played over her ribs.

"H-how'd I do?" Dallas panted, unable to catch her breath. She looked up, met his smoky gaze, and saw that she wasn't the only one who was disturbed by newly ignited passion. Nick's eyes said he was equally affected. And then, as quickly, his lashes lowered and his eyes said nothing at all. "Nick? Was that . . . I mean, was I all right?"

Nick sucked in three forcefully slow breaths and prayed the burn of hot, dry air would cleanse the desire from his soul. It didn't, but it helped stop his head from spinning. He glanced down at Dallas long and hard, then thrust himself to his feet. "Yeah, Squi—you did fine," he said curtly. "You're a real quick learner. Parker'll be thrilled."

He started to turn away, and though Dallas knew it would be wise to let him go, she couldn't. She craved Nick's company. She wanted Nick-Langston-The-Friend to explain why she'd lost all control the second his lips touched hers. His second kiss had been wild and wonderful; it had unleashed a strain of desire in her so strong that it surprised and frightened her. Dallas needed to understand this new sensation.

Then there was one other reason she didn't want Nick to go yet. Pride. This man had just kissed her breathless, and now he was turning his back on her. Her pride, always acute, chaffed under the curt dismissal.

"Nick?" she called out when he took a step away. His boot heels crunched in the dirt as he took another step. Another. The sound ceased abruptly when, as though coming to a reluctant decision, he stopped. His fists straddled lean, denim-clad hips, and the ragged fringe of his hair scraped the broad shelf of his shoulders when he tipped his head up to acknowledge her. He didn't look back. "You said David would be pleased. Did you mean it?"

His shrug was casual. The abrupt straightening of his spine was anything but. His stance looked tense, rigid. It was the stance of a man who half expected a rabid mountain lion to leap out of the trees and pounce on him.

"Do you think he'll be pleased enough to kiss me twice?" she pressed.

Nick dragged a palm down his jaw, as though the gesture itself could loosen the hard line of muscle that bunched there. Though he knew he should have kept on walking when he'd had the chance, something in Dallas's tone kept his feet rooted to the spot. His need to hear where this conversation was going was almost as strong as his desire not to. He'd regret listening to her, he knew, yet he shrugged and stayed where he was.

151

Dallas pushed herself up to a cross-legged sit. She would have stood, and saved herself the blissful agony of having to look up the sinewy length of Nick's body to get to his eyes, but she didn't trust her knees to support her yet. She was beginning to wonder if she'd ever be able to trust them again; they still felt weak and watery and shaky.

Clearing her throat, she continued bluntly, "I guess what I'm trying to say, Nick, is that if David likes my kisses well enough, he might want more." Her gaze was riveted on the back of his head, and Dallas tried hard not to notice the way the moonlight turned the color and texture of his hair to spun gold.

"And . . . ?" Nick growled. He plowed all ten fingers through his hair, waiting tensely for her answer. Only it wasn't an answer at all, it was another damn question!

"Well, what should I do if he *does* want more? Should I . . . ?" Dallas hesitated, a blush warming her all the way to her toes. She was trying to ask advice from Nick-Langston-The-Friend, but was having a devil of a time looking past Nick-Langston-The-Man to see him.

Nick felt like a punch had been planted solidly to his gut. The air pushed from his lungs with force. He staggered back a step, coming around on his heel to face her. *"Goddammit, Cameron, what the hell's the matter with you?! Don't you know better than to be asking a man that sort of question?"*

Dallas came up on her knees, instantly defensive. Her index finger made a stabbing motion at his chest.

"I'm not asking a man, Langston. I'm asking *you!* There's a difference."

"Like hell there is!"

"Like hell there *isn't!*"

Nick couldn't remember ever loosing his temper quite so quickly and thoroughly. He wanted to strangle the little witch for having the nerve to ask him that question in the first place. She couldn't stop insulting men, could she? If not out-shooting a man, she was questioning his manhood.

He had to teach her that talking like this to a man could be damaging to her virtue. It was a lesson she needed to learn a lot more than she needed to know how to kiss!

Nick cleared the distance between them in two long, angry strides. Bending at the waist, he coiled his fingers around her upper arms and hauled her roughly to a stand.

"What the hell are you doing?" Dallas gasped, and steadied her balance by splaying her hands over his chest. His heart was beating double-time beneath the heel of her palms. She could feel each ragged breath tear through his lungs only seconds before the blast of hot air smoldered over the top of her head. The arms beneath her fingertips bunched until they felt like walls of muscle and flush beneath the too thin covering of his sleeves.

It wasn't until she repeated the question that Nick actually heard the words over the thundering of his heart in his ears. He glared down at the top of her head. "I'm going to prove that I'm a man, *Squirt*. Isn't that what you wanted? Isn't that what you were trying to goad me into doing?"

Dallas's breath caught. Is that what he thought? That she'd been *goading* him? Nothing could be further from the truth! Or could it? *Had* her bruised pride subconsciously egged him on? "No!" She tried to twist away, but his grip tightened. A knot of fear—the first she'd ever felt for Nick Langston—coiled inside her. It felt icy and cold, not at all welcome. "Let go of me, Nick," she said, her voice a little shaky. "You're scaring me."

"Good. You should be scared," he growled, his mouth close enough to her ear for his mustache to tickle her and his breath to rustle the tawny wisps that curled there. "Any woman who says to a man what you just said to me deserves to be terrified. You can't challenge a man's virility, then expect him to walk away. Any man worth his salt won't stand for it." The knuckle of his index finger hooked under her jaw. With a flick of his wrist, he jerked her gaze to his. "When you challenge a man's virility, you'd better be ready for him to prove himself out to you."

Dallas felt the knuckle beneath her chin scrape a slow path down her throat, coming to rest at the creamy base where her pulse beat throbbed against it. She wondered if he was going to "prove himself out" to her now. The muscle in his jaw jerked furiously, but his expression remained cold and impassive. There was no way to know for sure.

Nick's attention fixed on the length of her throat, and the stretch of sun-gold flesh there. He watched the gentle lift and fall of a swallow, and felt his gut tighten in response. His entire body seemed focused in the calloused tips of his fingers, and the satiny flesh beneath. The urge to slip his hand around her neck and draw her close was strong. The urge to claim her mouth again was stronger still. He fought both, but knew by the hot, insistent response of his body that it was a fight he would lose very, very soon.

"Go home, Dallas. Now. Before I do something we'll both regret," he ordered, his tone half husky purr, half snarl of self-contempt.

Nodding, Dallas took a step backward. She was still unsure of what she'd done to cause his anger, but she knew better than to push Nick any further. Maybe if she gave him time to think, and used the time to put her own confused feelings into perspective.

She turned to leave, padding barefoot through the soft, thick grass. No more than three steps had she taken before Nick's voice shot out from behind her. His unmerciful tone chilled her blood.

"You think long and hard before you decide to let Parker"—his tongue tripped over the words—"go further with you. *If* he proves interest, o'course." He hooked his thumbs in his belt loops and rocked back on his heels. "If that brat puts one finger on you—I don't care *who* started it—I'll kill him. Ian'll never get the chance. I'll beat him to it."

Dallas opened her mouth to argue, but the grim set of Nick's lips made her think better of it. Obviously, there'd be no reasoning with him tonight, not when he was in this kind of mood. She nodded quickly and left the clearing.

Nick watched her go. He couldn't help noticing the

way her hips swayed gently beneath the robe and nightgown. He couldn't drag his gaze away.

He waited until the crunch of her footsteps over leaves and twigs had faded in his ears before cussing soundly and turning his back on the moonlit trees.

His thoughts were not pleasant as he fished the makings of a cigarette out of his vest pocket, then crammed the thing into the corner of his mouth, unlit. Even with distance, and a little time, he found his anger hadn't cooled. His thoughts ran red-hot; his mind's eye replayed their kisses, and her passionate response, over and over until he thought he'd go crazy.

"Was it worth it," he grumbled under his breath as he snatched a match out of his pocket and dragged it with unnecessary force up the outer seam in his pants. He held the flickering light to his cigarette, inhaling until the end glowed an angry shade of orange. "Yeah, darlin'," he admitted dryly, if only to himself, "I'd say your kisses are worth my job and . . . hell, worth my life, too. Not that my life means a whole lot these days."

The worst part was, it was true. His life hadn't meant squat since he'd started comparing himself to David Parker . . . and found he came up short.

Parker had money, land, some schooling. What did Nick have? A checkered past, and a future that suddenly looked bleak and monotonous. He had nothing to offer a woman. Hell, he had nothing to offer *himself* but more of the same thing he'd always had: a saddle, a bedroll, and memories.

That was Nick Langston's life. It was all he owned,

all he was. He'd never wanted more out of life than he had . . .

Until lately. Until he'd noticed how nicely Dallas Cameron had grown up. Until he'd kissed her, tasted her sweetness, and found himself to be insatiably thirsty for her.

If only . . . ?

Christ, what *was* he thinking? Ian would never settle for a no-prospects cowpuncher like Nick for a son-in-law. Why had the thought even crossed his mind?

Nick drew deeply on the cigarette. As the smoke burned his lungs, he willed the sting of it to also burn away this unnatural desire he'd discovered he had for Dallas Cameron. A girl he'd hardly noticed two months ago. A girl who consumed his thoughts now.

He finished the cigarette with his mind forcefully blank. It was as he flicked the last of it into the water that he came to a decision.

The trail drive was only a few days away. He'd go because he'd promised Ian he would. But after the drive was over, he was going to start looking for another job. He didn't want to, resented having to—was angered that things had gotten this bad this fast—but he had no choice.

Tonight had proven nothing if not to show Nick that he had to put some sanity-saving room between himself and Dallas. For both their sakes. Before the situation backfired in their faces. Meanwhile, he'd avoid her like the plague. To hell with her "lessons." He couldn't go through with them anymore. The restraint—or possible lack thereof—would kill him.

Nick stalked from the clearing. His palms, he wasn't

pleased to find, still burned with the feel of silky flesh, and his lips still smarted with the memory of airy whimpers and the way he'd caught them in his mouth.

Hours later, settled atop his lumpy cot for the night, Nick dragged his tongue over his lips and thought he could still taste the honey-sweetness of Dallas Cameron's kisses. He had a feeling it was a flavor he would taste for the rest of his life.

Chapter Seven

Nick lifted the bottle to his lips and belted down two slugs of whiskey. He'd already drank two-thirds of the bottle; he was beyond feeling the liquid fire blaze a path down his throat. The whiskey formed a sizzling pool in the pit of his stomach.

That he was sitting here by the river, drinking alone, should have told him something. It may have, had he been sober enough to think straight. While not completely drunk yet, he was well on his way.

Nick wasn't much of a drinker. The only times he usually felt the need for a good, stiff shot of whiskey was at the end of a trail drive. Hitting the wild cow-town of Abilene did something to a puncher when he'd been out herding stubborn cattle for the better part of two months. Imbibing while on the Bar None was a rarity for him. The few times Nick had done it, he'd had a damn solid reason.

A sloppy grin tugged at the lips beneath his whiskey-dampened mustache. Tonight, he couldn't exactly say his reason was . . . solid. It was damn good, just not "solid." It leaned more toward the soft, sweet, and sexy as all hell side.

His reason tonight was Dallas Cameron. And the way the memory of her kisses had eaten at his mind and gut all goddamn day!

Nick propped the whiskey bottle against his hip and reached for his battered guitar. Purging Dallas from his mind was an excellent excuse to drink until he passed out. God knows, it beat his first plan, which was to find her and finish what they'd started last night.

His head might be buzzing, but not enough that Nick didn't recognize his first plan as the stupidest he'd ever had. What was he going to do? Strut into the house, into her room, and take her?

But she was Dallas Cameron, the boss's daughter.

Nick, on the other hand, was just another dirt-poor cowpuncher. A man who lived on meager wages. A man whose work-filthy hands had no right to touch a woman like her. Or so Ian Cameron always said. And so Nick always believed.

Until last night.

Dammit!

What was it about Dallas that clawed at him? Why did the sweet, sweet taste and feel of her lips grinding beneath his slice through him like a knife? Even in retrospect?

Nick didn't know, didn't ever want to find out. That's where the whiskey came in. The liquor was meant to intoxicate him enough so he could forget those two kisses had ever happened. Forget Dallas Cameron even existed.

Problem was, the whiskey wasn't doing its job.

Instead of helping Nick forget, it made him remember. Everything. He was recalling things tonight that he hadn't even *noticed* two weeks ago. Like the way Dallas's firm, round bottom filled out a pair of men's britches like nobody's business. The way her soft cotton shirts stretched enticingly over her breasts . . . and the way his palms itched whenever he toyed with those particular thoughts.

Nick's fingers poised over the guitar strings. His head dipped, his blurred gaze focusing on the dented old instrument his father had given him too many years ago to count. The tune he plucked out matched his mood. Wild and reckless and more than a little sloppy. It was a song usually reserved for a brightly lit saloon, not silvery moonlight. He couldn't remember ever hearing it being accompanied by a howling coyote or a croaking bullfrog before.

He paused playing now and again to belt back more whiskey, then carried the song to its end. By the time he was done, Nick's head was spinning and his thoughts . . .

Dammit, his thoughts had slipped right back to Dallas!

He couldn't stop thinking about her. Fantasizing about her. *Wanting* her.

With a grunt of self-disgust, Nick set the guitar aside and leaned his head back against the gritty cottonwood trunk supporting his back.

If he'd seen anything funny in the situation, he would have laughed. Here he was, hard-as-nails Nick Langston, sitting in the moonlight, drunk out of his gourd, mooning over a gal like Dallas Cameron. Who would've believed it? Not him two weeks ago, that's for damn sure!

His thoughts were starting to get jumbled. The more whiskey he drank, the better his first plan was looking. It was nine o'clock at night. Most of the ranch was already asleep. If he was quiet, no one would see him enter the house. No one would stop him.

Except himself.

And Dallas.

His eyelids fluttered closed, and a wolfish grin tugged at one corner of Nick's lips. Going solely by her response to his kisses last night, it was questionable whether or not Dallas would stop him. While she may not realize it yet, she wanted Nick as badly as he wanted her. If she'd shared his range of experience, Dallas might have recognized the need for fulfillment that coursed hot and strong through them both. And she might have known how to fight it, the way he did. Or, at least the way he was *trying* to.

The hell of it was, experience or not, it was a fight he was losing. He'd never felt desire this strong. It was tearing him up inside, driving him crazy. He was tired of fighting his baser instincts, and failing at every turn. He was a strong man, always had been, but his need for Dallas coursed white-hot in his blood, threatened to bring him to his knees. Physical desire was proving stronger than common sense, and a good deal more powerful than any brand loyalty he'd ever known.

Nick was starting not to care so much about who Dallas was. Who *he* was. He wanted her with an urgency that shook him. Hot and wet and ready for him, that's how he wanted Dallas. Beneath him. Thrusting in time to him, writhing an equally strong need. He ached to hear her moan his name when he buried himself inside of her, became one with her. He wanted . . .

What he couldn't have. *That's* what he wanted!

Nick's open palm slapped his thigh hard enough to make his skin sting.

"Plain and simple, Langston, you've lost your goddamn mind," Nick slurred under his breath. Only there wasn't anything plain and simple about it. When it came to him and Dallas—a relationship that used to be easy, but wasn't anymore—everything was so damned complicated.

Everything had changed. So drastically, so quickly, that it made Nick's head spin in a way vast quantities of whiskey never could. He sighed, shook his head, the nape of his neck dragging harshly along the gritty bark of the cottonwood. His brain registered the sting of pain as a fuzzy nuisance.

The snap of a twig snagged Nick's attention. Still, he didn't become totally alert until he heard a soft, husky voice in his ear.

"Hate to be the one to break this to you, Langston, but you lost your mind a long time ago. What took you so long to realize what everyone else on this ranch has known for years?"

One blue eye cracked open a slit. Without moving his head, Nick's attention snapped to the side. He blinked that one eye hard. The liquor-blurred shape of the woman standing not six feet away didn't waver.

Nor did she disappear, the way he'd hoped to God she would.

"Dallas?" Nick croaked. "Damn." Nick pinched his eye shut at the same time his hand groped for the whiskey bottle. He needed another drink. With luck, he'd pass out cold real soon.

"Are you feeling all right, Nick?"

"Dandy. Just . . . dandy." He lifted the bottle to his lips. His hand was shaking almost as badly as the rest of him. More whiskey trickled down his chin than pooled inside his mouth. Nick wasn't surprised. He also wasn't pleased. The erotic thoughts he'd been entertaining about this woman—coupled with the flesh and blood sight of her, standing too damn close—had shaken him up. Badly. "What do you want?"

"You."

Well, now, *that* got Nick's attention right fast! It also got both his eyes open. He struggled to pull her into focus, then wished like hell he hadn't bothered. She looked nice, all grown up and pretty as hell. She looked . . . ah, God, she looked too damn good, that's how she looked! "Beg pardon?"

"I want to talk to you," Dallas said, and took a step toward him. Another. A navy blue slit skirt fell from her hips in soft folds. The hem whispered around her ankles; the sound whispered down Nick's spine.

It was on the tip of Nick's tongue to tell her to stop, not to come another inch closer. He was drunk; God knows what he'd say or do. It wasn't safe for her to be here.

He would have warned her, except his abruptly dry,

tight throat prohibited speech. Her body heat penetrated Nick's side as he watched her plop down on the ground next to him. And in that instant, Nick knew it was too late to tell her anything. It had been for days.

"What'd you want to talk about?" Nick asked, his voice thick and husky and slurred. He was hoping that maybe, just maybe, he could find out quickly why she was here, then send her on her way as sweet and as pure as she'd come.

"Last night," she said. "When you kissed me, Nick."

"Don't tell me, let me guess. Now you want to *talk* about it, am I right?"

"Not exactly." She'd been staring at his profile. Nick felt a stab of relief when her gaze shifted, sweeping over the softly churning river. "I wanted to tell you that I've been thinking about what you said. And I agree with you. I-I've decided not to let David make love to me."

"Son-of-a-goddamn-bitch!"

"You don't have to yell at me, Langston! I thought you'd be happy to hear it."

Nick ground the back of his head against the tree trunk and stifled a groan. If only the pain would clear his head! But it didn't, didn't even come close. *"Happy?"* he growled. "Is that what you thought I'd be? Damnation!"

He may be drunk, but Nick's reaction time was still lightning fast. He twisted to the side, knocking the whiskey bottle to the ground, barely noticing when the liquor spilled out and soaked through his pants.

His hands snaked out, manacling Dallas's slender

165

upper arms. He heard her gasp, but he was too far gone with drink and anger to care. "Are you *trying* to drive me crazy, woman?" he yelled, his breath a hot blast of whiskey-laced air in Dallas's face. Nick saw her wince, but it barely registered. Nothing but white-hot fury—mixed liberally with white hot desire—was able to penetrate the liquor-fog in his head. "If so, you're doing a damn fine job of it."

Her brown eyes were huge as her gaze slipped up, locking with his. The trace of a confused frown creased her brow. "All I'm trying to do is talk to you, Nick."

"Bullshit. Talkin' isn't what you came here for, darlin'. We both know it."

"We do?" One tawny brow cocked high. "Then why don't you tell me what I *did* come here for . . ."

"You really have to ask?"

"I *am* asking."

Dallas glared at him. She didn't look like she was feeling any fear, and Nick thought that was a damn shame. If she'd shown only a trace of fright, he would have let her go, would have stood up and walked away before either of them did anything they'd both regret come sunup.

But Dallas wasn't afraid.

And Nick wasn't going anywhere.

Beneath the cotton shirtsleeve, her arm felt slender, fragile in Nick's abruptly slackened grasp. It also felt warm and soft . . . the hot flesh underneath tempting beyond reason.

Moonlight caressed her upturned face, softening and defining her features. The silvery glow danced over her hair, made the tawny braid draping her shoulder look like it had been woven from threads of raw silk. The need to unwind that plait, to comb his fingers through her hair, gather it up in fistfuls, rocked Nick to the core.

His gaze dropped to her lips. They were shell pink and lusciously full, moist from where she'd just dragged her tongue over them. Another, stronger urge clawed around inside him.

"You haven't answered my question," Dallas said. It might have been Nick's imagination, but he could have sworn her husky voice cracked. A shiver ran through the arm beneath his hands. Ah, now that damn well *wasn't* his imagination. "Why *did* I come down here if not to talk to you?"

Her hot, sweet breath puffed over his chin and neck, heating the fire that was already pumping through Nick's blood, his mind, numbing his good sense.

Why did she come? Wasn't it obvious?

It was the same reason he'd drank almost an entire bottle of whiskey, hoping to pass out cold. The same reason that, before Dallas had shown up, he'd come damn close to losing an inner battle with himself that would have ended with *him* seeking out *her*.

A vague, uneasy feeling told him that Dallas wasn't aware of any of that. In fact, Nick was starting to think she really had come here only to talk. At least, *she* believed so. Nick's whiskey-fogged mind, on the other hand, was convinced the only reason Dallas was here was to test his already frazzled patience. To drive him crazy. To tease and tempt him beyond reason. To snap in two the fragile thread leashing him to what was left of his normally good self-restraint.

She'd done it all. The second she'd said the words "make love," Nick had felt something inside him snap. Something that cut right through his liquor-induced haze and sliced him clean to the bone.

He scowled, trying to clear the liquor from his mind. He succeeded only marginally. Why had she come to him tonight? That was the question she'd put to him, wasn't it? Well, damned if he wouldn't tell her!

He would have softened the truth with sugarcoated words if he'd known how. Flowery speech was as foreign to a man like Nick Langston as a carriage ride through Central Park.

"You came here," he said finally, gruffly, "because you want me." Nick watched her brown eyes widen. A pink flush warmed her cheeks. Odd. He couldn't remember Dallas Cameron ever blushing before. It was a sight to be enjoyed and savored.

"Want you?" Dallas asked cautiously, then tried to chuckle. If she'd hoped to abolish the tension crackling between them, she failed. Her eyes narrowed. "Want you . . . *how?*"

The fingers wrapped around her arms melted away—but not before Nick felt her shiver again. A normal reaction to the sudden cold washing over flesh heated by a touch. He knew it, because he felt the same thing himself.

His hand didn't go far. Nick hooked the knuckle of his index finger under her chin, dragging her gaze back to his when she tried to glance away. "You want me the way a woman wants a man, darlin'," he drawled, his tone only slightly tight, only slightly strained, but still very slurred. "That's the way you want me."

Dallas lifted her hand, pillowing the back of his calloused knuckles with her palm. His flesh felt warm and rough. It felt good. Was it true? she wondered. *Did* she want him the way a woman wants a man? She'd never had a man, never wanted one. Until now.

"You're drunk, Nick."

"Very. Damn astute of you to notice, Cameron. Now look at me and tell me if you think I'm stupid. 'Cause I'd have to be not to see what's in your eyes right now."

His palm opened, cupping her cheek. Dallas responded instinctively by turning her head, nuzzling into the touch. The tips of his fingers grazed her earlobe. She drew in a shaky breath, and closed her eyes.

"It's true, isn't it?" he asked.

She shrugged, and Nick felt the swell of her breasts brush his forearm. His blood simmered.

"I don't know," she whispered softly. Her breath seared his wrist. His pulse leapt in response. "I'm confused. I don't know what I want anymore. Except . . ."

Nick cleared his throat. The world was swimming around him, but this time it had little to do with the whiskey. *Me. Say you want* me, *darlin'. As I am.* The thought burned through his mind, throughout the rest of his body, hotter and faster than a brushfire during a dry, rainless summer.

"Except?" he prodded hoarsely. Nick tried to pull his hand away, but Dallas's grip tightened. He was bigger, stronger than her. He could have pushed her away easily. Should have. Almost did. But then she placed a fleeting kiss on the center of his palm, and suddenly pushing her away was the last thing on his mind.

"I want you to kiss me again," Dallas admitted reluctantly. "I've wanted that ever since last night."

Nick was lost in those large brown pools of her eyes. Her eyes were expressive, always had been. Yet never so much as they were tonight, with the moonlight shimmering off them and turning the irises a rich shade of chocolate brown.

"What *did* you have in mind, Nick?"

Nick swallowed hard, and thought that, Christ! this woman could *not* be little Dallas Cameron. No, no. The Dallas Cameron he knew wouldn't have any idea how to flutter her lashes in a way that tore at a man's gut and made his lower body harden and throb. She wouldn't know how to flash that kind of secretive half smile, the kind that made a man want to lay down his life if it meant getting a chance to part those lips with his tongue.

Or would she?

Maybe his little Dallas Cameron wouldn't have known any of that. Then again, this *wasn't* his little Dallas Cameron. Not anymore. As Nick had been forced to realize since that night by the corral, the woman sitting with him now was exactly that; a woman fully grown. With a woman's lush, promising curves, and a woman's wants and needs.

Was he strong enough to hold onto a sliver of sanity? Enough to *not* satisfy those needs for her?

If Nick had been sober, the answer would have been an absolute yes. Come hell or high water, he wouldn't

170

touch Ian Cameron's little girl with his work-filthy hands.

But he wasn't sober.

Worse, she'd tapped his resistance dry when she'd placed that feather-light kiss on his calloused palm.

Nick wasn't near good enough to touch a woman like this one. He knew it. Just like he knew he was going to touch her anyway. Everywhere. Repeatedly. What's more, they were both going to enjoy it. Because Nick knew in his heart that something that felt this good and right was a memory to be savored for a lifetime; a Langston would never be this lucky again.

He was too drunk to stop himself, and Dallas didn't look like she was going to do the job for him.

Nick angled his head, and gazed deeply into her eyes. Dark brown, large, and so inviting. Her lips were already parted in anticipation. The moonlight struck her throat in such a way that he could pick out the pulse pounding erratically beneath her creamy skin.

He had to kiss her. His tongue stroked frantic paths over the back of his teeth, begging to taste of her sweetness this one more time.

Who they were suddenly didn't matter a bit.

What they were about to do mattered one hell of a lot.

"Nick," Dallas whispered raggedly, her mind lost to the feel of Nick's broad shoulder nudging her toward the soft, warm ground. Her hands came up, her fingers curling around his biceps. He felt big and strong, hot and hard. Feeling the corded bands of muscle beneath her fingertips was almost as intoxicating as smelling the tobacco and whiskey scent of him.

"It had to come down to this between us. Last night's kiss whetted my appetite for you, set my blood on fire, left me hungry for more. You must have known that, must have guessed."

"Yes, maybe I did," Dallas admitted softly, her gaze fixed on the lips almost concealed beneath his mustache. She marveled at the way his mouth moved to form words. The sight was erotically stimulating. Her own lips burned in expectation. Nick's kiss would be hungry and demanding, draining and devouring. She knew it, could taste it already.

She was laying on the ground, staring up at him. Her hands, Dallas noticed, had drifted downward and were now pillowed atop his thighs. His muscles flexed beneath her open palms, reminding her of Nick's dormant strength. The angle at which she viewed him emphasized the broad wedge of his chest and shoulders.

With the moon behind him, Nick's face was cast in shadows. Dallas didn't need to see his eyes to know they were on her. The hot tingle of her blood told her that. She knew exactly where and when his gaze touched her, for her body warmed there in unspoken response.

"If you asked me to stop, I would," Nick said as he eased down to her side. He slipped one hand beneath her head. His fingers tunneled into the soft tawny hair above the braid, his palm cradled her from the hard-packed earth. His other hand settled atop her stomach; it was a huge, pinning weight that didn't feel nearly as restrictive as it should have.

"I don't want you to stop." Dallas's voice caught

when she felt Nick shift, the center of his hips pressing urgently into the soft side of hers. The long, hard proof of his desire nudged her, and her heartbeat staggered. His lips were inches from her ear. When he spoke, his breath sizzled through the silky curtain of her hair, warming her already passion-fevered skin.

"Wrong answer, darlin'. You're supposed to kick and scream and claw at me. Demand I let you go." He nuzzled her ear, his hot, wet tongue sneaking out and tracing the curl. Her breath caught, then came fast and ragged. "Remind me that your daddy will shoot me for even *thinking* about touching you like this, never mind actually doing it." He nibbled her earlobe, then brushed it with the tip of his nose. His attention shifted as he nibbled lower, slowly biting his way down her neck, making tingly sparks of pleasure shoot through her. "Come on, darlin', tell me. Christ, say *anything*, just make me stop. I'm too damn horny, and too damn drunk, to stop myself."

Dallas's hands were now flanking Nick's hips. She felt raw sinew beneath the tough denim, felt him tremble. Or was it her hands that trembled? "I think we're both in trouble Nick. I can't stop this. I'm too drunk on *you* to stop myself."

His heartbeat jerked as he levered himself up on one elbow, staring down at her. Her eyelids were thick with newly awakened desire, but not as thick as his own.

Her hands curled inward, digging into his hips. She pulled, ground his rock-hard erection against her. Even through the obstructive clothes, it was a torture comparable to none.

Nick was hard and hot and more than ready. He

didn't need Dallas's touch to make himself crazed. Imagining it was enough to do that all by itself. The reality of it was even more devastating. "You're going to regret those words come morning, darlin'. You're going to regret not trying to stop me."

"I don't think so."

"Not now, maybe. But you will."

"What about *you?* Will you regret it, Nick?"

"I already do. Ah, God, more than you know."

"But not enough to stop." The words came out more as a question than a statement. Dallas's breath caught as she waited for his answer. If Nick stopped now, if he left her aching and wanting like this . . . "Do you?"

His answer was low and whiskey-rough. The words came from somewhere deep inside of him, as though they'd been torn from his very soul. "No, goddamn it, I don't."

Chapter Eight

He couldn't wait. He'd held back as long as he could, but he simply couldn't hold back a second longer.

Nick had given Dallas a chance to stop him. She hadn't. He wasn't sure if he should be glad about that or not.

One thing he was damned sure of, though . . . he had to kiss her.

Nick angled his head, and his mouth settled over hers. A groan rumbled low and deep in his throat. He knew he must have died and gone to heaven, because nothing on earth had ever tasted as good and sweet and right as Dallas Cameron's lips. Nothing.

He whisked his mouth over hers, letting the fringe of his mustache sensitize her skin, awaken her senses. He nibbled her upper lip, ran the tip of his tongue over her lower, then suctioned the latter into his mouth. He applied just enough pressure to stimulate yet not cause pain.

The gentle suckling drew an airy moan from her. Her breath poured like liquid fire over Nick's cheek and jaw. Her back arched, and he felt her breasts press against his chest as she wrapped her arms around his back and clung to him.

The restraint was torture, but he refused to increase the intimacy of the kiss. Soon, but not yet. Instead, Nick focused on heightening the anticipation of when he would. He wanted to drive Dallas wild, until the desire inside of her matched the one that was driving him.

Instinct said that wouldn't take long.

She wanted him. The way her body squirmed beneath his, trying to get closer than was possible, told him that. It felt good, but not good enough. It wasn't what Nick wanted and needed with every throbbing fiber of his body. He wanted more. He wanted her hot, burning with need until she couldn't stand it anymore. Christ, he was close to that point himself, and they'd barely started kissing!

All night last night, every waking minute of today, Dallas had dreamed of kissing Nick like this. But dreams weren't real, and they couldn't hold a candle to the actual thing.

He tasted of tobacco and whiskey, with an undertone of strong black coffee. It was a delicious flavor, one she savored.

The feel of his hard, hot body easing her to the ground was comparable to nothing Dallas had ever known before. She could feel him, everywhere, hard muscle and strength. When his body moved against her own gentle softness, she felt the contrast of hard and soft down to the quivering core.

She felt him shiver when his tongue skated moistly over her full lower lip. She absorbed his shudders with her palms, and her body. Reciprocal ones vibrated through Dallas when she thought that moist shaft was going to dip into her mouth—when she hoped and prayed that it would. It didn't, but continued to tease her unmercifully.

"Please, Nick," Dallas whispered raggedly against his mouth. She arched beneath him, into him. Her fingers tunneled inward, clawing impatiently at his back. "Please."

She didn't wait for his response. She couldn't. All she knew was that she could not, *would not,* be denied another second.

Taking the initiative, her tongue slipped urgently past her own lips. With the tip, she caressed the place where mustache and teasing mouth merged into one, in her innocence not realizing that in so doing she'd just turned a feminine wile on Nick that was older than time. It was an instinctive form of torture that, drunk or sober, no man could resist.

Nick wasn't of a mind to resist. He stilled, waiting to see what she would do next. And wondering all the while if he would be able to live through it.

It was Dallas's turn to coax and tease, to taste and test. She followed Nick's lead, nibbling on his lower lip, sucking it into her mouth, stroking it with her tongue until she felt the hot flesh quiver.

His hand released her hair, slipped lower. His fingers hooked over her shoulder, digging into her flesh as he lifted her up, crushing her to him as though trying to melt her body into his chest. They met thigh to thigh, hip to hip.

And the kiss Dallas had wanted, craved, finally came.

Nick devoured her, eating at her mouth as though he couldn't feel and taste enough of her. His tongue pried her lips apart. It didn't take much coaxing. She opened to him willingly. He plunged inside the hot, moist recess of her mouth, the strokes of his tongue deep and sweeping, claiming her, branding her as his own.

Nick's free hand was no longer content to pin Dallas to the ground. There was no need. She'd made it clear she wasn't going anywhere. And Nick sure as hell wasn't about to let her. Not now. It was far too late for that.

The palm he splayed over the outer curve of her hip strayed inward, cupping her waist, marveling at its taut, concave smoothness as well as how nicely it nestled into his hand. He felt her quiver beneath the cloth, felt her arch up, begging him to strip off the obstructive barrier of cloth, to explore every glorious inch of her.

She needn't have worried. Nick was determined to commit each soft, warm, satiny inch of her to memory in his eyes, hands, and mind. Before the night was over, he would know her sweet curves and valleys better than he knew the back of his own weathered hand.

His caress drifted over her waist, again tested the firm, rounded smoothness of her hip, strayed lower. Her thigh was long and shapely, athletically firm as it skimmed beneath his open hand. But as good as it felt, it wasn't good enough to hold his attention.

His mind had fixed on the feminine swells teasing his chest. Right now, that was where his hand wanted most to be.

His fingers shook when he lifted them to her collar. The buttons trailing down were tiny, awkward for his large hand. It was only his determination to strip her, to feel her hot, hungry flesh against his own, that gave Nick the patience and willpower to complete the chores.

He did so slowly, feasting his gaze on the tantalizing inches of creamy flesh that were slowly being revealed. By the time he undid the last button, his fingers weren't the only thing shaking. His entire body shuddered with need.

The placket of her shirt gaped open. Shadows hinted at and defined the shape and size of her breasts. As much as Nick wanted to see her, all of her, he didn't trust himself to just yet. A sight that stunning would undo him.

Nick wasn't ready to be undone.

The tips of his fingers snuck beneath her open shirt. He felt her skin, soft and warm, as he dipped in further. A little more.

A groan tore from his chest when, unable to resist, he covered her fully. Her breasts were the perfect size and shape to drive a man insane. He nestled her in his palm, marveled at the fit. His eyelashes flickered down, a shield from the pleasure-pain he felt when her nipple beaded against his calloused palm, begging intimate attention.

Nick couldn't have refused that plea if his life depended on it. With a flick of his wrist, he nudged the fabric apart. Opening his eyes, he filled his senses with the lushness he'd exposed. Her breasts were small and round and unbelievably firm, glistening a silvery shade of white in the moonlight. The rosy nipple stiffened and puckered invitingly under the heat of his gaze.

"To hell with Ian," he murmured, and lowered his head, tickling the pearled flesh with his mustache, "I'd gladly die for this."

Dallas moaned and twisted her fingers in his hair, urging his head downward. It didn't take much coaxing for Nick to take her into his mouth.

His teeth nibbled her sensitized flesh, his tongue laved and stroked, his mouth suckled. A shaky inhalation filled him with her scent. She smelled soapy, rainwater fresh and clean. The smell was more intoxicating than the best bottle of whiskey money could buy. Nick felt himself drown in the sweet aroma.

Dallas was drowning in pure, erotic sensation. Every time his lips tugged, a wave of heat spread through her stomach, seeped downward. She felt edgy, her muscles unbearably tight. A throbbing had started somewhere in her body. She was too dazed to trace the origin, she only recognized the sensation as insistent and urgent, sharpened by the way Nick's mustache whisked over and tickled her skin.

Her fingers fisted his hair. She couldn't take much more of this. His mouth was driving her wild, and his tongue . . . dear Lord, his tongue!

Desire was riding Nick hard. His hand strayed down, flattening over her bare stomach, his thumb rubbing the waistband of her split skirt. He couldn't bunch up the hem and sneak his hand beneath, the way he wanted so badly to do. His finger toyed with the fastenings on the side. He didn't undo them. He was afraid to. Once those closures had been freed, once his hand slipped lower still, touched what he wanted most to touch, there'd be no stopping.

His head spun, half from the whiskey, half from the raw desire clawing at his gut. He lifted his head, just a little, just enough to look at her. His fingers poised over the hooks holding her skirt closed. "Tell me to stop," he rasped, his voice a whiskey-slurred moan. "Please. We can't do this. It isn't . . . Damnation! It isn't right!"

Dallas's eyes had been closed as she reveled in the lightning-sharp sensations Nick's fingers brought her. Her lashes flickered up slowly, and she gazed up at him. Years of silent admiration softened her features. Years of wanting to be near this man in every way possible sparkled in her eyes.

A surge of emotion fired in her blood. Desire, tempered by something stronger, more enduring. Something wonderful and endless.

Until this very second, Dallas hadn't known how deeply her feelings for Nick ran, or how strong. She knew now, though, and the intensity of it made her voice throaty and rough. "It feels right to me, Nick. Very right. And you said yourself it's too late to stop now."

Nick searched her face, desperate to believe her. Afraid to. Did it feel right? Did his touch feel as good to her as *dreaming* about touching her this way was for him? "You said you'd never let a man who wasn't your husband touch you like this."

"I know." Of its own accord, Dallas's body arched insistently beneath him. "I changed my mind. It's a woman's prerogative."

"Change it back, Dallas. I haven't got a damn thing to give you other than this one night."

"That's all I'm asking for. All I want. Give me tonight, Nick. I—I want you to be my first."

"Why, Dallas? *Why?*"

Her palm felt hot and soft as she stroked it over his jaw. Nick shivered in response, and swallowed hard.

"I don't know," she admitted raggedly. She wanted to tell him that she didn't plan any of this. She didn't plan to touch him, or to like it so much when she did. That all she wanted was just one memory of him to keep her warm through all the long, lonely nights of what promised to be a very dull, very cold marriage. Instead she said, "Please, Nick. Please. I need you."

It was the "I need you" that cinched it. Nick Langston had never been able to deny Dallas anything. When she was a kid, he would have given her the moon if she'd asked for it. She wasn't a kid anymore, and she wasn't asking for anything as simple as the moon. Still, he couldn't deny her. Deny himself. Tomorrow he would dearly regret . . .

Ah, damn! Let tomorrow take care of itself. There'd be plenty of time then for recriminations and regrets. But not tonight. Not when he had this woman soft and willing in his arms.

With a stifled moan, Nick spread himself possessively on top of her. He shifted, covering her mouth with his. Unlike the last, this kiss was wild, unrestrained, demanding and draining.

For them both.

Nick's hands stroked feverish paths up and down her sides. She felt good beneath him. Perfect. Better than anything he had ever—*would* ever—know.

He ended the kiss abruptly. They were both breathless and flushed.

Quickly, Nick unfastened the waistband of her skirt with trembling fingers. His fingers slipped beneath. He lifted her slightly, cradling her back with one hand while the other swept the thing down her legs. The garment was carelessly tossed, instantly forgotten. Her chemise proved no obstacle. Soon, that too lay in a crumpled pile on the dirt.

Dallas shivered. The night air felt oddly cool against her overly warm flesh. Nick's hungry eyes were quick to heat her. His attention never strayed as she watched him all but tear off his own clothing, then join her on the ground.

With a groan, he scooped her to him, holding her close enough for their frantic heartbeats to mesh. Their breathing was harsh and ragged; it was impossible to tell where one breath left off, and the next began.

Nick eased Dallas onto her back until she was laying atop the ground, with him stretched out beside her. Her eyes were closed. Good. He couldn't bare to see his reflection in those liquid pools. It might make him stop, and he was no longer sure if he could—even if she'd asked.

Her creamy thigh skimmed like hot satin beneath his palm. She quivered when his fingertips grazed the tawny curls nestled at the junction of her thighs.

He felt her stiffen, and for a second Nick thought

she was going to ask him to stop. He almost, *almost* wished she would. Then his fingers slipped between her legs, and he felt the moist heat of passion against his fingertips. The tension of nervous discomfort was swiftly replaced by the tension of urgent need.

He nudged her thighs apart, and his fingers slipped up and into the warm, wet folds of her.

Her hips arched into his hand as he began to stroke her. His movements were long and smooth, meant to excite.

Dallas had never known sensations like this existed. Her entire body was on fire, focused on Nick's large hand, on the fingers that were intimately exploring and exciting her. He was stroking her to madness, fueling the heat inside of desire that he had created. Passion fanned, and burned out of control.

"Nick," she whispered. His name was a husky caress on her lips. Her hand clawed at his back, instinctively trying to urge him to her. She wanted him, all of him, and she wanted him *now*.

He moved. His chest dragged erotically over her breasts as he settled his hips between her legs. His hands slipped up, cradling her shoulders, holding her steady as his hot, throbbing flesh probed her sweet wet softness.

Oh yes, Nick thought, Ian was going to kill him for sure. But Nick didn't care. A long, slow, torturous death would be worth having felt sensations this wonderful and good just once. Oh, yes!

He arched forward and slipped inside of her. She was tight, and hot, and wet, stretching around him,

184

gloving him, urging him onward. Nick probed gently deeper, and met instant resistance.

Easing most of his weight onto his elbows, he nuzzled her earlobe with his nose. "I don't want to hurt you, darlin'."

"This doesn't hurt," she murmured silkily.

"Yet. But it's going to. Brace yourself, darlin'. I promise I'll make it good for you, just . . . ah, God, hold onto me, lady!"

Dallas wrapped her arms trustingly around Nick's back. The soles of her feet caressed the back of his shins before her legs intertwined with his. She turned her head, her tongue stroking a moist path up his neck. "I trust you, Nick," she whispered, her hot breath caressing his flesh, dampened with her tongue.

Nick shivered and nodded as he lowered himself atop her. Her breasts made an all-too-wonderful cushion for his chest. He gave Dallas a second to prepare for the invasion. When both their breathing had almost regulated, he moved, almost withdrawing from her.

Sucking in a shaky breath, he braced himself. In one possessive stroke he plunged into her again. Deeply. Fully.

She gasped and stiffened in his arms.

His head turned, his lips capturing her startled cry, absorbing it into his mouth the way his body absorbed her tender quivers. His kiss was soothing and gentle, a direct contrast to his body's urgent need. He didn't dare move yet. Not until Dallas's body had a chance to get accustomed to the intrusive feel of him buried inside of her.

Nick's tongue slipped into her mouth. Dallas didn't respond at first. He swirled and coaxed, teased and tantalized, until he finally felt the hesitant touch of her tongue against his.

He groaned, deepened the kiss. His arms supported his weight as he lifted slightly, and dragged his chest against the tips of her breasts.

Hard male strength against warm female softness. It was a heady, irresistible contrast.

Dallas squirmed beneath him. Her hips arched. Tentatively at first, then, when she encountered no more pain, eagerly.

Nick moved with her. He pulled from her silky softness. When she whimpered, and her arms tightened around his back, he thrust forward again, rocking into her as far as he could go. Again, this time the pace a hairsbreadth faster. And again.

Of all the women he'd known, none had prepared him for this. Dallas surrounded him, her body milking a response from his, while her soft, panting breaths milked a response from his very soul. He quickened the tempo, thrusting into her, no longer able to restrain his movements or his desire. She arched to meet him, and her hips writhed beneath him, instigating a rhythm of her own.

Her breath whisked hotly over Nick's shoulder, seeping into his skin, into the blood that pounded through his veins. Her fingers raked his back, her nails slicing his skin. His body tightened in response, straining his already terribly weakened self-control.

A strange throbbing gathered within Dallas. She felt ready to burst, as though she was on the very edge of.

. . . What? She didn't know. But the sensations Nick's body ignited as he pulsed inside of her promised a gloriously fulfilling answer.

He moved, just enough so his mouth could reach her breast. His hair fell forward, scraping over Dallas's skin as he suckled a nipple into his mouth, his hips still rocking hard and fast against her.

The twin feelings, each emanating from very different parts of her body, was all Dallas needed to throw her over the edge she'd been clinging to. A sensation, raw and unfamiliar, started low in her body. It swept through her with lightning speed, leaving a trail of fire in its wake. The sensation spiraled higher, consuming her.

The explosion she'd been waiting for came. It burst through her, heightening her every nerve ending until she tingled from the inside out. The places where she touched Nick tingled the most.

He felt her quivers start around him. And as good as that felt, it was nothing compared to hearing Dallas cry out his name in the same instant waves of completion washed over her.

Nick closed his eyes and savored the sound. It was all he'd been waiting for. All he wanted. To give this woman pleasure. Now, it was his turn.

He kissed a path up her throat, over her chin, then settled his mouth on hers. The movements of his stroking tongue matched the insistent rhythm of his hips; long and fast and smooth.

He didn't want it to end. Being buried inside of her felt too good. He wanted to drown in these feelings, in *this woman,* forever. But he couldn't. His body wouldn't let him. His need for completion refused to wait a second longer.

Forever was right here, right now, upon him before he knew it, before he could prepare for it. Afterward, he would think there was no way to prepare for sensations that exquisite.

His climax was nerve-shattering. Sharper, more intense than anything he'd ever felt. The blinding spasms went on and on, pulling from him, draining a part of his soul and spilling it into her. He didn't think the waves of pleasure would ever stop.

Dallas's arms had grown slack. Her breathing wasn't nearly regulated, but close enough to it. Nick should be so lucky! He didn't think he would ever breathe right again.

His arms trembled, then collapsed, refusing to hold him. He eased all of his weight down on Dallas. For just a second, he allowed her warm, soft curves to be his bed, her shoulder his pillow. He dragged great lungfuls of her clean, fresh scent into his lungs, letting them purify him.

How long they lay like that, Nick couldn't say. He lost track of time. However long it was, it wasn't long enough. He could have lain like that, with her, forever. It wasn't until he felt Dallas squirm uncomfortably beneath him that he forced himself to ease the intimacy of his embrace and rolled to the side, laying back on the ground.

Dragging her with him was a natural thing. It never occurred to him to roll away from her, but to insist she roll with him. The bottom of his chin nuzzled the top of her head. Her silky hair tickled his skin.

"I'm sorry, darlin'," he murmured against her, not really meaning it, but feeling he had to say it. He felt her shift and mold herself more closely to him. "It shouldn't have happened. I shouldn't have let it happen. Maybe if I wasn't so drunk . . . ah, hell, it probably wouldn't have mattered."

She shook her head. Nick felt her shoulders tremble. The warm trickle of a tear skated down his chest.

Oh God, she was crying. Dallas Cameron was crying!

If he hadn't felt like a heel before, Nick certainly felt like one now. No, make that worse. He felt much, much worse than he would have believed possible. He wouldn't blame Dallas for hitting and kicking him and calling him all sorts of atrocious names right now. He deserved all that and more for what he'd allowed to happen between them tonight.

To his surprise, she didn't do any of those things. What she did was ten times worse. She lay in his arms, clinging to him while she cried silently against his chest.

Her sobs tore Nick apart. He couldn't have hurt more if she'd stuck a knife in his heart and twisted the blade. He sucked in a sharp breath and coaxed her chin up with his hand.

Her eyes remained closed. Silvery moonlight glinted off the fat tears spilling from beneath the thick fringe of tawny lashes. The wet drops slipped over her cheeks, and splashed onto Nick's wrist.

This was the first time he had ever seen Dallas Cameron cry. Ever. It had a powerful effect on him. Nick's heart convulsed. His hand opened, his palm cradling her moist cheek. "Dallas, sweetheart . . . God, darlin', I'm sorry. So sorry."

Dallas swallowed back a groan. If Nick said that one more time, she was going to hurt him. Didn't he know that she wasn't crying because she was sorry about what had happened, but because *he* was so obviously sorry about it? Didn't he know her at all?

"Christ, but I've made a mess of everything, haven't I?" he growled. While his words were savage, his touch was not. The calloused fingers caressing her face were gentle and soothing. Dallas sought shelter in that touch. "I'll make this up to you, Dallas. I swear to God I will. Somehow."

"There's nothing to make up *for*," she whispered huskily, and mentally forced her tears to stop. Crying would get her nowhere with a man like Nick Langston, she was sure of it.

His thumb had been stroking the sensitive spot between her jaw and earlobe. The tender rubbing came to an abrupt halt. "What are you saying?" he asked tentatively.

Dallas wiped her tears away with her fist. Her shrug was tight and strained. She forced her voice not to crack, and almost succeeded. "Dammit, Langston, don't be an idiot. In case you haven't figured it out yet, I'm not the least bit sorry about what happened."

"No?" Nick scowled darkly. "Well, you should be."

"I'm not. We both know I could have stopped you if I'd wanted to. I didn't want to. It felt good. *You* felt good. Nick, don't you see? I *enjoyed* it. You promised you'd make it good for me, and you did. I'm . . ." she

190

released an airy sigh, "I'm crying because I'm glad you were my first."

She hadn't hit or kicked or screamed at him, but she might as well have. Dallas's words, coupled with the way she glanced trustingly up at him, was the next best thing to being clipped in the jaw. Nick's head reeled from the blow. "You're confused, darlin'. You don't know—"

"Don't tell me what I do and do not know. What I do and do not *feel*. Stop treating me like a child, Langston! I'm a woman now."

Nick didn't need to be reminded of that fact, since he was the brute who'd just forged her way there. "Then act like one, Cameron. I've just ruined you. Let me take responsibility for it."

Dallas squirmed until she was facing him squarely. His arms circled her loosely. She tried not to notice the way his chest hairs tickled her breasts, but it wasn't an easy sensation to ignore. "And what, exactly, have you ruined? Nothing that I can see."

"No?" One golden brow tipped up. The curl of his lips beneath the mustache was menacing. "Well, look a might closer then. What do you think your daddy's gonna say when he finds out about this?"

She shrugged but refused to drop her gaze. "There's no reason he has to find out. *I'm* not going to tell him."

"You won't have to. Ian isn't stupid. What do you think he's gonna say when you refuse to chase after Parker and beget his grandsons? He'll know there's a reason. It won't take long for him to put two and two together, and figure out it equals one night with Nick

191

Langston. He'll be after my hide with a loaded shotgun faster'n you can spit . . . after he's done tannin' your backside."

"He won't know," Dallas repeated tightly.

"You don't think so?"

"I *know* so." Dallas sighed. Nick had promised her this one night, and she would never ask him for more. She wouldn't ask for anything that wasn't given freely. "I don't plan to stop chasing David, Nick. Our picnic is in a couple of days, and if it goes the way I think it will, David should propose shortly after that."

Her gaze lifted, locking with his. If she'd seen just a glimmer of warmth, of something that even resembled caring in his eyes or his expression, Dallas would have rethought her plans on the spot. But she didn't. Nick's eyes were filled with hot-blue fire, and his expression was strained, but not at all loving.

Without warning, Nick jerked to a sitting position. He dragged her up with him, but then quickly let her go. He wanted to reach out and shake some sense into her, but he didn't dare. As angry as he was, he didn't trust himself to touch her again.

"You'd do that?" he growled. "You'd go to Parker after what just happened here . . . with *me*. He can't give you what I just did, Dallas. He can't make you tremble and moan and cry out the way I just did. The pansy wouldn't know how."

"There's more to life than having the earth move," she said softly. Her eyes stung with tears she refused to shed in front of Nick. Why, oh why wouldn't he hold her in his arms and promise to keep her for his own?

It was all she wanted. All, Dallas realized suddenly, she'd ever wanted in her life.

"What, Dallas? What more is there? Money? Land? Does joining the TLP to the Bar None mean *that* goddamn much to you?" Nick sneered. Money. Land. It was only two of the many things he didn't have. Two of the many things that David Parker *did*. That, and a name to be proud of, stability . . .

The list was endless. It made Nick's head buzz thinking about it.

Dallas shook her head. No, joining the two ranches didn't mean that much to her. Winning her father's respect by marrying a man Ian Cameron could be proud of did. There was no way to tell Nick that, though. No way to phrase it so that he would understand.

"I have to go," she said, deciding it would be best not to answer him at all.

Nick's eyes narrowed to furious blue slits. He watched closely, but didn't stop her when she gathered up her clothes and tugged them on. His palms itched, and his need to reach out for her was strong but he held himself in check. What would be the point? She'd made her wishes painfully clear. She wanted better for herself than a man like Nick Langston.

Well that was just dandy. If that's what Dallas Cameron wanted, that's what Dallas Cameron could have. He'd be damned if he'd stop her.

Dallas hesitated when she reached the border of trees. She glanced back over her shoulder in time to see Nick reach for the bottle that had tipped over what seemed now like a lifetime ago. Most of the contents had spilled into the dirt. But not all.

Their gazes met and held, the bottle poised against his lips.

Dallas was the first to look away.

With a resigned sigh, she turned and walked into the woods, toward the ranch, toward the life her father had mapped out for her.

She didn't look back. Not only because the sight of Nick was simply too painful to bear, but because more tears were streaming down her cheeks, and she couldn't have seen him through the blur anyway.

Chapter Nine

The rain was coming down hard. The pounding of raindrops on the porch roof swallowed up the agitated clomps of Dallas's boot heels as she paced from one side of the porch to the other. A full, unwieldy calico skirt billowed around her legs with each abrupt turn. Already the cloth felt damp, weighty, as though it sagged from waist to ankle instead of falling in airy cotton folds the way it was supposed to.

Despite the rain, the temperature was hot enough to bring a flush to Dallas's cheeks. The humidity that hung heavily in the air made the tawny curls resting against her brow spring into tight coils. A trickle of perspiration ribboned down the side of her throat, trickled beneath her collar, sliding warmly between the shadows of her breasts.

She felt hot and uncomfortable. Anxious. Of course, those feelings might have nothing to do with the weather at all. They could easily have been born of frustration.

David was an hour late for their picnic. The delay

was beginning to eat at Dallas's already frayed nerves.

Where was he?

Had the storm caused his delay? Had he decided today would be a bad day for their picnic after all? And, if so, wouldn't it have been only polite to *let her know?*

This morning she'd received a curt note from David telling her that their picnic would be today, at noon, or not at all. It was the first she'd heard from him since the fire. So where was he? There was no way to know what was keeping him so long. The only thing Dallas could be sure of was that she had been tripping over this aggravating skirt for the past hour, and that it was driving her nuts!

Five minutes, she decided as she plopped onto a weathered old rocking chair. The wood groaned beneath her, and her spurs chinked softly as she shoved with her booted feet and sent the chair speeding to and fro. If David wasn't here in five minutes, she'd go back inside, change out of this damnably uncomfortable getup, and go back to work. Then, tomorrow, she would start looking for someone else to marry. Someone with a ranch as impressively large as the one David stood to inherit. Someone who needed a wife.

Someone who had the consideration to let a body know when he would be late for an appointed meeting!

That settled, Dallas leaned her head back against the chair, closed her eyes, and concentrated on the sound of rain hammering onto the roof. Water sluiced over the sides, dribbled down the gutters before splashing loudly into muddy puddles. It was a soothing sound.

In stark contrast, the sound of Nick Langston's voice wasn't soothing at all.

"Mind telling me what the hell do you think you're doing, Cameron?"

The fury in his tone was overridden only by the sound of his boots clomping up the steps. His angry strides brought him to the side of her chair. Not that Dallas needed the click of his boot heels to know where he was; her suddenly alive, suddenly too-sensitive nerve endings told her exactly where he stood.

Where he stood was much too close to her.

"Christ! I've got three men sick, a yearling stuck up to its belly in a mud hole down by the Deadwater, and where the hell are you? Sitting on a rocking chair *daydreaming!*" A long, tense pause was followed by, "Saddle up, Cameron. We ride out in ten minutes."

Those were the first words Nick had spoken to her in the last four days. Ever since their night together, he'd avoided her. He wasn't even taking his meals with the family anymore—which caused no end of speculation among Ian, Lisa, and Maria.

Dallas didn't realize how much she'd missed the sound of Nick's voice until she felt the gritty timbre curl like a hot slice of heaven down her spine. When his words, not to mention his tone, sank in, she bristled.

She sucked in a calming breath, and released it slowly. Not a wise idea, she realized too late. With her eyes closed, Dallas's other senses honed themselves, each becoming more alert.

Now, not only did she have the enveloping heat of Nick's anger—and the sensuous warmth of his *body*—

to deal with, she also had a breath suddenly trapped in the region of her throat that smelled sharp and spicy and thoroughly male. Her lungs burned with the distinctive scent of Nick Langston. In turn, the smell of him burned away a little of her indignation.

She shivered. Her eyes snapped open, and her gaze locked hard with narrow, stormy blue. "You'll have to take someone else with you today, Langston. I'm not going."

"What?" Nick's jaw bunched hard, the muscle in his cheek jerked. He looked like he was on the verge of dragging her from the chair, as though the only thing stopping him was a restraining fear of what he would do to her should he dare.

Dallas's gaze challenged him to try. "I said I'm not going."

"Like hell you're not! Did you hear what I said? I said there's a yearling—"

"You can stop shouting at me, Nick. There's nothing wrong with my ears, but obviously there's something wrong with yours. For the last time, I-am-not-going!"

The curse that slammed past Nick's lips would have made the devil blush. Dallas, used to his spontaneous cusses, didn't even blink. Her only sign of discomfort was the fingers she curled tightly around the chair arm. The wood bit into her palm, and her knuckles whitened from the strain of her grip. Her voice remained low and tight. "Swear at me all you like, Langston, it won't do you a bit of good. I won't change my mind. I have plans for this afternoon . . . and digging a yearling out of a mud hole isn't one of them."

Nick, in the middle of telling her exactly what she could do with her day, snapped his mouth shut. His stormy gaze lowered, the indigo irises darkening with each inch of the familiar calico dress his gaze drank in. His expression wasn't the only thing that tightened, so did the hands that curled into tight fists at his sides. The muscle in his cheek jerked furiously as his gaze lifted, capturing hers.

"Parker?" he growled. It wasn't a question, but a raw, hard statement of fact.

Dallas nodded, and forced her tone to remain neutral. Years of experience had taught her that the only way to deal with Nick Langston's temper was to ignore it. Though it shortened his fuse, it didn't make bearing the brunt of his anger any easier to bare. "Do you have a problem with that?"

"When it interferes with your work? Yeah, I sure as hell do have a problem with it. A *big* one." With jerky movements, he swept the hood of his oilskin slicker back from his head. The cloth crinkled. His hair was wet and water-dark, the strands plastered to his scalp.

Dallas's gaze trailed over the crystalline raindrops clinging to Nick's sun-kissed flesh. She sucked in an unsteady breath, smelled still more of him.

He leaned forward menacingly, bridging his hands over her wrists, one on each chair arm. His legs opened, his hips jutted forward until he was straddling her knees. A jolt went through Dallas at the feel of his thighs grazing hotly against her. The anger in Nick's gaze, she noticed, was equally hot.

She instinctively tried to retreat. The old wood creaked when she pushed with her feet, tipping the chair back on its rockers. She put three precious inches of space between them, but that was all Nick allowed her. Not that it mattered. There was nowhere to go. Except for her wrists, Nick didn't touch her. He didn't have to. His body was bowed threateningly over her. It was as good a restraint as having his rugged weight pinning her in place. Behind her, there was only hard, flat wood digging into her spine.

Nick angled his head until the tip of his nose was only inches from her own. His blue eyes were so close Dallas thought she could actually feel the heat of his furious gaze. She was only marginally surprised she didn't instantly combust, his glare was that hot.

His breath washed over her skin in harsh, choppy waves as he growled, "Two minutes, Cameron. You've got exactly two minutes to get your cute little butt into that house, get changed, and get on your horse."

"You're not my boss, Nick. You can't order me around like that."

"You're right, I'm not. But your daddy is, and he's been letting me order you around for years. When I said you've got two minutes, Cameron, I meant it."

"And if I don't?" she asked, one tawny brow cocked high.

It was on the tip of Nick's tongue to repeat his usual threat: if she didn't hurry and do what she was told, he'd tan her backside. And then Nick thought of the backside in question—round and full and so goddamn soft. His palms itched with the remembered feel of it cupped in his palms. His mind itched with the remembered, overpowering need to tear away the barrier of

200

clothes, to feel her, flesh against flesh. The threat wilted on his tongue. Such punishment—no matter how tempting—or satisfying—wouldn't do either of them a bit of good right now.

Then again . . .

Dallas saw the minute change in Nick's expression, and felt her blood quicken. She gulped, and decided it was time to lighten the mood. A false grin tugged one corner of her lips. Her chin unconsciously lifted, though she was careful to keep her head tipped back at an unnatural angle lest they touch. They could *not,* under any circumstances, touch!

"What's this?" Dallas prodded lightly when he said nothing, but continued to glower down at her. "No threats? Tsk, tsk, tsk, that isn't like you, Langston. Aren't you feeling well?"

"If you don't count being mad as holy hell, I'm feeling just dandy. Get inside and change, Cameron." His voice lowered a throaty pitch. If possible, the heat in his gaze intensified. "Now. Or else . . ."

"Or else what?"

"Let me put it this way, darlin'," he started. Nick's gaze narrowed, and his eyelids thickened, hooding the anger that hadn't diminished so much as grown. "The way I see it, you've got two choices. Either you go upstairs and change into working duds, or I swear I'll sling you over my shoulder and drag you out to the stables wearing that damn dress. Which'll it be?"

Dallas met his furious glare with a level one of her own.

Their combative gazes locked, and held for what felt like hours. The time was marked by the ragged give and take of their breaths, and the rain that continued to pummel the porch roof.

"I'll do neither," she said finally, and was surprised to hear how steady and strong her voice sounded. It shouldn't, Dallas thought. Not when her insides were churning and her heart was slamming double-time against her ribs. She tried to convince herself that her inability to breathe was due to the uncomfortably snug dress.

"You're making a mistake, Cameron."

"I don't think so. In the long run, the outcome of this picnic is more important to the ranch than one bogged-down yearling. I'm seeing David today. That's the end of this discussion."

With just the tips of his fingers, Nick lifted the front of the chair by the arms until Dallas's feet came off the damp porch floor. He heard her quick intake of breath, but the sound of it rushing in his ears wasn't nearly enough to satisfy the anger churning within him. No, his fury demanded more from her. A hell of a lot more. A *logical* explanation, for starters. "Ranch business always comes before pleasure," he growled. "You know that."

"Pleasure? Do you think I'm going on this picnic with David because it will be *pleasurable* for me?"

"Aren't you?"

"Of course not!"

Her answer was so quick, so forceful and spontaneous, that Nick's grip slackened. The front of the chair dropped. Dallas rocked forward with the motion. The top of her head accidentally grazed the smooth underside of Nick's chin. Her tawny hair felt like spun silk when it tickled his skin.

His flesh felt like rough velvet where it smoldered against her scalp. His broad shoulder was a mere inch from Dallas's nose. She could smell the spicy aroma of him clinging to the crinkling oilskin, and fought the irrational urge to bury her face in the familiar scent. Even though this wasn't the time or place—he was furious with her, after all—and she was angry in her own right—Dallas still had to fight not to drink that alluring male scent into her lungs, as though drinking in the very essence of the man it clung to.

Nick was fighting his own irrational urges, and they ran parallel with hers. Sweet and earthy-fresh, that was how she smelled to him as her scent invaded his nostrils. The smell of her was everywhere. The feel of her soft hairs tickling his chin and neck were a torture comparable to none.

He pulled back slightly, putting no more than two inches between them. The space was enough for the acidy scent of rain to waft between them, and to carry away the tantalizing aroma of the other.

Nick felt a sliver of sanity return, and he clung to it like it was a godsend. In a way, it was.

He didn't move his head as his gaze dipped. A scowl furrowed his brow when he noticed the tight coil of tawny hair pinned at her nape.

Good Christ, the kid had wound her hair into a bun! Though the observation shouldn't have affected him— *why should I care what she does with her hair?*—it did. Powerfully. The way the glistening strands had been swept back from her face seemed to age her, until she looked . . . well, until she looked her age, that's how she looked. Though he much preferred a braid bobbing at her waist, Nick had to admit she looked all grown up and pretty as hell right now. It was a dangerous sight. One he could have lived his entire life happy for never having seen.

Though his expression remained set firm, his husky voice softened a distracting pitch. "It isn't like you to shirk from work that needs to be done, Squirt. Does hitching up with Parker really mean so much to you?"

Dallas's gaze never wavered from Nick's shoulder, although she did feel a blush heat her cheeks. "I'm not the one insisting I get married. That was Papa's brilliant idea, remember? I was told what to do, and I'll do it, but no one ever bothered to ask me what *I* wanted."

Gently, his hand crept up. The tips of his fingers cradled Dallas's chin as he lifted her gaze. His eyes surprised her. The anger was gone from them. Not a trace of it could be found. The man she was looking at now was Nick Langston, her friend. Dallas thought no one had ever looked so good to her.

She sent him a timid smile. It wasn't returned.

His blue eyes darkened, searching her face. His hand dragged her chin up higher, pulled her head closer. Nick could see his own reflection floating in the dark brown depths of Dallas's eyes. He blinked hard, and wondered if the man staring back at him, the one who looked so nervous and uncertain, was really himself. *"I'm* asking, Dallas. What do you want? *Who* do you want?"

The answer was astonishingly simple. *You, Nick Langston. I want you.*

There was only one problem. She couldn't have Nick. Not now, not ever.

She was going to have to settle for David, who wasn't second best, third best, or even a close fourth compared to Nick. But David would have to do. He met Ian's requirements for a husband. Nick Langston did not.

To Dallas, that made no difference. To her stubborn father, it made a world of difference.

Ian Cameron had made it perfectly clear he would settle for nothing but the best for his daughters, and if either she or Lisa were content to settle for less, he would kick them off the ranch and disown them. No forgiveness, no inheritance, no future. About this, there would be no changing the old man's mind.

While Lisa may be the type of woman to sacrifice "all for love," Dallas was not. Her practical nature ran too deep, and her love for the Bar None was a driving force too solid to shake. She would not let one wild night of abandon and a girlish infatuation—that *was* what she felt for Nick, wasn't it?—ruin life as she knew it. Only a fool would do that, and Dallas Cameron was sure of nothing so much as that she was no fool.

Nick's fingers slipped down, cupping her chin like a vise. The feel dragged Dallas's attention back to him. His fury, she was surprised to see, had come back in force.

"Do you *want* to marry Parker? Do you?" he demanded, his hot breath blasting over her face in erratic waves. "Answer me, damn you!"

"I—"

"Dallas?"

The voice, not Nick's, cut a notch above the pounding rain and the whisper of words that clogged in Dallas's throat. Her reprieve came in the form of David Parker.

Nick's hand dropped. His spine straightened, and his stance went rigid. He plowed all ten fingers through his rain-dampened hair, his attention sliding over his shoulder just in time to see Parker step onto the porch. In all his life, Nick couldn't remember ever hating anyone as much as he hated this pansy right now.

Dallas, on the other hand, had never felt so relieved. The words she'd swallowed back, she realized only now, had been the truth. Incriminating in the extreme. She'd been on the verge of telling Nick that no, she didn't want to marry David. That just the thought of spending her life with the man filled her with a sense of boredom and dread that even the thought of joining their two ranches together couldn't overcome. She'd been close—so very close!—to saying she would much rather spend her life with Nick Langston by her side.

Thank God David had shown up when he did. One minute later and she would have ruined everything.

"What's going on?" David asked as he whisked the hood of his overcoat off his head, then shook briskly to swipe off the raindrops clinging to his shoulders. His gaze strayed curiously between Dallas and Nick. "Is there a problem here that I should know about?"

"Would you know what to do if there was?" Nick snorted derisively.

David opened his mouth to answer, but it was Dallas who spoke. "Nick was telling me about a yearling we have stuck down by the Deadwater. He asked me to go with him to free it. I told him I couldn't because you and I were going on our picnic." She prayed her smile was bright; Lord knows, it was forced. "He, of course, wasn't pleased to hear that." She shrugged, as though it didn't really matter. All three of them knew it did. "We were arguing about it when you rode up."

David nodded, but Dallas could tell he wasn't convinced. "And what did you two decide?"

"She's going," Nick growled.

In unison Dallas said, "I'm staying."

David dusted the rain from his suit. His grin didn't meet his eyes. "Well, glad to hear that's settled."

Neither Nick nor Dallas heard him. Their gazes had sliced to each other, and were now engaged in a hot but silent war. Her chin lifted. His gaze narrowed. Her jaw hardened. The muscle in his cheek jerked.

Dallas was the first to look away. Her gaze fell on David. "Are you ready to go?"

"Not hardly." It was Nick who answered. His cool, low tone added a brittle edge to his fury. His eyes sparkled dangerously. "Or did you forget, Squirt, that I still have some slinging to do."

Dallas flattened her back against the chair and glared up at him indignantly. "You wouldn't dare."

One corner of his mustached mouth quirked up, and one golden brow arched high in his sun-kissed forehead. It was Nick's only answer. It was enough. Wordlessly, he met the challenge and flung it straight back at her.

Spurs chinked atop the planks as Nick took a threatening step toward her. The sound of his boot heel clicking over damp wood sounded more ominous than the distant clap of thunder rolling in over the range.

"Don't touch me, Langston," Dallas said when she saw his hands snake out. "I swear, if you touch me you'll regret it."

If Nick heard her at all, he ignored her. His fingers wrapped tightly around her upper arms. With a yank, he dragged her to her feet. Yet his grip was tight enough, and he was holding her closely enough so that, even erect, her feet didn't touch the floor but dangled a few inches above it.

A cry of outrage bolted past Dallas's lips as she flung her head back and met his determined glare.

"Put her down!" David exclaimed.

"Put me down!" Dallas demanded.

Their voices tripped over each other's; the former too soft and timid to hear, the latter a loud outburst steeped in indignation.

It was the latter Nick answered. "I'll put you down, all right. When we get to the stables, and not a second before."

"I want you to put me down *now*," Dallas snapped.

The tips of her breasts were grinding into Nick's chest, telling him in no uncertain terms that this was no child's body molded into him, this was a woman fully grown. A woman with enough ripe curves to drive him crazy. God, she felt good! Already he could feel his anger fizzle. Against his will, the raw energy of fury channeled in a completely different, completely inappropriate direction. Desire for this woman cut through him like a knife. It rocked Nick to the core.

208

He seemed to have no control over it. Hell, he wasn't entirely sure he *wanted* control over it anymore.

His fingers uncurled. Nick set her down hard enough to make her teeth rattle.

Dallas stumbled back a step, and felt the groove of the rocking chair's seat cut into the back of her legs. Her hand shot out, steadying her quivering weight on the hard wooden arm. The second she'd seen the raw desire glinting in Nick's indigo eyes, her knees had liquified.

"Dallas, maybe it would be better if we had our picnic another day," David suggested. His voice was a harsh reminder that she and Nick were not alone.

How could she have forgotten David's presence? She wasn't sure, she only knew that when Nick had touched her, she *had* forgotten David. The second their gazes meshed her entire world tunneled down until it consisted of Nick Langston and only Nick Langston. The feel of him, the smell of him, the remembered taste of him. Their breaths had mingled with the driving sound of the rain until she could hear nothing except the throbbing beat of her own heart over it . . . and feel the answering rhythm of his slamming beneath her breasts.

Then Nick had released her, and David had spoken, and the magic of the moment shattered.

David cleared his throat and, when the two continued to stare at each other, said, "Dallas? Do you want to postpone the picnic? We can have it another day. It's no trouble. If Nick needs you to—"

"Nick doesn't need me for anything," Dallas said, cutting David short. Was it her imagination, or did

209

Nick's eyes darken? With effort, she tore her gaze from him and pulled David into focus. The sight of the man's tall, lanky darkness was unfulfilling. "Besides, the trail drive starts tomorrow. If we don't do it today, we'll have to wait until we get back." What she didn't say, but knew both her and Nick were aware of, was that she didn't have time for such a lengthy delay.

David's gaze strayed to Nick, and she could tell David was still uncertain. "What about the rain? Doesn't that put a . . . um, damper on the picnic?"

"No, not at all." Her smile was tight and strained. So was her shrug. It didn't help that Nick Langston's gaze hadn't wavered from her, or that the heat of his eyes was still warming her to a fevered pitch. "I—I've set up a blanket in the barn. If you don't mind, we'll have our picnic indoors instead of out. Your shooting lesson, of course, will have to wait."

David's grin was devilish. The way his eyes trailed from the top of Dallas's head, down the length of the dress that clung to her every curve, then back up again, was suggestive. By the time his eyes met hers, they were shimmering with newfound appreciation. "I can live with it if you can," he said, his voice a pitch huskier than normal.

Dallas felt a shiver race down her spine. It had nothing to do with physical awareness so much as mental disgust. Damn it! Now, if it had been Nick looking at her like that she would have . . . What on earth was she doing? She couldn't think like that. She wasn't marrying Nick, she was marrying David—she hoped. Comparisons between the two men would not only be unfair to David—there *was* no comparison—

but it would also be a danger to her very tenuous hold on sanity.

"You'll find someone else to ride out with you and free that yearling, right?" David asked Nick.

It was, in Dallas's opinion, a diplomatic way for David to end the silent battle that continued to rage between herself and Nick. Only Nick didn't look ready to surrender the fight yet.

"Dallas has a job to do," Nick growled. His blue eyes shimmered dark and dangerous as his gaze raked over the guilty flush spreading up from Dallas's neck. He watched her shift from foot to foot, and thought she wasn't squirming nearly as much as he'd like her to.

David refused to be put off. Straddling his fists on his lean hips, he continued to stare at Nick. "You mean to tell me there isn't any other hand on this ranch who can ride out with you? Only Dallas?" He shook his dark head, his gaze narrowed accusingly. "I find that hard to believe, Langston."

"I don't give a good goddamn what you believe, Parker. Dallas is my roping partner. Has been for years. Not only don't I wanna find someone else to ride out with me, but trying to break in another partner on a day like this would be risky. Not to mention just plain stupid."

"What about Rico?" Dallas asked, referring to the new hand who'd come to them by way of the Parkers. It was all she could do not to scream. What was wrong with Nick? Didn't he know that his continued stubbornness would ruin everything? Or did he know, and

211

not care? "You've roped with him a few times, and the two of you seemed to work well together."

"I don't want Rico," Nick said, and as the words rang in his own ears, he thought they sounded unusually petulant. Christ, why the hell was he fighting this so hard? Just let her go and be done with it!

"Nick, please, take Rico with you. Just for today." Dallas's gaze lifted. "I'll be back at work tomorrow, I promise."

She wasn't going to back down. He could see it in her eyes. The urge to throttle her was strong, but Nick wasn't sure if the desire was born from her defiance of him, or the way she kept insisting with her eyes that this picnic with Parker was so damn important to her. Whatever the reason, the thought of her being alone with Parker in a dimly lit barn churned in his gut. The thought of Parker kissing her the way Nick had done . . .

Nick's fists clamped at his sides, his knuckles were chalky white from the strain of his empty grip. Without a word, Nick spun on his heel and clomped down the porch steps. His boots slapped in the puddles and mud as he stalked across the yard and disappeared from sight around the corner of the stables.

He hadn't pulled up his hood. The rain pelted Nick's head, slicking the hair coldly to his scalp and running in icy rivers down his cheeks and neck. Nick barely noticed. The heat of his anger was enough to keep him warm, enough to make the moisture clinging to his skin turn to steam.

When he was safely out of sight, he stopped. The slicker crinkled as, oblivious to his wet state, he leaned his back heavily against the clapboard wall of the stable. His breath was coming in deep, ragged gulps. Each one cut through his lungs, but not through his blind fury. Damned if he couldn't still smell Dallas Cameron's earthy-sweet scent!

Scrunching his eyes closed, Nick scoured the lids with the heels of his hands. Dallas's image refused to be scoured from his mind. An emotion he didn't dare name tugged at him when he remembered the sight of the cracked leather toes of her riding boots peeking out from beneath the hem of the dress *he'd* bought for her. His ears rang with the remembered sound of her spurs chinking on the porch floor. She'd forgotten to take them off. By the end of the day, the spiky rowel wheel would have slashed the hem of the skirt to ribbons.

Damn it! Somehow even that unfeminine slight was endearing. Maybe it shouldn't be, but it was. Dallas Cameron was the only woman he'd even known who could wear riding boots, spurs, and a dress . . . yet still manage to look pretty and sexy and tempting as all hell.

Nick decided he'd lost his mind. To think Dallas Cameron was any of those things was a sure sign one was losing his grasp on sanity. He tried to will back the image of her with twin braids trailing down her back. He tried to picture her nose with a smattering of freckles peppering the bridge. The image came, but much too quickly faded. In its place, he remembered the feel of her mouth ground beneath him, the feel of her breasts crushed against his chest, her legs wrapped tightly around him, her body arching frantically to

213

meet his. It was only an image, a wispy memory, but the shock of it was strong enough to make him hard and hungry.

With a sigh of self-disgust, Nick pushed away from the wall and stalked toward the entrance to the stables. If he'd had any doubts before, he was now more certain than ever that after the trail drive he'd be looking for work.

All he had to do was keep his control, hold his desire in check for just a couple of months. Surely that wouldn't be too hard. Would it? Nope, not hard, *impossible*. The restraint would probably kill him—it was a pain inside him now just thinking about it.

But he'd do it anyway. But he had to. He could never have Dallas again, never touch her and feel himself buried in her hot, tight softness. Never again. No matter how badly his body and mind hungered for it.

Because if he did, if he weakened even a little, Ian Cameron would kill him.

It was a foregone conclusion.

Chapter Ten

"You look pretty today, Dallas."

"Thank you kindly, David. More tarts?"

Hazel eyes narrowed on the plate, heavy with sweet-tasting pastries that Maria had spent the day before baking, and that Dallas now waved temptingly beneath his nose. "No, thank you. If I ate another bite I'd probably bust. It all tasted good, though. Real good." This last was spoken as his gaze slid down the front of her body.

Dallas stifled a sigh and glanced away. He'd been doing that for the past hour, all through their meal. Their eyes would meet. His attention would stray over her. His gaze would linger on her breasts. He'd span the width of her waist with his eyes.

His scrutiny of her made Dallas uncomfortable, but not nearly as uncomfortable as her lack of a reaction did.

She kept waiting for her blood to heat, for a twinge of excitement to make her heart quicken. When David continued to stare at her, and she continued to be unaffected by it, Dallas started to feel vaguely frustrated. Where was that spark of temptation, that moistening of her palms and sudden inability to draw breath? She'd always felt it when Nick looked at her. Yet when David's gaze raked her appreciatively she felt . . . well, bored.

Perhaps if he kissed her . . . ?

Dallas's gaze settled on his lips. Unlike Nick, David had grown no mustache to cover his mouth. His lips were shaped nicely, even if they did look a bit full and feminine. Would his kiss feel hot and dry, she wondered, or cool and moist? Hungry and demanding, or slow and coaxing? Dallas found she really didn't care. In fact, the image her mind conjured up left her cold. Dammit!

To give herself a distraction, she plucked up one of the tarts, then set the plate aside. She nibbled on the yeasty crust and listened to the rain pelt against the roof of the barn. The sound was muffled, as was the clap of approaching thunder.

Mumbling something about large afternoon meals making him sleepy, David stretched out on his back on the light gray blanket Dallas had spread over the hay-strewn floor. His long legs were crossed at the ankles, his hands stacked beneath his head to form a pillow. With his eyes closed, she had the perfect chance to study his features without him noticing.

His dark, closely cropped hair glistened an appealing shade of black in the dimly lit barn. The color made a nice contrast to his sharply sculpted, perpetually sunburned cheeks and wide brow. A few stalks of hay had woven their way into his wind-tousled hair.

More dusted his shirt and loose-fitting brown trousers. The sight gave him a rumpled appearance that, while out of character for David Parker, was endearing all the same.

Though he wasn't what Dallas considered classically handsome, she thought most women would find David attractive. That she wasn't one of those women annoyed her.

Truly, there was nothing wrong with him. Nothing she could put her finger on, leastwise. His disposition was pleasant—except for those times when she purposely riled him—and, as Lisa had pointed out, his face wasn't hard on the eye. David was intelligent. She'd seen him hold his own in almost any conversation. At times, he was witty, but those times were rare and, in her opinion, nothing to be savored.

Simply put, David Parker was boring as holy hell.

Dallas set the tart back on the plate. She suddenly had no appetite for it. "How's your father feeling, David?" she asked when she realized the gap in conversation had stretched on for far too long.

His shrug assured her he wasn't asleep. "Better. It's only a matter of time, I know, but he does seem to be having more good days than bad lately. I'm thankful for that."

"Good," Dallas muttered, her gaze dropping to the hands she'd entwined in her lap. She dusted an imaginary crumb from her skirt, sighed, and tried to think of something else for them to talk about. Lisa had told her the topic of horses and cows was out. Likewise, roping and ranch work. That didn't leave much.

David, sensing her tension, opened one eye a crack.

"We're having a barn raising after the trail drive," he said, his gaze dropping to her breasts again. The way the calico molded over the generous swells that were usually hidden beneath a baggy shirt fascinated him. Never in his life did he expect to see such voluptuous roundness on Dallas Cameron's body.

"I figured you would," she said, and glanced at him. Noting where his eyes had strayed—again—Dallas stifled a groan. Her temples were beginning to pound from the way she'd gritted her teeth for the better part of the afternoon.

Another gap of silence stretched taut. It was broken only by a rumble of thunder, and the patter of rain.

Dallas found her mind straying to the Deadwater River. And Nick Langston. Had he freed the yearling yet? Was Rico giving him any trouble? Why, oh why hadn't she let Nick convince her to ride out with him? She regretted her decision. Freeing a yearling from a mud hole *had* to be more exciting than what she was doing right now!

The day's rain turned the dirt to slick mud, making the bank treacherous at best, deadly at worst. Rico's horse snorted, and lost its precarious footing on the slippery bank for precious seconds. The rope—one end of which was wrapped around Rico's saddle horn, the other looped around the cow's horns—grew slack.

From the corner of his eyes, Nick saw the horse jerk to the side and try to climb back up the bank. It was buried to the ankles in mud. The crinkling of Rico's oilcloth slicker spooked his mount. The horse's head tossed nervously from side to side as it snorted in agitation.

In that second, Nick knew why the Parkers had let this particular man go. Rico was an incompetent fool!

"Tighten the lead," Nick yelled as he quickened the pace of the shovel. His gauntlets had been left behind. His palms were raw with what would soon be a variety of fresh callouses. He paid no attention to the biting pain in his hands as he continued to shovel the mud. For each scoop he thrust aside, two more rushed in to fill in the gap. The thick brown stuff oozed forward, slurping at the frightened yearling's legs.

Nick's hood had fallen back. It sagged uselessly between his shoulder blades. Rain beat down on the top of his head, ran rivers down his face. Drops of it snuck past the grim set of his lips. It left a sharp, acidy taste on his tongue. The clothes beneath his slicker were heavy and wet. The day was sticky-hot and humid but Nick still shivered due to the strain of lifting the heavy shovel time and again.

Rico's horse whickered as it climbed back up the bank. The rope pulled taut. Too taut. The yearling bellowed as its head was swung around unnaturally on its neck. The animal pulled.

Nick felt its rump push against his thigh. He eased back a step toward the bank. Stuck as it was, the yearling couldn't get free no matter how hard Rico's horse pulled. But there was a very good chance the horns would be yanked from its head if Rico didn't let up the pressure soon. If that happened, Rico would have to rope it around the neck. Even on a dry day, with the animal's legs hog-tied, roping a piece of grown stuff by the neck could be dangerous to both the cow being roped, and the men who were roping it.

"Ease up. Not so hard," Nick ordered, his voice rising so it would carry to Rico over the pounding rain, and the protesting horse and cow.

Nick told himself not to think of how much easier this job would be had Dallas come with him instead of Rico. It wouldn't have taken her three tries to swing her loop around the cow's horns. She would never put a yearling through the stress of tug and release the way Rico kept doing. And another thing . . . she would never, *never* let her rope go too slack one minute, too tight the next. Dallas knew what the hell she was doing.

Christ, if she had come with him they'd have been done an hour ago. Right now they'd probably be drying themselves off near the stove in the bunkhouse. And laughing about the yearling's meager protests, and the situation in general. They'd be teasing each other about what could have happened if one of them had been partnered with someone else.

Well, Nick *was* partnered with someone else.

And he couldn't find a damn thing to laugh about.

The shovel was beginning to feel like it weighed more than his horse. His arms ached with each scoop and toss. His temples pounded from the worried gaze he kept volleying between the mud he was clearing, the cow, and Rico.

It wasn't humanly possible to look at everything at the same time, but Nick tried all the same. He didn't trust the mud not to swallow up more of him than his legs to midshin. He didn't trust the yearling not to bolt the second it was free. And he sure as hell didn't trust Rico to know what the hell he was doing.

Of them all, the one that presented the biggest threat of screwing up was Rico.

"David, I—"

"Dallas, did you—?"

Their mouths snapped shut as each gestured for the other to continue.

"Never mind," Dallas said. "What were you going to say?"

David pushed up on his elbows. His hazel gaze heated as it roamed over her face. "Only that you look pretty."

She smiled tightly. "You've already told me that. At least a dozen times."

"I know. And I meant it. You look real nice compared to how you usually . . . er . . . I—I mean, this is only the second time I've ever seen you wear a real dress. I just can't get over how different you look."

Dallas tipped her head to the side, and noticed the way David's eyes widened. That he actually meant the words seemed to surprise him almost as much as it surprised her. "It's still the same old Dallas under all this frippery, don't forget."

He pushed himself to a sit. Reaching out, he wrapped his fingers around her hand. His palm felt cold and clammy against her skin. Dallas sucked in a quick breath and forced herself not to pull away from him.

"That's another thing," David said, his gaze searching hers. "Do you realize you haven't insulted me once all afternoon? And you haven't talked about cows or water rights or anything like that." He shook his head, his gaze narrowing on her. "Christ, if I didn't know better I'd say you were turning into a real woman, Cameron."

Dallas resisted the urge to slap him hard. "Would that be so difficult to believe?" she asked. The sarcasm in her tone was tightly leashed, but by no means concealed.

"Yes. I mean no!" He squeezed her hand and shrugged nervously. "Come on, Dallas, you have to admit you aren't exactly acting like yourself lately." He nodded at the remains of their lunch, scattered over the blanket around them. His expression said that the Dallas Cameron he knew, and didn't particularly like, wouldn't have *thought* of a picnic lunch, let alone *arranged* one.

"People change, David."

"I agree, most people do. But you would be the last person I'd ever expect to change."

Her shoulders squared, her spine stiffened. She used her indignation as an excuse to slip her hand free of David's. Unfortunately, instead of his hand straying back to his own lap, it settled lightly on her knee. Dallas only thought about batting it away.

"Why not me?" she asked suspiciously.

"Why would you want to? You're happy living and working on the Bar None. Everything you want out of life you already have."

"Everything?"

David's gaze, which had strayed to her waist, lifted

and locked with hers. His hand strayed higher, boldly cradling the soft flesh of her lower thigh. "Don't you?"

"Not even close." Dallas's smile was weak, tinged with a sadness that was reflected in her eyes. She looked away before David could see it. When she closed her eyes she saw Nick Langston's face floating in the darkness behind her eyelids. His bittersweet image vanished the second her lashes swept up, but the ripple of emotion his face stirred within her remained for a long, long while.

David's thumb stroked circles on the calico covering her leg. He felt the instinctive tremors quivering through the softly molded flesh beneath his fingertip. "What could you possibly want that you don't already have?"

Nick Langston, Dallas's mind whispered so softly she barely heard it. What she said, however, was, "A husband, David. I want a husband. Children. A family."

"You?"

Her gaze sharpened on him. "Yes, me! Dammit, you don't have to look so surprised. I'm not so different from all the other women my age. Except," she muttered under her breath, "that I'm not married."

The harsh reprimand made him slam his gaping mouth shut. And was it Dallas's imagination, or had the natural pink color in his cheeks increased two vibrant shades? "I'm sorry, it's just that . . . well, I don't think of you in the same way I think of other women."

One tawny brow arched. Her eyes flashed chocolate-brown fire. "No? And exactly how *do* you think of me?"

David's lips thinned into a tight, grim line. "Do you really want to know?"

"Yes."

"Okay, then. I"—he sucked in a deep breath, and his hand stilled on her leg—"I try not to think of you at all. When I do, let's say I don't put you in a very favorable light."

"Because I rope better than you do?" she couldn't resist asking. Dallas didn't laugh when his cheeks reddened another shade, but she thought about it.

"I suppose that's part of it."

"And shoot better than you do?"

His left eye twitched. "That, too."

"And—"

"Stop it!"

"All right." Dallas sealed her lips around the barrage of other things she did better than David Parker—all of which sprang immediately to mind. Another thing that sprang to mind was that David's hand was no longer inactive. His thumb was stroking light circles on her leg, the upper arc boldly rising higher and higher.

Again, she waited for that familiar spark of desire to flame inside of her. Again, she felt frustrated and disappointed when it didn't.

"Dallas?" David whispered as he leaned toward her.

His breath was hot on her cheek, but by no means was the feel of it exciting. When she turned to look at him, she found his face uncomfortably close to her

MORE PASSION AND ADVENTURE AWAIT... YOUR TRIP TO A BIG ADVENTUROUS WORLD BEGINS WHEN YOU ACCEPT YOUR FIRST 4 NOVELS ABSOLUTELY *FREE*
(AN $18.00 VALUE)

Accept your Free gift and start to experience more of the passion and adventure you like in a historical romance novel. Each Zebra novel is filled with proud men, spirited women and tempestuous love that you'll remember long after you turn the last page.

Zebra Historical Romances are the finest novels of their kind. They are written by authors who really know how to weave tales of romance and adventure in the historical settings you love. You'll feel like you've actually gone back in time with the thrilling stories that each Zebra novel offers.

GET YOUR FREE GIFT WITH THE START OF YOUR HOME SUBSCRIPTION

Our readers tell us that these books sell out very fast in book stores and often they miss the newest titles. So Zebra has made arrangements for you to receive the four newest novels published each month.

You'll be guaranteed that you'll never miss a title, and home delivery is so convenient. And to show you just how easy it is to get Zebra Historical Romances, we'll send you your first 4 books absolutely FREE! Our gift to you just for trying our home subscription service.

BIG SAVINGS AND FREE HOME DELIVERY

Each month, you'll receive the four newest titles as soon as they are published. You'll probably receive them even before the bookstores do. What's more, you may preview these exciting novels free for 10 days. If you like them as much as we think you will, just pay the low preferred subscriber's price of just $3.75 each. *You'll save $3.00 each month off the publisher's price.* AND, your savings are even greater because there are never any shipping, handling or other hidden charges—FREE Home Delivery. Of course you can return any shipment within 10 days for full credit, no questions asked. There is no minimum number of books you must buy.

4 FREE BOOKS

TO GET YOUR 4 FREE BOOKS WORTH $18.00 — MAIL IN THE FREE BOOK CERTIFICATE T O D A Y

Fill in the Free Book Certificate below, and we'll send your FREE BOOKS to you as soon as we receive it.

If the certificate is missing below, write to: Zebra Home Subscription Service, Inc., P.O. Box 5214, 120 Brighton Road, Clifton, New Jersey 07015-5214.

FREE BOOK CERTIFICATE

4 FREE BOOKS

ZEBRA HOME SUBSCRIPTION SERVICE, INC.

YES! Please start my subscription to Zebra Historical Romances and send me my first 4 books absolutely FREE. I understand that each month I may preview four new Zebra Historical Romances free for 10 days. If I'm not satisfied with them, I may return the four books within 10 days and owe nothing. Otherwise, I will pay the low preferred subscriber's price of just $3.75 each; a total of $15.00, *a savings off the publisher's price of $3.00.* I may return any shipment and I may cancel this subscription at any time. There is no obligation to buy any shipment and there are no shipping, handling or other hidden charges. Regardless of what I decide, the four free books are mine to keep.

NAME

ADDRESS _____ APT

CITY _____ STATE _____ ZIP

( )
TELEPHONE

SIGNATURE _____ (if under 18, parent or guardian must sign)

Terms, offer and prices subject to change without notice. Subscription subject to acceptance by Zebra Books. Zebra Books reserves the right to reject any order or cancel any subscription.

ZB0394

GET
FOUR
FREE
BOOKS
(AN $18.00 VALUE)

AFFIX
STAMP
HERE

own. Her attention dropped to his lips. They were parted and moist.

Her gaze lifted, and locked with his. The hazel irises darkened perceptibly. Dallas recognized the emotion swimming in his eyes as one she had seen in Nick's eyes many times recently.

Nick. Dear God, she had to stop thinking about him!

It wasn't proper for a woman to initiate a kiss—or so Lisa had told her. But right now Dallas was beyond caring about what was and wasn't proper. What she did care about was wiping all thoughts of Nick Langston out of her mind. That was the only reason her back arched, and her chin tipped up. The only reason she closed the scant few inches between their lips.

Cool and moist. That's how David Parker's lips felt. She'd wondered, and now she knew.

"She's sliding again," Rico called out.

The raucous of sounds around Nick made it almost impossible to distinguish the accented thickness of Rico's voice. Though he couldn't make out the exact words, a quick glance told him what Rico had said. Nick did *not* throw the shovel into the mud the way he wanted to. Nor did he pull himself from the mud, and pull Rico from the horse by his throat. He wanted to do that, too.

"I said hold her steady," Nick yelled, his voice too calm and even for a man who was furious. His tone, he noted, made Rico sit up straighter in the saddle. The stubbled jaw he saw peeking from beneath the Mexican's hood—the jaw Nick ached to sink his fist into—bunched with indignation. None of that affected Nick's anger one bit.

"I said hold her steady!" Nick barked when he saw the horse slide a few more precious inches down the slippery bank.

The rope went slack. Again. Nick was in the process of sending a shovelful of mud onto the bank. His shoulders were turned so his upper left arm ran down from midchest to taut belly. His spine was twisted at an unnatural angle as he completed the fluid motion.

A bolt of lightning cut down from the sky. Thunder blasted around them before the jagged tip of light even had time to hit the earth.

Nick's attention flickered to the mud he splattered over the bank. His attention left Rico, the cow, the horse for only a fraction of a second.

A fraction of a second was all the time it took for the yearling to shake the loop of Rico's rope off its horns.

The sounds were the first thing to reach Nick. Thunder, loud and deafening. Rico's horse neighing. Rico himself shouting a warning, the words swallowed up by another blast of thunder, this one so loud the ground literally trembled with the raw fury of it.

As the rumble receded, Nick heard the yearling. A mewl of terror rumbled from its chest as the cow heaved to the side. The pool of mud sucked at its legs, trying to coax the animal back to its sticky depths. But the cow was acting on fear. Its actions were stronger than before. Terror was riding it hard enough for the yearling to jerk its hooves forward and propel it closer to the bank.

Closer to Nick.

Nick's head came around just in time for his vision, blurred by the driving rain, to fill with the sight of the crazed cow charging toward him. There was no time to think. He barely had time to react.

The mud sucked at his legs, weighing him down more than the heavy, unnatural water-weight of his clothes. He wouldn't reach the bank in time, he knew it. His fingers tightened around the shovel. The rough wood bit into his already tender palms. He felt warm stickiness ooze between his fingers as he raised the weapon high over his right shoulder. Half of his mind knew his palms had started to bleed. The other half knew but didn't care—that was the part that just wanted to stay alive.

The cow was close enough for Nick to think he felt the hot, frantic wash of its breath through the slicker. He pushed back a step, coming closer to the bank.

The mud lessened a bit here. Fortunate for the cow, since that made it gain speed. Unfortunate for Nick, for exactly the same reason.

From the corner of his eye, he saw Rico's horse near the bank, coming up behind him. What the hell was the idiot doing? If the cow got past Nick, it would make a beeline at the first thing that moved. And the first thing it saw would be Rico.

Rico shouted something that Nick couldn't hear. Or didn't try to hear, he wasn't sure which. His full attention never wavered from the yearling that seemed to be taking forever to get to him. But that was getting to him much too fast.

The muscles in his arms screamed a protest at the

dead weight of the shovel, poised above and behind his shoulder. Only when he judged the cow close enough to get in a good, solid hit did Nick finally let the shovel arch down.

A movement snagged the corner of Nick's eyes. Though he didn't dare look toward it, the sight itself was distracting.

The shovel was halfway to a point dead center between the yearling's eyes. It would be a perfect hit. Enough to stun but not kill. Nick widened his feet as quickly and as far as the mud would allow. He braced himself for the impact.

The impact didn't come.

Instead, just before the shovel should have hit the yearling square in the head, Nick felt the shovel stop. It hung, poised in midair for a split second, then reversed direction. The force of the handle biting into his palms made Nick wince, but that didn't stop him from increasing the pressure of his grip.

The shovel jerked, as though being snapped backward by an invisible force. In the blink of an eye, Nick tore his gaze from the charging cow. And fixed on the stout wooden handle. And widened. The sight of Rico's rope wrapped around the circular handle was too incredible to be believed.

Then he felt the shovel being yanked through the air, as though it was hauled back by some invisible hand. Felt himself being hauled right along with it. And Nick believed.

Two things happened at once. Rico's horse turned to the side and yanked. And the cow reached Nick just as he fell, his spine twisted, face first into the mud.

Nick barely had time to suck in a great gulp of air as his head went under. The mud closed around him like a thick, impenetrable blanket. He couldn't move, couldn't breathe. But he could hear. The mud clogging his ears vibrated, echoing the muffled thumps of the charging cow that, with any luck, had veered past him by now.

He moved his right leg, ready to push himself up. But the yearling hadn't gone past him. The knowledge sliced through Nick's head in the same instant pain sliced through his extended left leg.

His lips parted. The mud sucked up his agonized scream as his spine jackknifed.

There was only one pain comparable to the one he was feeling now. It was a pain Nick was intimately acquainted with. It was the pain of wanting something he could never have. The pain of trying, but never being quite good enough. It was the kind of anguish that ate at a man's gut . . . but then, so was the physical agony that was slicing through his body. While the one form of torture emanated from his head, the other rippled out from his leg.

Both hurt bad.

Nick's last lucid thought was that the clinging blanket of mud had nothing over the black velvet lining of unconsciousness. The former robbed him of breath. The latter robbed him of physical and mental anguish.

It never occurred to him to fight the darkness as the last of his air bubbled up through the rain and mud, tearing from his burning lungs.

* * *

David's mouth was cold and fleshy and moist as, after his initial shock faded, he moved his lips against hers. His mouth remained tightly closed. His head barely moved. He made no threat to whisk her mouth with his tongue. Dallas would have wondered why, had she not felt so relieved.

Except for the hand on her thigh which had grown suddenly very still, David didn't touch her. A corner of her mind stupidly remembered Nick's kisses—hungry and devouring. His hands had been hot and urgent, impatiently roaming her body as though he couldn't feel enough of her, as though he was trying to absorb the heat of her untamed passion through his palms.

Her reaction to David's kiss wasn't right. She *had* no reaction to it. None. Nor did Dallas feel the slightest inclination to strain against David the way she'd strained against Nick. The feel of Nick's muscular chest pushing into her breasts had been wonderful, something to strain *for*. The feel of David's lanky frame was something she didn't want to fight to feel. She knew it without even trying.

Perhaps if he wrapped his arm around her waist, the way Nick had done . . . ?

Dallas reached down and took David's forearm into her hand. She felt hardness in her palms, but it was the rigidity of bone, not muscle and strength. Dallas tried not to dwell on that not so subtle difference as she took his limp arm and slipped it around her waist.

Squirming to her knees in the dirt, her mouth and hands coaxed David to follow her up. He did, though she could sense his confusion in the way his soft mouth paused over hers. With frustrated movements, she

230

took his free hand and dragged it around her neck. She forced his fingers to tunnel in her hair, to cup her scalp.

Breathlessly, she waited. When Nick had done that, her scalp had burned at the feel of his palm and fingers holding her so closely. When he'd held her against him, wedging her hips between his thighs, she'd felt as though her body had been torched. And when he'd eased her down on the ground, when he'd spread himself out beside her and she felt the hot evidence of his arousal grinding against her thigh . . .

Nothing.

David inspired nothing in her.

His hands stayed tentatively where Dallas had placed them, but they didn't move. He showed no signs of curiosity to explore.

Unlike Nick.

Nick hadn't asked permission, nor had he seemed overly concerned he might frighten her. He'd wanted a taste of her and he'd taken it. His hands, his mouth, had explored her hungrily. And she'd been starved, urgent for his touch.

Now the only urgency Dallas felt was to end this kiss. The need to do it—*now!*—was as overpowering as it was strong. It was not to be ignored.

Her hands came up, tightening into fists that she used to push against the exaggerated hollow beneath the narrow shelf of David's shoulders. She levered herself away from him. As space came between their bodies, she saw that his head was still tipped, his femininely curved lips still puckered with a kiss he hadn't yet realized she'd ended.

His lips even *looked* moist and cold. Every bit as

uninviting as they'd felt, Dallas thought as she watched him open his eyes.

David blinked hard. A scowl puckered his brow as he dragged her into focus. His hazel eyes swam with a mixture of confusion and, perhaps, his own form of muted passion.

"Dallas?" he asked, and his tone shook.

The breath Dallas sucked into her heaving lungs shook harder. "I'm sorry, David, I didn't mean to—"

"That's all right." His sunburned cheeks reddened as his narrow shoulders rose and fell. "What I mean is, I don't mind that you kissed me. Not at all."

Her tawny brows arched. She resisted the urge to wipe the feel of his lips off on her sleeve. "You don't?"

"No. Should I?"

It was Dallas's turn to shrug. "Lisa says—"

The hay crinkled beneath the blanket as he crept on his knees toward her. The hand he splayed over hers felt cold and clammy. "I don't care what Lisa says. What do you say, Dallas? Did you . . . well, did you like it? Kissing me, that is."

"Like it?" she asked, and winced when her voice squeaked.

His eyes searched her face. Dallas blanched at the lie that automatically sprang to her lips, the one she knew she would have to push past her tongue if she ever wanted to get this man to marry her. The words tasted sour. A lot like David's kiss, come to think of it.

"Did you?" he pressed, his fingers squeezing her hands.

The lie wouldn't come. Oh, it was there, she could taste it, but no matter how hard she forced herself, the words wouldn't spew forth. She sucked in a sigh and lowered her gaze to their hands, linked together on her lap. What she saw was a splash of rose and yellow calico. What she thought of was Nick Langston, the man who'd given her the dress.

"You know," David murmured as one hand came up, the moist palm cushioning the line of her tightly set jaw, "I've been thinking about kissing you ever since that night when I saw you wearing this dress. I'm glad you did it. I don't think I would have had the nerve."

"I—"

"Shhh," he said, slashing his long, smooth index finger over her lips. "You don't have to say anything. If you liked kissing me, darling, then kiss me again and prove it."

"Again?" she asked weakly, praying she'd heard him wrong, knowing she hadn't. What she heard— really *heard*—was Nick's gritty tone, and the way his tongue curled and caressed the word "darlin'." Even that plain, simple endearment sounded dirty and exciting the way he said it. The way David said it made it sound flat and hollow. "You want me to kiss you again? *Now?*"

He nodded. His head angled to the side. His eyes closed expectantly. "More than I want to breathe. Yes. Right now."

Dallas's heart plummeted to her toes. It was quite a different sensation from the one she felt whenever Nick touched her. Then her heart may have sunk, but it also floated. With David, her chest felt weighted

233

down and heavy. Like she was drowning. And there was no one around to save her.

Her gaze dropped to his mouth. The pink flesh still glistened wetly from their kiss. She watched as his tongue darted out, moistening his lips still more. Her stomach rolled, and she knew she wouldn't be able to kiss him again. Just the thought made her shiver in revulsion.

"David, I—"

She would have given him some excuse—*any* excuse—to postpone the inevitable, had the door to the barn not crashed open at exactly that second.

Dallas jumped, startled by the sound of wood slamming against wood. Her head snapped around. She squinted at the short, thin shape of a man standing framed in the wide doorway. His yellow slicker was a bright splotch of color against the dreary sky he was outlined against. His hood was pulled down low over his face, making his features unrecognizable.

"What the—?" David sputtered as he started to push to his feet. "Who do you think you are barging in here like that? You're lucky I don't—"

The man sent David a quick glance, then ignored him. Though she couldn't see his eyes, Dallas could feel the heat of the man's gaze boring into her.

"Nick's hurt. Come quickly."

That was all the apparition said before spinning on his heel and disappearing back into the storm. It wasn't much, but it was enough to tell Dallas two things. Rico was the man who'd been standing there— she recognized his thick Mexican accent and short but cocky stance. And Nick was hurt.

234

Dallas was on her feet in a heartbeat. She was out the door in two.

David called out to her, demanding she take a blanket as protection from the driving force of the rain that continued to lash down from the sky. Dallas's heart was beating too loudly to hear more than the sound of his voice, and the loud clap of thunder. She didn't try to hear the words. She didn't care.

My God, Nick was hurt! That was all she cared about, all she was capable of thinking about. That, and getting to his side as fast as she could. Nothing else mattered.

David's fingers fisted in a white-knuckled grip around the blanket. The material felt coarse and hot against his palms. His green eyes narrowed, and his jaw hardened as he gritted his teeth and watched Dallas disappear into the storm.

"Bitch," he hissed between clenched teeth as he chucked the blanket to the hay-strewn floor. His nostrils flared in anger. His breathing became heavy and labored as he fought to control his temper.

He was tempted to stomp after Dallas, wrap his fingers tightly around her scrawny little neck, and *drag* the bitch back here. This silly picnic was her idea, damn it! And everything had been going so well! She'd been softening toward him, he was sure of it. Until . . .

The way she'd run out on him made it obvious that David Parker wasn't as important to Dallas as a hired hand. Especially if the hired hand in question was Nick Langston.

David snarled and gave the blanket a vicious kick.

He was going to have to make his move, and make it soon. The bill collectors were getting more demanding; some were already threatening foreclosure. Time was running out.

Chapter Eleven

Dallas closed the bedroom door behind her. The latch clicked into place, the sound loud in the silence that was broken only by rain pounding against the outer wall, streaking across the window. A slash of gray light snuck in through the part in the curtains. The shaft sliced a murky line over the planked floor. The effect was minimal; the dim glow scarcely touched the shadows clinging to the room. It illuminated nothing.

The air felt chilly and damp against her cheeks. It penetrated the wet gown clinging to her body, penetrated the hair plastered to her head and made her scalp tingle.

Dallas shivered, and leaned back heavily against the door. Her legs felt shaky. Her knees threatened to buckle. Her heart throbbed beneath her breasts. Her breaths came in deep, erratic gulps—because of the way she'd bolted up the stairs, or because of the *reason* she'd taken the narrow wooden stairs two at a time? She didn't know.

Locking her numb, icy thumbs behind her back, she

twisted her grip and flattened her palms against the hard wood grinding against her spine and hips. Her gaze narrowed, scanning the room.

To the right, she could see the outline of her bed, to the left; the shadowy form of her dresser. The room's twisting shadows swallowed up any details of either.

"Nick, are you in here? Nick?"

She heard a noise. What was that? She shook her head, dismissing it. Her concern for Nick made her overlook the sound as she continued to search the shadows.

The silence stretched taut. The lack of sound emphasized the rain drilling into the window, pattering like hail against the slippery sheet of glass. If there was another noise to be heard, the rumble of distant thunder masked it.

Dallas lifted her chin and pushed away from the door. Again, her knees threatened to buckle. Force of will kept them locked and rigid with each step she took toward the bed.

She noticed two things at once.

The first was the sharp smell of blood; it grew stronger the nearer she got to the bed. The second was the unusual shadow—long and broad—atop the bedspread.

The shadow separated and defined itself as she drew closer, and the more her eyes adjusted to the scant light. Slowly, a big, rugged body took shape against the backdrop of pale ivory comforter.

Seeing Nick Langston's sinewy body sprawled atop her bed sent a jolt through Dallas. She stopped at the foot of the bed, and leaned her shoulder heavily against the thick, spindled bedpost. A sharp corner of the wood bit into her skin through the thin, damp sleeve of her dress. She barely noticed. The solidity of the bedpost was the only thing keeping her erect at that moment.

Nick was half laying, half sitting on the bed. The small of his back was cushioned by the pillow—*her* pillow—that he'd balled up and wedged between his spine and the low, carved headboard. His shoulders ground against the top molding as he grunted and adjusted his weight, leaning his head back against the headboard.

His hair clung to his scalp in unruly, water-darkened waves. When he turned his head to the side, reaching for something on the nightstand, she saw the wet outline of his head against the papered wall. Her gaze dropped. His clothes were equally as wet as well as muddy. Dark smudges marred the once clean bedspread beneath him.

Dallas sucked in a quick, shallow breath. Her reaction had nothing to do with anger over the mess he'd made out of her room. She couldn't care less about that. It had everything to do with the way she noticed the rest of Nick. From lean hips down.

Someone had sliced away the left leg of his pants, just below the hip. The tube of denim that had once encased his heavily muscled thigh now lay wrinkled and discarded beside his hip. The tube of cutaway pants leg looked flat, hollow, empty.

So did the penetrating blue gaze that burned out of the dingy shadows, and fixed on her.

Their gazes met and held for a beat. Dallas was the

first to look away. Her attention returned to his exposed leg.

His sinewy, sun-kissed thigh and calf was a stark contrast to the pale bedspread beneath him. So was the smear of blood caked to the deep, half-clotted gash snaking down his leg from midthigh to midshin. His knee looked bruised and mangled. The lower half of his leg protruded from that swollen joint, twisting out at an unnatural angle.

A sharp pain speared through Dallas's heart. Her fingers curled around the bedpost. Her knuckles stung from the pressure of her grip.

"Papa said you refused Hickory Pete's help," Dallas said finally. "Mind telling me why?"

"Yeah. Now that you mention it, I would." His voice was cold, hard, emotionless. The rough timbre was foreign to her. "Let's just say it ain't none of your damn business and leave it at that."

She heard the sound of a cork being unplugged from a bottle. Her gaze lifted in time to see Nick turn his head and spit. The cork pinked onto the floor. Dallas heard it roll over the planks, but didn't track its progress. Nick obviously didn't care where it landed . . . which meant the bottle probably wouldn't need a cork by the time he was through drinking.

Glass clinked against glass. What little light there was in the room bounced off the bottle he held in one hand, and the shot glass he held in the other. Dallas smelled the whiskey fumes even before she saw him splash a goodly portion of the dark amber liquid into the glass.

Nick's fingers shook as he lifted the filled-to-the-top

shot glass to his mouth. The cold rim rested against his lips. The liquor dampened the tips of his mustache. He didn't drink it. Not yet.

His gaze lifted, locking hard with hers over the glass. His lips twitched, as though he was about to say something.

Dallas waited, but apparently Nick had just as quickly changed his mind. Still holding her gaze, he shrugged and downed the fiery contents of the glass. He didn't shudder, didn't even flinch, as he swallowed and tipped the bottle, refilling the glass.

Some of the alcohol spilled over. It washed over Nick's hand, soaked into his already wet shirt. The bands of muscles in his arm, outlined by the wet sleeve plastered to it, bunched and flexed when he lifted that hand to his mouth. His tongue darted out, licking the whiskey off the stretch of tanned flesh on the back of his hand, and then off his thick, calloused knuckles.

With effort, Dallas shook off the trance his actions had enfolded her in. Her narrowed gaze volleyed between his blue, blue eyes, which were now contemplating the whiskey bottle intently, and his mangled leg.

Swallowing hard, she eased away from the bedpost and made to step to the side of the bed. She'd cleared half the distance when his cold voice shot out from the shadows, freezing her to the spot.

"You can leave any time," Nick sneered. He paused only long enough to toss the second drink down. Then a third. "You've seen what you came here to see. Now get the hell out."

"It's my room."

"Fine. Then I'll go."

"Nick, be serious. You aren't going anywhere and we both know it. Or haven't you gotten a look at that leg yet."

"I've gotten a look at it. It's bad. Real bad. I've seen men lose a leg for lesser injuries. So've you. We both know a one-legged puncher's about as useful as a slicker without oil." The bottle was slammed onto the nightstand with enough force to make the small clock there jump. With a violent curse, Nick sent the shot glass hurtling into the wall. It exploded on contact, raining a thousand razor-sharp slivers to the floor. The tinkling sound they made against the planks was over-ridden by the deep, erratic breaths pumping through Nick's lungs.

The mattress crunched and creaked when he pushed away from the headboard. His torso pivoted until he was facing her, but his legs didn't move.

Dallas fought the urge to hurry to his side and push him back down on the bed. She would have done just that, had she not been so afraid the movement would hurt him more than he was already hurting himself. Sitting the way he was had to be excruciatingly painful.

Her eyes had completely adjusted to the dimness in the room now. The gray light made Nick's cheeks look paler than they really were. Sweat beaded on his brow, caused by the supreme effort it had taken to move himself.

As she watched, he sucked his lower lip between his teeth and bit down hard. His fingers were poised a mere inch from his mangled leg. Dallas read the inde- cision in his face, and knew he was weighing how much pain it would cost him to move the leg against how much pride it would cost him to be seen trying . . . and failing.

He was in agony, she knew, but she had to admire the way he gritted his teeth against the pain and refused to cry out. His fingers clenched and unclenched the bedspread in white-knuckled fists. That was the only indication of the pain wracking his body. That, and the telltale darkening in the indigo gaze that refused to lift, refused to meet hers.

He didn't get off the bed. Nor did he lay back down. In fact, he didn't move at all. He just continued to sit there, staring at his twisted, bloodied leg.

"Did you come to gloat?" he growled once his breathing had returned to normal. "What? Isn't my pain enough for you? You gotta rub my face in it, too? Is that it? You wanna gloat? Well, go right ahead. Do it. We both know you and dear Daddy have been waiting for this day for years. Hell, the whole damn ranch has been waiting for the day Nick Langston screwed up. Well, here's your chance, darlin'. Enjoy it while you can, 'cause it sure as hell won't come 'round again. Laugh your cute little ass off . . . *then get the hell out of here!*"

The raw hatred in his voice made Dallas flinch. Her head snapped back, as though he'd physically slapped her; she could actually feel the sting of it against her cheek. Her spurs clinked against the floor as she took an involuntary step backward. "Nick, please. Think about what you're saying. You know me and my family better than that. You know I would *never—*"

"Shut up!" His head came up fast. His blue eyes

narrowed to shimmering slits that flayed her from head to toe. When his gaze again captured hers, his eyes were as cold as ice. Like his voice, they were unfamiliar to her. "I don't want to hear any of your lies, woman!"

"I'm not lying," Dallas said, so softly she thought she was the only one to hear. Even if Nick's irrational anger had allowed the words to register in his mind, she didn't think he would believe her. He was too furious. In too much pain. He wasn't thinking right at all. None of what he said was true, yet his grim expression said he believed every word of it.

The muscle in his cheek throbbed as he plowed ten muddy, shaking fingers through his hair. He yanked the wet strands back from his face, slicking them to his scalp. "Get out of here," he sneered. His voice was softer now, flatter. For some reason, the tightly controlled tone was all the more alarming to Dallas. "Do yourself a favor and get out now, Cameron, while I'm still able to let you go."

"No." Dallas shook her head, her wet hair flicking against her back. "I'm not going anywhere."

An emotion fired Nick's eyes. It came and went faster than the lightning that continued to cut through the stormy sky outside. Dallas barely had time to see the emotion before Nick doused it. She never had time to read it.

"Don't be a fool," he snarled. "The way I'm feeling right now, if you stay here, one of us is liable to get hurt."

Dallas tipped her chin up at a proud, determined

angle and, drawing on an inner reserve of strength, met his gaze unflinchingly. "A threat?"

"Hell, no, darlin'. It's a promise."

A shiver iced down Dallas's spine. With effort, she suppressed it. The Nick Langston she knew would never hurt her. But this Nick . . . she didn't know this Nick at all. "Fine. I'll take that as a warning . . . and I'll also take my chances. I'm not going to leave you alone right now, Nick. Not when you need me."

Very slowly, and with much effort, Nick turned and lowered his shoulders back to the headboard. With his weight more evenly distributed, he seemed to relax a bit.

Still holding her gaze, he reached for the bottle on the nightstand. He found it by feel alone. Closing his thick fingers around the neck of the bottle, he lifted the rim to his lips.

Nick drained back a healthy swallow, then smacked his lips and saluted her with the now half-empty bottle. "I'm not alone, Squirt, I've got some of Kentucky's best to keep me company. Better than any whore I've ever had, and twice as warm. I don't need you."

"Liar." Dallas's gaze narrowed. Fear of him, fear *for* him, was quickly redirecting itself into anger. Dammit, she was trying to help this man! And what did she get for her trouble? Insults and anger and ungratefulness.

"I *don't* need you," Nick assured her, so forcefully it made Dallas wonder if he was trying to convince her, or himself.

"Yes you do. You need me, Langston. More than

ever. And you know what else? I think you damn well know it."

"Wrong, Cameron. I *want* you. There's a difference. And you damn well know *that.*"

"Do I?" she asked, as she ignored the sudden heat that sizzled through her body at his words. She even managed to ignore the flush of crimson that warmed her cheeks. Only the hot, tingling flutter in the pit of her stomach, the one that seeped lower and lower, could not be ignored. But that, of course, could be hidden.

Nick's grin was crooked and liquor-sloppy. "Don't you?" One damp gold brow arched high, issuing a blatant challenge. It was minute compared to the challenge Nick issued with his next words. "I expect the next thing you'll be telling me is that you don't want me. Physically, that is." He studied her long and hard. His grin widened when he saw her squirm, and watched a guilty flush stain her cheeks. "Didn't think you could say it."

"I don't want you, Nick," Dallas snapped, surprised at how easily the lie slipped off her tongue. Judging by the look in his eyes and his dubious expression, Nick didn't believe her. "It's true. I don't. All I want is to take a look at your leg. I'll set the bone and stitch the wound, if you'll let me. But that's *all* I want right now."

The grin melted from Nick's lips. His eyelids lowered, hooding his eyes. His voice, when it came, was slightly slurred, and completely serious. "Yeah, right now maybe," he agreed huskily. "But that wasn't what you wanted the other night, was it, Dallas?"

Her spine went rigid. She clamped her mouth shut and refused to answer him. Her thoughts burned through her with almost as much heat as Nick's gaze did. Almost. What he said was true. What she wanted the other night, what she still, deep down, wanted was Nick Langston.

Nick shook his head. The wetness of his hair spread the damp spot that would probably always stain her wall. His fingers tightened around the bottle, except the calloused index finger, which jutted out and arrowed at a spot dead center of her chest. "I can tell you exactly what you wanted the other night by the river, Dallas. And exactly what you got. *I* can say the words you don't seem able to. Is that what you want? You want me to say them and save you the trouble?"

"No."

"Tough. I'm gonna say it anyway. About damn time one of us did, don't you think? Hell, we've been skirting around the issue for days. Right now, though, I think I'm just drunk enough to bring it all out in the open."

"Shut up, Nick," Dallas snapped angrily. His eyes were starting to look glassy, dazed—with pain, with whiskey. He couldn't mean what he was saying. Dallas was sure of that. Whiskey will grease a man's tongue with lies or not. "I'd rather you just shut up, Langston. Right now. Before you say something we'll both regret . . . something that will ruin our friendship forever."

His gaze lifted and locked with hers. The indigo depths of his eyes sparkled with a sincerity so intense it made Dallas shiver. "You know something, Squirt? The only thing I regret right now is that I'll never get another chance to make you feel the way I made you feel that other night. And as for us being friends . . ." His laugh was loud and brittle. It, like his expression, dripped sarcasm. " 'Bout time you faced it, Cameron. We haven't been friends for a long, long time. Fact is, we'll *never* be friends again."

If the planks underfoot had been covered by a rug, Dallas knew it would, at that moment, have been yanked out from under her. She felt weak, shaky, liquid. Her knees buckled. She shifted quickly to the side, and lowered her weight onto the very edge of the bed before she could embarrass herself by collapsing.

Her gaze shifted to the hands she clasped tightly in her lap. She didn't cry. She knew it, because she felt the wet sting of tears in her eyes, combined with the effort it took to blink them back. She heard Nick take another, longer drink from the bottle, but she didn't look up. She didn't dare.

"I know we haven't exactly been getting along lately," she admitted finally, forcing the words around the lump of emotion wedged in her throat. "But I think we could be friends again. If we both tried hard enough."

"And that's exactly the problem, Dallas," he said, his voice low and whiskey-raw. "Every time I look at you, I get hard as a rock. Without trying."

Dallas's head came up fast. Her watery gaze instantly dried. Shocked brown clashed with lusty blue. "I didn't mean—"

He sent her a sloppy wink. "But *I* did. Want me to prove it to you, darlin'? Or would you rather take my word for it?"

For the first time Dallas saw—really *saw*—his suddenly red cheeks, his glassy eyes, his whiskey-wet lips. His movements, when he lifted the bottle to his grinning mouth, were liquor-clumsy. Not at all the agile, fluid motions she was used to seeing in Nick Langston. The scowl of pain had been ironed from his brow, and the muscle in his cheek had stopped twitching.

"You're drunk!" Dallas found that, oddly enough, the observation was comforting. It made her feel better to think it was the whiskey talking, not Nick. Try as she did, though, she wasn't entirely convinced that was true.

"Yup," Nick said, and wiped his mouth on his arm. His shrug was unrepentant. "But not nearly as drunk as I plan to be. I've still got another half of this to drin— Where the hell do you think you're going, Cameron?"

"To get Hickory Pete. Maybe he can convince you to let one of us tend that leg."

"Like hell!"

Dallas had started to rise from the bed. Nick's left hand shot out with more coordination than she would have given his liquor-dulled senses credit for having at that point. His fingers curled around her wrist. They felt like tight steel bands biting into her tender flesh as he jerked her back down on the bed.

She landed hard enough for the mattress to groan beneath her . . . hard enough for Nick to wince as the pain of the movement shot through his injured left leg. His grip tightened reflexively. Her fingers went icy and numb.

It was in that instant that Dallas realized she'd had

about as much as she could take from this man. She'd tried to be calm and cajoling, sympathetic to his pain. She'd even gone against her nature and bitten her tongue while he abused and insulted her. But this man-handling was the last straw. Her patience snapped.

"You're not leaving this room until I tell you to go." Nick's voice was easy, careless. His gaze was ice cold. "I'm not near finished with you, darlin'. Haven't you figured that out yet?"

His words sent a chill down Dallas's spine. He meant more than the situation here and now, and she knew it. But how much more?

She tried to wrench free of his grip. She should have known better. Pain shot up her arm when he gave a reciprocal tug.

Of the two, Nick's had a greater effect. Where her yank didn't even loosen his grip, his shook her balance and sent Dallas sprawling face first onto the mattress. And onto Nick.

Dallas was too busy squirming, trying to stay away from his injured leg, to pay proper attention to what Nick was doing.

Nick was dragging her body up his chest.

Slowly.

He settled her against him, wrapping his arm around her waist to hold her steady. Her breasts were crushed against his chest. Dallas could feel his heart-beat slamming beneath hers. His breath, rushing over the top of her head, smelled whisky-sharp. It felt warm as sin.

"You know what Pete wants to do to me, don't you?" Nick asked, his voice a throaty rasp as he caressed the top of Dallas's head with his cheek. His lips whisked back and forth over the wet, tawny strands. He inhaled deeply, and Dallas felt the rise of his chest press him more firmly against her. With her very soul, she felt the groan that rumbled from within him.

"H—he wants to help you, Nick. That's all he wants. That's all any of us want." Dallas was trying so hard to fight the spicy male scent that had wrapped around her, and was holding her a prisoner as surely as the arms that pinned her close. It wasn't possible to fight either. Suddenly, she lacked the stamina and willpower to try. His grip on her, she noticed foggily, resembled a desperate hug. "Nick, listen to me. Please. I know you're half out of your mind from the pain. I know the whiskey's blurring your normally good sense. Fine. I understand that. But *you* have to understand that all I want is to help you."

The rumble that emanated from Nick's broad, hard chest this time, the one that vibrated straight through to Dallas's soul, had no foundation in anything but contempt. "Now why the hell would you want to do that, Cameron? I'm just a no-good cowpuncher. Easily hired. More easily fired. It shouldn't take Ian long to find someone to replace me. We both know it."

His grip loosened. Not much, but enough for the arms Dallas had flanked on both sides of his chest to stiffen. Slowly, she levered herself up, and looked down into Nick's face.

The unease she saw there darkened his eyes to a rich, piercing shade of midnight blue. It tightened his expression, adding still more weathered creases to his brow, and to the corners of his eyes. "You're more than that, and you damn well know it. You're my friend, Nick Langston. You have been for years. I'd do anything for you."

"Anything?" His gaze, which had been fixed sightlessly on the ceiling, slipped down. His eyes burned into her.

Dallas squirmed, but only a little. She felt Nick's stomach muscles pull taut. With a reluctant sigh, she admitted, "Yes, Nick, anything."

"Why?"

"Because I—I like you. I always have."

"And if I told you I didn't want you to like me? That I don't want to be your friend?" His hands stroked up her arms, hooking over the slender shelf of her shoulders. He exerted no pressure to pull her down atop him. "What would you say to that, Cameron?"

Her eyelids thickened, hooding her gaze. "That all depends. What would you say if *I* asked *you* exactly what it is you *do* want, Langston?"

"The truth," he answered. His voice was slurred, his tone hard but sincere. "I think I'm drunk enough now to tell you the truth to any question you ask."

One tawny brow cocked. Dallas tipped her head to the side, and noticed the way her wet hair dragged over her shoulder. And over Nick's. A shiver worked through Nick, telling Dallas she wasn't the only one who'd noticed. "Then consider yourself asked. Tell me what you want, Nick."

The hands holding her against him melted away. It didn't matter. She wasn't going anywhere. Nick's gaze held her pinned against him more firmly than his hands ever could.

Their gazes met, forming a tether that charged the air around and between them. It was a bond that had always been there, growing stronger throughout the years. It was a bond too strong to break. A bond that, in truth, Dallas didn't *want* to see broken. Ever.

Nick's roughened palms cupped her cheeks. He drew her head closer, but he didn't kiss her the way Dallas *hoped* he would. Instead, he rested her forehead against his and said, "I want you to stay away from David Parker. I want you to forget about marrying him. And then I want you to get the hell out of this room . . . and forget about *me.*"

She closed her eyes and sucked in a sharp breath. Staying away from David Parker, she could do without effort. Staying away from Nick Langston . . .

No, she'd rather die.

"I can't do that, Nick."

"Yes, you can. You *will.*"

"No, I—" Dallas shifted her weight to get a better look at Nick. And that was when she felt it.

The cold leather of his holster brushed her knuckles. Her hand turned inward, her fingers searching, but that was all she felt. The holster was empty.

As carefully and as quickly as she could, Dallas pushed herself to a sit. Her gaze scanned the bed. And fixed on the long, thin, blue-cast barrel of the Colt .44 that lay nestled in the place where the mattress dipped beneath his hip. It looked as though the gun had been shoved there quickly, like it had been hidden.

A rush of memory assailed her. It was strong enough to make the room spin. The noise Dallas had heard over the pounding rain when she'd first entered the room—the noise she'd forgotten in her haste to see Nick—now came rushing back.

Her horrified gaze drilled into the half-hidden pistol. The room swam around her as the remembered sound reverberated in her mind.

It was the sound of a pistol hammer being cocked.

Dallas's gaze lifted. She searched Nick's face, noticing the way he'd turned away from her. He was staring at the wall. His profile was sculpted hard by the twisting, murky shadows. His expression was impassive. "Nick?"

"Get out, Dallas. I want to be alone."

No, that wasn't what he wanted at all. Dallas sensed it, even as she sensed that what he truly wanted to do scared her witless.

With quivering fingers, she snatched up the gun. It felt cold and deadly in her palms.

The metallic click of chambers being jerked open grabbed Nick's attention. His head came around fast. Dallas could feel the heat of his eyes biting into her, but she ignored it. Instead, her gaze sharpened on the gun.

Five bullets were nestled inside. All of them gleamed eerily in the muted light.

With a flick of her wrist, she snapped the chamber closed. Her gaze didn't lift. She didn't look at Nick. She couldn't.

He was close enough, and strong enough, to wrestle the gun away from her. They both knew it. They also knew he was too drunk, and in far too much pain, to try.

Still, Dallas didn't dare take that chance. The stakes

were too high; the stakes were Nick Langston's life. That, she would never risk.

Her entire body tensed, ready to throw the gun to the opposite side of the room should Nick decide to fight her for it. In his condition, he'd never make it that far. He could try, but first he'd have to go through her to get to the pistol. And Dallas intended to put up one hell of a rip-roaring fight. The best fight of her life.

With self-conscious movements, she slipped her legs over the side of the bed and stood. Her knees shook as she pushed herself to her feet and crossed the room. She placed the gun on top of the bureau, turned, and leaned back against it. Crossing her arms over her waist, she sent Nick a disappointed glare. "You know, Langston, the one thing I never took you for was a coward."

"I'm not. I'm a realist. Always have been. I know that after they've chopped my leg off, and they're gonna have to, I'll heal. Physically. But what the hell good will it do me if I can't sit a horse? Can't rope cattle? Can't . . . dammit, can't do anything worthwhile and useful? I live for cowpunchin', Cameron. Take that away from me, and I'm nothing."

Dallas pulled in a long, slow breath. She forced herself to concentrate on the first part of what Nick had said, not allowing herself to dwell on the rest because it hurt too damn much. Did he really believe what he'd said? Did he really think he'd be useless just because he'd lost a leg? "Is that what you call what you were about to do with that pistol before I came into the room? Being a realist?"

"Yup." Nick was still looking away from her, his

gaze fixed on the rain that continued to pour in twisting streams down the windowpane. "I didn't expect you to understand."

"Damn good thing, because I don't. I don't understand this at all." Bunching her fists atop her hips, Dallas resisted the urge to charge across the room and slap some sense into this man.

What was wrong with him? This *wasn't* the Nick Langston she'd known since she was knee-high. Not even close. Her Nick wasn't a coward. Her Nick faced life head on; faced his problems and dealt with them. Her Nick would never even *consider* taking his own life—under *any* circumstances!

The turn of her thoughts brought Dallas up short. *Her* Nick? When, exactly, had she begun thinking of him as *her* Nick?! And—worse; much, *much* worse—*why* did it sound so perfect and right?

Dallas's anger deflated. She felt numb. That must have been reflected in her voice, because this time Nick turned to look at her when she spoke. "You've got a broken bone and a very bad cut, Langston. That's all. Believe it or not, you *will* heal . . . given half the chance."

"You really believe that?"

"Don't you?"

"Do I look stupid?" His hand sliced through the air, stifling her immediate reply. "Forget I asked."

"Tough, Langston. I'm gonna tell you anyway." Her chin tipped up. Her jaw hardened. Dallas watched his sun-bleached brows arch high when he recognized the words—*his* words—that she now flung back in his face.

256

She sucked in a deep breath, and plucked the gun up from the bureau. It felt heavy, dragging from her hand as she retraced her steps. She didn't sit down this time. Rather, she stood towering over the bed. Towering over Nick.

She waited until his gaze lifted, traveled up her body, then locked with her own before she spoke. Her words were as hard and as cold as any he'd said in the past half hour. "I think you're a real son of a bitch, Nick Langston. You're a yellow-bellied coward, that's what you are. What's more . . . I'm ashamed to know you."

Her gaze dropped to the gun. It dangled heavily from her fingers when she lifted it, then she let it drop to the bed. It made a lifeless thud as it bounced atop the mattress, then came to rest against his hard, denim-clad hip. "There you go. You don't want to fight? Fine. You want to take the easy way out of this? The *coward's* way out? Be my guest. I won't stop you."

Nick felt his gut twist. The whiskey-fog burned away a bit under the onslaught of his confusion. He watched the water-heavy skirt slap at Dallas's legs when she spun on her heel and stalked toward the door. The sound of her spurs and boots clicking atop the planks matched the frantic rhythm of his heart, hammering in his chest.

The urge to call her back was strong. He almost surrendered to it. And then Nick wondered what the hell he would say to her if he did give in and call her back.

He could tell her she was right, but they both already knew that. What would be the sense in arguing the point? Besides, that wasn't really the problem. The problem was trying to make someone like Dallas understand the desperation knifing through him—desperation that was a hell of a lot sharper than the throbs of pain emanating from his leg! How could he make her understand the agony—both physical and mental—that was cutting him up on the inside?

He couldn't. He wasn't a wordy man. He didn't know how to convey his feelings. What's more, he had no right to try to, but . . . ah hell, he was going to try anyway. He owed Dallas that much.

"Wait."

Dallas's hand was on the doorknob, but she didn't turn it. Her spine went rigid, but she didn't look back at him. She stood stiffly, waiting for him to continue.

Even from across the room, Nick could feel the tension radiating from Dallas's body, seeping into his. It warmed him, boiling through his blood. And, yes, it reheated his anger. All the things he'd planned to say when he'd called her back wilted on his tongue. Her stance was rigid, slightly masculine, and annoying as hell. His tone dipped threateningly low. "You have nerve, Cameron, I'll give you that."

Dallas's hand dropped away from the doorknob. Her palm slapped her thigh as she spun around to face him. "And what the hell is that supposed to mean?!"

"It means that it might not be such a bad idea for you to open your eyes and look at the people around you every now and again. Not everyone lives the perfect little life Dallas Louise Cameron does. Some of us poor folk have to work for a living. We don't have the luxury to pick and choose spouses like we do a fresh melon. We can't decide not to work one day because we'd rather go to a picnic. *Not all of us are as lucky as you!"*

"Lucky?" she shouted back at him, her cheeks hot with renewed fury. "Is that what you think I am? *Lucky?* I'll have you know I work around here, Langston. You know I do!"

"Wrong. What I *know* is that you're a spoiled rotten little brat who could stand a healthy wallop on that cute little ass of yours." It wasn't the truth, and Nick knew it, but he needed to lash out at someone and, God help him, Dallas was available.

Her brown eyes narrowed, shooting fire. "Oh really? And who's going to do it, Nick? *You?"* she sneered. "Ha! You can't even get up off the bed. Besides, in three minutes, if you have your way, you won't be around to do much of anything."

Her gaze wasn't the only one that narrowed. So did Nick's.

If Dallas hadn't been so damn furious, she might have seen the dangerous glint in his eyes. The rhythmic jerking in his cheek meant trouble. So did the tight, grim set of his mouth, and the fists he twisted tightly in the bedspread.

"And *you* called *me* a coward," he growled. Nick shook his head, and ran a palm down the length of his whisker-darkened jaw. "Well, ain't that the pot calling the kettle black? Those are real big words to be speaking from across the room, Cameron. Bet you can't come over here and say 'em to my face."

As he'd planned, Dallas stalked the distance between them before he could draw in another breath.

What he hadn't planned on was the way she planted balled fists on her hips and leaned threateningly over him.

The angle made her breasts heavy, made them strain for freedom against the wet calico bodice. Her hair slipped over her shoulder, and over his cheek. The tip of one thick tawny curl tickled the end of Nick's nose. It felt wet and silky. It smelled earthy and fresh.

Dallas met his gaze and shouted, *"When the hell are you going to stop feeling sorry for yourself, Langston? Bad things happen to all of us. Learn-to-make-the-best-of-it!"*

Nick's hand came up. He fisted the very end of the curl that was tickling him and driving him crazy. "I've been making the best of things all my life, Cameron. Mind telling me what it's gotten for me so far?"

Dallas's scalp burned when the lock of hair Nick had seized was pulled taut. She glanced down, her gaze fixing on the tawny strand, and the way it was slowly being wrapped around Nick's fist. His skin looked dark, tough. Her hair looked like a delicate spider's web in comparison.

Not all of the fight went out of her—their discussion was too important to let go of all of it—but she felt a goodly portion drain away.

Her gaze lifted, and meshed with his. "I can think of a dozen men who would kill to have what you do. You've got a good job, Nick. You pull decent wages. You're healthy . . ." she hesitated, and blushed, "relatively speaking. You've got your pride, and your self-respect, which is a hell of a lot more than a lot of men can claim. What more could you possibly want?"

"A hell of a lot. Christ, lady, I want things you couldn't even begin to imagine. People like you Camerons are handed things that people like us Langstons can only *dream* about having."

"Things?" she asked cautiously. "What kind of things?"

Nick shrugged. The lift and fall of his broad shoulders was strained and tight. "Land for one. A few possessions besides my saddle and a sack full of memories for another. You know, Cameron, I don't even own my own horse. Your daddy owns it." His gaze darkened when it dropped to her lips. His eyes smoldered hungrily over her mouth. His tone turned husky and raw. "Ian Cameron owns everything I've ever wanted and could never have. Everything."

"Y—you've never said anything like that before," she whispered, her voice unaccountably breathless. The way Nick's gaze continued to taste her lips was making Dallas feel all hot and tingly.

"You never asked." Nick continued to turn his fist slowly end over end, wrapping the hair around his hand as he went, reeling her in. "As I recall, you never cared to know anything about me, until recently. Isn't that right . . . *Squirt?*"

"I would never ask, Nick," Dallas countered, and tried to pull back. He wouldn't allow it. The most she could do was bow her spine forward, trying to keep as much distance between them as she could. "You know how uppity the men around here get when someone asks a personal question. Most consider it an invasion of privacy. I know that, and I respect it. Besides, you, more than any man on this ranch, have always been stingy with information about yourself."

"Not with you, Dallas," he corrected, and tugged her a hairsbreadth closer. "I've never been stingy with you. You could've asked me any question at all, and I would have answered you."

Dallas swallowed hard. Her heart was racing, but that was only because she'd been tugged down another inch. The tips of her breasts brushed the hard bed of Nick's chest. She knew she shivered; she wasn't sure if Nick did.

"And now?" she asked softly, shakily. "Can I ask you anything now, Nick?"

He nodded, but his attention was no longer on her. Well, no, that wasn't exactly true. His attention was focused on her lips, and he looked incapable of thinking about anything else at that moment. His eyes were slitted, the blue depths lusty and bright and hungry. Her mouth tingled, with awareness, and with a reciprocal hunger.

Now wasn't the time or place—they had other, more important matters to attend to—but . . .

God, how she wanted Nick to kiss her. Dallas wanted to feel him, to taste him. She wanted Nick to kiss her hard, and make her forget about his injury, and about what he planned to do with that gun. She wanted . . .

She wanted Nick Langston to make things all better for her; the way he always did.

Only this time, it was *she* who should be doing that for *him*.

"The gun, Nick," she murmured, even as he pulled

her lower still. Her breasts were pressed intimately to his chest. Her mouth moved against his. She smelled the whiskey on his breath, tasted the bitter sting of it when she dragged her tongue over her lips. And she tasted Nick. The latter was the more potent flavor; the one that lingered.

"What about the gun, Dallas?" he rasped, and shifted beneath her. The corded muscles of his chest dragged over the beaded softness of hers.

A sensation bolted through them both. The contact was electric, sizzling and intense.

"You said you'd answer me anything," Dallas clarified huskily, and thought that, dear God, the feel of him was driving her crazy! Another minute, and she was going to kiss him, whether he wanted her to or not. Of course, the observation was moot. He wanted this just as badly as she did. If nothing else, Dallas was positive of that.

"Ask me anything, darlin'. I'll answer." As he spoke, Nick's hand gave another insistent tug on her hair.

Dallas's scalp burned with the pressure, but she craned her neck, refusing to let their lips meet. If she kissed him now—the way she wanted so desperately to do—words would be forgotten. The world, and everything in it, would recede and melt away. She couldn't let that happen. Not yet. But soon. Very soon . . .

"I want the gun. I want you to give it to me of your own free will, and I want to bring it with me when I leave this room." The unnatural tilt of her head made Dallas's neck ache. Still, she didn't move, but instead looked down her nose and straight into his abruptly guarded expression. Her fingers curled around fistfuls of his wet shirt. It was all she could do not to shake some sense into his stubborn head. "Please, Nick. Will you let me do that?"

"You're asking a hell of a lot from me, Squirt. You know that, don't you?"

Dallas shook her head, wincing at the sharp tug on her scalp. Nick's grip hadn't loosened. If anything, it grew more biting, more intense. "All I'm asking is for you to give yourself a chance. That's all I want."

He scowled darkly. "A chance for *what?* What kind of life do you think I'm gonna have after this?"

He nodded down to his mangled leg. Dallas didn't lower her gaze. In fact, her attention never wavered from his. The pain she saw there was incredible. Some of the agony was physical, but most of it wasn't. All of it looked to be tearing Nick Langston apart.

"A broken leg isn't the end of the world, Nick."

"It's the end of mine," he growled furiously. "I won't be able to ride now. And forget anything but ground roping—*if* I can walk." He grumbled a vicious, explicit cuss. "My life is now, and always has been, on the back of a horse, Dallas. Take that away from me, and I have nothing."

"No! That isn't true. You have—" She snapped her mouth shut before she said something they'd both regret.

Nick's gaze sharpened on her. His free hand lifted, his fingers manacling her slender upper arm. "Finish it. Tell me. What do I have?"

Her mind raced. She couldn't tell him the truth. She didn't know what the truth was anymore. Instead, she

264

placated him by substituting something she *knew* to be true. "A job on the Bar None. No matter what, you'll always have that."

"Even if I can't ride?"

Dallas nodded vigorously. "Even then. There's always work to be done around here. Papa will find something for you to do, even if it isn't on the back of a horse. But all this is supposition, Nick. You're the only one who says you'll never ride again."

"I'm the only one drunk enough to admit the truth."

"No, you're the only one too drunk to *see* the truth."

The grip on her hair loosened, but didn't fall away. Nick relaxed back against the pillow, although there was very little of him that was truly relaxed. He seemed as though he wanted badly to be convinced of what she was saying, but was wary of letting himself be.

"I've seen my leg, darlin'," he said finally, wearily. His voice was slurred again, his tone limp. "That tells me all I need to know. I've seen guys lose limbs over lesser injuries. So have you. No reason to think I'll be any different."

"But you *are* different, Nick," Dallas whispered hoarsely, even as she felt the fight drain out of her. Her body went limp atop his. His chest felt hard and firm beneath her. It felt wonderful. "You always have been different. That's one of the reasons I've always liked you so much."

She felt him stiffen beneath her, but she was too tired to fight him any longer. It wasn't doing any good.

The second she left, he was going to do what he wanted anyway.

"Any other reasons?" he asked, and his voice cracked. Just a little, but she heard it. And responded to it.

Again, Dallas levered herself over him. "Give me the gun, and I'll give you a dozen."

One blue eye narrowed under a skeptically tilted brow. "That's blackmail."

She shrugged, and thought that maybe this time he might actually do it. She was afraid to hope. "Whatever it takes."

A tense moment passed, and then Nick shifted. She felt his left hand fish between them. The solid pressure of the pistol was nudged against her stomach. It felt hard and cold.

Dallas held her breath, and took the gun before Nick had time to change his mind. She moved, and tossed the pistol to the floor, far enough away so he'd have to struggle to get to it.

A shudder of relief rippled through her as she turned back toward him. For the first time since she'd entered the room, she smiled.

His voice, when it came, was thick and low. "Reasons, Cameron. You promised me reasons. If I'm gonna have to live like a cripple for the rest of my life, then you'd damn well better make it worth my while. Tell me why you've always liked me."

"If I do, will that be enough for you, Nick?"

"Hell no. But it'll do for starters." His gaze dipped, fixing on the way her breasts swayed, heavy and tempting as all hell, over his chest. He could pull her

266

down now, and feel that ripe softness pressing into him, or he could wait. Either way, he *would* feel it again. It was inevitable.

In that instant, Nick decided that if he had to live—and this woman seemed hell-bent on seeing that he did—then he'd be damned if he wouldn't carve himself a new dream. Something to work for, something to cling to.

His new goal in life came to him as automatically as breathing. It carved itself quickly and sharply into his soul.

To hell with the ranch, he thought. And to hell with Ian Cameron. No matter what Dallas said, with his mangled leg, Nick knew that he wouldn't be working for Ian much longer anyway. Once he'd been fired, Nick would owe the Bar None no brand loyalty. He'd owe the Camerons nothing.

Good. That would make his new goal in life all the easier to attain.

His new goal in life was to have Dallas Cameron again. Naked and hot beneath him again. Writhing. Moaning his name over and over as he rocked intimately against her.

Once set, Nick Langston always achieved his goals. Eventually. Ask anyone.

Dallas watched the play of emotions as each shifted over Nick's face. She scowled. What had he been thinking of to make his expression go so all-fired determined? What thought had put that sparkle back in his eyes? She didn't know. And when those brilliant blue eyes turned on her, her breath caught in her throat and she forgot to wonder about it.

His grip on her arm tightened. "Reasons, darlin'. You promised."

"I know." Dallas rolled her lips inward and shrugged. How much should she tell him? There were thousands of good, solid reasons she'd always liked Nick. Most of them, she was only now realizing, were extremely personal. "I . . . I like you because you're honest, hard working, and loyal."

Nick grunted, shifted, and snatched up the whiskey bottle. After belting down another two shots, he grumbled, "Put like that, I sound like a goddamn dog!"

Dallas did *not* grin, but she thought about it. Was he joking with her? If so, the whiskey must be doing its job. Finally. Now, if she could just get him to drink until he passed out cold . . .

"I like dogs," Dallas said, her tone falsely bright. "And so do you."

"As much as the next guy, I suppose. That *doesn't* mean I like to be compared to one. Especially when it's a woman doing the comparing."

"How about if I told you . . . ?"

The bottle paused on the way to Nick's lips. His head didn't move, but his gaze swung back to her. "What?"

Dallas's gaze was fixed on his lips. She was mesmerized by the way the liquor left them wet and shiny beneath his mustache. Her tongue curled back, eager to lick the wetness away.

She opened her mouth to say something, then quickly closed it again. Dallas frowned and thought that no matter what she said or did now, Nick was too drunk to remember it come dawn. She could tell him anything. Couldn't she?

She cleared her throat. With her free hand, she stroked his cheek. She felt him tremble against her palm. Then again, it could very well have been the palm that trembled. Or both. "How about if I told you I like the way you make me feel, Nick Langston? How about if I told you I've been dreaming and fantasizing about you ever since that night at the river?"

His lips, which she'd been watching intently, curved up in a liquor-sloppy grin. Nick belted down another shot of whiskey. Dallas didn't realize the bottle was empty until his hand draped over the side of the bed, and she heard the hollow clink of glass hit the floor.

Nick's gaze, deep and penetrating, never left hers. "How about if *I* told *you* I've been thinking about the same thing, Dallas Cameron?" The hand that held the bottle came up to cushion the back of hers. This time Dallas was sure; they both trembled. "I have, you know. Night and day. Every hour, every minute, every second . . . that's all I've thought about. Kissing you. Holding you. Touching you."

"But you haven't done any of that."

Nick shook his head, although it was clear he was agreeing with her. How could he deny it? "Uh-uh. I wouldn't dare. Once was bad enough but . . . well, I won't make the same mistake. Not while I worked for your daddy." His grin was whiskey-slow, and devastating. It made Dallas's heart throb, and her blood flow hot. "But after what happened today . . . well, looks to me like I don't work for your daddy no more. Which means—"

"Which means," an intrusive third voice boomed from the doorway, "that you've got one hell of a lot of explaining to do, Langston. If you're planning to quit the Bar None, *I* damn well want to hear the reason why."

Nick's reaction time was slowed by the liquor he'd consumed, and by the pain that continued to eat at him.

Dallas had no such problem. The mattress crunched beneath her as she bolted guiltily into a sitting position, and scooted to the side of the bed. Were the shadows thick enough to hide the way she'd been lying, sprawled atop Nick? She prayed they were, and that they would likewise cover the blush heating her cheeks.

Ian Cameron took a commanding step into the room. He looked as though he was about to slam the bedroom door hard enough to rattle its hinges. But he didn't. His gaze came to rest on Dallas, and he froze.

"You set the boy's leg yet?" Ian asked coldly.

Dallas shook her head. "No, I was waiting for the whiskey to take hold first."

One bushy white brow cocked. Dallas didn't need to see her father's gaze to know it had come to rest on Nick. Nor did she need evidence of the accusation shimmering in his eyes to know it was there. She felt it.

"Leave, girly," her father ordered sternly. "I want a word with Nick. *Alone.*"

"But . . ."

One glare from her father was enough to push Dallas off the bed. Her legs felt shaky beneath her, but somehow they held her weight. She glanced quickly over her shoulder, and saw Nick nod toward the door. His gaze was fixed on her father, however, and his blue eyes were cold and hard.

Dallas bent and picked up the gun. Turning so her father wouldn't see what she was doing, she tucked it into her pocket.

Her gaze volleyed uncertainly between her father and Nick. When neither of them acknowledged her, she turned and left the room.

The door clicked into place behind her. The sound was swallowed up by Ian Cameron's booming voice. "So, you think that little scratch is reason enough to quit on me, do you, Langston? Well, think again. I don't let my best hands go so easily. You, of all people, should know that!"

The thickness of the door might have been what muffled Nick's reply. But Dallas didn't think so. Her heart was beating too loudly for her to hear much of anything. She knew why. Her hand had just slipped into her pocket, and her fingers had curled around the gun.

Nick's gun.

The gun that, had she not entered the room when she did, would have ended his life by now.

A shiver trickled like ice water down her spine. It was as cold and as sharp as the pain that knifed through her heart.

The closeness of what might have happened scared her. Only knowing that it *hadn't* happened, that she'd prevented Nick from taking his own life, gave Dallas the strength to put one foot in front of the other.

On treacherously weak knees, she walked away from the door.

Away from Nick Langston.

For now.

She would come back. And knowing that Nick would be there waiting for her—in *her* bed, his golden head resting atop *her* pillow—when she did, lightened Dallas's steps. And her heart.

Chapter Twelve

Hickory Pete had made the base and top of the crutch out of a thin but sturdy branch. It was shaped like a long, narrow T. The stick of it was gnarled in the center. Lisa had wound old rags around the top, making a thick, padded cushion to prevent chaffing.

Nick had told her not to bother. The thing couldn't have if it wasn't used . . . and he damn well didn't intend to use it.

Lisa had smiled indulgently, then ignored him. She'd padded the crutch in spite of his wishes. Then she'd propped the thing against the bureau.

That had been two weeks ago.

The crutch hadn't been moved since; it just leaned against the bureau, collecting dust.

Nick could see it from his bed, but he couldn't reach it. He didn't want to reach it. Didn't intend to ever *touch* it.

The crutch served only one useful purpose that he could see. It made a good focal point. Something to stare at when he was bored.

Like now.

Like yesterday.

Like the two weeks' worth of yesterdays that had dragged very slowly by.

With an aggravated grunt, Nick flopped onto his back. The mattress crunched beneath him. The pillow, soft and full, rose up on either side of his face to cradle his head. His narrowed gaze was fixed on the ceiling, but he didn't see it.

His mind was blank. Totally and completely blank. And that aggravated the hell out of him.

To say he was bored would have been an understatement. Quite simply, he was very slowly, very quietly, going out of his cotton pickin' mind!

There was nothing to do that he hadn't already done. Twice. He'd read and reread every dime-store western Ian had ever bought. He'd even read some of the books that belonged to Dallas and Lisa.

Like their personalities, the sisters' tastes in reading material were opposites. Lisa's Emily Bronte novels had provided temporary amusement, but hadn't held Nick's interest. Dallas, on the other hand, had brought him her own personal favorite: a dog-eared copy of the latest Sears catalogue. Nick had ogled the section on women's undergarments, and carefully perused the hand-tooled saddles and holsters, but the catalogue hadn't entertained him for long.

And why should it?

Everything in the damn thing cost money, and Nick was painfully aware he no longer had a job.

Ian hadn't said it, not in so many words, but Nick knew. He'd be shown the property markers just as soon as he was healed enough to get out of bed. And as for what Ian had said the day of the accident . . . well, that was sympathy talking. Ian would come to his senses soon enough, and see what Nick already knew. Ian was, first and foremost, a businessman. And no businessman worth his salt kept a deadbeat in his employ. You either earned your way, or you were fired. That was just the way it was, no matter how close you got to the family you worked for.

Nick had gotten damn close to the Camerons. Closer to any family he'd ever worked for. But that didn't change a thing. Business decisions had to be made for the good of the ranch, and in business decisions personal preferences weren't worth squat.

When it came right down to it, there wasn't a damn thing on the Bar None that Nick could do anymore. Not with a bum leg that, according to Hickory Pete, at the very least would leave nagging pain and a permanent limp. *If* he was ever able to walk again. Okay, so he'd been lucky enough to keep the leg. And maybe he should be grateful for that much. But . . .

Nick wasn't grateful, damn it! Not at all.

What he was was bitter. And angry. Damn angry. Angrier than Dallas had been when Ian had told her she couldn't go on the trail drive, that she'd have to stay home and nurse Nick instead. Angrier than Lisa had been when she'd been told *she* would be going on the drive in Dallas's place. And, yes, he was even angrier than Dallas had been when, only moments after leaving Nick the day of the accident, she had stormed out to the barn and fired the incompetent Rico on the spot.

The last two weeks hadn't been easy on anyone, but as far as Nick was concerned *no one* had suffered as much, or had as much right to be angry, as he did.

Dallas would get over her disappointment at missing the drive. Lisa would survive the unaccustomed roughness—hell, it would probably do the girl good, add some grit. And Rico would be rehired just as soon as Dallas's anger cooled.

But what did Nick Langston have?

Same thing Nick Langston always had.

Nothing.

Make that *less* than nothing, since the accident had even robbed him of the freedom to stand up and walk out the door if he wanted to.

The plain fact was, he would never walk again. Hickory Pete hadn't told him that. Then again, the old coot didn't have to. Nick knew.

His healing leg throbbed a protest when he flipped onto his side, and slammed a fist into the pillow beside his cheek. His entire body hummed with fury.

A hot, dry breeze puffed the curtains at the open window. Muffled shouts echoed from somewhere outside.

Nick closed his eyes, and mentally tracked the noise down to the split-rail corral. He smiled, imagining the punchers who hadn't gone on the drive trying to break in one of the new mavericks. His grin broadened when he imagined himself down there with them. Where he belonged. Where he would be right now, if only . . .

The image was so real he thought he could almost feel the roughly hewn rail under his elbow, feel the sun pounding down on his head, warming his scalp through his hat. He could taste the gritty dirt the maverick's hooves kicked up, and hear the—

A click of boot heels and jangle of spurs sounded in the hall. Footsteps paused outside the bedroom door. The knob rattled, then turned.

Nick's eyes snapped open. His gaze was watery. He told himself that was due to the sting of sand his imagination had all too accurately conjured up. He almost convinced himself it was the truth.

A slice of lemony sunlight cut a rectangle over the bed. The light stabbed through Nick's eyes, making his temples ache. He blinked hard and scowled when the comforting vision that had taken root in his mind disintegrated, and scattered like so much dust. Had he ever felt so empty and alone before?

The mattress crunched beneath his shifting weight as, with an aggravated growl, he tossed onto his back. His slitted gaze snagged on Dallas.

She was standing in the open doorway, hands on hips, glaring at him. The color in her cheeks was high. The glint in her eyes said she was furious.

Nick wasn't feeling very patient himself right now. For the past two weeks he'd been spoiling for a fight. The look on Dallas's face said she was going to grant his wish. She looked primed and ready to do battle. Nick almost grinned.

His glare had a minimal effect on her. Her chin came up, her jaw hardened, and her gaze grew savagely bright, but that was her only reaction.

To a man whose feelings had been simmering for the better part of two weeks, her reaction wasn't enough. It wasn't satisfying. Nick wanted more. He didn't want her indignation, he wanted her fury—if only so he could match it with his own. He wanted, *needed,* an outlet for the emotions that had been whipped into a veritable storm inside of him.

"What do you want, Cameron?" he growled, his tone low and acidy.

Her chin hiked up another stubborn notch. The fists straddling her hips tightened until her knuckles paled. "Same thing I've wanted for the past four days, Langston," she snapped. "You. Out of that bed."

"Good trick. Or did you forget . . . *I can't walk?"*

"How would you know?" Her gaze strayed to the crutch, still propped against the bureau. The top sported a thick layer of dust, telling her it hadn't been moved, let alone *used.* Dallas wasn't surprised. Nor was she pleased. "You haven't even tried."

"Why the hell should I? Only a fool tries something he knows damn well he's gonna fail at. I'm many things, darlin', but I ain't no fool." Nick's pause was long and tense. "I'm *not* getting out of this bed."

Dallas's gaze, still fixed on the crutch, swung slowly back to him. Her brown eyes were narrowed and combative, but no more so than the stormy blue ones she locked onto. "Wanna bet?"

"That depends. You wanna fight?"

She tipped her head back and chuckled, her unexpected laughter cold and sarcastic. "Come on, Langston, give me a little bit of credit, would you? I'd *never* pick a fight with a cripple. Too easy to win. Where's the challenge in it?"

As was Dallas's intent, a low growl issued from the bed. The sound was animalistic and feral.

So was the glint in Nick's eyes.

The muscle in his jaw jerked furiously. His expression was strained, murderous. His fingers flexed, curling tightly around the sheet that covered his half-naked body from midchest down. She thought he would rather be closing his powerful fists around her throat.

Under normal circumstances, Dallas would have felt a very rational pang of fear. But these weren't "normal" circumstances, and instead of fear, she felt elated. Finally, *finally,* something she'd said to Nick got through his stubborn-as-all-hell skull!

It was about time. Cajoling and sympathizing had gotten her nowhere fast. Infuriating him, goading him into moving, was the only option left to her. And, as Dallas had suspected, it wasn't a hard option to follow through on. Lately, it seemed that infuriating Nick Langston came to her as naturally as breathing.

"That was pretty low, Cameron. Even for you."

"Was it?" She feigned a shrug. "Well, you know what they say, Langston. The truth hurts."

"Not nearly as much as *you're* gonna hurt when I take you over my knee and paddle your—" The spontaneous threat wilted on his tongue. Nick was surprised the sheet covering him didn't tear—his palms smarted from the abrupt tightening of his fists. The sensation had nothing to do with the death grip he had on the sheet. He only *wished* it did!

Dallas's heart skipped a beat. A wave of color that had nothing to do with anger warmed her cheeks. She'd already decided the best way to deal with Nick's unfinished threat would be to ignore it. That wasn't a problem. Now all she had to do was ignore the way his grittily uttered words made her feel all hot and breathless and tingly.

That was a problem. An insurmountable one. There was very little about Nick Langston she *could* ignore these days. Most especially a threat that had to do with his warm, calloused hand, and her sensitive bottom!

Dallas tore her gaze from his, and restlessly scanned the room. *Her* room. Rather, it had been two weeks ago. Except for the softly papered walls and ivory comforter, the place no longer looked familiar to her.

There wasn't an inch of space, not a stick of furniture, that didn't have Nick Langston stamped all over it in one form or another; from the gun belt looped around the bedpost near his head, to the clothes—*his* clothes—folded and neatly stacked atop the dresser. His mark was everywhere.

Sucking in an unsteady breath, she noticed that even the air smelled different. A sharp, spicy, thoroughly male scent filled her lungs. Dallas scowled, and realized with a jolt that her room now smelled like Nick Langston.

And so, she knew, would her bed.

Always.

Her gaze shifted, looking for something, *anything* that would take her mind off its present, rocky course. Her attention settled on the crutch. It was as good a distraction as any, plus it would bring her back to her original reason for this impromptu visit.

With trembling fingers, she picked up the crutch. It was heavy; the wood felt solid and rough beneath her fingertips. A puff of breath dispersed the dust clinging to the top. "Hickory Pete tells me you won't use this."

"Stating the blatantly obvious, ain't you?"

Dallas's gaze narrowed. Her grip on the base of the crutch tightened, and she welcomed the wave of anger that returned in force. "Don't get fresh with me, Langston. I'm trying to help you."

"Then put that damn thing down and get the hell out of here," he growled. *"That* would help me."

Dallas spun on her heel. The navy blue split skirt whipped around her legs. Her gaze locked with Nick's long before the hem settled in soft folds around her booted ankles. "Like hell! I've been coddling you all week, and look where it's gotten me. Nowhere. You're still laying in that bed feeling sorry for yourself."

"I've got a right to feel sorry for myself, wouldn't you say?" he shouted, and shoved himself up on his elbows. If he could have thrust himself off the bed and crossed the distance between them, he would have done it. His fingers itched to wrap around Dallas Cameron's long, creamy throat. "Or did you forget, *I'm* the one stuck in this bed with a busted leg? *I'm* the one who can't walk!"

"How could I forget when you keep reminding me of it every chance you get?"

"That's only because you keep barging in here insisting I get up."

"Well, *someone* has to! Believe me, I'd just as soon it wasn't me, too. Unfortunately, that grim disposition of yours has scared everyone else away."

The muscle in Nick's cheek twitched. His eyes narrowed. "Who? Tell me one person I've scared off."

"Maria," Dallas snapped. "Or haven't you noticed that *I'm* the one who has been bringing your meals lately? She refuses to get anywhere near ever since you threw that tray at her. And then there's Hickory Pete. I don't know what you said to him last night, Nick, but he hasn't come within ten feet of the house all day."

The strength went out of Nick's arms. He collapsed back atop the bed, his mind echoing every word he'd said to the old coot. He also remembered every word the old coot had said—make that shouted—right back at him.

"We had a disagreement," he grumbled as sheepishly as he was about to grumble anything on a day as lousy as today was turning out to be. In other words, not very sheepishly at all.

"I'll just bet you did. Mind telling me what this 'disagreement' was about?"

"That damn crutch."

"I thought so." Dallas shook her head and sighed. "Don't tell me, let me guess. Pete wanted you to use the crutch, and you, stubborn to the end, flat out refused."

"Something like that." Nick shrugged and averted his gaze out the window—as much to look away from Dallas as to look away from the crutch dangling from her fingers. Damn that crutch! Every time he looked at that gnarled piece of wood, it seemed to be laughing at him. It reminded him too clearly of the things he'd used to do; and would never do again.

Unfortunately, the change of view didn't help. His insides still churned. He'd hoped venting his anger on

Dallas would make him feel better. It hadn't. If possible, he felt worse. Knowing Dallas was right didn't sit well.

Now that he thought about it, her face *was* the only one he'd seen all day. Pete had left in a huff last night, and hadn't come back. His last memory of Maria was seeing the large Mexican woman ducking to avoid the heavy tray he'd hurled at her graying head.

It hadn't occurred to Nick to miss either Maria or Pete. Until now. Until Dallas pointed their absences out to him.

Damn and double damn, what was happening to him? He'd never been that callous in his life.

Then again, he'd never been a cripple before.

"I want you out of that bed, Langston. Today." What Dallas didn't say, but what her no-nonsense tone implied, was that Nick no longer had a choice. She'd given him plenty of time to come to his senses. Now, she was making the decision for him. "You've been lying there wallowing in self-pity for two weeks. Don't you think that's long enough?"

"No," he growled, his anger flooding back, "as a matter of fact, I don't. Lesson number eight, Cameron. Ladies don't argue with men; they smile, nod, and *agree.*"

"Oh God, are we back to that again?"

He grinned coldly. "Aren't we always? That's what started this mess to begin with, isn't it? Well? *Isn't it?*" He gave an aggravated huff. "Fine, don't answer me. I'll answer myself. You know as well as I do that if you hadn't asked me to teach you how to be a lady—as if I ever *could!*—you wouldn't have gone on that picnic with Parker. And if you hadn't gone on that damn picnic . . ."

Nick didn't have to finish the sentence. She'd known this man all her life. She knew him well enough to know what he hadn't said.

Dallas came very close to throwing the crutch at his arrogant head. A surge of self-restraint stronger than she thought herself capable of possessing was the only thing that held her back. But the temptation was undeniably there. "You rotten son of a bitch! Don't you lay the blame for what happened to you on *my* head. Don't you dare!"

"Why not? If anyone's to blame, it's you. We both know it."

Dallas's eyes darkened with fury. *"I* know no such thing."

"Then you're a blind little fool."

"The hell I am."

"The hell you're not!"

She sucked in three rapid-fire breaths. They didn't help. If Nick was trying to make her mad, he'd succeeded. Dallas's head spun, her fist begging to knock that condescending grin right off his handsome face.

"What's the matter, darlin'?" Nick asked, his voice heavy with sarcasm. "The truth hurt?"

"Not half as much as your jaw's going to when my fist hits it," she answered through gritted teeth.

"Big words, Cameron . . . coming from across the room." One of the hands pillowed atop his waist came up. The tip of his index finger tapped the hard, bristle-coated line of the jaw in question. The challenge was enhanced by the cold glint in his eyes, and one slanted brow. The thick curl of mustache didn't conceal his broadening grin. "Give me your best punch."

"Don't tempt me."

"I'm not. I'm *daring* you. There's a difference." His chin lifted another notch. His grin widened still more.

Few people knew Dallas Cameron well enough to know she never backed down from a challenge—directly issued, or merely implied. Nick Langston was, of course, one of those people.

Her gaze narrowed, the brunt of her attention focused on his jaw. That whisker-shadowed expanse of carved bone and sun-kissed flesh looked mighty tempting; too tempting to resist.

And why should she resist? Didn't he deserve at least one good slap for accusing her of being the cause of his accident? He did. And he deserved at least a dozen more for the aggravation he'd caused her in the two weeks since.

Dallas had worn herself ragged caring for Nick when everyone else refused to. And she'd still had the same amount of daily chores to perform on top of it. Although she didn't regret taking care of him—he would have done the same for her—that wasn't the point. The least Nick could do was be grateful for all the inconvenience he'd put her through.

He wasn't, and Dallas resented that almost as much as she resented the fact that, if not for Nick, she'd be on that trail drive right now. If not for Nick, Lisa would still be at home, where she belonged. If not for Nick, Dallas would never have lost her temper and fired Rico.

All of those reasons and more crashed through her

mind, fueling her determination to slap him soundly.

Dallas took another step toward the bed. The skirt rustled around her legs, her boot heels clicked atop the bare planks. Her spurs clinked. The sounds combined, and wove themselves into the thready wisp of a memory. The sound of Nick Langston's voice was the only thing able to burn through the anger clouding her mind.

Lesson number three: Women dress like women, not like ranch hands.

Dallas came to an abrupt stop. A scowl puckered her brow. "I suppose ladies don't punch men."

It wasn't a question but a cold, hard statement of fact. "A real lady wouldn't. But, hell, don't let that stop you, darlin'."

"Oh, I won't," she said.

But it did.

With a quick glance, Dallas measured the distance between herself and the bed. Two steps. Only two small steps stood between her fist and Nick Langston's rock-hard jaw.

It might as well have been a mile.

Her spine stiffened. She glared down the length of her nose, her gaze meeting and clashing with his. "Are you going to get out of that bed, or am I going to have to force you?"

Nick's eyes narrowed. The sweep of thick gold lashes hooded the brilliant blue depths of his eyes beneath. "Force me, darlin'. Just keep in mind that I'm a lot bigger than you. And stronger. Unless you brought help, I ain't going nowhere I don't want to go."

Dallas's fingers flexed. Her grip on the crutch was so tight her knuckles ached. But she did *not* move forward. She refused. "If I had enough time, I'd make you eat those words, Langston."

Nick's shrug was negligent. "I don't know about you, but I've got all day." All day? Hell, he had his *entire life.* The nagging ache in his leg said he wouldn't be going anywhere for a long, long time.

Dallas balled her hands into unladylike fists, which she planted firmly on her hips as she continued to glared at him. "Well *I* don't. David promised to call on me this afternoon, and I want to be washed up and changed before he gets here."

Nick's eyes narrowed. There was a painful tightening inside of him that could have been attributed to the constant throbbing in his leg. Then again, the pain had mysteriously moved up to the region of his chest, so maybe it wasn't his leg after all. "Parker was here the day before yesterday, wasn't he?"

"Um-hmmm. And the day before that."

"You've been seeing a lot of him, haven't you?"

Dallas's eyes narrowed. Now, what was he trying to do? "I have. So much, in fact, that before the drive started Daddy ordered four new dresses for me to wear—just for the times when David pays a call."

A flash of rose and yellow calico snapped through Nick's mind. God, even now he could see this woman's body outlined to perfection beneath the clinging cloth. The color had accented her healthy tan complexion, and made her brown eyes dance.

Then his mind focused on the dress itself, and his gut kicked. While it hadn't been fancy by any means

287

. . . hell, he'd gone a week without tobacco to pay for the damn thing. It didn't sit well to realize that Ian could not only replace the garment, but buy four *new ones* whenever the mood struck.

Damnation!

Compared to the Camerons, Nick had always felt inferior. But never so much as he did right now.

"Well, ain't that dandy," Nick drawled as he thrust himself to a sitting position. He grabbed the pillow and pummeled it to softness with his fist, then jammed the lump of feather stuffing and linen behind the small of his back. "You never told me what Parker thinks about all the changes in you, Dallas. Or hasn't he noticed?"

He wasn't talking about the obvious, ladylike changes Dallas kept struggling to remember and put into effect. The changes those shimmering blue eyes of his hinted at were decidedly *un*ladylike.

A flush spread up from her neck, splashing over her cheeks in a wave of pink color. The memories Dallas had been avoiding for the last two weeks crashed over her like a tidal wave. Every minute, every second of her progression from girl into woman was remembered in a flash. As was every warm, virile detail of the man who'd taken her hand and led the way.

"Of course David's noticed," she said finally, her voice unnaturally high and weak. "He wouldn't be calling on me if he hadn't."

"Maybe." Nick shrugged and reached for the pouch of tobacco on the nightstand.

He seemed in no hurry to roll the cigarette. In fact, while his motions were smooth and fluid, they were also abnormally slow, as though he was trying to emphasize his next words. He needn't have bothered. They would have had the desired effect on Dallas even without the tension-riddled pause.

"Then again . . ." he continued, pausing to wet the paper with his tongue. The moist, pink tip made darting motions beneath the curl of his mustache. Dallas's stomach knotted. ". . . you never thought about marrying the man until someone put a bug in your ear about joining the two spreads together. Tell me something, Squirt. Didn't it ever occur to you that maybe someone put the same bug in Parker's ear?"

"That's ridiculous," she answered half-heartedly. Her eyes were glued to the place where Nick's tongue and the paper met. "A—and you're making it sound as though I'm marrying David because I want to. We both know that isn't true. I'm doing it because Papa ordered it."

"Marrying Parker? Ian ordered that . . . *exactly?*" He jammed the cigarette into the corner of his mouth, then reached over his head and scraped a match against the headboard. The tip burst into flame, charring the air with a vague, sulphury aroma.

"No. What Papa said was . . . Well, you already know what he said. I told you once. I'm not going to repeat it again now."

"You don't have to." Nick held the match to the tip of his cigarette, instinctively cupping his hand around the flame as though warding off a gust of wind. He inhaled deeply, until the tip glowed bright orange.

Dallas stopped breathing. She watched, mesmerized by the way his cheeks pulled inward with the small, sucking motions. His lips were pursed, cupped around the end of the cigarette. The fringe of his mustache tickled the still moist paper.

A drop of fire sizzled through her blood when she recalled in breathtaking detail how it felt when his warm, silky mouth had done the same thing to her breast.

Nick glanced up sharply when the crutch slipped from her slackened grasp and clattered noisily to the floor. Scowling, he watched Dallas stagger across the room and plop down hard in the chair beside the window.

He shook out the match and tossed it into the dish he'd been using as a makeshift ashtray. "You all right?"

"Just dandy," she whispered hoarsely, and could have bitten off her tongue. That was a Nick Langston phrase if ever she'd heard one. God, she was starting to think like him! That wasn't a good sign.

"You sure? You don't look dandy to me. In fact . . ." He exhaled a cloud of smoke and squinted at her through it.

The gesture emphasized the appealing creases shooting out from the corner of his blue, *blue* eyes. It was all Dallas could do not to groan.

"In fact what?" she asked, not sure she wanted to know the answer, but sure she would do anything, talk about anything, if it would distract her from the arousing images flickering through her head.

"You look flushed. And you're"—with effort, he forced his voice not to crack when his gaze slipped down—"breathing a'might hard." His eyes darkened as a wave of hot, erotic memories washed over him.

"Am I?" Dallas asked, and took a quick mental note of her body. Nick was right; her breaths *were* sawing in and out of her lungs in quick, erratic gulps. "Hmmm, I hadn't noticed. It must be . . . the heat. You may not have noticed it because you've been lying in bed all day, but today is unseasonably hot."

Liar, Nick thought, but didn't say. Why bother? The proof was no farther away than the window. Today was hot, sure, but no hotter than any other day this time of year. They both knew it. Just like they both knew the weather wasn't even *close* to the real reason behind Dallas's sudden breathlessness.

At least, not the dry, blistering heat caused by the sun. The kind caused by steamy, erotic memories, however . . . well, that was something else again.

Nick grinned. Between them, he figured their passionate lovemaking had generated enough smoldering memories to thaw out the Rockies in mid-February. And certainly enough heat to put that becoming flush in Dallas's cheeks.

Nick leaned to the side, tapping the ashes off the end of his cigarette and into the dish. His watchful gaze never left Dallas. "Sure you're all right?" he said with a smirk. "You don't look—"

"Dammit! I already told you, I'm just dand—*fine.* I'm *fine.*" She leaned her head back against the wall, closed her eyes. "Can we please get back to the reason I'm here?"

"No we can't get back to it."

Dallas sighed and opened her eyes. She turned her head to look at him. And gulped. Hard.

Nick was busy whisking a few stray ashes from the white linen sheet that covered him from the midchest down. He wasn't looking at her, and Dallas was grateful for that.

She'd noticed he wasn't wearing a shirt the second she'd entered the room. Only a dead woman wouldn't have. But only now did she really, *really* notice.

At this angle, his chest look incredibly broad. And firm. And . . . nice. Very nice. The mat of dark gold hair pelting his sun-kissed flesh looked curly and coarse and tempting beyond reason. Her fingers curled into instinctive fists as her gaze strayed from his sinewy shoulders, down a firm wedge of solid muscle, to where his taut stomach dipped beneath the sheet.

A shiver skated down Dallas's spine. The blood tingled in her veins. She swallowed hard, then dragged in a steadying breath. It was a mistake. The air in this portion of the room smelled seductively spicy and male. It smelled like Nick.

Dallas averted her gaze, and at the same time realized she was breathing funny again. There was no need to be told she was blushing this time; she could *feel* the heat rising in her cheeks.

"You'll have to get up eventually," she said suddenly. Her voice was only a little high, only a little shaky. "I mean, you can't very well stay in that bed for the rest of your life. Surely you wouldn't want to."

"Normally I'd agree," Nick replied. The steely edge in his tone made the words sound less than casual. "But not this time."

"And what makes this time different?" A trickle of apprehension made Dallas shiver. He didn't answer her right away. For a few seconds, she suspected he wasn't going to.

She turned to look at him. Her gaze slipped slowly up the length of his body, until it met with his. And held.

Curious brown locked hard with burning blue.

The noises outside receded until all Dallas could hear was the sound of her own heart drumming an erratic beat in her ears. And Nick. She heard a faint hiss when he exhaled a cloud of wispy gray smoke through his teeth. And she heard his next words much more clearly than she would have liked.

"This time," he drawled, "I'm in *your* bed, darlin'. Exactly where I want to be. And that makes a whole world of difference."

Was it possible for hearts to stop beating? It must be, because that's exactly what Dallas's heart did—a split second before it thudded to frantic life. Her breath locked in her lungs. She couldn't have spoken right then if she'd wanted to; not only didn't she have the breath, she didn't have the voice. Nick's words, and the husky way he'd uttered them, had made her throat go painfully tight and dry. Even the whimper that bubbled up inside of her couldn't have snuck through.

Nick lifted the cigarette to his lips and inhaled thoughtfully. The smoke cut into his lungs while he observed the effect his words had on Dallas. Her eyes were huge, her cheeks as pale as a freshly laundered sheet. Her breathing was quick and shallow. He watched her entwine her fingers in her lap, but it was too late. He'd already made note of their sudden trembling.

"What's the matter, Cameron? The truth hurt?" It gave Nick perverse pleasure to throw her own words up in her face.

"I—"

"Or don't you believe me?" He angled his head to the side, and regarded her levelly. "I've never lied to you in the past, Squi—" The muscle in his cheek jerked as he cut the childish endearment short. "No reason to think I'd start lying to you now."

And that, of course, was the problem. That was the sole reason behind Dallas's sudden tension.

She knew Nick Langston well. Knew that if he was nothing else, he was an honest man. He hadn't lied to her. And that frightened her senseless.

Her fingers brushed the corral dust from her skirt as she averted her gaze to the door. "I don't want to talk about this, Nick. I—"

Nick reached to the side and smashed the cigarette out in the dish. "Tough. Like it or not, we're *gonna* talk about it. Christ, lady, we *should've* talked about it over two weeks ago."

Dallas's head came around. Her brown eyes shot him daggers, testimony to her swiftly returning anger. "Why? What good will talking about it do? It won't change anything. All the words in the world couldn't . . ."

Nick leaned forward, his gaze intense. "What? What couldn't all the words in the world do? Tell me, damn you!"

The chair legs scraped against the floor when she pushed unsteadily to her feet. Her fingers were still gripped tightly in front of her as Dallas walked shakily toward the door.

"Running away isn't gonna change anything," he taunted from the bed. "You can run, but you can't hide. Not from memories like the ones we made together."

"Maybe." Chin high, Dallas continued walking. She didn't glance at Nick. She didn't dare. Her knees were weak enough as it was. One look at that handsome face of his and they would buckle out from under her.

"Definitely. You go ahead and walk out that door, darlin'. We both know I can't stop you." His tone lowered a steely pitch. "Just like we both know that sooner or later, no matter where you go, you're *gonna* remember what it felt like to—"

She took a few shaky steps. "Don't, Nick. Please, don't say it."

He continued as though she'd never interrupted him. "—lay naked and hot and willing in my arms." He paused only long enough to draw in a sharp, furious breath, then growled, *"My* arms, lady. *Not* David Parker's!"

The erotic memories Nick's words conjured up shot through Dallas's head, and rooted her feet to the floor. She closed her eyes tightly, trying to ignore the way her blood pumped in hot surges through her veins, the way her every nerve ending was alive with Nick Langston's all-knowing gaze.

But she couldn't. There was no ignoring the way his

295

words honed her already acute awareness of him. Nor could she ignore the wave of sensuous memories she'd been struggling for the past two weeks to forget; memories that . . . Dear God, even now they had the power to make her feel tingly and weak and vulnerable.

Vulnerable.

It suggested weakness and femininity; neither was a quality that Dallas respected. Her eyes snapped open. Somehow, she managed to force her quivering knees to carry her to the door. The knob felt cold when she gripped it in her trembling fist. Sheer willpower gave her the strength to swing the door wide.

She took a step across the threshold, but again Nick's voice shot out from behind her, stopping her short.

"Never took you for a coward, Cameron."

Seven simple words, that was all he said. But it was enough to make her indignation roil. Enough to make her spin around to face him. He was sitting in the same lazy position. Only his head was turned. And his blue eyes were drilling into her.

"Where have I heard those words before?"

He grinned and shrugged.

"In case you haven't noticed, I haven't changed. I'm still the same Dallas Louise Cameron I've always been."

Nick grimaced. "Not quite. Or did you forget—"

"Nothing. I've forgotten nothing. I know what we did that night. Dammit! Do you think I could *forget?* But there's one thing you ought to know, Nick. What happened between us meant"—she sucked in a fortifying breath to give credence to the lie—"absolutely nothing to me."

Nick's gaze narrowed to dangerous blue slits. The muscle in his cheek jerked angrily. Was it her imagination, or did the cords of muscles in his arms and chest flex, then pull tight?

"Nothing?" he asked. The single word sounded raw and biting.

"Nothing," she confirmed, surprised that her tone held up so well. It shouldn't have. Dallas hated to lie to Nick. Even though she knew the circumstances demanded deception—she *couldn't* risk telling him the truth—the lie still tasted bitter on her tongue.

"Well, then . . . if that's the case, I don't expect you'll mind proving that out to me. Would you, darlin'?" The mattress crunched when Nick pushed himself up straighter. The sheet, intentionally or not, slipped down.

Large brown eyes automatically tracked the splash of white linen. Belatedly, Dallas realized it for the mistake it was.

The sheet was now puddled daringly low on Nick's taut, sun-bronzed belly. "I b-beg your pardon?" she breathed, and leaned back heavily against the door frame.

"You heard me, darlin'. I said prove it."

Nick's open palm slapped the narrow stretch of mattress beside his hip. Dallas paid little attention to the palm, her gaze snagged on the lean stretch of hip outlined beneath the sheet. Try though she did, she couldn't seem to tear her gaze away. "H-how would you suggest I do that?"

He shrugged. Only the muscle ticking in his cheek said the gesture wasn't as casual as it was meant to appear. "Come over here and kiss me. That should be proof enough that what happened between us didn't mean squat to you."

Dallas's breath hitched in her throat. It was all she could do to push her next words off her suddenly dry tongue. Even to her own ears, her response sounded weak and breathless. "And if I refuse?"

Nick grinned. The gesture didn't reach his eyes—cold blue and piercing, studying her intently. "Then you'll prove you ain't only a coward, you're a liar to boot."

He was goading her, of course. Nick knew her well enough to know how to challenge her into doing something Dallas knew damn well she shouldn't do. And yet . . .

He'd backed her into a corner. Worse, the glint in his eyes said he knew it, and that the knowledge pleased him tremendously.

Although Dallas would have loved to be furious with him, she couldn't find an ounce of anger to cling to. The threat of kissing him allowed only one sort of heat to seep into her blood; the slow, simmering kind that burned a body up from the inside out, that seduced a woman into doing things she'd be smarter not thinking about, let alone acting upon.

Her attention wavered between Nick and the door. When it came right down to it, she had only two options. She could waltz over there and kiss Nick—and prove what they both already knew; that she melted like butter under a hot summer sun the second his mouth closed over hers. Or she could walk out that door and *not* kiss him—and prove an even greater truth; that she was terrified to go near Nick again for fear he'd see how very much his touch—his kiss, his hot, smoldering caresses—affected her.

Either way, she was lost.

Nick was going to know the truth no matter what she did—or didn't—do.

Dallas shifted, her gaze straying past the open door. The stack of a dozen or so heavy ledgers she'd lugged upstairs with her were in the same spot where she'd left them, stacked in the hallway beside her bedroom door.

Her gaze locked onto the large, leather-bound volumes. The twitch of a relieved smile tugged at her lips. Maybe, just maybe she could take Nick's mind off of kissing her, and put his thoughts back where they belonged; on his imminent recovery.

The spurs attached to the heel of her boots chinked as she walked determinedly out the door.

From behind, she heard Nick grumble, "Little coward."

"Coward is it?" she grumbled under her breath as she squatted and began piling the bulky ledger books in her arms. "We'll just see who's the coward between us, Mister-I'll-Never-Walk-Again."

The ledgers were heavy. Dallas's arm muscles ached a protest as she pushed awkwardly to her feet and returned to her bedroom. Balancing the stack beneath her chin, she approached the bed.

Nick was eyeing her warily. "What the—!"

Dallas didn't give him time to say more. Nick was laying on the bed now, his dark head cushioned by her

299

pillow. She dropped the stack of books on him—aiming them toward his chest and stomach, and not his wounded leg. A whoosh of air rushed raggedly from his lungs at the collision. The sound was music to Dallas's ears.

Backing up a few steps so that he couldn't reach her without getting out of bed she surveyed her handiwork.

Nick glared up at her. He looked stunned. And more than a little furious.

Dallas grinned. "You want to stay in that bed for the rest of your life? Fine by me. However, I for one think it's past time you started earning your keep on this ranch . . . the same way everyone else does." She leaned forward, her eyes narrow and intent. "In other words, Langston, as long as you're on Bar None property, and drawing Bar None pay, you'll damn well make yourself useful." She jerked her chin toward the ledgers she'd toppled over him. "Well, don't just lay there. *Work.*"

Spinning on her heel, she stalked toward the door. On her way, Dallas paused only long enough to snatch up the crutch and toss it atop the bed near Nick's feet. The grin never wavered from her lips.

She was halfway down the hall when she heard Nick's first angry bellow.

"What the hell do you expect me to do with these, Cameron?"

She didn't break stride. "Fix them!"

"How? I don't know anything about keeping books."

"Learn. When you're done with those, let me know.

I have at least two dozen more just like those waiting for you in Papa's study."

The feral growl that emanated from her bedroom made Dallas pause at the top of the stairs. Her gaze drifted over her shoulder, fixing on the open door.

The angle didn't allow her to see Nick. Then again, she didn't have to. Dallas knew the muscle in his cheek would be ticking, and could picture with perfect clarity the murderous glint in his indigo blue eyes. It wouldn't surprise her if he had one of those big ledgers fisted in his big, calloused hand, ready to throw it at her head if she were stupid enough to peek in at him.

Nick did have a ledger poised in his grip. And he was ready to pitch it at her the second she stepped through the door.

Instead, Nick heard her retreating boot heels click atop the planked stairs. The sound combined with the increasingly distant chink of spurs.

Nick threw the ledger at the door. The force of the collision slammed the door closed with a resounding crash. Papers crinkled as the leather-bound covers opened, and the book fell to the floor.

As he glared at the offensive book, Nick could have sworn he heard a familiar, husky chuckle emanate from another portion of the house. Oh, how that rankled!

"Damn that woman to hell and back!" he growled beneath his breath. Sitting up fully, he swiped the remaining ledgers from the bed with his fist. They thunked to the floor.

As far as he was concerned, Dallas had no right to demand that he work on the ledgers. No right at all.

Wrong, Langston. As Ian Cameron's daughter, she has every right in the world to insist you earn your keep.

A dark scowl puckered his brow as he sat back hard against the pillow and reached for the leather pouch on the nightstand. Even as his fingers closed over it, his gaze drifted to the ledger he'd thrown. It had opened on impact with the door, and now lay face down on the floor.

Nick rolled a smoke from memory, his furious gaze never leaving the ledger. It took three matches to light the cigarette; his angry, jerky motions snapped the first two.

Inhaling the burning smoke, he leaned his head back against the headboard and fixed his glare on the ceiling.

He wouldn't do the ledgers. No, goddamn it, he would *not!* His job as foreman was grueling and varied, nine times out of ten carried out on the back of a horse. He'd never had anything to do with the financial end of the ranch. Christ, he didn't even know what the financial end of the ranch consisted of. Had never *cared* to know.

He took another fiery inhalation off the cigarette, exhaled a thick cloud of smoke through tightly gritted teeth, then inhaled again. The process was repeated until he got dizzy and couldn't breathe. He smashed the cigarette out on the dish.

He had to do something. If Dallas had been right about nothing else, she was right about that. His leg wasn't hurting him so much these days. The splint that encased him from midthigh to midshin cushioned the healing wound and made sure any unexpected movements kept the pain to a minimum. And, like she'd said, it was past time he started earning his keep again—at least until he could find out what a cripple could do to support himself.

But working ledgers?

Damnation!

That was a sissy job if ever there was one. Oh, sure, it was necessary—on a ranch this size, *someone* had to do it!—but it was a job usually reserved for a no-good pansy. A man too soft to earn his livelihood riding the range.

A man . . . like David Parker.

Oh yeah, Parker'd be *perfect* for the job. But not a man like Nick Langston. The inactivity involved in pushing a pen would likely kill someone who instead thrived on pulling long, hard hours in a saddle. Just the thought of sitting in front of ledger books, pen in hand, back hunched over a desk, made Nick wince. A bad case of saddle sores would have been preferable.

But what else could a cripple do?

Not a whole hell of a lot, as far as he could see.

If he wanted to earn his keep—*wanted? Hell, he* needed *to do it; his pride* demanded *it!*—then he'd better start considering a menial task that didn't involve horses or longhorns, fresh air or sunshine. He'd better start giving serious thought to those ledgers, is what he'd better do.

Before the drive started Papa ordered four new dresses for me to wear—just for the times when David pays a call.

Nick gritted his teeth together, and his gaze unconsciously swung to the ledger book lying open near the door. The one that was marked *Household Accounts* in Lisa's dainty, swirled handwriting.

His eyes narrowed in speculation.

How *did* Ian afford to buy four new dresses at the drop of a hat? Was the Bar None earning that much? Oh, he knew the ranch turned a profit, but he'd never really been concerned with how big the profit was. So long as his monthly wages came to him on time, he'd always been satisfied.

Nick was the Bar None's foreman. He ran things, saw that everything went as smoothly as possible. He handled problems with the herd, the drives, roundups and branding. He also settled minor disputes between the hired hands on the few occasions one cropped up.

Ian, on the other hand, was the ranch's owner. He took care of the ledgers and anything else that had to do with the business end of things. Ian was the one who decided where the cattle should be driven, and arranged the selling.

Though the two men discussed bad or good years, the details of both ends of the business were left to the one in charge of it. Both had faith in the other's abilities.

It stood to reason, then, that when two properties bordering the ranch had become available a few years back, Nick had never questioned how Ian had come by the money to purchase the deeds. Nor had he wondered how, not one to put stock in credit, Ian had paid for them in cash.

Only now did Nick wonder how Ian had done it. How, when so many other ranches depended on credit for survival, Ian Cameron had *always* managed to do his business transactions in cold, hard cash.

And, most of all, Nick wanted to know how the hell the man could afford to buy his daughter four brand new dresses in a blink! *That* was what Nick really wanted to know.

A surge of curiosity prompted Nick to push away from the pillow and ease his long legs awkwardly over the side of the bed. The splint made his left leg stick out parallel to the floor, but he managed to work around that and collect the ledgers he'd sent careening to the floor. He stacked the big, rectangular books on the bed next to him.

All of them, that is, except the one near the door. The one labeled *Household Accounts*. The one he really wanted to see.

The one he couldn't reach.

His open palm smacked the top ledger of the stack. The mattress shook with the blow. The crutch, which had been precariously balanced on the edge of the bed, clattered to the floor.

Nick frowned. His gaze automatically tracked the gnarled piece of wood.

"Goddamn woman probably planned this," he grumbled, and reached for the crutch. He had to stretch and twist, since the contraption had fallen almost out of his reach, but eventually he managed to retrieve it.

The unaccustomed activity surprised his body, which had lain dormant for two weeks. While he hadn't gone soft by any means, Nick was definitely weak. By the time he had the crutch in his hands and had straightened, the muscles in his arms and back ached, and he was out of breath.

Gritting his teeth against the ache in his left leg, Nick wedged the padded top of the crutch beneath his left armpit, and pushed to his feet. All of his weight was on his right leg, since his left leg had taken to throbbing painfully just from the change in position. Every surge of blood pumping through his leg was felt all the way down to the bone.

His brow beaded with sweat. He almost fell over, but quickly grabbed the very top part of the crutch before both he and it could careen to the floor. His fingers wrapped around the wood in a white-knuckled fist. He scowled when he felt grooves bite into his palm where the wood should have been smooth.

Once the dizziness had passed, and the pain in his leg had receded a bit, Nick sat back heavily on the bed and held the crutch up in front of him. There, an inch below where the two pieces of wood were joined, Hickory Pete had whittled a horse and rider. Beneath that, Nick's name had been etched into the wood—spelled the way Pete always spelled it: NEK

"Loony old coot," he muttered, while fondly tracing the perfect carving with the tip of his index finger.

Then his gaze focused on the ledger, and his mind flashed him a picture of four new dresses . . . on Dallas's tempting little body.

Did she look like a lady when she wore them, he wondered. Did she pile all that silky, tawny hair up in the alluring way she had the day of her picnic with Parker?

Nick closed his eyes, and rolled his lips inward to

stifle a groan. His gut kicked when he remembered in detail how she'd looked that day.

Her hair was gathered in a twist just loose enough to make it look as though the silky strands had been mussed by a lover's hand. Wispy curls bounced against her brow and cheeks, and something about the style had made her brown eyes look huge. And hungry.

Though he'd seen her look that way only once, the sight was memorable. Burned into his mind. Nick loved it when she wore her hair that way. It was so . . . *un*Dallaslike. So . . . soft and feminine and alluring.

The bodices of the four new dresses Ian had bought her probably wouldn't fit Dallas as snugly as the calico frock he'd provided her with. But Nick figured that would be all right, too. Just so long as the cloth cupped the generous swells of her breasts, hinted at the lush fullness it concealed while emphasizing a waist he now knew damn well his hands could span without stretching. So long as the hems whispered around her long, shapely legs, and made that seductive, rustling sound when she walked. So long as . . .

Spurs.

Nick opened his eyes and grinned. Knowing Dallas the way he did, he was pretty sure that no matter how fancy the dresses were which her daddy had bought, she'd wear her boots and spurs beneath them. And she'd slice up the fancy fabric with the spiky rowels in no time.

The thought pleased Nick immensely as, with a grunt, he shoved the crutch under his arm and pushed clumsily to his feet. His gaze was again fixed on the ledger book, and this time his blue eyes were bright with determination.

He wanted to know how Ian Cameron could afford so much. How the man who'd come to Texas twenty years ago with only fifty greenbacks in his pocket had managed to make such a name for himself.

And he wanted to learn all this information first-hand—in a way that would show him how a man like Nick Langston, a dirt-poor cowpuncher and cripple to boot, might be able to apply some of those same smarts into being able to afford those things, too. Someday.

Chapter Thirteen

"What the hell do you think you're doing?" Nick roared, at the same time ripping the bottle out of Dallas's hand.

He was towering by the side of Lisa's bed, standing with the aid of the crutch shoved under his left arm. In the soft flicker of lamplight, his blue eyes looked narrow, and dangerously bright.

Pity Dallas was in no mood to let his anger affect her. She rearranged the nightgown around her legs, then settled against the lacy pillows tucked behind her back. She returned his icy-blue glare measure for furious measure. "What am *I* doing? What are *you* doing? Langston, for a man who was never going to walk again this afternoon, you're sure doing a fine job of it tonight!"

Her tawny brows arched. Angling her head, Dallas's gaze dipped, raking him. She regretted the impulse instantly. When their gazes again collided, her cheeks were a hot shade of pink. The warm color had nothing to do with anger. Rather, it was caused by what Nick was—make that *wasn't*—wearing.

His only covering was a dingy union suit, cut away high on his left thigh to make room for the cumbersome split. Though the light flannel covered him from broad shoulders to tapered ankles, it didn't cover nearly enough. Instead, the thin cloth molded and shaped, defined and outlined, cupping and emphasizing his—

Nick lifted the bottle to his nose and sniffed. He winced when the fumes made his eyes water. From the smell of it, this wasn't any bottle of old whiskey. Hell, no. This was a bottle of Ian Cameron's finest. It would seem that when little Dallas Cameron set her sights on getting drunk, she did it in style.

He glared down at her. "I don't believe this. Whiskey? You're drinking whiskey? *You?*"

"Stating the blatantly obvious, ain't ya, Langston?" she said nastily.

"Watch your mouth, brat, or I'll take you over my knee and . . ." Nick didn't finish the thought—with either his mind or his mouth.

Lifting the bottle to his lips, he downed two fiery slugs, holding Dallas's gaze the entire time. The liquor burned a raw path down his throat, then settled in a sizzling pool in his gut.

Dallas crossed her arms over her stomach, and rested her head against the headboard. "You know, Langston, in all the years I've been hearing that threat, I can't remember a single time you doled out the punishment."

"Yet," Nick growled, then downed another slug. He

310

wiped off his mouth on the back of his hand, exhaling a half gasp/half sigh. The whiskey was twice as smooth as the firewater he was used to.

Dallas stared up at him. "Can I have my bottle back now?"

"Nope. From the looks of it, you've had enough."

"Enough? I haven't had *any!*"

"I know. That's what I meant."

"It's my bottle, Nick," Dallas snapped through gritted teeth. "You have no right to take it away from me."

Nick waved the bottle in question at her, but not close enough so Dallas could grab it. "Wrong. This bottle belongs to your *daddy*. And because he ain't here, I have every right in the world to stop you from making an ass out of yourself." His blue eyes narrowed. "And speaking of your daddy . . . what do you think Ian'd say if he knew you were sitting in your sister's bed trying to get drunk?"

"Damned if I know," she grumbled, then added tersely, "and damned if I care. Right now, all I want is to get my bottle back."

"Ain't that a damn shame. Hate to tell you this, Cameron, but since your daddy ain't here to watch over you, the responsibility falls to me. Don't think for one minute that I'll just sit idly by and watch you get three sheets to the wind, because I won't."

"It's not your decision."

"It is for as long as I'm the one holding this bottle, and don't you forget it."

Dallas's anger had been simmering just below the

surface all day. It only took Nick's persistent obstinacy to goad her over the edge.

Flattening her palms atop Lisa's frilly bedspread, she shoved herself up until she was kneeling on the bed. Dallas wasn't on eye level with Nick but she was close enough to give him a good smack, should she so desire.

But her gaze had snagged on the crutch, and on Nick's hand. His knuckles were white from strain. He seemed to sway a little, but Dallas wasn't sure if that was an illusion caused by the flickering lamplight. One thing she *was* sure of: his cheeks were chalky, and his lips were edged blue and tightly compressed.

She glared up at him. "Why'd you come here, Nick? To prove you can walk, or to faint at my feet?"

Dallas's eyes widened when he looked like he was about to do the latter. Concern rushed in to replace anger. In a flash, she measured how much time it would take her to scramble off the bed and catch him if he fell. Well, maybe not catch him, but at least ease his big body to the bed or floor, whichever was closest. The distance was too much, the chance too risky. She decided it would be quicker to play on his inborn sense of responsibility, and goad him into not fainting.

"I'm warning you, Langston," Dallas barked in a voice that had made more than one cowpuncher cringe respectfully in the past, "you faint now, and that bottle's mine. I'll have it out of your hand before you hit the floor."

As expected, that snapped Nick's eyes open—and added a steely blaze to them. The crutch tapped against the floor when he swayed, then staggered toward the bed.

Dallas lurched to the side, her arms outstretched. She tensed, ready to spring into motion, prepared to shove Nick toward the bed should his momentum somehow propel him away from it. Failing that, she was ready to use her own body to cushion his fall.

The crutch clattered to the floor. The mattress dipped under the onslaught of his weight.

Dallas hadn't expected that. One second she was kneeling precariously on the bed, the next her world tipped, and she lurched to the side.

Before she could catch her balance, she was flung face first over Nick Langston.

She lay completely still, hoping her fall hadn't hurt him, yet at the same time afraid to ask and find out. Perhaps if she waited for him to say something . . . ?

When he didn't, she began to wonder if Nick had indeed fainted. No, she didn't think so. Beneath her stomach, she felt his breath sough in and out of his lungs; swift and erratic. His heart throbbed against her lowest rib. Did an unconscious man's heart pound that fast and hard? She had no idea.

Then Dallas felt a tremor ripple through the hard muscle beneath her, and she felt . . .

Dallas closed her eyes. She caught her lower lip between her teeth and bit down to stifle a groan. It was either that, or surrender to the urge to look back and see exactly how much of her legs were exposed.

A warm draft—uh-oh, that was no draft, it was *Nick Langston's breath!*—wafted over the backs of her legs. Very high up, from the feel of it. The fall, she realized numbly, had shoved the hem of her night-gown indecently high.

"Are you all right?" she asked weakly, and winced at the high, squeaky sound of her voice. *Please, God let him be unconscious! And if not unconscious, then at least—*

"Dandy," he grumbled. "Just . . . dandy. And your-self?"

Nick's voice sounded hoarse. Dallas barely noticed. His answer had sent another hot blast of breath over her abruptly hotter skin. Her blood sizzled, pumping frantically in her veins, pounding in her ears. She wasn't trembling—yet—but that was only because she was utilizing sheer force of will. She *was* breathing funny, however, and her skin felt . . . Oh God, she was tingling again.

She felt him tense, felt him lift up, felt his gaze drilling into the back of her head. The muscles in his stomach pulled taut, they felt like a chunk of molded steel beneath her. *So much for not trembling!* she thought, as a shudder of awareness wracked through her.

"Dallas!"

"What!"

"I asked if you were all right."

Dallas longed to say she was great, fantastic, just "dandy," but she couldn't. This was Nick Langston she was sprawled over, after all. Lying to him didn't come naturally, it had to be strategically planned in advance. Right now, she was beyond strategically planning *anything*.

"Well?" he prodded. "Are you or ain't you?"

She sighed. Her entire body melted atop him. The frilly bedspread felt soft beneath her cheek—quite the opposite of the hard, rugged body pinned beneath her. "No, Nick, now that you mention it, I don't think I am. In fact, I think I'm decidedly *un*dandy."

"Damnation. How much of this did you drink?"

"I already told you. None," Dallas repeated, and wished she'd drank half the bottle. After what had happened this afternoon, God knows she could use one! Also, having had a drink could easily have explained why she abruptly felt so light-headed and dizzy and . . . sensitive. Yes, her entire body felt sensitive. Her every nerve ending felt alive, in tune to each inch of rigid muscle and hot flesh touching her.

"You ain't gonna be sick, are you? Lisa had to beg your daddy for six months to buy this bedspread. She'll kill you with her bare hands if you get sick on it."

Dallas wisely kept her opinions on Lisa's frilly, impractical belongings to herself. "No, I'm not going to be sick," she said. What she didn't say was that there was a very real possibility *she* might faint—if only from pure sensation. The pleasure of feeling so many hard male contours, blanketed by her own soft, feminine curves, was truly too good a feeling for any woman to be expected to live through.

Feminine. Oh, God, there was that word again. Perhaps she was going to be ill after all?

"I think you'd better get off me. I can't breathe."

"I'm not that heavy," she replied shakily.

It took Nick a second to respond. When he did, his

315

voice was low and husky. "I know. Unfortunately, that ain't the problem."

"Then what—?" The words withered on Dallas's tongue.

What was the problem? Did she really have to ask? Maybe a few weeks ago she wouldn't have recognized sexual changes in a man's body, but she wasn't that innocent anymore. She not only recognized the physical changes in Nick, she felt them.

The left side of her waist grazed the front of his hips. Her breath caught when she detected a certain firmness there. The curved tip of him felt warm, pulsating and hard. Her nightgown and the flannel union suit offered no barrier. Nor did the cloth absorb the intense heat radiating from that portion of Nick's body. But Dallas's side did.

She felt a sharp, reciprocal heat fire through her.

With arms that felt liquid and weak, Dallas lifted up until her body was bowed over his. Her head turned, her gaze automatically sought his face.

The flickering orange lamplight danced over his features, angling the already hard lines of his cheeks and jaw. A jaw, she noticed dazedly, that had very recently been scraped clean of its stubble. The lips almost hidden beneath the downward curl of his mustache were tightly compressed. From pain? No, Dallas doubted it.

She watched the index finger and thumb of his right hand scour the eyelids he'd pinched tightly closed. The muscle in his cheek ticked furiously. In a nick of time, she checked an impossibly strong urge to smooth the worried creases from his weathered brow.

Swallowing hard, Dallas averted her gaze. Her attention fixed on the bottle of whiskey fisted in Nick's outstretched left hand. How he'd managed to hold onto it through all of that, and not spill a drop, was beyond her.

Before she could change her mind, she pushed herself away from him. She smoothed the skirt of her nightgown primly around her legs, then grabbed the bottle. His fingers tightened, but the reflexive gesture came a split second too late.

The glass felt smooth in her palm, still warm from Nick's hand. Dallas's fingers trembled when she lifted the bottle to her nose and sniffed. The fumes alone were enough to make her gag!

"If you've gotta drink, darlin', at least do it right."

Like a chunk of steel being dragged to a compelling magnet, Nick's husky tone snagged Dallas's gaze. She lowered the bottle and glanced at him, only to find his indigo eyes studying her intently. "You mean there's a 'right' way to get . . . what did you call it?"

"Three sheets to the wind. And no, there ain't no right way. Well, not exactly. But what you're doing is definitely wrong."

Her tawny brows arched, and her eyes flashed curiously. "And what am I doing?"

"Smelling it. Christ, anyone who'd smell that stuff and still drink it can't be all there. Just put the bottle to your"—he swallowed hard—"lips, hold your breath, and drink."

"That's all there is to it?"

"Yup."

It sounded easy enough, Dallas thought. Doing it was another matter. And not only because the thought of *drinking* the horrible smelling stuff was so repulsive, but because the ability to swallow had abandoned her the second her gaze had clashed with Nick's.

The hot glint in his eyes—combined with the way it made her heart stutter and her stomach churn—was what finally prompted Dallas to lift the bottle to her lips. Her gaze met his as she tilted it back, sucking in a bitter-tasting mouthful.

Goddamn, that hurt!

The whiskey flamed in her mouth. Dallas squinted against the sudden tears in her eyes. Grimacing, she forced herself to swallow—and wished she'd spit instead. She felt every raw inch of the burning path the liquor cut from the back of her throat to her stomach. Once it had settled, she wheezed in three choking breaths. It didn't help. The fumes had set her lungs on fire. If she could have coughed she would have. As it was, she was afraid her lungs would explode if she tried.

"I can't . . . believe . . . you drink this . . . stuff," she wheezed hoarsely. "It's awful."

"Nah. It's an acquired taste. Take a few more swigs, you'll see what I mean."

"One sip is more than enough, thanks. Here." As she'd seen Nick do, Dallas wiped her mouth on the back of her hand, then passed him the bottle.

The mattress dipped and swayed when Nick rolled carefully to his side. Propping himself up on one elbow, he reached for the bottle.

They were both careful to make sure their hands did not touch.

Nick swirled the amber liquid around, but didn't

drink any more. He remembered too clearly what had happened the last time he'd gotten drunk.

Dallas tucked her legs beneath her, closed her eyes, and leaned back against the pillow. Her breathing was still strained and choppy, and her throat still felt as though it had been scraped raw, but at least the burn had faded. The whiskey, she noticed absently, had gathered in a radiant puddle in her stomach. Her arms and legs felt cool, and unusually light.

"I take it things didn't go well with Parker?"

Dallas cracked one eye open, and glanced at him. Nick wasn't looking at her. Instead, he seemed fascinated with the way the whiskey slickened the inside of the glass. "Actually, things went very well."

"Then he isn't the reason you're drinking?"

Both of Dallas's eyes opened then, though not all the way. "He's part of the reason."

Nick glanced up. Their gazes locked for a full minute before he again looked down at the bottle. "And the other part?"

"You." Though he didn't move a muscle, Dallas felt Nick's sudden tension. It mingled with the heat twisting through her; artificial heat from the whiskey, and natural heat emanating from the man laying much too close to her legs. "I'm . . . confused is all. I thought maybe getting drunk would make me see things clearer."

His shrug was tight and strained. He didn't glance up, but kept his blue eyes fixed on the bottle, and the whiskey he was now swirling in jerky, erratic motions. "It won't. All drinking's likely to do is make you sick as a dog come morning. It rarely solves problems."

Dallas leaned forward, pillowing her elbows on her thighs. "Then why were you drinking, Nick? I've wondered about it a lot, you know."

"No, I didn't know." His pause was tense, his expression hard. He didn't look pleased to hear that she'd thought of that night often in the last two weeks—the same way he had. "I was drinking to forget," he added tersely.

"And did you?"

Nick gave a short, derisive chuckle before shaking his head. "Nope."

Dallas's gaze dipped, and fixed on the bottle Nick had set atop the bed. No, that wasn't entirely true. She did look at the bottle, but only for a second. She looked at the strong hand holding it steady for much longer. "What were you trying to forget, Nick?"

His gaze slipped to hers. He took three long, slow breaths before answering her. "You."

Dallas leaned closer. "Wh-what about me?"

Nick shifted, and lifted the bottle to his lips. He must have changed his mind, for he scowled and didn't drink any. With a muffled curse, he thrust the bottle at her. Dallas took the bottle and set it on the bedside table.

The mattress trembled as Nick dragged his body up higher, so that he was now laying across the bed with just his bare feet hanging off the edge. His gaze never left her when he lifted his hand. She felt the heat of his index finger before she felt the calloused tip trace the delicate line of her jaw.

One of them shivered.

"What were you trying to forget about me, Nick?" she asked again.

He sighed. "Everything. Like how nice you look in a pair of boy's pants. And how pretty and grown up you look in a dress. Mostly, though . . . mostly I was trying to forget how it felt to kiss you." His gaze slid to her lips, his voice lowered a husky pitch. "Like I said, it didn't work. I can't forget."

"Neither can I," she murmured hoarsely.

Nick stroked her sensitive earlobe between his index finger and thumb. Dallas shivered. Her eyelids thickened, her chin tipped up. His caress drifted downward, fluttering against her jaw. Then he slipped his fingers around the side of her neck. She sucked in a sharp breath when she felt her pulse hammer against the heel of his calloused palm. He fingered the delicate tawny wisps curling beneath her tightly woven braid.

She trembled, and Nick's fingers stilled, cupping her neck. He didn't exert pressure, didn't draw her closer. He didn't have to. Dallas leaned forward of her own accord.

"I've been telling myself for the last two weeks that your skin couldn't possibly have felt as soft as I remembered," he admitted thickly. "That the whiskey I'd drunk had fuddled my mind, and only made me *think* you felt like silk. Christ, but was I ever wrong."

"My skin doesn't feel like silk?" she asked breathlessly.

He shook his head. "It feels better."

Nick's fingers flexed as his gaze delved into her very soul. For a second Dallas thought he was going to push her away. He looked as though he wanted to leave, but couldn't quite bring himself to do it.

Dallas swallowed hard, and wondered how she would stop him if he did try to go. How could she get him to stay? And, more importantly, how could she convince him to kiss her again, and prove that what *she'd* been telling herself for the past two weeks hadn't been true. That his kisses weren't magical. That his touch was not as earth-shatteringly wonderful as she so clearly remembered.

She wrapped her fingers around his sinewy forearm, just to assure herself he wouldn't stop touching her. The skin beneath his sleeve felt hot and tense. Her gaze dipped, and fixed on the powerful chest outlined to perfection beneath the clinging gray flannel.

"I like it when you touch me, Nick," she said softly, feeling his hand tremor against her neck. "It makes my blood tingle and my breasts—"

"Ah, hell." Nick's tone was too gritty for the words to have their proper impact. He opened his mouth once, twice, as though he was going to say something but changed his mind at the last minute. Finally, he said, "Do you have any idea what it does to me to hear you say that?"

Dallas shook her head, making the thick tawny braid draped over her shoulder bounce against her breasts. She didn't miss the way Nick's gaze tracked the movement, or the way his eyes darkened hungrily. "Tell me what it does to you, Nick. Please."

His hand drifted down, hooking over her shoulder. His grip was tight, his strong fingers tunneling into the tender flesh beneath her nightgown. "It ties my gut up in knots, Dallas," he answered huskily. "It . . . Christ! It makes me want to kiss you so damn hard, to crush you beneath me, to touch you and to . . . well, to do things I ain't got no damn right doing to Ian Cameron's daughter. *That's* what it does to me."

"And that's bad?"

"Damn straight it is!"

Dallas nodded, and would have argued, but she couldn't. It was difficult to talk around the sudden lump of joy wedged in her throat. It was even more difficult to breathe. Nick's admission sizzled through her, igniting a reaction that was almost but not quite comparable to having his roughened palms stroking her flesh.

Holding his tormented gaze ensnared, Dallas moved her hand, stroking a slow path up his arm. Her fingertips worshiped the thick muscles beneath his sleeve, the ones that bunched to steely cords beneath her touch. Leaning forward, she breached his shoulder, cupped his thick neck, then opened her fingers and plowed them into his thick golden hair. Lord, he felt good!

Nick tensed, and reached up to encircle her wrist in a bracelet of loose, calloused fingers. "What the hell do you think you're doing?"

"Touching you." He tipped one golden brow, prompting Dallas to explain. "You said you had no right to touch me. You didn't say I couldn't touch you."

Nick closed his eyes and sucked in a shaky breath. When his lashes flickered up again, his gaze was determinedly dark. "I didn't think I had to. You know as

well as I do that your daddy would kill you for wanting to touch *any* man who ain't your husband. Just
like he'll kill any man stupid enough to . . . well, stupid
enough to be thinking the things I am right now."

"You didn't care about what Papa thought two
weeks ago."

"I did care. Only I was drunk. So drunk I couldn't
think straight. If I hadn't been, maybe I would have
realized what the hell I was doing—*who* I was doing it
with—and put a stop to it."

"And now?" Dallas asked as her hand slipped from
the circle of his fingers. Her palm cupped his cheek.
The corner of his mustache tickled her skin, and made
her pulse hammer.

"I'm only *wishing* I was drunk," he admitted huskily
and tugged her toward him. "Maybe then I'd forget
about that kiss you owe me from this afternoon." He
eased her closer another inch. Another. Their gazes
met, and Dallas saw that the blue depths of his eyes
were still shimmering with determination, but in a
different way. "You remember that kiss, don't you,
Dallas? As I recall, it was supposed to prove that what
happened between us didn't mean squat to you . . .
before you turned chicken and ran out."

"I didn't—"

Nick shook his head, and lifted up higher on his
elbow. His lips mere inches away. His spicy, soapy
scent wrapped around Dallas like a warm, familiar
blanket.

"Here's your chance," he said, his words a hot blast
of whiskey-soaked air on her face. "Kiss me, darlin'.
Prove how much I don't affect you."

Nick yanked Dallas forward. Her head was tipped, her lips parted in hungry anticipation of his kiss.

With a growl, Nick slanted his mouth over hers.

His kiss was hard and punishing, demanding and possessive. He cupped the back of Dallas's head, pressing her close as he rolled onto his back, dragging her with him. A spasm of pain jolted through his left leg when she twisted. He tightened his grip, thinking she was trying to fight him.

Only Dallas wasn't fighting him at all. Just the opposite, she was rearranging her position, meshing her tempting curves to the hard angles of his chest.

They met chest to chest, hip to hip, thigh to thigh. Nick felt each ripe inch of her breasts crushed against him. Her body heat burned through the cotton, through the flannel, and branded the hard muscle and flesh beneath.

His right hand flattened over the small of her back, then drifted lower. Her nightgown felt thin and smooth, her skin hot and firm under the negligible barrier of cloth.

His fingers curled inward. He roughly kneaded the rounded flesh, arching his hips up while pulling her closer to the rigid source of heat she'd sparked within him. He guided her hips, rubbing her against him in hard, then soft, then hard again strokes.

Nick felt Dallas shiver, and captured her pleasured groan with his mouth. He turned her response to his advantage by parting her lips with his tongue and plunging hungrily inside.

Her hips picked up the tempo his hands inspired, even as her tongue mated with his. She drove him crazy with her wild, curling strokes. One minute she was timidly returning his thrusts and parries, the next she was instigating them, sucking and laving his tongue and lips until his blood bubbled in his veins.

Nick's fingers flexed inward, curling around fistfuls of the delicate nightgown, crushing the cloth into wrinkled clumps. His hands trembled as he yanked the skirt up. The cloth tore, but their ragged breaths and pounding heartbeats masked the sound.

His palms stroked the backs of her thighs, the curve of her bottom, the small of her back. Her hot flesh quivered beneath his fingertips, the same way her shallow breaths quivered against his cheek.

It wasn't enough. What he felt was good—*damn* good—but it wasn't nearly enough. He had to feel more.

Pinning her close, Nick rolled Dallas onto her back. His mouth lifted from hers. He rained damp kisses on her jaw. His tongue laved her tiny earlobe before he sucked it into his mouth and nibbled on it.

Her hands were cupping his shoulders now, her fingers tight and trembling. Her back arched, pressing her breasts more fully against him time and again. His hand skimmed over her flat stomach. With the tip of his index finger, he traced her bottom ribs, prolonging her agony. Prolonging his.

The tip of her braid tickled his fingertips. Nick made short work of the frayed ribbon securing the plait. He loosened the braid quickly, then tunneled his fingers through the thick tresses. With a husky groan, he lowered himself fully on top of her, burying his face in the waterfall of tawny silk. His lungs burned when he sucked in deep, shaky breaths of her fresh air and sunshine scent.

He turned his head, and stared at her profile. Her eyes were closed, her expression serene. Her lower lip was kiss-swollen and moist. It trembled. Nick's stomach knotted.

He cupped her cheek in his palm and turned her face toward him. "Open your eyes, lady. Look at me and tell me that what happened between us that night, what's happening between us now, doesn't mean squat to you."

Her long, thick lashes flickered up. Their gazes collided. She opened her mouth, then closed it again.

Nick's gaze dipped, focusing again on her tempting lower lip. He fought a strong urge to lower his head and suck that lip into his mouth. To nibble it with his teeth. To . . .

"Say you don't care for me, Dallas," he ordered, at the same time his left hand came up to settle possessively over her breast. Her nipple had already puckered into a hard bead that burned the center of his palm. He closed his fingers, kneading her, flicking the nipple beneath the cloth with his thumb before rolling it back and forth.

She groaned. Her back arched as she closed her eyes and turned her head away.

He allowed her that much, but no more. His hand released her, but it didn't go far. His big palm slid down her stomach. A calloused index finger dipped into her navel, but didn't tarry there long.

Her nightgown was bunched around her waist. She was wearing nothing underneath.

Nick's hand skimmed her creamy thighs, then slipped between them. She whimpered when he fingered the source of her heat. He separated the moist, velvety folds, dipped deeply inside. He stroked and teased until her back arched and her breaths came choppy and quick. Her legs closed, hugging his hand. Her fingers curled around his forearm in a tight grip that begged him to finish what he'd started.

But Nick Langston was nothing if not persistent. He played with her until she shivered and cried out in frustration, but he wouldn't ease her torment. Not until she eased his.

"Say you don't care for me, Dallas," Nick repeated through tightly clenched teeth. His hand lifted. He toyed with the tawny nest of curls nestled in the junction of her thighs. "Say this means nothing to you. That *I* mean nothing to you."

"Y-you've always meant something to me, Nick. Always," she murmured, so low that he barely heard her.

"What do I mean to you? Tell me."

When she didn't, his fingers slipped beneath the hem of her nightgown. He swept his hand up and, shifting his weight to the side, cradled the firm undercurve of her other breast. Again she arched up, but not into his hand. He lowered his head, and the tip of his tongue moistened the hard, rosy peak. She groaned when he took possession of her with his mouth.

He tasted and nibbled, causing pleasure and pain at the same time, but not too much of either. It still wasn't enough for him. Nick opened his mouth and sucked in as much of her as he could. Her left hand was trapped beneath his waist. He felt it close on the bedspread in a tight little fist.

Her right hand cupped the back of his head, her fingers twisting in his hair.

But her lips remained silent.

She exerted pressure when he lifted his head, but Nick was too strong for her struggle to have much effect. He gazed down into her face, and saw that her forehead was beaded with sweat. More dotted her upper lip. "What do you feel for me, Dallas? Tell me, damn you. Tell me!"

"I . . ." His hand shifted, and his fingers again played with the springy curls between her thighs. Dallas sucked in a sharp breath, licked her lips, and whispered, "I . . . don't know."

He separated her legs, then stroked and teased. Only when she whimpered did he finally plunge his finger up deeply inside of her.

"I know what you feel for me, Dallas," he said as he stroked her. His gaze was fixed on her throat. He saw her pulse leap erratically, saw her try to swallow and fail. Her jaw was hard from grinding her teeth. What he could see of her expression was pinched. "I know. Your body's telling me right now. But it's not enough. I want to hear you say it."

"Nick—"

"Say it!" He increased the tempo of his hand. He stroked deeper, and felt her moist core shudder with anticipation. His gaze fixed hard on her tightly compressed lips. He willed her to part them, to say the words he needed so desperately to hear.

Nick should have known better. Dallas Cameron

329

was just as stubborn as he was. He swore inwardly when she didn't utter a sound.

Nick pulled away from her and sat up. Dallas clutched at him, but he brushed her hands away. The bulky splint made peeling off the union suit take more time than he would have liked. But it was time well spent. The night air wafted over him, cooling his fevered flesh and handing him back a thin, tenuous thread of self-restraint.

The fringe of golden hair scraped his shoulder when he glanced back at her. Dallas's eyes were open, and she was staring with open admiration at the muscles ripping in his back. Sensing his stare, her gaze lifted to his. The shimmering brown depths spoke the words her lips refused to form.

Pity that, like everything else, it just wasn't enough. Not anymore.

Her big brown eyes, sparkling in the lamplight, could tell him every emotion she harbored in her heart, but that wasn't what he wanted from her. He wanted more. He wanted everything. And he was determined to get it.

The mattress creaked as he rolled on his spine and lay back atop the spread. He cupped his hands behind his head and stared, unblinking, at the ceiling.

The touch of her hand on his upper arm was tentative. The heat in her fingertips burned through muscle and bone, seeping into his blood. It took effort, but he kept his gaze locked on the timbers crisscrossing the ceiling.

"Nick?"

When he didn't respond, her hand slipped over his

chest. Her fingertips hesitated amid the curling mat of golden hair there, as though measuring the erratic beat of his heart, then her touch strayed upward.

She cupped his cheek, and turned his head toward her the same way he'd done to her only a short while ago. Nick capitulated, but made it seem like it was a reluctant gesture. God, if she only knew the truth!

Her gaze was fixed on his mouth. She ran the tip of her tongue along her lips, then swallowed. Slowly, her gaze lifted, and locked with his. When her thumb traced the curl of his mustache, and the lips hidden beneath, it was all he could do not to suck that finger into his mouth.

"I . . ." Dallas closed her eyes and sucked in a breath, finishing the statement on a shaky rush of air that blasted hotly over his face. "I love you, Nick Langston. I can't think of a single day when I didn't love you."

Her words were soft and airy, and so damn sincere it made Nick's heartbeat stutter, then slam against his ribs. No one in his life had ever said those words to him before. That Dallas should be the first felt touchingly right.

His hand came up, blanketing the back of her knuckles with his open palm. "When did you grow up, Squirt?" he asked hoarsely.

"The first time you kissed me, I think."

"I shouldn't have done that."

"And I should never have asked you to teach me how to be a lady. But I'm glad I did." She smiled, and her lashes lowered coyly. "Make love to me, Nick. Please."

His muscles tensed. Never had the splint encasing his leg felt as awkward and unwanted as it was now. "It'll have to be different this time."

"I don't care. I just want you to make love to me. Please?"

He didn't have to be asked twice. Slipping an arm beneath her, he lifted her and settled her atop his chest. Her knees parted, flanking his hips. To have her sitting astride him, with her long hair falling all around her, all around him, took Nick's breath away.

His gaze darkened as his hand plowed through her hair. He cupped the back of her head and yanked her down. With a groan, he sealed their mouths together.

Dallas melted against him. Their heartbeats entwined. What began as a soft, tender kiss quickly turned hungry and demanding, on both their parts. Their tongues meshed and mated.

Neither had patience for preliminaries. Their bodies were too hungry to wait.

He arched beneath her. She strained against him. His curling chest hairs teased her nipples, making them pucker. Her hips teased something intricately male, making it rigid and hard.

Nick settled his hands on her hips, his thumbs pointing upward. He exerted little pressure, just enough to coax her back into arching. She twisted and wiggled atop him. He groaned, and felt a fire light in his blood. A burning flame that only her sweet, sweet body could douse.

Dallas splayed her hands against the hollow beneath his shoulder. Her fingers tunneled into his sunbronzed flesh as she glanced down at him inquisitively.

He didn't use words to answer her. He used his body.

He eased her into position. Their gazes held as he arched his hips upward in one sure, claiming thrust. His stiff, swollen flesh drove into her dewy warmth, even as he pulled her down, impaling her fully.

He heard her surprised inhalation, felt her fingernails slice into his skin. The pain brought pleasure—in the form of her wide-eyed, astonished expression.

"I didn't know . . . *oh!*"

Nick grinned as he gripped her hips and started to move her. He coaxed her upward, then very, very slowly, back down again. She shuddered when he repeated the process, then varied it. He moved her from side to side, then in slow, torturous circles. He watched Dallas's face, and thought he'd never seen anything as beautiful as the way her shocked expression melted to one of heavy-lidded desire.

She caught on quickly. Too quickly, if his rapidly dwindling self-control had anything to say about it.

After a few experimental wiggles, Dallas lifted her legs and shifted, burying him deeper still. She moved slowly at first, then quicker, settling finally on a sensuous rhythm that made them both moan.

"Does this . . . feel as good to you?" she panted.

He arched his hips, just as she was grinding hers against him. They both gasped. "Does that answer your question?" he rasped, when he could finally breathe.

"Dear God, yes!"

"Good, then ask it again, darlin'. I liked that, too."

She did.

And he did, answering her this time by reaching up and cupping her breasts in his hands. He rolled her nipples between his index fingers and thumbs, tugging gently.

It was too much. Having such exquisite sensations pouring into her from her most sensitive places threw Dallas over the edge. The tightness gathered in her thighs in throbbing waves. The pace of her hips grew frantic and hard.

Nick matched it. Doubled it.

His hands were never still. Neither was Dallas's body.

Unlike two weeks ago, this time when the shudders started low in her body, in the place where they were joined, Dallas knew what was happening. She welcomed the feeling, welcomed the sweet, sweet promise of imminent release.

She moved faster, arching her spine so that Nick could cup her breasts more fully in his hands. He kneaded one, while the fingers of his other hand kneaded her soft, sensitive bottom, urging them both to an even wilder pace.

The ultimate of pleasures gathered in her, in him. They arched together, apart, together . . . their ragged breaths soughing, hot breath fanning even hotter flesh. Their bodies strained one final time.

Their mutual cries of release mingled, and stirred the late night air.

When it was over, Dallas collapsed atop Nick's chest. His arms wrapped around her, hugging her close. Their skin was warm and slick where they pressed together.

Nick nestled her head beneath his chin. Dallas softly kissed his chest. Both sighed. And both trembled.

Chapter Fourteen

"Are you going to move that thing, or am I going to have to sit on it?" Dallas asked, flashing Nick a saucy grin. She glanced down at his left leg. Except for his head and shoulders, it was the only part of his body not covered by Lisa's frilly green bedspread.

"Darlin', please feel free to sit on any part of me you want, any*time* you want." Though Nick didn't move his head, his gaze slid up to hers. His blue eyes were dark with lurid insinuation.

Dallas's grin broadened. "If I wasn't holding these cups of coffee, I'd take you up on that. Now scoot over, Langston. I refuse to sit on any man who looks so damn good swaddled in green lace."

Nick's lips pursed ruefully as he shifted to the side. The mattress dipped under Dallas's knees as she climbed onto the bed, then handed him one of the mugs she was carrying before settling back against the pillows.

She absorbed the heat of her own mug with her palms, and looked over at him. Nick was taking a tentative sip from his, while glancing at her from the corner of his eye. His appreciative gaze sizzled through her; it was steamier than the coffee in either of their mugs.

He swallowed and, leaning his head against the carved oak headboard, sighed with satisfaction. "You brew a damn fine cup of coffee, Squirt. Glad to see that something I taught you stuck."

Dallas shrugged and raised her mug to her lips. The coffee burned her tongue when she took too big of a sip too quickly.

A couple of comfortably silent minutes were ticked off on the gold filigree clock sitting on Lisa's nightstand.

The mattress dipped again as Nick shifted, rearranging his splinted leg beneath the bedspread. "I—er—took a look at the ledgers you tossed at me this afternoon."

Dallas turned a disbelieving stare on him. "Did you?"

Nick grinned, and tapped her nose with the tip of his index finger. "You don't have to look so stunned, Squirt. I can read."

"I know that. I just thought . . . Never mind. It doesn't matter."

Setting her cup on the bedside table, Dallas tucked her legs beneath her, then turned eagerly back toward Nick. He wasn't looking at her, but studying the rich, dark coffee in his mug. That didn't matter. The fact that he'd gone through the ledgers and not thrown them back at her was a good sign.

"So, what did you think?" she asked. "Will you be

able to bring the accounts up to date? I'd do it myself if I had time, but with both Papa and Lisa gone, and with you . . . well, things have been pretty busy around here lately. I've barely had time to sleep, let alone study the accounts."

Nick's gaze slid up to hers. Dallas thought she saw a shimmer of guilt lurking in his beautiful blue eyes. "I've caused you a heap of trouble in the last two weeks, haven't I, Squirt?"

She grinned, and thought that as long as he called her "Squirt" in that endearing drawl of his, he could cause her all the trouble he wanted. The only thing she liked better to be called was "darlin'," in the huskily seductive way only Nick Langston could.

She shrugged almost casually. "Let's just say you don't make a very good patient, Langston, and leave things at that. Now, about those ledgers. Do you think you can do them? It would help tremendously if you did."

Dallas was positive that it was Nick's desire to help her—perhaps even to somehow make up for the two weeks of trouble he'd spoken of. After a thoughtful pause, prompted his reluctant nod. "I reckon I could give it a try. But don't blame me if the columns don't add up right when I'm done with them. Counting horns is about as much arithmetic as I've ever done."

"That's fine. Really it is." Dallas reached out and touched Nick's upper arm reassuringly. She shivered. His skin felt warm and dry and smooth. The muscles beneath tensed under her fingertips, but she didn't pull her hand away. "I'll make a deal with you, Nick. If you put the columns of figures together during the day, I'll add them up at night." She hesitated and, afraid she may have offended the staunch Langston ego, rushed to add, "Only for a while, mind you. Until you get a little better with figures. How does that sound?"

"Like you're stretching to find a way to keep me busy, and keep me from causing any more trouble. You don't have to, you know."

Her hopeful expression melted to one of concern. Dallas's fingers unconsciously tightened on Nick's arm. "You're no trouble, Langston," she said softly, sincerely. "Not to me. You never have been."

He held her gaze for the length of a heartbeat, then averted it to the mug he'd lifted to his lips. He took a tentative sip of coffee, then swore long and hard when the potent brew burned his tongue.

Dallas swallowed a grin when he slammed the mug down on the nightstand. The small clock again bounced with the force of the blow. Nick's cussing didn't bother her. It assured her his recovery was progressing quite nicely.

This time the moments of silence that passed between them were tighter, strained.

Finally, Nick shifted to look at her. His blue eyes were inquisitive. "Why'd you bring me the ledgers, Squirt?"

"Isn't it obvious?" When he didn't answer, Dallas shrugged and said, "I thought it was high time you found out that roping and riding weren't the *only* jobs to be done on a spread." She pursed her lips and glanced away. When Nick's penetrating blue eyes continued to drill into her, she sighed and continued reluctantly, "All right, Langston. The truth of the matter is, I wanted you to feel useful again. I got sick and tired of seeing you wasting away in that bed. You've never been the type of man who was happy lolling around. I knew the inactivity had to be killing you, but since you refused to get out of bed, I . . . Ah, damn, Nick. Don't you see? It hurts *me* to see you hurting so bad, both physically and mentally."

Now that she was talking, Dallas couldn't seem to stop herself. If Nick wanted her reasons, her *real* reasons, she'd give them to him.

"After the day of the accident," she said, "I started wondering if you would really have had the guts to use that gun. Knowing you as well as I do, I figured you did. Nick, it drove me crazy. I'd lay awake late into the night, waiting to hear a gunshot. Even during the day, when I was out roping, I'd listen for it." She shuddered. "Every time I walked into your room—my room—*your* room—I was scared to death about what I'd find. I thought that maybe, just maybe, if I gave you something to live for you wouldn't . . . well, you know."

"Put a bullet through my head. End my misery. That sort of thing."

Her gaze swung back to him. Her brown eyes were hot with indignation. "Don't laugh at me, Langston. Don't you dare. I've spent the last two weeks without sleep worrying myself sick over you."

"I ain't laughing."

Dallas looked deeply into his eyes, and saw that

341

Nick wasn't lying. He wasn't laughing. In fact, he looked dead serious as he held her gaze. She leaned back against the pillows, but she didn't relax. She felt tense, like a fiddle string wound taut, ready to snap.

This time, the pause that fell between them was more than merely tense. It was strained and awkward.

Dallas started to turn her head, only to have Nick's roughened fingers bracket her jaw. Gently, he tugged her attention back to him. Her gaze lifted, meshed with inquisitive blue.

"Ask me, Squirt," he said finally, flatly. "I know you're dying to."

He was, of course, telling her to ask whether or not he would really have done it. Whether he would have put that gun to his head or in his mouth and pulled the trigger. It was a question Dallas had tormented herself with a thousand times in the last two weeks. One she was pretty sure she already had the answer to. After all, Nick was still here, wasn't he?

"Well?" he prodded. His grip on her jaw loosened. The calloused tip of his thumb abraded her skin as it swept over the curve of her chin. "You gonna ask or not?"

"All right," Dallas said, her gaze dropping, fixing on Nick's lips. The fringe of his mustache was damp from the coffee. Swallowing hard, she wondered how it would taste to lick that moisture away. She shivered, knowing exactly how it would taste. Warm and rich and male. It would taste wonderful.

Her shaky tone was her only outward indication of the erotic thoughts she was trying so hard to push away, and failing. "Why didn't you ever get married, Nick?"

His thumb stopped in midstroke. His golden brows lifted. "Beg pardon?"

"Why aren't you married?"

He scowled. "Why are you asking?"

Dallas shrugged, and hoped the gesture appeared casual. God knows it didn't feel it! "Because I want to know. Because I've always wanted to know. But, since we usually talk cows and ropes and horses, there never seemed to be a good way to bring the subject up."

"And you think *that* was a good way of doing it? Asking out of the blue, when you knew damn well I was expecting an entirely different question?"

"You're cheating, Langston. When someone asks you a question, you're duty bound to answer it, *not* shoot two more back at them. Of course, you can always tell me to mind my own business."

Nick's expression said he was seriously considering doing exactly that. He surprised her by, after a brief hesitation, sighing and visibly relaxing. "I don't know why I never got hitched. Just never found a woman I wanted to spend my whole life with, I expect."

Like he'd done with her earlier, Dallas stared at Nick hard, willing him to continue. He hadn't told her his entire reason. She knew it, just as she knew she wanted—needed—to hear the rest.

Nick whisked his thumb across Dallas's kiss-swollen lower lip. The skin was moist and warm from where she'd nervously wet it with her tongue. A tremor vibrated through his hand, up his arm, before he quickly lowered his hand to his lap.

"I never got married because I ain't got a single thing to offer a woman," he admitted gruffly. *"That's why. Subject closed."* Nick clenched his teeth and made a visible effort to relax. "Now, let's talk about why you were so hell-bent on trying to get drunk when I came in here earlier. That's something *I've* been wondering about."

Dallas's gaze dipped to the fingers she'd tightly entwined in her lap. The reason she'd ferreted out the whiskey seared through her mind. It wasn't something she wanted to talk to Nick about. Not right now. For the first time in weeks they were actually getting along. Now that things between them felt almost right again, she realized how badly she'd missed Nick's easy company, his comfortable friendship.

No, she would *not* risk spoiling this moment by mentioning something that she had already decided hours ago would never happen.

Dallas's hair had fallen forward over her shoulder, curtaining her expression from view. Nick's calloused fingertips felt hot when he reached out and gently tucked the thick tawny tresses behind her ear. His hand dipped, cupping her chin, tipping her face toward him.

Dallas could easily have lifted her chin, pulled away from his touch. She didn't.

After a second, her gaze lifted to his. Did she look as nervous as she suddenly felt? She hoped not. She wouldn't ruin this time with Nick for anything. Especially not by something that had faded to inconsequential from the second he'd kissed her.

"The truth, Squirt. Why were you drinking?"

"I . . ." Dallas's mind raced. What, besides the truth, could she tell him? She said the first thing that entered her mind, then winced when it came painfully close to the truth. "I'm trying so damn hard to be a lady, Nick. Really I am. It just . . . oh, hell, it's not working too well."

"Did Parker say that?"

"No," she answered miserably.

"Then what makes you think it isn't working?"

She glanced at him sharply. "You remember those dresses I told you about?"

Was it her imagination, or did his fingers flex? "I remember," he drawled, his tone low and noticeably edgy. "What about 'em?"

"I ruined them. I forgot I was wearing my boots and my spurs slashed the hems of two of them all to hell. Then I dropped a dollop of jam on . . . I'll thank you to stop laughing, Langston. This isn't funny." Dallas swatted Nick's arm hard, but his pleasant baritone laughter filled the room, and skittered nicely down her spine. "Nick, please. Papa spent good money on those dresses. He's going to be furious when he finds out. *Nick!*"

"Sorry," Nick mumbled. He wiped his hand down his mouth, attempting to smooth out his grin. It didn't work. "I've been—er—meaning to tell you not to"— he smothered another chuckle—"wear your spurs when you're dressing up. I"—he cleared his throat, twice—"guess it slipped my mind."

"Lesson number nine?" Dallas asked. Her voice lacked the sarcasm she'd meant to imply. Of course, grinning back at him didn't help get Nick to take her

345

seriously, either. But that couldn't be helped. It had been so long since she'd heard this man laugh. Longer still since she'd been able to laugh with him.

Though his grin didn't go completely, it did fade. "I thought I said I wasn't giving you any more lessons?"

"You did." She shrugged, and glanced at him hopefully. "I was hoping to change your mind."

"Were you? And *how* were you planning to do that, I wonder?"

His tone had dipped, thickened with lewd suggestion. A bolt of awareness shivered down Dallas's spine. Suddenly, she was very much aware that Nick was stark naked beneath the frilly green bedspread. And that she was wearing just as little beneath her nightgown and wrapper.

"I haven't decided yet." Dallas looked at him levelly, knowing her gaze was just as warmly inviting as his tone had been. "But I'm open to suggestions. What *could* I do to convince you to start teaching me again, Nick? Hmmm, *I* wonder."

She leaned a bit closer to him, and saw his eyes darken lustily. All traces of laughter were gone now, in both of them, replaced by lightning-hot awareness.

Dallas reached up, surrendering to the urge to trace his hard, square jaw. Her fingertip stroked his freshly shaved jaw, so fine and warm and smooth.

Nick encircled her wrist with his fingers. Dallas was free to pull from his grasp if she wanted. She obviously didn't want to.

They stared at each other for what felt like hours. His eyes were trying to tell her something, Dallas was sure of it, but she didn't know what. She'd never seen

346

that expression on Nick's face before, didn't know how to read it.

Nick must have sensed her curiosity, for in a low, husky voice, he said, "You told me you loved me. Did you mean it?"

Dallas swallowed hard and nodded. "Yes. Very much."

"Then . . ." Nick stumbled over his next words, as though they were in a foreign language he didn't know quite how to pronounce. His tone deepened another pitch, his voice sounded gritty. "Marry me, Dallas."

Dallas's eyes rounded. She opened her mouth to give voice to the answer that immediately leapt to her mind. She didn't get a chance.

Before she could utter a sound, Nick leaned forward and silenced her with a kiss. His lips were soft and tender and coaxing.

While the kiss lasted only a few too short seconds, it was more than enough time to drain the voice and breath out of Dallas.

Nick pulled away and planted a kiss in the center of her palm. Dallas's skin sizzled when his tongue flicked out, caressing her flesh. He sighed, moved her hand to his shoulder and leaned toward her, into her.

His face was mere inches from hers, his expression serious, but guarded. His blue eyes were completely emotionless, as though he was afraid of what her answer would be.

"Before you answer," he said gruffly, "I want you to know that what I said before was the God's honest truth. I ain't got much to offer a woman, and I've got less to offer you. I know you want land and money,

Dallas. I don't have any of that. Christ, even the name I'm offering you don't mean dirt to most. But I'm hard working and honest and . . ." His gaze dipped, lingering on her lips. He seemed to have to force his next words off his tongue, but that didn't make them any less sincere, or any less touching.

"But I do love you," he admitted, then smiled, as though surprised to find it hadn't hurt him to say those three words as much as he'd expected it to. "If you give me half a chance, I think I can make you happy. I'd . . . Oh, shit! Now I've gone and made you cry. Goddammit!" Nick plowed his fingers through his hair, and growled, "Look, let's just forget I ever asked, all right?"

Dallas shook her head. She swallowed hard, trying to work her voice around the wedge of emotion lodged in her throat. She clutched Nick's forearm when he started to roll away. "No, you don't understand. I— What was that?"

She tensed when a shout cut through the early morning air. It sounded like it came from the yard near the corral. Listening closely, Dallas heard the thunder of approaching hoofbeats, then more shouts. Voices mumbled outside; their tone was tense, panicky. Though they were still too far away for her to be positive, Dallas could have sworn one of the voices was feminine.

What on earth was going on outside?

"Something's wrong," Nick said, mirroring her thoughts as he shoved the frilly spread off. He reached for the union suit, which was lying in a crumpled heap at the foot of the bed. With jerky, awkward movements he tugged it on. He cursed constantly as he worked the abbreviated leg hole over the splint.

Dallas was on her feet and standing at Nick's side, his crutch grasped in trembling fingers, before he'd worked closed the first button. She shifted from foot to foot impatiently. It seemed to take forever for Nick to work the buttons closed. More than once, she had to bite back the urge to brush his fingers aside and do the chore herself.

The voices were getting closer. Downstairs, she heard a door slam. A barrage of footsteps clomped toward the stairs. Dallas heard Lisa's voice. A bolt of fear sizzled through her.

Dallas automatically surrendered the crutch when Nick took it from her, then used it for leverage to push to his feet.

Dazed, she turned to look at him. Nick's cheeks paled to an ashy shade of white. His lips were compressed tightly, his stance shaky as he leaned heavily on the crutch.

Taking his right hand, she draped his arm around her shoulder. She wrapped an arm around his waist and leaned into him, taking on as much of his weight as she could. In that fashion, they managed to stumble to the bedroom door and out into the hallway.

Dallas had just propped Nick against the wall in the hallway, and was in the process of closing Lisa's bedroom door, when the first person cleared the top step and rounded the corner.

Her attention snapped to the side, and fixed on Hickory Pete. The old man was raking bony fingers through his wispy gray hair, trying to smother the coarse, sleep-wrinkled strands that stuck up from his scalp at odd angles. He stopped short when he saw her and Nick.

Dallas's gaze met Pete's. Her heart stopped for a beat, then pounded to frantic life. A shiver of alarm skated through her when she saw that the weathered creases shooting out from Pete's eyes had deepened to thick crevasses of concern and sympathy.

Dear God, what had happened?

Deep down, Dallas felt that she already knew.

Hickory Pete opened his mouth, but before he could say a word, Lisa rounded the corner. She stopped short behind the old man, her worried gaze melting with relief when she caught sight of Dallas. "Thank God you're here."

"What happened? What's wrong?" Dallas asked shakily, her gaze volleying between her sister and Hickory Pete.

It was Lisa who answered. "It's Papa. I don't have time to explain. Three of the punchers are carrying him up here right now. Dallas, you get him settled in bed while I ride over to the TLP and get David. Sit with him until I get back, and for Heaven's sake, Dallas, keep him calm."

Lisa slammed a limp-brimmed hat atop her golden head and spun on her heel. Only then did Dallas notice her sister's male attire. But the sight barely registered.

Keep him calm, Lisa had said. That meant Papa was still alive. She felt a shiver of hope warm her. "David?" she called out to Lisa shakily. "Why are you getting him?"

Lisa didn't glance back. She vanished around the

corner, her feet slamming on the bare planks in a most unladylike fashion as she barreled down the stairs. Only her voice drifted up the stairwell, and it sounded mildly derisive. "Because he's been attending one of the best medical schools in Boston for the last three years, Dallas. *That's* why. You take care of Papa. I'll be back within the hour."

Lisa's voice receded along with her footsteps. Dallas heard the front door being wrenched open. It closed with a resounding crash that seemed to snap something deep inside of her.

She swayed, and felt a surge of black rush around her.

A strong hand wrapped around her upper arm. The grip was tight and steadying and comforting. As though in a daze, Dallas glanced down at thick, sun-bronzed fingers. Nick's hand, she realized foggily, was the only thing between her standing erect, or her fainting to the hallway floor.

"You all right, Squirt?"

Dallas nodded weakly. She couldn't talk.

The front door opened again. More voices, male and gruff, pierced the hot night air. Feet stomped up the stairs.

"I'll go with you," Nick said.

Dallas started to nod, then thought better of it. Nick was still weak. This was his first day on his feet, she couldn't forget that. As much as she wanted him to come with her—*needed* to feel him by her side through what she was about to face—she knew he wasn't up to it. She couldn't risk him overexerting and damaging his leg any more than it already was.

351

"No, I'll be fine," she said, shaking her head. "Let me get you to your room and then I'll go—"

"Pete can do it," Nick said, cutting her words short.

Was his voice granite hard all of a sudden? And were the looks Nick and Pete exchanged riddled with tension? Dear God, Dallas couldn't tell. She was so worried about Papa that she just couldn't think straight!

"Yeah," Pete grumbled finally, "I'll get him settled. You go to yer pa, Dallas."

Dallas opened her mouth to protest, but the men carrying her father had just made it to the stair landing.

The sight of Ian Cameron's limp body and ghostly pale face made Dallas's breath catch and her heart twist. When Nick nudged her shoulder, she stumbled forward a few steps. She had to lean heavily against the wall to steady her precarious balance.

"Go on, Cameron," Nick insisted gruffly.

Dallas scowled, trying and failing to keep her thoughts on two unconnected paths when she didn't really want to think about anything at all. "Nick, what we were talking about before . . ."

"Ain't important."

"It is!"

"No, it ain't. In fact, far as I'm concerned, the subject wasn't worth mentioning in the first place. Go to your daddy, Dallas. That's where you belong."

Dallas glanced at Nick from over her shoulder. His face was hard, unreadable. What had happened that she hadn't noticed? "But . . ."

Nick was no longer listening. Hickory Pete had

moved to his side, and was wrapping Nick's arm around Pete's own gaunt shoulders. Nick didn't look at Dallas as he allowed himself to be helped back down the hallway.

Dallas felt a very strong need to rush to Nick's side and find out why he was treating her this way. She also felt an equally strong obligation to rush to her father's side and reassure herself he was going to live.

She stood in the hallway, feeling so damn torn.

One of the men carrying her father slammed his foot against Ian's bedroom door and sent the panel of wood crashing open. As they carried Ian across the threshold, Dallas saw her father's snow-white head loll limply to the side. In a weak, quivering voice he called her name . . . and in so doing forced her into a decision.

Dallas glanced back down the hallway, only to find it deserted. Pete had gotten Nick into her bedroom, and the bedroom door was closed. She didn't even have the sight of Nick's rugged body to comfort her now.

With a shaky sigh, Dallas pushed away from the wall. A good dose of Cameron determination was the only thing that kept her knees from buckling as she hurried toward her father's room.

Chapter Fifteen

Nick was sitting in a chair beside Ian's bed, his splinted leg propped so his heel dented the mattress beside Ian's hip. To an observer, his demeanor would have looked casual; posture slouched, hands laced negligently atop his stomach, head lazily cocked to one side.

In truth, he was anything but. Inside, Nick was a bundle of raw nerves. Nothing, absolutely *nothing* about tonight had gone even close to the way he'd planned. First with Dallas, then with Ian, then . . . Damnation! Who knew Parker was going to medical school?

Out of them all, Ian taking sick like this had been the least expected. And the most disturbing.

Ian.

Nick's attention shifted to his employer. It might have been his imagination, but it looked like Ian Cameron was having one hell of a good time.

The old man was sitting up in bed, his back propped against a bunch of softly plumped pillows. The pillowcases were as white as the man's hair. Ian's cheeks were still ashy gray, and he looked a might haggard, but the sparkle in his green eyes was as sharp as ever.

The green eyes in question were right now volleying between the two other occupants of the room. Nick Langston and David Parker.

"Well?" Ian grumbled, and shivered when David placed the stethoscope's disc dead center of Ian's hairy chest.

David winced at the booming voice, and sent Ian a silencing glare.

Ian huffed, but shut his mouth. He breathed when David told him to breathe, coughed when David instructed him to cough. It was only those sharp green eyes that said the tasks were performed grudgingly.

"Well?" Ian barked again when David dislodged the earpiece and stepped away. "Am I going to live or aren't I?"

With a shrug, David tucked the stethoscope away in his black leather bag. "In my expert opinion, I'd say you've got at least another five or ten years in you, Ian."

"I'm expected to take the 'expert opinion' of a kid who couldn't rope straight to save his life?" Ian grumbled from the bed. "Not hardly."

Though Ian had looked at Nick when he spoke, the words were obviously meant to be overheard. And they were, if the slamming shut of David's medical bag was any indication.

David's gait was stiff as he turned and carried a small, cork-lidded bottle over to the bed.

Though David glanced meaningfully at the foot

Nick had propped atop the mattress, he was smart enough not to tell Nick to remove it. In Nick's currently sour mood, an order like that would have been all the motivation he'd need to kick the red-faced little pansy into tomorrow.

"Ian, I want you to take one teaspoon of this medicine every six hours. Precisely," David said, and placed the bottle on the already cluttered nightstand. He continued as though instructing a child, "I mean *every* six hours. Do you think you can do that?"

"Depends. Do you think *you* could talk to me like an adult?" Ian countered tersely. "I'm sick, Parker, but I sure as hell ain't stupid. And there's nothing wrong with my hearing. If you say to take one teaspoon of that stuff every six hours, then that's what I'll do."

David stiffened under Ian's hostile tone, and his cheeks darkened another ruddy shade. "I'm going to have a talk with Dallas. I'm sure *she'll* see to it that you take your medicine when you're supposed to. Where is she?"

"I sent her downstairs to make tea," Ian replied grumpily. "Her hovering was driving me crazy."

David nodded, and turned away. "Fine. Then I'll go help her."

"Why? My girl may not be anything like the society ladies you're used to, but she can damn well brew a decent cup of tea *by herself.*"

David looked as though he was about to say something, then changed his mind. He grabbed his leather bag up off the chair, then stalked to the door. His boot heels made meticulous little clicks atop the bare, planked floor. "If it's all the same to you, I'd like to see Dallas anyway. That is, unless you can think of a good reason that I shouldn't be speaking to my fiancée in private."

Nick had been noticeably silent up to now. Tonight's unexpected events—all of them—had put him on edge. The emotions roiling through him inhibited rational conversation. He was in pain, he was tired, and he was confused. Worry over Ian was exceeded only by worry over what Dallas had thought of his impromptu proposal.

Parker, however unintentionally, had just pushed him past the breaking point. "Fiancée?" Nick growled, his voice low and extremely controlled. He pushed himself up straighter in the chair.

It was Nick's sharp, gritty tone that snagged David's attention and made him freeze, his hand poised in the act of turning the doorknob. He glanced over his narrow shoulder, then dearly wished he hadn't. If Nick Langston's brilliant blue eyes could shoot bullets, David's back would have been riddled with lethal holes.

"Fiancée?" Ian said, when the two younger men did nothing but glare at each other. "Are you saying that you proposed to my girl, Parker?"

David, grateful for the distraction, averted his gaze to Ian. He nodded, and swallowed hard when he felt a pair of hot blue eyes burn into him. "I am. And she accepted. Do you have a problem with that?"

"I'd say it's more likely *you're* the one with the problem, Parker," Ian grumbled. "Especially if you're seriously thinking about settling down with my girl. In case you haven't noticed, Dallas ain't the easiest person to get along with. She's stubborn as a mule, and opinionated as all hell. As far as she's concerned, there's only one way to do things: *her* way. She'll make your life hell, Parker. You know that, don't you?"

"No, I can't honestly say that I do," David replied flatly. "I'll admit to being aware of some of her . . . shortcomings, but I'm convinced that after we've had more time together, she'll come around to my way of thinking. Eventually." David scowled, then reluctantly turned his attention back to Nick. His green eyes glittered meaningfully. "I won't lie and say this is a love-match. Dallas and I have never gotten along, that's common enough knowledge. But there's no reason we can't set our differences aside now that we're going to be man and wife. Dallas and I have come to an understanding. She told me herself that I can give her things a lot of the other men around here can't. Things that are much more important to her than love."

"Things?" Nick sneered furiously. "I'd be interested to hear what kinda 'things' a pansy like you thinks he can give a woman like Dallas."

David's grin was cocky and arrogant; it chafed Nick raw. "Land, money, a respectable name . . . for starters. In return, she can give me sons."

An image burned through Nick's mind, hot and intense. It wasn't Dallas and David's future children that had him shoving himself out of the chair, it was the picture of David and Dallas *making* those kids.

Blind fury pumped through Nick's blood and combined with an even stronger urge to rip David

Parker apart with his bare hands. Not a normally violent person, the urge—the infernal *need*—to commit violence right here and now was so strong it was staggering.

Nick shoved the crutch under his arm so hard it hurt, and stalked across the room. He was pleased to see David's ruddy cheeks drain to a deathly shade of white, pleased to see the way the pansy let go of the doorknob and flattened his back against the door.

The lump in Parker's throat bobbed up and down, scratching against his starched collar. David hugged the black leather bag to his chest as though it offered protection from the approaching storm that was Nick Langston.

Nick stopped when he was toe-to-toe with Parker. David's wide hazel gaze had to travel upward to meet furious blue.

Fisting the crutch in a grip that made his knuckles sting, Nick shifted his weight and reached out with his free hand. He grabbed a chunk of Parker's perfectly pressed shirt in his fist and yanked the boy forward. The tips of their noses grazed.

"Let me give you a friendly piece of advice," Nick growled into Parker's face. With supreme satisfaction, he watched the pansy blanch, then gulp. "Touching Dallas Cameron wouldn't be a safe thing for you to do, Parker."

"I'm going to marry her, Nick. I can't very well sleep in the same bed with her every night and not—"

The rest of David's words were cut off by the fingers Nick wrapped tightly around the man's scrawny throat. He applied only a minimal amount of pressure.

Not enough to cut off his air supply, but enough to threaten it at any time.

Nick congratulated himself on his self-restraint. It was all he could do right now not to give in to the urge to throttle the brat on the spot. "I think you've got things backward, kid. You ain't gonna be sleeping with Dallas because you ain't gonna be *marrying* her." Parker opened his mouth to refute. Nick glared at him and increased the pressure on his neck. "Period. End of discussion."

"Not quite. You see, Langston, it isn't your decision to make," David croaked, using what little air Nick allowed him to draw into his burning lungs. The green gaze darted to the bed, his eyes wide and pleading. "It's *Dallas*'s. Isn't that right, Ian?"

"I reckon you've got a point there," Ian said, his voice rich with amusement. "Better let him go, Nick. His lips are turning blue."

Although Nick loosened his hold, he didn't release Parker. He couldn't. Fury was humming through him, clouding his normally good sense.

Dammit! Dallas had *known* Parker had proposed to her before he'd even entered Lisa's room tonight. Hell, she'd even accepted the pansy's proposal. Yet she hadn't told him. Worse—much, *much* worse—she'd let him seduce her, even after she'd said yes to Parker.

Was she ever planning to tell Nick about Parker, or had she intended for him to find out on his own so that she wouldn't have to face his anger? Nick had never taken Dallas for a coward, but then, he'd never *ever* planned on being attracted to her so strongly, either. He'd been wrong on both counts.

Another thought came to Nick then. The repercussions of it tore him up from the inside out. His fingers shook against David Parker's throat, and his grip loosened still more.

Had Dallas lied when she'd said she loved him? It didn't bear thinking about, but Nick had to know. He hated the immediate answer that bubbled up inside of him, but there was no avoiding it or the feelings the realization evoked.

She'd lied to him, Nick thought bitterly. Actions always spoke louder than words—and Dallas's actions had been to accept Parker's proposal, not his. Nick closed his eyes and sucked in an unsteady breath. The pain that cut through him was excruciating. It sliced into his heart, and left an immediate scar that he doubted would ever heal.

Nick gritted his teeth and moved back an awkward step, dragging Parker with him. Balancing his weight on the crutch, he leaned forward and ripped open the door with enough force to send it slamming against the bedroom wall.

He glared at David Parker for a full minute before spinning the boy roughly around. When Parker was facing the hall, Nick flattened his palm between the boy's bony shoulder blades and shoved. Hard.

David yelped, and staggered out into the hall. The black bag clattered to the floor, and David scrambled to pick it up. He kept a watchful eye on Nick the whole time, but to his immense relief, Nick didn't look like he was going to tear him to shreds—the way those hard blue eyes of his said he badly wanted to.

"You want her? Fine. She's all yours," Nick

sneered, his chin jerking in the direction of the stairs. "Far as I'm concerned, the two of you deserve each other." His murderously bright gaze seared into Parker. "If you've got half a lick of sense, you'll get Dallas and get the hell out of here. Find Preacher Thomas and get hitched tonight. Because, by God, if I get my hands on that woman first, there won't be anything left for you *to* marry."

Nick slammed the door in his face before Parker could utter a sound. Nick heard feet shuffle in the corridor, felt Parker's indecision seeping through the slats in the door.

Eventually the footsteps moved off, thumping slowly down the stairs.

Nick turned, and looked at Ian. The older man was staring at him, but not a single emotion came into play on his pale, weathered face.

That wasn't a good sign. Ian Cameron was an emotional person, always had been. When he was riled, people knew it. Except for when he was furious.

"Ever think I may have some say about when and who my girl marries?" Ian asked, his voice too calm and controlled for Nick's comfort.

Nick's gaze narrowed. "You got a problem with the way I handled things, Ian, just say so."

"Would it matter if I did?"

"Probably not." His leg was starting to ache badly. Nick hobbled back to the chair, hoping that taking his weight off of it would help. It didn't. Nor did it soothe his inner turmoil. His gut was kicking up a storm, his temples were throbbing with the whirlwind of his thoughts, and even sitting, he still felt every pulsing throb rushing through the veins in his knee.

He stretched out in the chair, again propping his leg on the mattress. His gaze slipped up to Ian's. "What the hell's your problem?" he gritted accusingly. "You got what you wanted. You should be happy as a pig in shit."

"I'm thrilled," Ian replied flatly.

Nick nodded. "And so you should be. Dallas is getting married, just like you said she had to. Give her and Parker a couple of years and she'll probably fill up this house with the grandsons you're so goddamn desperate for." Beneath his breath he added, "That is *if* Parker can figure out what it's for and where it goes."

The image of David Parker and Dallas together, intimately, came back to haunt Nick. He could feel his cheeks heat, feel the strong tide of anger flood back, threatening to drown him.

While he may be furious with Dallas for lying to him, that didn't make the image of her and Parker in bed—*doing the same he and Dallas had done not two hours ago*—any easier to accept. Nor did it ease the inexplicable constricting pain in his chest, the lonely ache in his gut.

Feeling Ian's gaze on him, he glanced up. The old man was eyeing him so intently it made Nick do something he *never* did.

Nick squirmed and glanced guiltily away, his hand straying to the pocket of his shirt for that familiar leather pouch . . . which, come to think of it, he'd left back in his—no, *Dallas*'s—room. Dammit! He needed a cigarette, some fresh air, and a goodly piece of distance between himself and this ever worsening situation. In that order.

Unfortunately, Ian looked like he wanted to chat. Nick didn't think it likely he was going to get any of those things in *any* order for a while.

"You feeling all right, Langston?"

"Yup, just dandy," Nick growled, his terse tone saying he felt anything but . . . and that the subject was *not* open for debate.

Either the older man didn't sense Nick's worse-than-sour mood, or he chose to ignore it. "You're sure about that?"

"Uh-huh."

"Funny, you sure as hell aren't acting like it. In fact, you've been acting downright ornery ever since they hauled me in tonight. Did something go on here while I was away that I should know about?"

"Nope." *Not unless you count me making hot, wild love to your daughter, old man. Other than that, not a damn thing happened that you need to know about. And you sure as hell don't need to know about that.*

"You ain't upset about anything?" Ian prodded.

"No, goddamn it, I'm not!" *I'm furious.*

"Hmmm. Gotta say, Langston, for a man who claims he isn't upset, you sure got mad at Parker fast. Can't say I've ever seen you threaten a man like that before." Ian sent Nick a level glare. "You still sticking by that story about not being upset?"

Nick grunted noncommittally. *Simple, Ian. It's your traitorous little girl,* Nick thought, but didn't say. *It's the way she told me she loved me, and didn't mean it. The way she made me humble myself and propose to her when she had no intention of ever accepting.* That's *what's eating at me!*

Not that he'd ever tell Ian any of that, of course. The emotions could simmer inside of Nick, but so long as they *stayed* inside, there wasn't a chance of Ian killing him for having taken liberties with his baby girl.

Affecting an air of indifference that he didn't feel, Nick shrugged and said, "There's nothing eating at me, Ian. My leg hurts. I'm worried about you. Other than that, my life's just dandy."

Ian chuckled dryly. "You don't really expect me to believe that, do you?"

"Can't think of any reason why you shouldn't."

"Oh, there are reasons, all right. Several, in fact. Knowing you the way I do is the main one. You don't fly off the handle like that over nothing, Langston. And you of all people wouldn't threaten to strangle a man for no good reason."

"I'm having a bad day."

"Uh-hmmm. You don't seem too thrilled with the idea of Dallas and David getting married."

Nick's gaze snapped back to Ian. He scowled at the older man, trying to decide whether or not that was a hint of a grin he detected wedged in the corners of Ian's mouth.

Nick laced his hands atop his stomach and, resting his head back, closed his eyes and shrugged almost easily. "Dallas is a big girl, Ian. She can marry whomever she pleases. Don't mean squat to me."

"Bullshit."

One blue eye slitted open. The golden brow above arched high. "Beg pardon?"

The bed creaked when Ian sat up and leaned forward. His green eyes were narrow and intent. "I said bullshit, Langston. B-u-l-l-s-h-i-t. I think it matters one hell of a lot to you. What I can't figure out is where the harm is in you admitting it. You've been my girl's best friend for almost fifteen years; like peas in a pod, you and Dallas. A man's apt to feel protective over any woman he spends so much time with. Stands to reason you'd take an interest in who she marries. Hell, it wouldn't seem right if you *didn't*."

Nick didn't reply, but that was only because a lump of emotion he'd rather not have felt had lodged in his throat.

For the last few weeks, his thoughts about this man's daughter were anything *but* friendly. Hot, erotic, mind-boggling sexual; those would have been better descriptions.

What, Nick wondered, would Ian say if he knew any of that? What would Ian *do* if he knew how far Nick and Dallas's relationship had progressed? And did he even have to ask that question? Hell, no! The second Ian found out Nick was bedding his daughter—and both of them were liking it just fine—Ian would live up to the promise he made all the hands when they hired on.

He'd shoot Nick Langston, then fire him for good measure.

Ian sat back against the pillows, his fist unconsciously rubbing away the lingering pain in his chest. He knew he should take some of the medicine Parker had left, but he didn't. The stuff would make him

367

sleepy, and he didn't want to sleep. Not right now. Not until after he'd finished talking to Nick.

"Why don't you want Dallas to marry David?" Ian's voice took on a sharp edge of paternal defensiveness. "What's the matter, Langston? Don't you think my girl's good enough for a Parker?"

"In my mind, it's Parker who ain't good enough for her." Nick shifted in his chair, his hand gingerly massaging the cramp out of his bad leg. "Dallas would never be happy with a pansy like Parker. You know it, Ian, and so do I. Hell, I think if Dallas ever gave it serious thought, she'd know it, too. But she ain't thinking too clearly these days . . . and that's your fault, old man. The ultimatum you gave her sent her into a tailspin. She's so desperate to win her daddy's approval she would do damn near anything, including marrying Parker, and making the single biggest mistake of her life."

"I didn't say she had to marry *him,*" Ian huffed indignantly.

"No? Well, she seems to think you did." Nick's gaze narrowed on Ian. He'd always liked and respected the old man, but . . . God, right now he didn't care for Ian Cameron and his nagging, interfering ways one bit. That's what had started this whole mess in the first place. "Dallas has it in her head that you'd be right proud to have David Parker as a son-in-law."

"She's right. I would."

"Have you told her that?"

"Many times."

The muscle in Nick's jaw jerked. "Well then, there you go. You know, sometimes I think all Dallas has ever wanted out of life is for you to be proud of her. In case you haven't noticed, she's turned herself inside-out for you over the years. Working this ranch the way no woman I've ever known would. Roping, wrangling and, in short, trying her damnednest to be the son you always told her you wanted and were cheated out of. Now, she finally sees a way to make you proud, to give you something you desperately want—her married, and grandsons to bounce on your knee—and she's making the effort. What she doesn't seem to realize is that her efforts ain't gonna mean squat to you. No matter what she does, she'll never be your son."

Ian's expression melted to one of stunned disbelief. He stared at Nick for a full minute, absorbing the younger man's words, knowing in his heart they were true. Then he blinked hard and looked away.

Shaking his snow-white head, Ian said gruffly, "Any dream I had of having a son of my own came true the day you swaggered onto this ranch and demanded a job, Langston. I thought everyone knew that."

Nick sat up straighter in the chair, a dark scowl puckering on his brow. A trickle of unease shivered down his spine when he asked, "Now what the hell's that supposed to mean?"

Ian shrugged and sighed. It was a tired, resigned gesture and sound. "What it means is that I've always considered *you* my son."

"I'm no relation to you, Ian. I'm a puncher, bought and paid for, just like—"

"Oh, settle down and hear me out." Ian waved Nick back into the chair when it looked like Nick was going to get up and stalk out of the room. Maybe even out of their lives. The pain in Ian's chest clenched tight, telling him there were words that needed to be said. Words that he might never get another chance to utter. "I'm not talking about the flesh-and-blood kind of son, Langston, I'm talking about the close, trustworthy, always-there-in-a-pinch kind. I knew the second I set eyes on you fifteen years ago that you'd grow into a man I could be proud of." Ian scowled, and turned his gaze back to Nick—who looked, quite simply, stunned. "Why the hell do you think I hired you on when nobody else would?"

"Because you sensed I was a damn good worker, and that I'd always be brand loyal?"

"Sure, that was part of the reason. A *small* part." He shook his head, and ran his thick, trembling fingers through his thinning white hair. "I hired you because I liked you. I knew in the years to come you'd do me proud, and you didn't disappoint me there. I took you on because . . ." Ian cleared his throat and swallowed hard. Not a man to open up easily, he found he literally had to shove the words off his tongue. "I took you on all those years ago, Nick, because I saw something of me in you. And because you were everything I'd ever imagined a son of mine would grow up to be."

Nick absorbed all this, and for the first time that night, he felt a smidgen of elation. Ian thought of him as a son. *Him?* A dirt-poor cowpuncher like Nick Langston? Christ, didn't that beat all! "But I thought—?"

"Wrong. You thought wrong. Just like it would seem my girl's thought wrong all these years. Yes, I want my grandsons. I can't deny that. But getting them had absolutely nothing to do with the reason I ordered Dallas to get married. And just to set the record straight, I never told her *who* she had to marry."

"From what I hear, you weren't real specific about that."

"I told her no hands, but that's the *only* stipulation I gave her. I don't know where she got the idea that only Parker would do. I never said that."

Nick sat back in his chair and studied Ian assessively. The man looked tired. The way Ian kept rubbing at his chest was starting to alarm Nick. Instinct told him to leave now, let Ian get some rest. They could talk in the morning.

But first, Nick had one more question he needed answered.

Cushioning his elbows atop his thighs, Nick leaned forward. Ian was staring blankly out the window. Somehow, not having those sharp green eyes drilling into him made the words a lot easier to say. "What've you got against us cowpunchers, Ian? Why don't you think we're good enough for your little girl?"

Although Ian was looking away, Nick could see his profile. As he watched, the very corner of Ian's mouth tipped up in a crafty smile.

Ian reached out and reluctantly picked up the bottle David Parker had left for him. He uncapped it and took a swig he imagined to be a teaspoon's worth of the awful-tasting stuff. Then he plugged the bottle, set it aside.

When Ian figured Nick Langston had suffered long enough, he finally turned his head and looked at the younger man. His green eyes sparkled in the flickering lamplight, and he grinned again. "I said hand, Langston. Correct me if I'm wrong, but I don't recall ever saying that the Bar None's *foreman* wasn't good enough for my daughter."

Chapter Sixteen

"Damn it, what's taking so long?" Dallas paced beside the kitchen table, her arms crossed tightly over her waist, her spurs chinking on the planked floor with each nervous stride. "David's been up there for over an hour."

"These things take time," Lisa assured her sister. Her strained tone said she was every bit as anxious for news about their father as Dallas was. "Have a seat. I'll pour you a cup of tea and—"

"I don't want any tea."

"Okay," Lisa said patiently. "Then I'll brew some coffee."

"I don't want coffee, either." Dallas shook her head. The last thing she needed right now was coffee. Her nerves were strung taut enough as it was. "What I *do* want is for David to get his ass down here and tell us Papa is going to be all right. I think I'll go up there and—"

"Dallas!"

Dallas hesitated on her way to the door. She glared at her sister. "What?"

"Look, I know you're upset. So am I. But do you have to use such language?" Lisa pushed to her feet, smoothed the snug, fawn-brown pants over her thighs, and shook her head. "You're not going anywhere. In the mood you're in, you'll only upset Papa more. I'll go up and see what's going on. *You* stay right here."

Dallas opened her mouth to argue, then snapped it shut again. Lisa was right. She watched her sister leave the kitchen. Why was it that even trail-dusty male attire managed to shape to Lisa's slender form like tailored silk?

With a groan of frustration, Dallas plopped onto the chair Lisa had just vacated. Truly, Dallas hadn't even realized she'd cussed until Lisa had pointed the fact out to her.

Her frown deepened to a scowl.

Ladies don't swear.

Had that been one of Nick's "lessons?" If not, it was probably a planned one for the future. It was something Dallas thought she should have known instinctively, not needed to be taught. Lisa never swore.

Dallas sighed. It was no use. Like she'd told Nick earlier, acting lady-like was beyond her, a skill she'd never, no matter how hard she tried, be able to master. She was becoming more convinced of that by the second. Nick would probably agree. Hadn't he been saying much the same thing for weeks?

Nick.

Even though the kitchen was hot, Dallas shivered. Vividly, she remembered the feel of Nick's hands—

hot and strong and urgent—scouring her naked body. Even now, hours later, her flesh still burned, branded by his touch . . . the same way his huskily uttered words of love and marriage were branded forever into her mind.

A guilty flush warmed her cheeks. She should have told Nick about David's proposal. And her acceptance of it. She'd wanted to, almost had a few times, but . . .

One thing had stopped her.

The instant Nick's warm, whiskey-tasting lips touched hers, Dallas had known she couldn't possibly go through with marrying David Parker. Not when her heart was elsewhere.

Her heart belonged to Nick Langston.

For as long as Dallas could remember, she'd loved Nick in one way or another. First as a teacher. Then as a roping partner, a friend, a confidant. Now, finally, as a man and her lover.

Go to your daddy, Cameron. It's where you belong.

Dallas winced. Even in retrospect, those words sliced into her like a knife buried to the hilt, the blade being viciously twisted. So did the impassive expression Nick had worn when he'd growled them at her.

Had he already learned of David's proposal?

Groaning, Dallas rested her elbows atop the table and buried her face in her hands. Her cheeks felt hot as she cradled them in her trembling palms.

Dear God, if Nick already knew—

"Dallas?"

The unexpected voice startled her.

Dallas sprang out of the chair and spun on her heel,

her breath coming in shallow gasps as her gaze swung toward the door. She tried to ignore a stab of disappointment she felt when, instead of Nick, she saw David standing there, scrutinizing her oddly.

Thoughts of Nick didn't evaporate from her mind—they couldn't—but they were momentarily shoved aside, overridden by concern for her father. "How's Papa? Is he . . . ?" She couldn't say it, couldn't even *think* it.

David crossed the room and set his black bag down on the table next to Lisa's dainty porcelain teacup. He looked paler than usual, Dallas noticed, and he looked tired.

"Dead?" David finished the sentence for her, and shook his head when she winced. "No, no. Ian will be fine, just so long as he takes his medicine the way he's supposed to." His gaze bored into Dallas. "I'm counting on you to make sure he does."

"He will," she assured him, even as she sat back down heavily in the chair. Dallas didn't know until that very second that relief could flood through a body so strongly that it left one feeling light-headed, dizzy, and weak. The last time she'd felt anything remotely similar had been when Nick had willingly handed over his gun to her the day he'd gotten his leg broken.

Dallas glanced up at David, her brown eyes sparkling with promise. "I swear to you, if it takes me and Lisa and Nick and Pete, combined to hog-tie him and pour it down his ornery throat, then that's what we'll do. Papa *will* take his medicine."

Was it Dallas's imagination, or did David stiffen at the mention of Nick Langston? A shadow seemed to flicker in his eyes, but it came and went too quickly for her to decipher.

"Dallas," David began, then hesitated. The way he cleared his throat seemed tense and nervous. Elbowing his medical bag and Lisa's teacup out of the way, he took one of her hands in his.

Dallas forced her fingers to go limp. It was either that, or surrender to the urge to snatch her hand away from his. His skin felt cold and clammy. Unappealing. Keeping her voice as neutral as her expression, she prompted, "Yes . . . ?"

"I—I know this isn't the time or place, considering, but I have to ask. You, um, remember me telling you about that barn raising we're having this weekend?"

Dallas nodded vaguely. The nervous glint in David's eyes, and the uneasy way he squirmed in his chair, was beginning to alarm her. His too-soft fingertips trembled against her palm, and again she fought the urge—stronger this time, harder to deny—to pull her hand back.

"I remember," she murmured, her eyes narrowing cautiously. "What about it?"

"Well, I was thinking it would be an excellent time for us to get married."

"David, I—" Dallas cried.

He sliced his free hand through the air, and Dallas lapsed into a reluctant silence. Inwardly, she groaned, *Oh, Lord, what had she done?* The second she'd realized she couldn't marry this man, she should have told him. But, the way things had happened, there'd been no time.

"Please, Dallas, just hear me out, okay? Think

377

about it. You've already agreed to marry me. All we need to do now is pick a date. The barn raising makes perfect sense, because everyone we'd invite to the wedding is going to be there anyway. Besides . . ."

David grinned. His gaze slipped downward, caressing the firm thrust of her breasts beneath the shirt she'd hastily put on earlier. All traces of fatigue left his face. His gaze heated, and the color in his cheeks came back in force.

Dallas swallowed hard. She felt ill.

"I don't know about you, honey," David murmured, his attention lifting, "but I don't want to wait a day longer than necessary for us to get married."

David started leaning slowly toward Dallas, at the same time tugging on her entrapped hand and drawing her toward him.

Oh, God, he was going to kiss her.

Dallas knew it, just as she also knew that so much as a fleeting touch of his lips on hers would make her scream.

The memory of Nick's mouth devouring her lips was achingly clear in her mind. It felt blasphemous to even *think* about kissing another man besides Nick. Especially if that man was David Parker.

The hell of it was, Dallas wasn't thinking about kissing David. At that moment, all she could think about was how to *prevent* such a thing from happening.

Do something, her mind screamed as David's mouth—his lips cool and wet and fleshy—inched threateningly closer.

* * *

Nick was pushing himself too hard, and he knew it. His first day on his feet, and here he was tackling stairs. Well, hell, Helen Langston had always bragged that her son never did anything by half measures. When it came to Nick, it was all or nothing at all.

His left leg was killing him. Throbbing bad when he walked, not as bad when he didn't, yet always throbbing to one extent or another. Pete had warned Nick the pain would dull in time, but that he'd never be rid of it entirely. It was the price Nick would have to pay for being lucky enough to keep his leg at all. Men had lost limbs over wounds less than his.

Nick grunted as, the majority of his weight on the crutch, he maneuvered his stiff, aching body down the stairs. The wooden planks creaked under his weight as he stepped onto the bare, flat floor and breathed a sigh of relief.

Massaging the pain in his wounded leg, Nick glanced up the stairs. He swore under his breath. If going down had been so hard and painful, he could just imagine what it was going to be like trying to climb back up there again. It was going to be a bitch, plain and simple.

Nick figured there wasn't any physical pain imaginable that could match the emotional pain he had experienced when David Parker said that Dallas had accepted his marriage proposal.

Nick would be damned if anything ever had—ever could!—hurt that bad.

He gritted his teeth, his jaw bunching hard. His blue

eyes narrowed and his gaze locked on the kitchen door, just down the short, narrow hall. Lamplight flooded out of it, splashing dimly over the hallway floor. The sound of murmured voices tickled his ears. Ignoring the voice he immediately recognized as David Parker's, Nick instead concentrated on the whiskey-sweet timbre that was Dallas's.

His heartbeat staggered and his breath caught. If he wasn't so confused, Nick would have been humiliated.

How could the mere sound of her voice stir such raw emotion in him? He didn't know, it just did. No woman had ever had such a devastating effect on his senses. He doubted any woman besides Dallas ever would.

One thing Nick was damn sure of, and that was that no other woman would ever be given the chance to hurt him the way Dallas Cameron had hurt him tonight. Never again would he open himself up to a woman that way, open himself up to the kind of pain that felt like his heart had literally been clawed out of his body and stomped into the dirt. Never.

The tip of the crutch clicked softly on the hall floor as Nick hobbled toward the kitchen. With each agonizing step, his resolve strengthened.

Maybe it was irrational, but then, "rational" wasn't one of the emotions pumping hot and fast through Nick's veins right now. He'd endured the agony of going down those stairs for one reason, and one reason alone. There was no way he was going back up them again until he'd gotten what he'd come down here for.

He wanted, *needed,* Dallas to look him in the eye

and admit that she'd agreed to marry David Parker. He had to hear the truth from her own traitorous lips, had to hear in that seductively smoky voice of hers the words she should have spoken *before* she'd allowed him to make love to her earlier . . . but hadn't!

The voices in the kitchen stopped just as Nick reached the doorway.

Years of working the range had trained Nick to adjust his eyes from darkness to light in a heartbeat. It was a trick that came in handy now as, in a blink, he squinted and accustomed himself from the shadowy hallway to the lamp-lit kitchen.

Nick stopped, frozen to the spot.

The scene playing out before him made his blood run cold.

And his fury burn red-hot.

Dallas pulled back an instant before David's lips would have touched hers. His mouth shadowed the movement, and she held up a hand, shuddering fiercely when his lips grazed her open palm. "Don't."

David's eyes had been half closed. They now snapped open and flamed with . . . what? Frustration? Anger? She couldn't tell.

He asked, "Don't what?"

"Don't kiss me."

"Why not?" David sighed, then frowned. "Dallas, darling, in less than a week you're going to be my wife. Really, it's all right to kiss me."

Dallas shook her head and yanked her hand back. She detested the way David's mouth moved against her, the way his breath felt hot and clammy against her flesh. "No, it's not all right. David, I've been meaning to talk to you. I've—"

"Well, ain't this cozy?"

The husky voice that shot out from the doorway snagged Dallas's attention. She hadn't realized she and David were no longer alone in the kitchen, until she looked up . . . right into Nick Langston's furious blue glare.

Her breath caught, and her heart and stomach did that odd little somersault they always did when she caught a glimpse of Nick. At least, that had been her normal reaction to the sight of him lately.

"Nick," Dallas breathed, unaware that she'd sighed his name aloud. She was unaware, also, that her cheeks had flushed with excitement, and that her breathing had recommenced with a vengeance, one breath lapsing right into the next without pause.

Nick was aware of it, though. He was also aware of the way David Parker's glare turned on him, and narrowed furiously a split second before his cheeks flooded with hot crimson color and the man glanced away. If he didn't dislike Parker so much, Nick would have felt sorry for him.

"Don't look so guilty, Parker," Nick said as he hobbled into the kitchen and seated himself in the chair next to Dallas. He would rather have died than let either of them know it wasn't the agony in his leg that insisted he sit, but the agony of having seen them about to kiss. "Like you said, the two of you are gonna be husband and wife in less than a week. No reason you can't kiss each other."

Nick's gaze slid to Dallas. Had he been in a better mood, he might have enjoyed the way she flushed and squirmed.

"Nick, you don't understand," Dallas said. "I was just about to tell David that—"

Nick shook his head, cutting her short. "I understand perfectly, darlin'."

Darlin'. The warm endearment now sounded cold and dead on his tongue. Just hours ago, when Nick had rasped the word against her bare skin, it had sounded anything but.

Dallas flinched. She had to make him understand. She *had* to. "Nick, please, if you'll just let me explain . . ."

"Explain what? That you and Parker are getting hitched? No explanations necessary, darlin'." Nick's eyes narrowed, his gaze probing deeply into hers. "It's what you wanted all along, isn't it? Even a no-account cowpuncher like me could see that. Hell, I'm *happy* for you."

Dallas stared at Nick blankly. "You are?"

"Sure. Any reason I shouldn't be?"

"No reason at all," David inserted nervously. "Why, we're happier than two melons in a patch. Isn't that right, Dallas?"

David received no response. Both Dallas and Nick were staring at each other, acting as if they hadn't heard him, as if they'd both forgotten he was in the same room with them. David didn't know what was happening between these two, but the undercurrents that sizzled in their gazes bothered him. Whatever was happening here, he didn't like it.

Neither Dallas nor Nick noticed the way David's eyes narrowed to murderous green slits. His gaze, which grew stormier by the second, alternated between them. The natural flush in his cheeks deepened with his mounting rage.

"You're lying, Langston," Dallas snapped. She plucked up the spoon Lisa had used to stir her tea and fiddled with it, her fingers needing something more constructive to do than wrapping around Nick Langston's arrogant throat—the way they wanted badly to do. "There are plenty of reasons for you to be anything *but* happy about me marrying David."

Nick shrugged. The casualness of the gesture cost him in the way of pride; it was something these two would never know about, or understand. "Name three."

"Easily." Dallas smiled coldly and counted off the reasons with a jerky tap-tap-tap of the metal spoon on the tabletop. "One, you just made love to me not two hours ago. Two, you told me that you loved me. Three, you asked me to marry *you.*" Her gaze sharpened on him, and her tone rose in agitation. "Are those reasons good enough for you, Langston, or do you want more? I've got plenty!"

"Go ahead, Cameron. Give me every reason you've got, because, no, those ain't good enough."

The desire to strangle Nick where he sat was getting stronger. "Not good enough? Ha! They were good enough for you a few hours ago. They were good enough for you that night by the riverbank when you made love to me. They were good enough for you when—"

"Excuse me, darlin'? Exactly who made love to whom . . . ?"

If his intent was to pop the bubble of her anger, Nick succeeded.

Dallas had the decency to blush and glance guiltily away. Accidentally, her attention fell on David. His face was unnaturally pale, and he was staring at her blankly, as though unable to believe what he'd just heard.

Dallas swallowed hard. Her heart plummeted to her stomach. Oh, Lord, what had she done?

Every word she and Nick had just exchanged suddenly replayed themselves in her mind, slowly and vividly. While Dallas could believe she'd said what she did, what she was having a hard time coming to grips with was the fact that, in her anger, she'd said it all so *openly.* In front of David. This was one hell of a way for David to find out she couldn't marry him—not at all the way Dallas had planned on delivering the news.

"Damn you, Langston. *Now* look what you've done!" As far as Dallas was concerned, this whole mess was his fault. If not for Nick's goading, she would never have gotten mad enough to say the things she did, so mad she'd forgotten poor David's presence entirely.

Poor David?

Dallas brought herself up short, and thought that the stress of the day—Nick's lovemaking and proposal, her father's sudden illness—was finally getting to her, making her irrational. Why else would she feel even a smidgeon of pity for a tenderfoot like David Parker?

As though to make a bad situation even worse, the delicate sound of a throat being cleared intruded upon the tension-riddled silence.

Dallas looked up, a groan escaping her tightly compressed lips as she slammed the spoon on the table hard enough to make her palm and wrist hurt.

Lisa was standing framed in the doorway. Judging by her sister's rigid stance, wide-eyed expression, and flushed cheeks, it was a safe assumption that the girl had heard every incriminating word.

Well, wasn't that just dandy?

For a split second, Dallas was glad her father was laying upstairs, too sick to leave his bed. The only thing that could make things worse would be to spot Ian Cameron looming in the shadows of the hallway behind his youngest daughter.

"Am I interrupting?" Lisa asked softly, her fingers toying nervously with the two coffee mugs she was holding. Dallas recognized the mugs as the ones she and Nick had left in Lisa's bedroom earlier.

So much for things not being able to get worse.

Dallas opened her mouth to reply, but never got the chance. It was Nick Langston who answered Lisa.

"Not interrupting a thing, sweetheart. Mosey on in and sit a spell. Things are just starting to get interesting." Nick's big, open palm patted the empty chair to his right invitingly. His gaze left Lisa's, shifted, collided with Dallas's. "I was congratulating your sister and Parker on their upcoming nuptials. Isn't that right, Squirt?"

"Right," Dallas agreed tightly. "And I was just

about to tell Nick that there are no upcoming nuptials to congratulate us for."

"What?" David asked, confused. "But, but . . . What's going on, Dallas? I asked you to marry me this afternoon, and you said yes."

"I know," Dallas replied on a sigh. She turned to David, her gaze searching his, begging him to understand, even though she knew he couldn't. "I was wrong. I never should have said yes. I—I can't marry you, David. Not next Saturday, not next year . . . not ever." He looked crestfallen, and Dallas felt a stab of guilt. She shook her head, and her thick blond braid swayed against the rigid line of her spine. "I'm sorry. This isn't the way I wanted to tell you."

"Hey, Parker, don't look so glum," Nick said sarcastically. "At least she's *telling* you. That's a hell of a lot more than she did with me."

"I was going to tell you, Nick," Dallas snapped. Her barely suppressed anger rushed back in a flood. He was doing it again, making her so mad she couldn't think straight. And he did it so effortlessly!

"Is that so, darlin'?" Nick growled. "And when were you planning to do that? Before you went on your honeymoon . . . or after?"

"Dammit, Langston, I just told you that I'm not getting married!"

"Oh my," Lisa murmured from the doorway. "I think I do need to sit down after all." She crossed the room and, instead of taking the chair Nick had offered, perched daintily on the one next to David. The mugs rattled together as she placed them carefully on the table next to David's black bag. "Dallas," she said finally, and as calmly as her confusion would allow, "I thought you *wanted* to marry David? I thought . . . ?"

"I know, so did I," Dallas admitted miserably. "But I was wrong. I don't." Her gaze lifted, meeting Nick's. His blue eyes were hooded, his gaze as impassive as his expression. "I can't."

"Dallas," David said in a reasonable tone that grated on Dallas's already chaffed nerves almost as much as the way he again took her hand in his, "if you're worried that I won't want you after"—he swallowed nervously—"what's happened between you and"—this time he swallowed twice and nodded in Nick's general direction—"him, you're wrong. Darling, I love you. I want you to be my wife. It won't be easy, I admit. Still, I know in my heart that, in time, I can find it within myself to forgive your one—er, two minor indiscretions."

Dallas groaned and slipped her hand from his. David was talking prissy again. Oh, how she hated that; she always had to struggle to keep up, never quite understanding what he was trying to say, because he never just came right out and said any of it!

Absently, Dallas noticed that the outer corner of David's left eye was ticking rhythmically. A sure sign he was lying.

He could never forgive her "minor" indiscretions—*dammit, there had been nothing minor about them!*—and Dallas knew it! If anything, it was more likely David would hold them over her head for the rest of her life. *If* she changed her mind and decided to marry him, which she wasn't going to do, couldn't. Not after what she'd shared with Nick.

And speaking of Nick . . .

She glanced at him. Nick's face and gaze were still stony and unreadable. He seemed to be waiting for her to make some sort of reply to David. A look at Lisa said her sister was waiting for the same thing.

Dallas felt trapped. What did they expect her to say that hadn't already been said? And, as far as she was concerned, what had been said already was far too much. "While I appreciate it, David," Dallas said finally, choosing her words with care, "my answer is still no. I can't marry you."

David's jaw clamped hard, and the ticking in his left eye increased. His hands clenched and unclenched in tight fists on top of the table. "You're sure?"

"Positive."

"And there's nothing I can do or say to change your mind?"

"Nothing," Dallas assured him.

"All right then." David stood quickly, with enough force to unbalance the chair he'd been sitting in. The chair toppled to the floor, clattering noisily on the bare planks as he snatched up his medical bag.

David hesitated only long enough to split a hot glare between Dallas and Nick before spinning on his heel and stalking out of the kitchen, down the hallway. A few seconds later, the front door slammed shut. The sound reverberated throughout the abruptly quiet house like a clap of thunder.

"Well, that was . . . interesting." Lisa shifted uncomfortably when Dallas and Nick made no reply. The two of them had commenced glaring hotly at each other again, and looked like they'd be happy to continue doing so all night. The tension in the small kitchen was palpable; it made Lisa uneasy. "David seemed awfully upset. M-maybe I, um, should go talk to him . . . ?"

"Good idea," Dallas said, her voice husky and strained. She barely noticed when Lisa stood nervously, placed the mugs in the sink, and hurried out of the kitchen.

Dallas picked up the spoon again, and began picking at the edge of the metal handle with her thumbnail.

Lisa closed the front door much more quietly than David had.

Dallas waited until she heard the latch fall into place, and was sure her sister was out of earshot, before allowing herself to vent the anger that had been boiling inside of her. Her eyes sparkled a murderous shade of brown. "I hope you're happy with yourself, Langston, because you've just gone and spoiled everything!"

"Happy? Oh, yeah, Cameron, I'm tickled pink," he sneered. "It always thrills me to find out, *by accident,* that the woman I just made love to and proposed to went and got herself hog-tied to another man and forgot to tell me. Yup, can't think of anything that would make me happier."

"Damn it, Nick! Weren't you listening to anything that I just said? Hell, it seems like the whole rest of the house heard me! How many times do I have to tell you, *I'm not marrying David Parker!* And I didn't forget to tell you a thing. There was nothing *to* tell!"

"Is that so?" The muscle in his jaw worked furiously.

Dallas hesitated long enough to suck in a couple of deep, sanity-cleansing breaths. She forced herself to calm down before continuing. "Listen to me, Nick. Please. I'm telling you the truth." Her free hand lifted, and her fingertips gently skimmed her lips, remembering. She could still feel and taste Nick Langston's claiming kisses. "Tonight, when you kissed me," she continued breathlessly, "when you touched me . . . when we . . . Damn it, Nick, I knew then and there that I could never marry David. It just didn't seem like the right time or place to tell you about something that I knew damn well was *not* going to happen."

"The whiskey," Nick said suddenly.

Dallas frowned. "What about it?"

"That's why you broke into your daddy's liquor cabinet tonight, isn't it? You were drinking because the pansy had proposed."

Dallas wrapped both hands, cold and shaky, around the spoon handle. Lowering her gaze, she nodded. "Yes. I knew I should have been happy. No, I should have been *ecstatic*. David had asked me to marry him, and I'd said yes. I'd gotten exactly what I wanted." She sighed heavily. "The thing of it is, I *wasn't* happy. Oh, Nick, I was so damn miserable!"

"Why?"

Dallas's gaze lifted, meeting his. Nick was scrutinizing her, as though ready to read a lie into even the most minute expression or gesture. She shook her head, confused. "Why . . . what?"

"Why were you miserable?"

"You don't know?"

"I'm pretty sure I do." His attention dipped, sliding over her lips.

Dallas's blood tingled warmly in her veins. She shivered, feeling as though the calloused tips of his fingers had singed her flesh, not merely the onslaught of his gaze.

"Tell me why you were miserable, darlin'," Nick prompted. His gaze darkened and heated. He cursed under his breath when he felt his respiration go rapid and shallow. Not that he was surprised. Lately, this was a normal, physical reaction to Dallas Cameron's nearness. A reaction Nick wasn't entirely sure he'd ever get used to, but knew he'd welcome the opportunity to try. Softly, huskily, he said, "I want to hear you say it."

Dallas leaned forward. Dropping the spoon, she reached out and cupped Nick's cheek in her open hand. She could feel the muscle just beneath his chiseled cheekbone jerk erratically against the heel of her palm.

She shivered as, meeting and holding his gaze, she confessed, "Because, Langston, you've got me so damn crazy in love with you that I can't think straight anymore. Because the idea of marrying David Parker, when the only man I've ever loved and wanted is you, had me tied up in knots on the inside. I knew what I *should* do—marry David—and what I *wanted* to do— be with you. I also knew that I couldn't do both. The indecision was eating me up."

"Couldn't have hurt more than when Parker told me and your daddy that the two of you were getting hitched."

"H-he told Papa, too?"

Nick nodded.

Dallas rolled her eyes and groaned. "What did Papa say?"

"That he was thrilled." Nick intentionally didn't mention the flat tone of voice Ian had used, or the conversation that came afterward. His mind still echoed the words insistently back to him, though.

Ian thought of Nick Langston as a son? Thought Nick was good enough to marry his little girl? Nick's head still spun from that unexpected revelation.

After so many years of being good, but never quite good enough, he was finding it hard to believe that now, for reasons that eluded him, he suddenly was.

The idea . . . dammit, the whole thing just didn't sit right!

Doubt pulled and nagged at Nick. What if Ian had said those things only because he was afraid he was dying? What if, once the old man figured out he wasn't, Ian changed his mind and decided that a dirt poor, crippled ex-foreman—a fair step *down* from a dirt poor, healthy cowpoke, in Nick's estimation— wasn't near good enough for his baby girl after all? What then?

The muscles in Nick's gut fisted. He wanted so badly to take Ian at his word. He wanted . . . things that were out of reach. Things he simply could not have.

He wanted Dallas Cameron.

In the worst possible way, he wanted her. Maybe he wanted her even more because she was so damn far out of his reach? No. Nick had a gut feeling that, even if

Dallas was within reach, he'd want her as badly as he did now.

Nick's gaze strayed over Dallas, and his emotions twisted.

He remembered the feel of her hair tickling his bare belly, the erotic feel of her bare legs wrapped tightly around his hips as he buried himself deeply inside of her. He remembered how her breaths misted a warm brand on his skin, remembered how wonderfully their bodies had fit together, and how she'd moved in perfect time with him. He remembered . . .

Ah, God, he remembered too damn much!

You even think *about touching one of my daughters in a less than brotherly fashion, boy, and what's left of you will be shown the property markers come sunup.*

"Nick?"

Nick shook off the memory and glanced up sharply. "Yeah?"

"What's wrong?"

"Nothing, why?"

Dallas frowned. "Because two minutes ago I told you that I love you, and you haven't said a word."

"What's left to say?"

"You could tell me that you love me, too."

"Yup, I could do that."

"Well? Are you going to?" Dallas's pause was thick and tense. "Nick?"

"No. I can't. It just . . . it ain't right."

Despite the slicing pain in his leg, Nick pushed himself to his feet and snatched up the crutch from where he'd propped it against the side of the table. He needed a cigarette and a drink, not necessarily in that order.

He'd left both upstairs. He'd have to settle for some fresh air. Maybe *that* would help clear his head.

Nick was halfway to the kitchen door when Dallas's soft, shaky voice stopped him cold.

"What do you mean, it isn't right? *What* isn't right?"

"You and me, darlin'. It ain't right, and it won't work." Nick wondered if it hurt Dallas half as much to hear the words as it hurt him to say them. No, he decided, it couldn't possibly. "Go find Parker. Tell him you've changed your mind about marrying him."

"What?" A bang of metal on wood told him Dallas had just slammed the spoon down on the table again. "Dammit, Langston, I don't want to marry David, I want to marry *you!*"

Nick winced. How could emotional pain cause such acute physical agony? Even on his worst days, his leg never hurt as much as his heart did at that moment. It would be better for them both, Nick decided, if he took the reins and ended what was between him and Dallas here and now, and ended it quickly. "Pity we don't always get what we want, isn't it, Cameron? Tell your daddy I'll be riding come dawn."

"You're l-leaving?"

"Yup."

"But why? Where will you go?"

"Haven't rightly decided yet," Nick answered tightly. "Right now, darlin', about the only thing I'm dead-set sure about is that I have to get the hell off this ranch and away from you."

Nick heard a gasp and a muffled sniffle, and he knew Dallas was crying.

A second ago, he would have sworn he couldn't feel any worse. He was wrong.

In a slow, limping gait, Nick hobbled to the doorway and, after a heartbeat's hesitation, melted into the cool midnight shadows of the hallway.

He didn't look back at Dallas.

He didn't dare.

Chapter Seventeen

"Nick?" Dallas broke through the stand of cotton-woods, her steps faltering. The moon was bright and full, bathing the small clearing in a soft silver haze. Her heartbeat staggered when she remembered all too vividly . . .

No, dammit, she couldn't, *wouldn't,* think about any of that. Not right now.

Shaking the highly erotic memories aside, Dallas scanned the clearing. Her gaze searched and found Nick.

He was sitting on the riverbank with his back to her, in the same spot where she'd taken a tumble into the water what seemed now like at least a lifetime ago. His boots and stockings were tossed atop the ground beside him. The pants leg that wasn't cut off had been rolled sloppily up to hair-dusted midshin. His feet were bare. While his splinted leg didn't bend, instead extending perpendicularly with the water, his other foot was in the water, making small, restless circles and gently stirring the otherwise placid surface.

Dallas half expected to see a bottle of whiskey propped against his hip. Wasn't that how she'd found him here the last time? "Nick?"

If she'd wondered before if he'd heard her, now Dallas was positive he hadn't. At the sound of her voice, his spine went rigid, and his broad shoulders squared. His head had been bent, as though he'd been staring vacantly at the water; his chin now jerked sharply upward. Beneath his shirt, she saw the muscles in his back, shoulders, and arms pull taut.

"What the hell are you doing here?"

Nick didn't glance back at her as he *growled* the words. Dallas was unsure if she should be pleased or disappointed.

"I'm looking for Lisa."

"She's not here."

"I can see that. Has she been here?"

"Nope. Last I saw of her, she was chasing after Parker."

Dallas sighed and nodded. "That was the last time I saw her, too. And I haven't seen her at all since. Nick, I'm starting to get worried. I've looked all over, and I can't find her anywhere."

"So?" Nick's shrug was strained. "What's the problem? She probably went for a walk."

"At this hour?"

"You're here, aren't you?"

"That's different. I'm not Lisa. Lisa never goes for walks at night. You know that."

"Yup. I also know Lisa never goes on cattle drives, but she did that recently, too."

"Only because Papa *made* her."

"Wrong." Slowly, Nick's head came around. The moonlight glinted off his eyes, making them shimmer an arresting shade of blue. Dallas's breath caught. His gaze bored hotly into her. "Lesson number . . . ah, hell." Nick gritted his teeth and shook his head. "Dammit, Cameron, I gave you credit for being smarter than that. Don't you know that no one can *make* someone do anything they don't, deep down, want to do? Haven't you figured that out yet?"

Nick wasn't referring to Lisa taking an unprecedented midnight stroll. Instead, his words, his tone, hinted at a deeper, more complex meaning. One that warmed Dallas right down to the shivering core.

Picking her words carefully, Dallas said, "You mean that you wouldn't have agreed to give me lessons in how to be ladylike if you hadn't, deep down, wanted to?"

"No. What I *mean* is . . ." Nick sucked in a ragged breath, and raked his fingers through his hair. His foot made restless, churning circles in the water. "Damnation, I don't know what the hell I mean! You've got me so tied up in knots I can't think straight."

"I know."

"Like hell you do!" he growled hotly.

"Like hell I don't!" Dallas countered, just as hotly.

She crossed to where Nick sat, kneeling on the ground beside him. Her hand lifted, poised a fraction of an inch from touching his shoulder. Her fingers trembled when his body heat seared into her palm. After a beat of hesitation, Dallas sighed and lowered her hand limply to her lap, the contact never made.

"Do you think this isn't tearing me up, too, Nick?"

she asked. "Do you think I planned for any of this to happen? Well, it is, and I didn't. All you were supposed to do was teach me how to be a lady. Period."

"So you could rope Parker to the altar," Nick prompted tightly.

"Right."

"So what's the problem? You did it. The pansy proposed. As always, Dallas Cameron got exactly what Dallas Cameron wanted."

"The problem," Dallas clarified softly, "is that Dallas Cameron doesn't want David Parker. She wants Nick Langston."

Nick's foot stopped in midswirl. His heartbeat had sped up the second Dallas knelt beside him and the heat of her body, the fresh, clean smell of her, invaded him; the rhythm still hadn't ironed itself out. He doubted it ever would.

"We've been over this territory before, Cameron. I've got nothing to offer you," Nick said finally, his tone forcibly flat as he glanced down at his bad leg. "Less than nothing."

"Nothing? You're sure about that?" With the tip of her index finger, Dallas traced the line of his jaw.

It was a simple touch.

There was nothing simple about Nick's reaction to it.

The feel of Dallas's skin sliding over his own sliced into him like a bolt of lightning. His breath caught, and he shivered.

Her touch felt good. Ah, Christ, it felt *too damn good!*

Reaching up quickly, he banded her wrist with his

fingers, yanking her hand away. Beneath the heel of his palm, Dallas's pulse throbbed. The beat, he noticed, was every bit as heavy and erratic as his own.

His gaze lifted, locking with hers. "Don't."

"Don't what?" she asked, her normally husky voice a pitch huskier. "Don't talk to you? Don't touch you? Don't . . . what, Nick? You'll have to be more specific."

"Any of it." He shook his head. "All of it. I—"

"Love you," she said, cutting him short. "I love you, Nick. I always have, always will. When are you going to get it through that thick-as-all-hell skull of yours that the only thing I want from you is . . . you?"

Nick looked at her, wanting with all his heart to let himself believe what she said, yet at the same time unable to. She was the boss's daughter, he reminded himself forcefully. Ah, but he was having the devil's own time remembering that!

. . . I don't recall ever saying that the Bar None's foreman *wasn't good enough for my little girl.*

Ian's words—the disbelief and elation Nick had felt when the old man uttered them—cut through Nick like a knife. His voice low and gritty, he said, "And Dallas Cameron always gets what Dallas Cameron wants. Isn't that right, darlin'?"

Dallas's grin was steeped in an innately feminine confidence that Nick would never have given her credit for knowing . . . a few weeks ago. Before their lessons had commenced. She knew it now, though. He'd taught her too damn well!

She lifted her chin, leaned toward him.

"Always," Dallas whispered, her breath hot and misty against his mouth.

The temptingly firm swell of her breasts pressed warmly against Nick's upper arm.

He groaned.

The night was warm and dry, but that didn't account for the beads of sweat that abruptly dampened his brow. His body felt like it was on fire in all the places where it touched Dallas's . . . and so cold everywhere else. He felt himself harden and he shook his head. He shouldn't want her again. Not here, not now, not *this badly*.

But he did.

She cupped his face in her hands, tugging him closer. He offered no resistance, couldn't. Nick's foot stilled in the water. He dragged in a deep, harsh breath when Dallas leaned more closely into him and brushed her lips softly back and forth over his.

His hands lifted, his fingers tunneling into her hair, cupping her scalp as he angled his head and kissed her deeply. The tip of his tongue dragged along her lower lip before plunging into her mouth, dancing and mating hungrily with hers.

Ah, but she felt and tasted so good!

Nick was beginning to think he'd never grow tired of touching this woman, kissing her, making love to her. He was starting to think he'd never want to tire of it. And he was also starting to think that maybe, just maybe, he was good enough for her after all.

His bad leg was aching. Nick took his other foot out of the water, then carefully shimmied back on the bank. His mouth never leaving her, he lay down on the warm, damp ground.

As he moved, Nick slipped his hands over Dallas's shoulders, absorbing the violent tremor that ran through her with his palms. He coiled his fingers around her upper arms, dragging her body down on top of his.

He deepened the kiss to a fevered pitch, reveling in Dallas's unabandoned response. Through the barriers of their clothes, he could feel her heat and softness. Her hair floated down around them like a thick, tawny cloud. The strands tickled his skin like threads of moon-shot silk.

Nick's blood hummed, throbbing in his ears. The desire to rid them quickly of the obstruction of clothes, to feel her flesh to flesh again, hit him like a punch. It drove the air from his lungs and all sense of caution and reason from his mind.

He had to have her. His need to bury himself inside her wet heat was as uncontrollable as it was strong. He couldn't fight it. He no longer wanted to.

Nick pulled back slightly to look up at her. Dallas's cheeks were flushed, her gaze hooded, her breathing every bit as ragged and labored as his own.

She'd never looked more beautiful.

"This is madness," he said huskily.

"I know. But it's the most wonderful kind of madness I've ever known." Dallas's gaze lowered, caressing Nick's lips even as she ran the tip of her tongue over her own. She tasted him on her tongue, and shivered. "No one can make me feel the way you do, Nick. No one."

"Your daddy . . ."

Dallas slanted a finger over his lips to silence him, his mustache tickling her skin. She shook her head. Her voice low and throaty, she said, "Agrees with me."

"How do you know that?"

"While I was looking for Lisa, I stopped in his room to talk to him. Papa told me what you two said earlier. He said there's never been a question in his mind of you not being good enough, and that the only person who's never been able to see that is you. He's right, Nick. I don't know why you think you're not good enough, I'm not even sure the reason matters anymore. Whatever happened in your past to make you the way you are, I don't care. The way you are, *who* you are, is fine by me. You—"

A throat cleared loudly. That, coupled with the rustle of leaves and crunch of fallen branches beneath booted feet as someone trampled through the moonlit stand of cottonwoods, made Dallas stiffen and glance up sharply.

Lisa?

It was Dallas's first thought, and her heart picked up speed with relief. Maybe Nick was right. Maybe Lisa had decided to take a late-night stroll after all.

If so, the girl hadn't strolled down to the river. Dallas knew it the second she saw a tall, rangy figure emerge from the trees and step into the clearing.

That was not Lisa. Even though the intruder stood mostly in shadows, his wispy gray hair and loose, bowlegged gait made his identity obvious.

"Pete?" Dallas asked as, suddenly realizing her and

Nick's position, she scrambled quickly to her feet. "What are you doing down here?"

Nick sat up and frowned. Something was wrong. He could feel it. Pete wasn't the sort to wander around at night; the old coot worked damn hard all day and he cherished his sleep. For Pete to be here at this hour of the night spoke volumes.

Nick picked up his crutch, propped it on the ground, and used it to push himself awkwardly to his feet. "What's wrong? Another fire?"

"Nope." Pete shook his head and scratched under his grizzled chin. His gaze volleyed between Dallas and Nick. "Worse."

Dallas paled and took a leadened step forward. "Oh, no. Not Papa."

"Your daddy's fine, Dallas. It's your sister who . . . ain't so fine."

Dallas had been in the middle of taking another step toward Pete. His words hit her like ice water, freezing her in midstep. "What's happened to Lisa?" she demanded, her voice cracking with the panic that washed over her in cold waves.

"Dunno. Parker took her."

"What do you mean he 'took' her?" Nick asked insistently.

"Just what I said. One of the punchers saw Parker and her riding past the Bar None property markers hell-bent for leather on his horse." His scowl increased the number of sun-cracked lines in his weathered face. "Since she was tossed over the saddle in front of him like a sack of grain, and putting up one hell of a

405

rip-roarin' fight, from the sounds, I'd say she didn't exactly want to go with him."

"You mean David *kidnapped* her?" Dallas cried.

"Ayup," Pete said. "That'd be my guess."

Dallas's thoughts whirlwinded. Goddammit, what was going on? Why would David kidnap Lisa?

She tried to swallow back a surge of panic. Her knees felt weak and shaky; she refused to allow them to buckle, the way they threatened to. While Dallas's fear and confusion were strong, there was no time to acknowledge or indulge in either emotion. What was needed now was swift, sure action.

"Which way were they heading?" she asked.

"Toward town," Pete replied. "The puncher seemed to think that Parker didn't know he was being watched, so there's a good chance he ain't trying to cover his tracks."

"Has my father been told about any of this?"

Pete looked stunned. "Hell no!"

"Good." Dallas nodded slowly, thinking. She felt Nick come up behind her, and while their bodies didn't touch, the heat and nearness of him helped to fortify her courage. She kept her attention locked on Pete. "Has anyone gone after them yet?"

"Nope. Just found out about it myself, Dallas. First thing I done was come down here to fetch you and Nick."

That Pete had thought to look for both herself and Nick by the river, at this hour of the night, struck Dallas as odd. Why did he naturally link them together in his mind? Had Nick told him . . . ? As quickly as the thought came to her, Dallas shook it off, deeming it unworthy. She knew Nick Langston better than that; he never bragged about his bed partners.

Oh, Lord, what was she doing? There wasn't time to worry about anything so trivial right now!

Lisa had been kidnapped, and Parker was still near enough to catch. If she rode fast and hard. *That* was what she needed to concentrate on.

A sly grin tugged at Dallas's lips. David Parker rode about as well as he roped. Which meant not well at all. Plus, his horse was burdened with two people, one of whom was struggling—the thought made Dallas cringe inwardly. That in itself would slow him down.

Why he was heading for Green River was anyone's guess, but Dallas was determined to catch up with him and get Lisa back before he ever made it into town. There was a very good chance she could accomplish that, too. But not if she wasted any more time here!

"Pete, give me your gun." Dallas held her hand out expectantly. The old man complied without hesitation, reaching for his holster and unstrapping it with weathered, work-roughened fingers.

"What are you going to do?" Nick asked.

"Go after them. What else?" Dallas glanced back at Nick impatiently. "I can't very well sit back and do nothing, Langston. Goddammit, the pansy took my sister!"

"Which means he's not as much of a pansy as we thought. I'm going with you."

"No, you aren't, Nick. You can't. The shape you're in, you'll only slow me down."

Nick swore loudly and fiercely, his eyes darkening to a furious shade of midnight blue, his narrowed gaze piercing her. The slight flush beneath the tan in his cheeks spoke for itself.

Nick knew that Dallas was right. Admitting it hurt more than the reason for it.

Pete draped the gun belt over Dallas's hand, and she immediately set to work buckling and tieing it into place. When she was done, he shoved a box of ammunition into her hands. She looked up at him, surprised.

"Figured you'd be needing it." Pete smiled a crooked-toothed grin and hiked a thumb over his shoulder. "Your horse is back there, tethered to a cottonwood. So's mine . . . along with a shotgun and plenty of shells for it. I ain't letting you go after Parker alone, Dallas. Maybe Nick can't go with you, but I can."

Dallas regarded her old friend levelly. "You're not as good a rider as I am, Pete, and you know it. You'll slow me down, too."

"Dang it all! Keeping up with you isn't what I had in mind, girl." Pete's wiry shoulders rose and fell in a tight shrug. "Watching your back *is.*"

Dallas hesitated for a beat.

If Pete wanted to come with her, fine . . . so long as he knew from the outset that she would *not* keep a slow pace on his account. The glint in the old man's eyes said he understood that, and was determined to go with her anyway. So why not let him? While he wasn't as good a rider as she was, the fact remained that he was a damn good shot. Also, the appeal of having someone to guard her back was as strong as it was undeniable.

There was no way to know David's reason for kidnapping Lisa . . . or if he'd acted alone. Just because only the one rider had been spotted didn't mean there were not more who hadn't been seen.

Dallas nodded briskly. "Let's go." She sent Nick a quick glance, whispered softly, sincerely, "I'm sorry," then sprinted toward the trees.

Pete turned to follow her, but Nick's fingers curling around the old man's thin upper arm stopped him cold.

"Dammit, Pete, if anything happens to her . . ." Nick growled.

Pete glanced up at him, his normally narrow eyes narrowing still more. His gaze raked Nick's face assessively. A grin twitched at one corner of his mouth, and a flash of realization glinted in his watery green eyes. His only response was a curt nod.

Nick forced himself to let go of his old friend's arm.

Gritting his teeth, the muscle in his jaw jerking, Nick watched as first Dallas, then Pete, were swallowed by the shadows cast by the stand of moonlit-cottonwoods.

In the past few weeks, Nick Langston had thought he'd come to know what it felt like to be worthless.

He was wrong.

Nothing compared to the emotion that tore through him like a sharp, jagged icicle when Dallas had said, "You'll only slow me down."

And he'd realized she was right.

Chapter Eighteen

"If you don't stop whining and squirming, so help me God, I'll tie you up and gag you!"

The way David Parker sneered the words at her, at the same time yanking her unceremoniously off of his horse, made Lisa gasp.

The blood rushed from her head as she was placed on her feet. Lisa swayed dizzily, her stomach churning. Only the bite of David's fingers digging roughly into her upper arms kept her from keeling over.

For the last half hour she'd been flung face first over a saddle; her body ached from the hard ride and the way the pommel had ground into the side of her waist with each jarring stride of his mare. Right now, the only thing she felt more than soreness was fear.

Good Lord, what was going on?

One minute she'd been standing in the yard, talking to David and trying to console him over Dallas's refusal to marry him. The next thing Lisa knew, David had savagely muttered something about "setting things right one damn way or another," then without warning hoisted her up and tossed her, struggling, over his saddle.

But *why*?

"Tell me what's going on," Lisa pleaded as soon as she was able to catch her breath and keep her voice marginally steady. "What's wrong?"

"Nothing anymore. Come on."

With that cryptic response, David spun on his heel. His grip on one of her arms fell away, while the fingers of his other hand slipped down to vise her wrist.

Lisa winced. David's grasp was bruisingly tight as he gave her a tug, dragging her roughly up the boardwalk stairs leading into McFee's, Green River's lone saloon. The muscles in her legs were sore, screaming a protest as she was forced to stumble in step behind him.

"What are you doing?" she cried. Lisa tried to yank free of his punishing grip, even though she knew it was useless. When that didn't work, she tried clawing at his fingers. That didn't work, either. David only tightened his grip, but never bothered to glance at her, let alone once break stride. "David, please, *let me go!*"

David's open palm smacked determinedly into one of the swinging doors. The collision shoved the door open with enough force for it to swing back and crash hard into the interior wall of the saloon.

The patrons of McFee's must have been used to such abrupt entrances, Lisa thought, for only a rare few bothered to give David a first, never mind second, glance. If they noticed the dainty, diminutive figure cowering behind him, they showed no sign of it.

Tinny harpsichord music and the bark of harsh

male laughter hit Lisa like a slap. She cringed and coughed. Her eyes stung and watered, and her nostrils burned as a thick fog of cigarette smoke assailed her.

While she'd seen McFee's Saloon often enough, it had always been from the outside. Unlike Dallas, she'd never stepped foot across the threshold, nor had any desire to.

"Hey, Parker," someone bellowed from across the room; the man had to shout to be heard over the commotion. "Mosey on over here and I'll buy you a shot of rotgut. Sure to grow some hair on your chest. The good Lord knows you could use some!"

"Yeah," another, equally abrasive voice called out. "That and some shootin' lessons."

"Nah," the first man hollered back, "leave that to Dallas Cameron . . . if'n she ain't taught the boy already."

"Oh, she done taught him something, all right," the second said. "But it weren't how to shoot!"

A few men laughed heartily over the exchange.

Lisa felt David's body go stiff. While she had no idea what was going on, or why he'd hauled her off the Bar None in such a fashion and brought her here, she suspected that the men's nasty teasing wasn't going to lighten his mood any. Or help her situation.

"David, please," Lisa whispered anxiously, "let's get out of here."

"Not yet," he replied through tightly gritted teeth. "Not until we've done what I brought you here for."

His voice was rough, uncompromising; if Lisa didn't know better, she wouldn't have recognized it as belonging to David Parker.

413

She shivered, and a drop of fear trickled down her spine like ice water. Squirming to stay hidden behind him as best she could, afraid someone would see and recognize her, she asked timidly, "Why *did* you bring me here?"

David glanced back at her then, and Lisa wished suddenly that he hadn't. His gaze was as hard and as ruthless as his answer. "To get married, of course."

"To . . . *what!*" Lisa cried. Shock made the response come out much louder than she'd intended.

The sound of her voice over so much male talk and laughter silenced those in the immediate vicinity. Men glanced up from behind their hands of poker, while others dragged their thoughtful attention away from half-empty glasses, searching for the source.

They found it quickly.

David gave Lisa's wrist a vicious tug, and she stumbled out from behind him. She groaned, as much from the pain that shot up from her wrist as from the feel of dozens of lewd, curious gazes biting into her.

A blush heated her cheeks. Thirteen-year-old girls didn't enter saloons at this hour of night. Not decent ones, leastwise, so Maria said. Shame burned Lisa to the core; it was matched with equal parts of fear that David Parker meant every word he'd said.

"You heard me," David replied, his tone confident, and loud enough for anyone nearby to hear him. "Just as soon as Preacher Thomas has been fetched, you and I are getting married. Tonight."

Had she not been so shocked, Lisa would have resumed her struggles. As it was, all she could do was stare up at him with large, beseeching eyes. "You're joking?"

"Do I look like I'm joking?"

No. Oh, Heavens, he most definitely did not!

The rhythm of Lisa's heartbeat kicked into double-time. She had to swallow hard before she was able to speak. Even then, her voice was low and shaky. "I don't want to marry you. I'm not *old enough* to marry you."

David's grin was so predatory and cold that it froze the blood in her veins. He leaned toward her and, for a split second, Lisa feared he was going to kiss her.

Instead, David whispered loud enough for only her to hear, "Do you think I give a hoot about your age, Lisa? I don't. All I care about is getting my hands on the Bar None. Dallas was a means to that end, but I should have known she'd mess things up somehow. Luckily, I'm not picky. As far as I'm concerned, one Cameron's as good as the other."

"I—I won't do it," Lisa stammered. "I . . . I'll fight you. I'll scream and kick and make sure everyone in this place knows that I do *not* want to marry you."

"No you won't." If possible, David's smile became degrees icier. Reaching up with his free hand, he stroked the back of his knuckles over the curve of her cheek. "And do you want to know why that is, Lisa?" She swallowed hard and nodded mutely. "Because if you do, if you say so much as a word or let on in any way that you don't want to marry me . . . I'll kill you."

She paled.

His grin broadened. "They may have taught me in medical school how to heal people, but I also learned something else. How to kill. I can snap that pretty little neck of yours in less than a second. You'll be dead before you hit the floor. What's more, sweetheart, I can make it look like an accident." His eyes narrowed to dangerous green slits. "You'd better think long and hard before deciding to fight me. I'll do it. I've got nothing to lose."

Lisa's knees, which had been watery since she'd been hauled off the horse, buckled. She collapsed weakly against David's side, her breathing shallow and rapid enough to make her head spin and her stomach churn.

Lisa could see conviction burning hotly in David's eyes. If she protested in any way, he *would* kill her. She knew it.

Mustering her courage, Lisa glanced furtively around the room. Her gaze fell on a man sitting in the corner. She could barely make out his features through the veil of cigarette smoke and shadows that cloaked him. She squinted, bringing him into sharper focus, and the breath left her lungs in a rush when she recognized him.

It was Rico. The cowpuncher whom Dallas had fired the day Nick Langston got hurt.

Did the man still feel even a smidgeon of brand loyalty to the Bar None? Would he offer her help?

Dear God, Lisa hoped so!

"Damnation!" Nick slammed the cover of the ledger closed. The clock sitting next to the book atop the

study's thick, solid oak desk shivered with the vibration of the blow.

How could he concentrate on adding up long, tedious columns of numbers when all he could think about—*worry like hell about!*—was Dallas?

She'd been gone for over three hours.

With each minute that ticked very slowly, very tensely past, Nick felt the fingers of concern tighten around his heart, constricting his chest until he could barely breathe.

Christ, he hated waiting!

Tonight was the first time he'd been on his feet in weeks, and the pulsating pain in his leg told him he'd overtaxed himself at least four hours ago.

That pain was nothing compared to the agony of wondering—worrying, worrying, *worrying!*—about what had happened to Dallas in the time she'd been gone.

Dammit, what was wrong with him? How could he have let her go after Parker and Lisa with only Hickory Pete along as protection?

The muscle in his cheek ticking erratically, Nick massaged his wounded thigh and grimaced.

How could he not have? He sure as hell was in no shape to go with her, and there'd been no time to fetch anyone else.

Time had been of the essence. He'd known it as well as Dallas did.

The second Nick had gotten back to the ranch house he'd rounded up a couple dozen sleepy cowpunchers and sent them after her, but he doubted their help would do much good.

Dallas was a damn fine rider. The best on the Bar None—second only to himself, back when he could sit a horse. The help he'd sent would never catch up to her in time.

With a savage curse, Nick brought his fist down hard on top of the closed ledger book. Resting his elbows on top of the desk, he plowed all ten fingers through his hair. The sigh that pushed from his lungs was ragged and torn.

He *should* be by Dallas's side right now, facing whatever was happening to her, not sitting impotently behind Ian Cameron's big oak desk in Ian Cameron's study! He had no right to be in this room, in this house. No damn right at all.

Yet here he was.

And here he would remain. Until Dallas got back, and he'd seen with his own eyes that she was unharmed.

The fist around his heart tightened painfully. Nick refused to contemplate another scenario, couldn't.

Dallas had been right about one thing, wrong about another.

She'd been right in thinking Pete wouldn't be able to keep up with her. Right now, the old coot was a good mile behind her, even as her horse dashed hell-bent down the center of Green River's only main street, its hooves kicking up clouds of dry Texas dust.

What she'd been wrong about was thinking she could catch up with David Parker before he reached town. She hadn't, although Dallas didn't think he was very far ahead of her. Ten minutes at the most would be her guess.

That surprised Dallas, and left a nagging doubt in her mind.

If she'd underestimated David's riding ability, what *else* had she underestimated about him?

At this hour of the night, the town was mostly deserted. Except for McFee's. Dallas had visited the saloon—usually snuck in as a joke by a few drunken cowpunchers after a particularly long and arduous trail drive—enough times to know there should be rowdy music and harsh male voices pouring out of the saloon's swinging doors right now.

There wasn't.

Except for the light shimmering out the door and through the big front window, the place might have been empty. The saloon was quiet. Too quiet.

Her gaze scanned the horses and buckboards lined up in front of the boardwalk. She frowned and slowed her mount when she spotted David's mare tethered to a post.

What the . . . ?

David had kidnapped Lisa and brought her to McFee's? For what purpose?

She didn't know, but she was going to find out.

With a flick of her wrist, Dallas guided her stallion toward the saloon. Dismounting lithely, she tethered the horse next to David's, then cautiously climbed the boardwalk's steps. Only the hushed murmur of a few male voices snuck out through the swinging doors and whispered in her ears.

While Dallas's first instinct—strong and hot—was to barge right into the place, she quenched the urge.

Something out of the ordinary was going on in there. The lack of commotion told her that.

While her need to get to Lisa was strong, Dallas didn't want to do anything rash or stupid. She had to wait until she knew exactly what was happening in there before making her presence known. It was the only way to keep the advantage of surprise on her side.

Oh, how she wished Nick was here. He'd know what to do!

But he wasn't, Dallas reminded herself staunchly as she crept quietly to the door.

She plastered her back against the cold, hard, clapboard wall and listened intently. It was difficult to hear much over the throbbing of her heart in her ears, but she heard enough . . .

Soft, feminine sobbing.

A male voice—David's—snapping for the girl to shut up.

Both were almost drowned out by the reluctant drone of Preacher Thomas reciting wedding vows.

The words cut through Dallas like a knife. Her eyes widened in shock. Her breath caught in her throat, and her blood ran cold. Realization hit her like a slap, dumping a dose of adrenaline into her bloodstream that was so strong it made her aching muscles shiver with the need to *do something*.

David was forcing Lisa to marry him.

Dear God, the girl was only thirteen years old!

A wave of self-recrimination crashed over Dallas. She should have known Parker was up to something.

420

He'd never been so nice, so complimentary, as he'd been these last few weeks. She remembered the look on his face when she'd told him she wouldn't marry him. Remembered the glint of raw fury she'd seen sparkling in his eyes a split second before he found the self-control to mask it.

How had she missed all of that?

And did it really matter now?

Dallas shook her head determinedly. No, it did not. She couldn't control the past, but she could damn well do her best to control the future.

What mattered right now was getting Lisa away from Parker, back to the Bar None and to safety, *before* the final vows were spoken.

But how . . . ?

Holding her breath, Dallas leaned to the side, peeking into the saloon. She assessed the situation in a glance.

Parker and Lisa were at the far end of the room, near the bar, standing in front of the tall, dark, imposing form of Preacher Thomas. Even from this distance, Dallas could see the way her baby sister was shaking; the sight cut through Dallas like a knife.

From this angle, there was no way to tell if David was holding a gun to Lisa, but Dallas thought it smart to presume he was. Better safe than sorry, especially where her sister's life was concerned.

Her attention quickly scanned the rest of the room. The other patrons of the saloon were still scattered at the numerous tables, drinks and hands of cards set aside. Most were silently watching the unexpected ceremony taking place.

Dallas's hand slipped the pistol from its holster as a movement in the right corner of the room snagged her attention. She glanced quickly in that direction, then swerved her attention back to Lisa and Parker.

As recognition dawned, Dallas's gaze shot back to the corner again, honing in on the man who was sitting in the shadows there.

Rico.

Dallas's fingers tightened around the butt of the gun as her gaze caught and held Rico's penetrating black one.

Rico's expression was impassive. His eyes were puffy and bloodshot, indicating he'd been drinking. But he wasn't drunk. The way his attention shifted unerringly from herself, to Parker, then back again told Dallas that.

Rico hesitated, then gave a quick, brisk nod of his head.

Dallas released the breath she only now realized she'd been holding. She nodded back at him.

Her heartbeat stammered with renewed hope, and the knowledge that she was no longer in this situation alone. She'd fired Rico; he no longer owed the Bar None an ounce of loyalty. Yet he was giving it anyway.

Preacher Thomas cleared his throat and said reluctantly, "If there is anyone here who knows just cause why these two should not be joined in the state of Holy matrimon—"

"There isn't," David snarled, cutting the preacher short. "Get on with it."

The muscles in Dallas's body pulled taut as her gaze

shot back to Rico. He was in there, he knew the situation better than she did. Hate though she did to wait, Dallas forced herself not to act until he'd given her some sort of sign that the time was ripe.

Rico wasn't looking at her—his narrow black gaze was rooted on Parker's slender back—yet Dallas knew he was still very much aware of her presence.

Again, Rico nodded his dark head, this time more firmly. At the same time, he pushed to his feet with enough quickness and force to send the chair he'd been sitting in careening into the wall behind him.

Dallas's reaction was instantaneous. She'd been braced, ready for action, and now she followed through on that impulse without a second thought.

Simultaneously shoving her shoulder hard against the swinging door and bringing the pistol up, she burst into the saloon.

Parker, holding a crying and squirming Lisa against his side, spun to face the sudden noise and intrusion.

Lisa gasped when she saw her sister, then whimpered when her gaze dropped to the gun in Dallas's hands. The barrel was aimed expertly at David Parker's forehead.

From the corner of her eye, Dallas noted that Rico's gun had also been drawn, cocked and aimed.

"Wrong," Dallas snapped as she yanked the hammer of the pistol back with her thumb. The *click-click-click* of chambers revolving into place sounded loud in the unnaturally thick silence. "I can think of several reasons for this 'marriage' not to take place. One is that the bride is only thirteen years old. The other is that she doesn't want to marry you."

"Let her go, Parker," a thickly accented voice said as Rico stepped around the table he'd been sitting at to take better aim. A few of the patrons closest to him were wise enough to hustle out of the angry Mexican's way.

David's eyes glinted, his cheeks flushing with fury as his gaze shifted between Dallas and Rico. His right hand came away from Lisa's waist, edging toward his gun.

Dallas's gaze shadowed the movement, and she smiled coldly as she took a step forward, her aim never wavering. "Do it," she urged icily. "Go ahead, pull your gun. After what you've just done, I'd take any excuse I can get right now to put a bullet in you."

David hesitated, and moved his hand to Lisa's throat, his thin fingers curling threateningly around the light, creamy expanse of skin.

Dallas forced herself not to react to her sister's whimper of fright.

"I can kill her without a gun," Parker said confidently. The tone of his voice was belied by the way he shifted, moving Lisa's body to shield the front of his. Lisa was smaller than Dallas; her sister's body didn't shield enough of him, even though David hunkered slightly behind Lisa's quivering form. "We both know I can do it."

"No, David, we both know you can *try,*" Dallas corrected him flatly as she took another step forward. "We also know I'm a damn fine shot. I've proved it to you and everyone else in this place time and again. I'll put a bullet between your eyes before your fingers can even flex."

"And if she doesn't," Rico added as he also took a step toward the pair, "I will."

David was panicking. Dallas could tell by the way the corner of his left eye began to twitch, and the way his gaze nervously darted between herself and Rico.

If pressed, Dallas wouldn't have been able to say exactly what she expected David to do next. Her index finger remained steady against the trigger of the pistol; she was tense and leery and ready for anything.

Anything, that is, except for the way David growled savagely . . . then shoved Lisa toward Dallas.

Dallas had barely enough time to lift her gun up in the air before Lisa screamed and collided with her. The blow made Dallas's index finger convulse.

A bullet tore from Dallas's pistol, burying itself harmlessly in the timbered ceiling. Shards of wood splinters rained to the floor.

Freeing one hand, Dallas pulled her sobbing sister close, and at the same time saw Parker trying to run for the door. That son of a bitch! She lifted the gun, pivoted slightly, squinted and took aim.

Another shot cut through the night.

This time the bullet did not come from Dallas's gun, it came from Rico's.

Parker went down hard.

All hell broke loose among the saloon's patrons. It was as though the gunshots had finally unfrozen them and thrust them into motion.

A few went over to David, who was writhing on the floor, clutching his bleeding leg. One particularly burly puncher placed a solid kick in Parker's side before reaching down and hauling Parker to his feet. David

425

screamed in pain, but the man showed no mercy as he yanked David's gun from its holster and tossed it to someone else.

Lisa clung to her sister, crying hysterical, hiccupy sobs into Dallas's shoulder.

Dallas uncocked her gun and holstered it. She wrapped her arms around Lisa, hugging her sister's trembling body tightly. Lisa's tears soaked warmly through Dallas's shirt, wetting the material and plastering it to her skin.

A handful of men, including Preacher Thomas, came over to make sure the women were both all right. Dallas simply nodded, distracted as her attention searched the saloon.

Where was Rico?

At first, she was afraid he'd left before she could thank him. Rico was tucked somberly away from the commotion, in the chair behind the table in the corner where she'd originally spotted him.

Their gazes met and held.

Understanding and gratitude passed wordlessly between them.

Rico grinned and, in silent salute, lifted the shot glass Dallas only now realized he was holding.

Hugging her sobbing sister close, Dallas tried to take a step through the gathering of men toward him. She was distracted by the swinging doors banging open.

Hickory Pete stood framed in the doorway, his wiry arms spread wide as he propped both doors open. A frown creased his leathery brow, his watery gaze narrowing angrily on Parker . . . who was being dragged, quite literally and loudly, out of the saloon.

The old man's attention shifted to Dallas and Lisa. A relieved grin cracked his grizzled features. Rubbing his gnarly hands together Pete hooted, "Ooo-eee! Just wait till Nicky hears 'bout *this'un!*"

Chapter Nineteen

"Nick? Nick!"

After swiftly checking the lower rooms of the ranch house, and not finding Nick in any of them, Dallas dashed up the stairs. Her spurs chinking atop the bare, scarred planks, she jogged down the corridor.

Toward her bedroom.

Toward Nick Langston.

Lisa was downstairs. The girl had fallen into an exhausted, stress-ridden sleep on their way back to the Bar None, curled up like a wilted flower in her sister's protective arms. Dallas had held Lisa protectively close, riding slowly. She'd been adamant on carrying Lisa back herself, afraid to let her sister go.

Only once they'd reached the ranch house, and Pete had taken a few minutes to go talk to Nick, could Dallas finally be persuaded to leave her sister's side.

Lisa was in the parlor, curled up on the sofa sleeping. Rico and Hickory Pete stood guard beside the girl to make sure no one disturbed her.

Now that her sister was safe, Dallas's concern channeled in a different direction. It turned inward, focusing on what *she* needed.

What she needed was to see Nick Langston.

The urge to hold Nick, and be held by him, had never been stronger; it pumped hot and strong through her veins. Dallas needed to feel his heavily muscled arms wrap around her, clutching her shelteringly close. She wanted to rest her head against his hard, broad chest and hear the comforting beating of his heart drumming in her ear.

She needed to draw from Nick's strength and warmth, and let it replenish her own.

Her needs were too overpowering to deny.

Dallas had come heartbreakingly close to losing her sister tonight. She shuddered at the thought and quickened her stride. Had she ever been so scared? No. For the first time in her life, Dallas Louise Cameron felt soft, weak, vulnerable.

It was an uneasy feeling; she couldn't seem to rid herself of it.

Dammit, she needed Nick Langston!

That was it, plain and simple. She *had* to see and touch and talk to Nick. Only then would her abruptly off-kilter world right itself.

The lamp in her bedroom had been lit. Soft orange light spilled out of the slat where the door stood ajar, slicing over the hallway floor in a long, narrow rectangle. Movement could be heard from inside the room.

A rustle of cloth.

The *tap-tap-tap* of a cane.

The slow shuffle of labored footsteps.

Dallas stopped in front of her bedroom door. She

allowed herself a few seconds to regulate her breathing—that and her heartbeat always went awry at the thought of seeing Nick Langston—then pushed the wooden panel open with a splayed palm.

The smile on her face melted.

"What the hell do you think you're doing?" Arms crossed tightly over her chest, Dallas stepped over the threshold and entered the room. Her spurs chinked angrily on the planked floor as her attention sharpened accusingly on the half-filled canvas sack lying open atop her bed.

"What the hell's it look like I'm doing, Cameron?" Nick countered, just as tightly.

The answer was obvious.

Nick was packing.

The son of a bitch was *leaving!*

Nick had been in the process of pulling shirts, jeans, underclothing and socks, from the top drawer of her dresser. That drawer was the only one his possessions had occupied since he'd taken up residence in Dallas's bedroom. It was a drawer that, for the rest of her life, she would always think of as "Nick's."

His pause when she burst into the room was infinitesimal. He didn't even bother to glance up. Instead, Nick turned and walked awkwardly toward the bed. A fresh batch of haphazardly folded clothes was tucked in the crook of his arm, while the fingers of his free hand were curled around the crutch in a white-knuckled grip.

His face was pale, his jaw hard, his lips thinned and strained. He gritted his teeth with every jarring step.

Dallas winced, feeling Nick's pain as acutely as if it were her own. In the most integral way, it was.

Her first instinct was to go to him, wrap her arms around his waist and unselfishly take on the bulk of his weight with her own body to ease the agony that must be tearing through his leg right now.

With effort, Dallas suppressed the urge. She knew Nick Langston well. He was as brave as he was stubborn; he'd shun sympathy and assistance of any sort. No, with Nick a different approach was in order.

Dallas crossed to the bed and perched on the edge of the mattress. Absently, the tip of her index finger traced one of the many slashes her spurs had made in the cream-colored bedspread. Her tone forcefully flat, she asked, "Where will you go?"

Nick shrugged, and punched the clothes sloppily into the canvas sack with his fist. "Haven't decided yet."

"Well, now, doesn't that make sense? You're running out in the middle of the night, no destination in mind. Yup, real brilliant of you, Langston." Her gaze narrowed on Nick, and she noticed a bit of angry color seep into his cheeks. Dallas suppressed a grin. "Tell me something. Have you let Papa know you're going, and why? Or were you planning to sneak out the back door and not even say goodbye to a man who's trusted you to run his ranch, and been paying your wages, for the last fifteen years?"

"Oh, that's low, Cameron. Even for you."

Dallas laughed coldly and shook her head, her braid bobbing against her waist. "Running out in the middle of the night is a lot lower. In fact, it's a pretty cowardly thing to do, if you ask me."

"No one asked you," he growled. Leaning heavily on his crutch, he maneuvered himself back to the dresser.

Dallas watched him, feeling the pain of every step Nick took like a knife slicing right down to the bone. Keeping her tone neutral ate up all her concentration, but she did it. "You know, I never took you for a coward, Nick."

"I'm getting real sick of hearing those words. And I ain't no coward."

"No? You're running, aren't you? That speaks for itself. Running is what cowards do, Langston. They come up against a wall, they get scared, they run." Dallas hesitated, frowning as a thought occurred to her. Even though she instantly dismissed it, the notion kept coming back and gnawing at her until she couldn't resist asking, "Tell me something else, Nick. What exactly are you running from? The Bar None? Papa? Me?" She paused meaningfully, studying his reaction. "Or yourself?"

Nick's steps faltered. He teetered on his good leg, almost losing his balance. A groan ripped from his throat when his elbow collided hard with the sharp corner of the dresser drawer. "Isn't it time you left . . . Squirt?"

"Why? It's my bedroom. I can come and go as I please."

The irony of that statement was not lost on Dallas.

She glanced to the side, and she saw the dark impression his wet hair had left on the wallpaper over the headboard of her bed. A ragged Sears catalogue sat open on the nightstand, its sketches proudly displaying hand-tooled saddles that Nick Langston would probably never have a use for.

There was the top drawer of her dresser. *Nick's drawer*. And the seductive, spice-and-tobacco-laced male scent of him on the warm night air.

This room felt like anything *but* Dallas's bedroom. It was as though it had never belonged to her at all. Or, if it ever had, never would again. She would never be able to look at anything in this room with the same eyes with which she would have seen it only a month ago.

No, she couldn't find an inch of this room, not a stick of furniture in it, that wasn't firmly stamped with Nick Langston's imprint in one form or another. Dallas would never be rid of it. Never be rid of him.

In the future, whenever she walked into this room, she would be slapped with the memory of Nick Langston's presence. Never again would she be able to take even a quick glimpse at her own soft bed and not see his rugged body laying there, the open Sears catalogue tented over his hard, flat, naked belly while the hot summer sunlight snuck in through the window to caress his tanned skin while he napped.

Dallas sighed. The fingers she'd been using to pluck at the spur slices in the creamy bedspread moved, grazing the gun that was still strapped to her hip. The butt felt cold and hard as it brushed against her palm. It was no colder or harder than her resolve.

Nick had gathered up another, the last armful of clothes, and crossed back to the bed. He put these into the canvas sack the same way as he had the last load.

It was then that Dallas stood and walked resolutely around the foot of the bed. At the same time, she slipped the unfamiliar pistol from its equally unfamiliar holster.

The weapon felt heavier in her hands than it had when she'd aimed it at David Parker. She wondered why.

"Here."

Nick angled his sandy head, looked at her. His gaze narrowed, slipped down and locked on the pistol, narrowed still more.

Dallas's fingers, curled around the steely barrel, trembled slightly as she held the weapon out to him. "Take it," she insisted.

Nick's breath caught, and his heartbeat sped up as his gaze lifted to hers. "Why?"

She returned his stare levelly. "Because I'd rather you killed me now, quickly and cleanly, and got it over with."

"What the hell are you talking about, Cameron?"

Dallas shrugged, and wondered how she managed to make the gesture look so loose and casual when she felt anything but on the inside. "I don't want to live without you, Nick."

"Look, if this is some kind of trick to get me to stay . . . ?"

"No, what it is is the truth." Dallas reached up and brushed the pad of her thumb lightly over the muscle ticking erratically in Nick's jaw. Ah, but his flesh felt so smooth and warm and wonderful skimming beneath her own! How could she live knowing she'd never be able to touch this man again? "I love you,

435

Nick," she said softly, huskily, sincerely. "I always have. If you leave, it will break my heart."

"Is that a fact? Well, what about me? What about how I feel? Or doesn't that count?"

A shiver of hope curled down Dallas's spine. Her heartbeat quickened, dumping a surge of adrenaline into her bloodstream. "What about you? Nick, you've told me so many times you aren't good enough for me that, while I don't believe it, I've decided I'm going to have to accept it." She paused, swallowing hard. "I've told you how I feel about you. Hell, I've thrown myself at you twice! But you keep pushing me away. I have my pride, you know. I won't beg . . . and I won't chase after any man who obviously doesn't want me."

Nick's gaze swept assessively from the top of her tawny head to the tips of her booted toes. He drew in a shaky breath, shook his head. Finally, almost reluctantly, he reached out and took the gun from Dallas's hands, checked to make sure the hammer hadn't been cocked, then tossed the weapon aside. It bounced once before coming to rest on the bed.

"Pete says Lisa is okay," Nick said flatly.

Dallas nodded, frowning at the abrupt change of topic. "She's downstairs sleeping. The poor kid's exhausted."

"And Parker?"

"He's in jail. Most of McFee's customers . . . ahem, 'escorted' him to his cell. He won't stand trial until the circuit judge comes this way again. This is one mess I don't think Winston Parker can buy his son out of."

"The pansy's lucky he's around *to* stand trial," Nick growled and plowed his fingers through his hair. An emotion fired in his indigo eyes that Dallas couldn't read. "It's a good thing I couldn't go with you tonight. I would have killed the son of a bitch with my bare hands."

"When I saw the way he was holding Lisa, saw the way she was shaking and crying, I was tempted to do that myself. Not with my bare hands, but with a bullet between his beady eyes."

"But you didn't."

Dallas shook her head. "No."

"Why?"

"Because Rico shot first." She shivered at the memory—still much too clear and fresh in her mind for comfort—that washed over her.

"And if he hadn't?" Nick prompted.

Dallas's gaze had drifted past Nick's broader than broad shoulder, fixing on the impression his head had left on the wallpaper over her bed. Grudgingly, her attention now returned to Nick. Her shrug was not casual. "Who's to say? Maybe I would have killed David, maybe I wouldn't have. There's no way to know for sure, because I wasn't forced to make that choice. I *do* know I was *capable* of killing him when I saw what he was doing to Lisa."

"More than capable," he corrected gruffly. "Or did you forget who taught you how to shoot?"

"I didn't forget." A sad grin tugged at one corner of Dallas's mouth as her gaze locked with his. "*You* taught me how to shoot. You taught me . . . everything. And I'll never forget any of it." With the pad of her thumb, she traced the curve of his chin. Her voice soft and throaty, she whispered, "I'll never forget *you.*"

Nick's thick fingers curled around her wrist. Dallas waited, prepared for him to yank her hand away.

Instead, Nick closed his eyes, inhaled a deep, shaky breath.

He turned his head, and pressed his mouth against the center of Dallas's palm.

His mustache feathered over Dallas's skin, tickling slightly. His lips were warm and moist as they whisked against her. She felt pure sensation shudder up her arm. The raw emotions even this seemingly innocent contact evoked wrapped like gossamer threads around Dallas's heart, squeezing tightly.

Nick sighed. His breath felt warm and misty against her flesh. It felt more than wonderful.

"Ah, Christ, I should have been there, Dallas," Nick groaned against her hand, his voice so soft she almost didn't hear him. Almost. "Dammit, I should have been there!"

His fingers flexed around her wrist, as though he was afraid to loosen his grasp for fear she would pull away from him. His grip was not painful so much as insistent. Dallas surrendered herself to it without a second thought.

"Is that why you're leaving? Because you couldn't ride into Green River with me tonight?"

"It's not the only reason. But it's one of them," Nick admitted. He lifted his head and looked down at her, his gaze shimmering with irritation and . . . something else. "Your turn to tell me something, Cameron. Tell me what good am I to the Bar None in this condition? Tell me what I can do on this ranch that would make a damn bit of difference, or that any cowpuncher with two good legs couldn't do. If I stayed—and I do mean *if*—I'd only be in the way. A charity case. Hell, I'd rather—"

"Stop it," Dallas snapped, stiffening angrily as she cut his tirade short. She jerked her wrist free, glaring up at him. "You know what, Langston? I'm getting sick and tired of hearing that stupid, self-pitying, I'll-never-be-useful-again speech of yours."

"You and me both!"

The intrusive third voice—loud and booming—drew both Dallas and Nick's startled attention to the door.

Ian Cameron stood in the doorway, his shoulder leaning heavily against the wooden frame. His weathered complexion was pale, his snowy hair as disheveled as his sleep-wrinkled clothing. Only his stare was level and steady. That stare was aimed directly at Nick Langston.

"Papa!" Dallas took a concerned step toward her father. Only the hand Ian held up, palm out, stopped her from rushing to his side. "You're supposed to be in bed, resting."

"Like hell! You think I'm going to lollygag around in bed while one of the best punchers I ever had runs out on me in the dead of night? No, I won't." Ian's gaze fell accusingly on the canvas sack laying atop his daughter's bed. "That *is* what you were about to do, isn't it, Langston?"

"I'd planned to stop by your room and say goodbye before I left, Ian," Nick offered stiffly.

"Uh-huh." Ian's gaze glinted shrewdly. "And while you were there, were you going to bother giving me a reason for why, after fifteen years of hard work, loyalty, and trust, you were up and leaving"—he snapped his fingers—"just like that?"

Nick shifted his weight uneasily on the crutch. "Seems to me it would be pretty damn obvious."

"What? Are you referring to all the rubbish about you being a useless cripple that you were spouting to my girl here? Don't look at me like that, Langston, I could hear the two of you yammering all the way down the hall. You were handing Dallas a bunch of crap, and we both know it. Now you're trying to hand it to me. Don't bother wasting your breath, or my time. I ain't stupid enough to fall for it."

Nick stiffened defensively. "What I said to Dallas was the truth."

Ian stared at Nick long and hard, then shook his head slowly. "Well, I'll be damned. I do believe that's the first time you've ever lied to me, Langston." His bushy white brows furrowed in an intimidating scowl. "And, make no mistake about it, it damn well better be the *last*. Now why don't you tell me the *real* reason you're leaving the Bar None? After fifteen years, I think you owe me at least that much."

Dallas's attention volleyed between her father and Nick. The two men were staring at each other hotly, their jaws set in identical hard lines of stubbornness. She might as well not have been in the room for all the attention they paid her.

Dallas exhaled sharply. All right, that did it. She was as tired of being ignored as she was of being

440

rejected. Both of which had been happening far too often lately!

Spinning on her heel, her spurs chinking, Dallas went to the bed and snatched up the canvas sack. She felt the heat of both men's gazes shift to her as she carried the sack over to where Nick stood.

Returning Nick's gaze with a level one of her own, Dallas slammed the bag into his stomach hard enough to threaten toppling him over, but not hard enough to actually do it.

Nick stumbled back a painful step. His crutch scraped the scarred plank floor as he simultaneously tried to regain his balance and hold on to the sack.

"I have had it!" With a toss of her head, Dallas planted her balled fists atop the slender shelf of her hips. Her glare on Nick turned furious. "You want to leave, Langston? Fine, do it. And good riddance! I no longer give a damn what you're running from, or what you're running to. You've made it crystal clear that neither of them is me. As for all that tripe about you loving me and wanting to marry me," she sneered, "I guess I'll have to assume that you were lying to me, the same way you were lying about you being a worthless cripple."

Nick stared down at her, stunned. The sack dropped from his abruptly slack grasp, spilling clothes onto the floor.

Dallas spun on her heel toward the door. She took a step, fully prepared to stalk out of the room and out of Nick Langston's life. Forever. She didn't want to— God knows, her heart ached unmercifully at the thought—but she had no choice. She was not going to throw herself at this man again. She was tired of being rejected by him. It hurt too much and . . .

Dammit, she had her pride!

"Wait!" The power in that single word was reinforced by the fingers that Nick snaked firmly around Dallas's upper arm. He stopped her before she could retreat a second step. With a quick tug, he turned her around to face him. "Look, darlin', I've done a lot of things in my life that I ain't proud of, but lying's not one of them. I *never* lied to you." He glanced past her shoulder briefly, his indigo eyes dark, his expression sincere. "Or you, Ian."

Dallas's breath caught in her throat. Her gaze lifted and met Nick's.

His eyes glistened with an honesty that she wanted with all her heart to believe, but was afraid to. The pain of possibly losing him was too fresh and raw.

It took effort, but Dallas managed to erase all emotion from her voice and her expression as she said, "You told me you loved me, Nick."

"I know."

"Are you saying that wasn't a lie?"

Nick hesitated, the lump in his throat bobbing up and down when he swallowed hard. Twice. A tinge of red crept into his tanned cheeks. Dallas's palms itched to reach up and cup them, to feel the heat that burned there, but she resisted. If she touched Nick now, she knew she'd never *stop* touching him . . . nor would she ever hear what he had to say.

Dallas *had* to hear it.

She *had* to know.

Nick closed his eyes, inhaled slowly, deeply. If he'd

hoped the lingering breath would help to clear his head and heart, he was mistaken. The warm night air was laced with Dallas Cameron's sunshine-sweet scent. The aroma surrounded him, engulfed him.

His leg was throbbing mightily, but Nick was past feeling the pain. Right now, all he was capable of feeling was the heat of Dallas's nearness . . . and the almost overpowering urge to draw her body to his.

He opened his eyes, looked down at her. A fist of emotion clenched tightly in his gut. Dallas was trying to mask her feelings from him, but couldn't. Maybe from someone else, she might have been able to. But not from Nick. He'd known her too well for too long. He saw her hopeful expression, saw the hunger for his answer—the *right* answer—shimmer like hot brown fire in her eyes.

Nick gritted his teeth. Like a twig in a hurricane, he felt something deep inside snap.

What he'd told Dallas was the God's honest truth. Dammit, Nick Langston was no liar! Oh, sure, he didn't doubt he could stumble over a lie if he *had* to. But he wouldn't. Couldn't. Not now.

To lie now wouldn't just hurt himself—that, Nick could bear—but it would hurt Dallas even more—and that, he couldn't bear to even think about, let alone *do*.

The realization of how hot and strong and deep his feelings for this woman ran hit Nick like a punch to the jaw, leaving him stunned and numb, his senses reeling. If the physical and mental anguish he'd experienced at the thought of leaving her didn't prove it, then the sudden knowledge that he'd lay down his life rather than hurt her any more than he already had, did.

"Well?" Dallas asked softly, breathlessly. "Tell me, Nick. Please. Were you lying to me when you told me that you love me?"

"No." It was a single, simple word, yet Nick found that he had to literally push it off his tongue; it reeked of a commitment he wasn't entirely sure he was ready to make. Still, knew in his heart that he couldn't lie. He *did* love Dallas. So much so, it scared the hell out of him!

"Then say it," she insisted.

Nick frowned. "Say what?"

"That you love me. I want to hear you say the words."

"I just did!"

Dallas shook her head. "No. You agreed that you didn't lie to me the last time you said it. That's not the same thing. I want to hear you say it, Nick. Please."

"I . . ." His voice trailed off, the words evaporating in his abruptly parched throat. If he said what she wanted to hear, then there would be no turning back. And no leaving her side.

Ever.

Nick adjusted his weight awkwardly on the crutch, his gaze straying to the doorway, looking to Ian for help. He should have known better. One snow brow was cocked high, and the old man's eyes glistened with amusement as he watched the scene unfolding before him. No help would be coming from that quarter!

Nick's gaze shifted back to Dallas, trailing over the fringe of tawny bangs, the straight line of her nose, the sensuous curve of her mouth. He licked his lips, remembering all too well the erotic taste of her.

He wanted to taste her again. And again. And again. For the rest of his life. And only her.

Only Dallas.

The truth of those words cut through Nick's mind like a bullet, hummed hot and fast through his blood.

He wanted Dallas. Only Dallas. Not the lady she'd been trying so hard to be, but the gal who could shoot and ride a horse better than most. The gal who could rope like nobody's business. He wanted the smart-mouthed little hellion who could stand toe-to-toe with any puncher on this ranch, including himself, and give as good as she got. Usually better.

Dallas shifted her weight anxiously, waiting.

Nick heard the soft chink of her spurs on the bare plank floor.

Despite himself, his mouth curved up in a grin. The jingle of the spiked rowel wheels conjured up an instant mental image of stubbornly tattered hemlines. In the end, the sound and memory combined to melt away what was left of his reluctance.

One by one, his fingers loosened. The crutch clattered to the floor as he reached for Dallas. His arms slipped around her waist as he hauled her body roughly against his.

Angling his head, Nick's mouth slashed hungrily over hers. He kissed her deeply, thoroughly, until they were both flushed and breathless.

" 'Bout time we got *that* straightened out. Hmph! I'll round up a puncher to fetch Preacher Thomas," Ian muttered. Rubbing his chest, he pushed away from the doorway and left, closing the door quietly behind him.

Dallas was barely aware of her father leaving. Nick was kissing her, nothing else mattered.

After the initial, unexpected shock of feeling his mouth on hers wilted, she moaned deep in her throat and curled her arms around Nick's neck, melting into him hungrily as she fit her soft curves to his hard planes and angles. Her mouth flowered open, her tongue meeting and teasing his as she returned his kiss with equal fervor.

After what felt like a very long, very pleasurable lifetime, Nick pulled back slightly, only far enough to whisper against her kiss-swollen mouth, "Ah, Squirt, I've never lied to you. I do love you."

Nick felt her lips curve up in a smile against his own and, to his surprise, tasted the salty tang of her tears on his tongue. With his thumbs, he gently stroked the moisture from her cheeks.

"I know," Dallas said as she impatiently kicked aside the canvas sack and spilled clothes. Enfolding Nick's hand in hers, and meeting his passion-dark indigo gaze, she guided him over to the bed. "But there's one thing I still need to prove to you."

"What's that?"

Dallas looked up at Nick, her love for him shimmering in her eyes. "That you aren't as worthless as you think you are."

One sandy brow cocked high. He sighed and shook his head. "I don't think I'll ever truly believe you, darlin'."

"That's fine." Dallas smiled, and Nick felt a stab of

warmth cut through him. "I've got the rest of our lives to prove you wrong. And I intend to do exactly that. Now come here."

"But—"

Dallas cast a mock frown up at him. "No 'but's about it. Now, hush and listen up, Langston. This is important. Lesson number one: Husbands *never* argue with their wives. Better practice it now, because it's something you're going to need to know."

Dallas lay down on the bed, shifted, making room for Nick to join her.

She patted the expanse of mattress next to her invitingly.

It was an invitation Nick couldn't resist. He eased his weight down on the bed beside her, groaning as he adjusted his position to take pressure off his left leg. "What's lesson number two, darlin'?"

Dallas's smile widened. Her gaze and voice steeped in a husky, feminine seduction that Nick knew damn well *he'd* never taught her, she said, "Kissin'. Until Papa fetches that preacher, lesson number two is kissin'."

Nick returned her smile, scooped Dallas's warm, soft, willing body into his arms, pressed her back against the bed, and proceeded to practice his second lesson with breathtaking skill.

"What's lesson number three?" he rasped hotly against her mouth a long while later.

"That one, you'll get from your wife, Langston." The twinkle in her eye was both mischievous and seductive. "And knowing Papa, class will start in about an hour. Please make sure you're not tardy."

447

"Oh, darlin', don't you worry about that," Nick whispered, his voice low and husky.

His concentration was diverted to practicing lesson number two to its fullest . . . and all the while entertaining hot, erotic thoughts about a lifetime of lesson number threes. With Dallas Louise Cameron Langston. His wife.